More praise for Nevada Barr's award-winning Anna Pigeon mysteries . . .

"Well-baited suspense." —*People*

"Gripping adventure . . . [An] exceptional series."
—*The Denver Post*

"Nevada Barr writes with a cool, steady hand about the violence of nature and the cruelty of man."
—*The New York Times Book Review*

"A truly harrowing series of tight squeezes."
—*Chicago Tribune*

"Heart-pounding . . . Barr combines primo mysteries with what always feels like a virtual reality tour of one of the parks . . . There is beauty here. Still, Anna never loses her edginess in a world where your life depends on having a backup light for your backup light." —*Detroit Free Press*

"Evocative and suspenseful . . . Thoroughly satisfying—thanks to the writing and plotting talents of a master."
—*Publishers Weekly* (starred review)

"Barr's descriptive prose is a constant source of pleasure."
—*San Francisco Chronicle*

"From the fabric of fiction she creates real worlds, sometimes beautiful, sometimes terrifying, but always convincing."
—*The San Diego Union-Tribune*

"Nevada Barr is one of the best." —*The Boston Globe*

Park Ranger Anna Pigeon returns to face her most duplicitous foe—human nature—in the latest entry in Nevada Barr's bestselling, award-winning series . . .

The quiet beauty of autumn on Mississippi's Natchez Trace is swiftly shattered when Anna answers a call to Mt. Locust, once a working plantation and inn, now a tourist spot. But the man Anna finds in an old bedroom is no tourist in distress. He's nearly naked and very dead—his body bearing marks consistent with sex games gone awry. On a writing table nearby is an open Bible with ominous passages circled in red.

There are secrets that prominent men in this God-fearing country wish to keep under wraps—and Anna has stumbled into a nest of them.

HUNTING SEASON

"A true original . . . like a combination of Henry David Thoreau, Mark Twain, Sherlock Holmes and Maureen O'Hara, the engaging character of Anna Pigeon is the only reason most readers will need to return to this series again and again. But it doesn't hurt that Barr can write rhapsodic passages about America's beautiful parks and cobble up page-turning whodunits." —*The Denver Post*

"The edgy, fast-paced tale generates plenty of tension . . . and Barr does a good job of developing the character of Anna, adding romance to the mix and giving the ranger plenty of opportunity to display her slightly dark, off-center wit." —*Booklist* (starred review)

"First-rate . . . Barr outshines most other authors in the mystery genre." —*Publishers Weekly*

Please turn to the back of this book for a special preview of Nevada Barr's

FLASHBACK

Available in hardcover from G. P. Putnam's Sons!

HUNTING SEASON

·

NEVADA BARR

BERKLEY BOOKS, NEW YORK

This is a work of fiction. Names, characters, places, and incidents either are the product of the author's imagination or are used fictitiously, and any resemblance to actual persons, living or dead, business establishments, events, or locales is entirely coincidental.

HUNTING SEASON

A Berkley Book / published by arrangement with the author

PRINTING HISTORY
G. P. Putnam's Sons hardcover edition / February 2002
Berkley mass-market edition / February 2003

Copyright © 2002 by Nevada Barr.
Interior map by Jackie Aher.
Cover design by Wood Ronsaville Harlin, Inc.
Cover illustration by Rob Wood.

ISBN: 0-425-18878-7

BERKLEY®
Berkley Books are published by The Berkley Publishing Group,
a division of Penguin Putnam Inc.,
375 Hudson Street, New York, New York 10014.
BERKLEY and the "B" design
are trademarks belonging to Penguin Putnam Inc.

PRINTED IN THE UNITED STATES OF AMERICA

10 9 8 7 6 5 4 3 2 1

*For the people of Clinton, Mississippi,
who welcomed me into their lives and supported my work*

ACKNOWLEDGMENTS

Thanks to Sheriff McMillan for his guidance, and apologies to the sheriff of Jefferson County for handing his jurisdiction over to Adams County.

0 ___ 10 kilometers
0 ___ 10 miles

LOUISIANA

Sunken Trace

NATCHEZ

Port Gibson District Headquarters

Emerald Mound

Grindstone Ford

NATCHEZ TRACE PARKWAY

Rocky Springs

Future Terminus

Mount Locust

Bullen Creek

Port Gibson

Magnum Mound

Owens Creek Waterfall

ANNA'S DISTRICT

North

MISSISSIPPI

HOMOCHITTO NATIONAL FOREST

55

Historic route of the Trace

MISSISSIPPI RIVER

Barnett's

TRACE PROPERTY LINE

Woods

Old Slave Cemetery

Maintenance building

Eric's Garden

Ranger station

Mt. Locust Stand

Visitors Center

Parking lot

VICKSBURG

Mount Locust

North

NATCHEZ TRACE PARKWAY

Lower Choctaw Boundary

Battle of Raymond

CLINTON

20

Dean's Stand

Clinton Pullout

55

JACKSON

© '01 jackie aher

1

The priest was droning on inexorably toward "till death do us part," and Anna began to get nervous. At some point over the years, the well-worn phrase had come to feel more like a sinister threat than a romantic promise.

Death had parted Anna from her husband years before, sudden and pointless death delivered by a cab driver on Ninth Avenue in Manhattan. Judging from the internal damage to Zach's body, the NYPD accident investigator estimated the cab was traveling at fifty to sixty miles per hour on a city street. The impact had knocked Zach out of his shoes. They were found, still laced, sixty feet from his body, a detail Anna hadn't needed to know then and didn't like remembering now.

Nearly a hundred people had witnessed the accident; a baker's dozen stayed to tell their story to the police. No one had gotten the cab's license plate number. No one heard the squeal of brakes. There were no marks on the asphalt to indicate the cabbie had tried to stop or even swerve.

"Drunk or high," the accident investigator had offered. "Or maybe just didn't know where the brake pedal was. Some of these guys get their driver's licenses off Froot Loops boxes on the boat over from Iran."

Six hours after Zach died Anna identified his body at the morgue. Despite the violence of the collision, his body was almost completely unmarked. Still, he'd not looked as if he were sleeping. That was a story invented for comforting children. Without life inside, the human body looked like the awkward and asymmetrical compilation of parts it was. At the time she'd known seeing the face in death would eclipse a thousand memory pictures of him in life. And so it had.

Alarmed by the return of morbid visions she'd not suffered—or, as her sister Molly might have said, indulged in—for a long while, Anna shook herself, the tremor of an animal ridding its hide of biting flies.

A plump brown hand bearing a squirrel's weight in gold and semi-precious stones patted her knee reassuringly. The stately black matron beside her on the pew was a stranger, but this was Mississippi. In the South there were still people who believed "what you do to the least of these, you do also to me." Solace was not strictly reserved for friends and family.

Startled, Anna smiled at her benefactress and received a nod in return, a minute dipping of a fabulous crimson hat with a prow like a pirate ship, sequins glittering like plunder. On a white woman it would have looked absurd. Atop this substantial black woman it was grand and subtly defiant.

Made uncomfortable by random kindness, Anna looked away. Alarm at harboring funereal thoughts at a wedding crept up on her in the form of superstition, a race memory of evil fairies come to christenings with curses for the princeling child. She crossed herself, then felt guiltier still. She wasn't Catholic. She wasn't even Christian. It was merely a habit picked up from the nuns during her years at Mercy High.

Contemplating her megrims, Anna realized she'd not been in a church of any stripe in more years than she cared to remember. The Restin-Wells nuptials were oddly timed—a morning wedding with a brunch following. For the uninitiated, being at a holy edifice at 9 A.M. before one was properly fortified with sin and coffee was taxing.

St. James Episcopal Church in Port Gibson had been built in the 1800s. Dark wood and vaulted ceiling, glass stained with saints, most of whom died grisly deaths, invited belief, if not in the divine, then at least in a human history steeped in blood.

A laugh boiled hot in Anna's lungs. She only just caught it before it blew past her lips and she made a spectacle of herself. Who was she kidding? Gods, demons, death in its myriad forms, none of it scared her. Marriage was what gave her the willies. A marriage performed by Paul Davidson, the man it was possible she was vaguely, carefully falling in love with, was even creepier.

She was used to seeing Paul in his comforting gun-toting persona as the sheriff of Claiborne County. Knowing he was also an ordained Episcopal priest was one thing. Seeing him in the collar, a Bible in the blunt, capable hands, as sunlight filtered through glassine lambs and shepherds, dying his blond hair three shades of Paschal green, gave the whole experience the unsettling feel of a drug-soaked dream.

Naming her demons freed Anna of them, and she returned her attention to the ceremony. Lonnie Restin, one of Paul's deputies, was the groom. Anna had worked with him on the Posey murder the previous spring. She'd seen him face the corpse of a child and a crazy lady racist, but she'd never seen him as nervous as he was sliding a band of gold onto the finger of his young bride.

As Lonnie murmured "with this ring," Paul looked up for an instant. His eyes locked with Anna's, and she felt a jolt stronger than touch and heard the quick hissing intake of her breath. Then Paul was back with the bride and groom, eye contact broken. It was as if he had vanished from right before her to reappear forty feet away.

This sudden warping of the space-time continuum left her tingling. It took several seconds to realize at least part of the sensation was promulgated by the pager in the side pocket of her dress vibrating against her thigh. Though it made no sound, Anna was conscious that, in carrying it at all, she had become one of *them,* a member of the army battering down the last feeble remnants of graciousness, taking the final step in the cant of the "me" generation by dragging pagers and cell phones into theaters, churches, AA meetings, dinner parties and wakes. Ringing and buzzing declared priorities: My convenience takes precedence over your paltry event.

Now at Lonnie's sacred moment, Anna's thigh was vibrating with other peoples' priorities. She excused herself from the ranks of Miss Manners's nemeses by telling herself she *needed* to carry the beeper. The Trace from Natchez to Jackson was uncovered till she came on duty at noon. Randy Thigpen, one of her GS-9 field rangers, had demanded the four to midnight shift. The other, Barth Dinkins, on 8 A.M. to 3:30 P.M., had taken four hours of sick leave to visit the dentist.

Needed.

Sure.

As if beeping her in church could stop a crime wave or a spurting artery.

What the activity in her pocket might augur flashed through her mind as she steadfastly refused to fish the beeper out and look at it, at least not before the bride and groom had gotten their share of rice thrown. Highway death. Hunting accident. Domestic dispute. Visitors center out of toilet paper.

Lonnie and Showanda Restin were presented. Applause carried them down the aisle. Not rice but rose petals, handed out in paper cones before the ceremony, showered the newlyweds. Ushers began emptying the church pew by pew, starting at the front. Paul disappeared; after the service the priest was superfluous. He'd scuttled into a priestly sort of bolthole to slip into something less godly before going to brunch.

Paul was understanding of Anna's discomfiture with anything that smacked of The Cloth. He'd given her explicit instructions as if she were a small child in danger of becoming lost in the woods: "After the ceremony stay put. Don't move. I will come find you."

The kindly Christian in the crimson cap weighed anchor and was sailing out with the tide of people leaving the church. Anna slipped the beeper from her pocket. On the digital read-out was the number of Mt. Locust Visitors Center followed by 911. Not toilet paper.

She sat back down and rummaged through her purse. The South and dating again had had a feminizing effect. Several dresses now hung in her closet, along with an accumulation of National Park Service uniforms, and she was growing accustomed to female accoutrements. Her watch was in an inside zipper pocket. It read 9:22 A.M. Without even thinking about it, she registered the time she first got the call for the inevitable report that would follow.

The church emptied quickly and she was left along with saints, shepherds and chrysanthemums. Even in a church peace came with solitude. Anna let her mind float with the dust motes on the dyed sunbeams. Minutes passed and Paul emerged from some inner sanctum to the left of the altar. As he walked, he rolled up the sleeves of a green woolen shirt, exposing his forearms. When Anna's sexual triggers were set, during those confusing years between birth and senior prom, along with strong hands, the smell of Scotch whiskey and sun-warmed cotton, rolled sleeves on brown arms had been factored in.

For a moment she stayed still in the shadows, merely enjoying the sensation of enjoying watching a man.

"That's a pretty dress, is it new?" Paul said as he walked down the side of the pews to where she waited, jewel tones from the stained glass washing across his face and hair.

The dress was pretty. And it was new. This wasn't the

first compliment Anna had received from Paul Davidson. All the same she felt an upwelling of self-consciousness that only bald-faced truth could quell.

"Bought it new to impress you," she said, and he smiled in a slow southern way that reached deep into his eyes. "I can't make Lonnie's brunch," she said abruptly, not liking to feel in a church the sensations that smile engendered. "Duty calls." She showed him the beeper by way of explanation.

A shimmer ran through the denim blue of his eyes. The smile widened fractionally, then relaxed. The light was uncertain but Anna had seen relief enough times to know it. Intellectually, she couldn't blame him. There was a Mrs. Davidson who had crawled out of the woodwork. Paul and his wife had been separated for nearly four years: each with their own homes, jobs, finances, friends, and if you believed Paul, and Anna did, no conjugal visits to talk over old times on either side of the sheets. But no divorce. Mrs. Davidson had not wanted one and Paul let it be. Till he'd met Anna and filed. Mrs. Davidson was contesting. Along with football and hunting, Mississippi still revered the institution of marriage and had hammered that reverence into law. There were three grounds for divorce in the state: commission of a felony, cruel and unusual treatment, and adultery. There had been adultery, but too damn little of it, as far as Anna was concerned. Sheriff Davidson had succumbed once or twice but in the end Father Davidson prevailed. A man who was true to his principles wasn't much comfort on hot summer nights.

Anna never pushed. She, too, had principles, though they hadn't been sanctioned by the bishop. She wouldn't be a part of Paul being defrocked for behavior unbecoming a representative of the church, and she wouldn't play a part in a scandal that would lose him his upcoming re-election for sheriff. Once she'd thought she'd never willingly form any part of a triangle, but it was too late for that. By keeping her clothes on and sleeping alone, she hoped to retain the dignity and self-respect they would both need if they were to be able to meet without shame after the divorce.

Though she was relieved they would not have to share a romantic social event while steadfastly being neither romantic nor social, Paul's obvious relief stung. Heart and ego are not big proponents of logic.

"Let me know what's happened." Paul touched her arm.

"Sure," Anna said, wondering if she would. She'd want to call—that was unfortunately a given—but she'd lost her taste for soap opera sneakings, however justified by the sneakers, somewhere between her sophomore and senior years at Mercy. Cloaking it in the trappings of job interaction didn't count for much in the world of karma.

"You can use the phone in the office," Paul said.

Anna made the necessary calls. John Brown Brown, the Natchez Trace Parkway's chief ranger, doomed to a life of redundancy because his mother's maiden name and her husband's surname were the same, would inform the superintendent, currently out of pocket at a regional meeting in Atlanta. Dispatch was given her ETA at Mt. Locust. The park aide who'd paged, a seasonal interpreter named Sherry or Shelly, was soothed, then instructed to stay away from the inn and keep visitors out. There was nothing more to be done till Anna was on scene.

Needing to keep her mind from speculating on the report the park aide had babbled over the phone lest she arrive with preconceived ideas, Anna concentrated on history and nature as she drove south.

Both were a balm. History because its sins had already been committed, nature because she was supremely indifferent to the petty hysterias of the human race.

Mt. Locust was thirty miles south of Port Gibson on the Natchez Trace Parkway. Once it had been a producing plantation with the attendant kitchen and slave quarters. In the early 1800s it became one of the first of over fifty "stands"—rudimentary inns—serving travelers between Natchez and Nashville. Of these stands, Mt. Locust was the only one remaining and, built about 1780, arguably one of the oldest structures in Mississippi. The outbuildings and detached kitchen had been reduced to rubble and memory. All that remained to tell of the many slaves who labored in them was a recently discovered cemetery out beyond the kitchen garden, bones without names or markers.

In the past year, Ranger Dinkins, with the help of the park archaeologist and historian, had undertaken to find out who was buried there. So far they had eleven names. With the tendency of Mississippians, both black and white, to settle close to home, it was hoped that through deeds of purchase, oral history and DNA testing the descendants could be found. The graves would then be marked and commemorated, a piece of a people's violently fractured history put in place.

Anna drove with the window rolled down, breathing in the essence of autumn: an exhalation of a forest readying itself for sleep, a smell so redolent with nostalgia a pleasant ache warmed her bones and she was nagged with the sense of a loss she could not remember.

Most of the leaves had been stripped from the trees by a recent hard rain. The sweet gum and sassafras were bare, winter branches etching a sky still summer blue. Pin oaks and black oaks clung to their foliage though it was sere and brown and clattered rather than rustled when the wind blew. Along the shoulders of the narrow two-lane road, grass as green as springtime was neatly mowed to tree line. Here and there, in hollows where the mechanical slash of the bush-hog couldn't reach, the soft blue of chicory shimmered. The delicate yellow daisy that an enemy of botany and poetry had named tickweed touched the higher ground with earthen sunlight.

Anna savored the thirty minutes of the drive, the beauty flashing by at a speed the original travelers of the Trace would never have dared even imagine lest they be accused of witchcraft. Soon enough the darker side of being a park

ranger would assert itself. She wanted to absorb all the antidote she could before she drank in whatever poison
awaited. A poison that she knew from experience and ob-
servation was addicting. Actors weren't the only ones who
thrived on drama.

Before ten on a Saturday morning in November, Mt. Locust's parking lot was blessedly empty. The park aide was
outside the small visitors center, a brick building with the
one-room bookstore to the left, bathrooms to the right and
a breezeway between. The aide was a tiny woman,
scarcely bigger than a child. Anna's thoughts flashed on
her maternal grandmother as she pulled the Rambler into
the shade of an oak tree, one of several left on a center island when the asphalt was laid. What Anna's grandmother
had lacked in stature she'd made up for in venom. Anna
wished she'd taken more time to know this seasonal interpreter so she'd know which way the little woman might
break under pressure.

As she walked toward the visitors center, the aide
stopped pacing, her eyes fixed on Anna. They were blank
and slightly hostile.

"Hi," Anna said, needing to make a connection.

Shelly Rabine—Anna had come close enough to read
the name tag—stood squarely in front of the breezeway
and crossed her arms on her chest. "I'm sorry. Mt. Locust
is closed. You can't go up to the house," she said.

Her voice was high and strained, a mouse squeaking authority, a kindergartner putting her foot down. Stress
showed in the hunch of her shoulders and the way her
hands cupped her elbows as if the crossing of arms was not
only to keep the world out but also to hold herself together.
Regardless of the trauma she'd sustained, Shelly was determined to hold the fort till the cavalry came. Anna admired that.

"It's me, District Ranger Anna Pigeon," Anna said. She
waved a hand at the red dress and red-and-black high heels.
"I'm disguised as a normal person. It was a wedding."

Shelly Rabine blinked rapidly. Large exothalmic eyes,

so light brown as to be nearly yellow, were framed in chin-length parenthesis of stick-straight dark hair. Her face was wide and slightly squashed, the brow and chin narrow bands. Clear pale skin and perfect brows rescued her from plainness.

The fluttering lids stopped. Information was processed. "What took you so long? I called hours ago. I'm not going back."

"Good job calling me right away like you did," Anna said. "That was quick thinking." The shoulders lowered fractionally. "I'm going to go on up now and take a look." Anna put the humdrum of normalcy in her voice. "Why don't you keep on with your work down here. Keep any visitors from heading up to the house. That would really be a big help to me."

Miss Rabine was wound tight. The sight she'd been greeted with coupled with what, to her, seemed an unconscionably long wait, put her in fight mode. Had Anna asked Shelly to come with her up to the old stand, she had little doubt there would have been an altercation centering around "that's not in my job description" or "that's what *you* get the big bucks for."

Left comfortably where she was with only boring peripheral responsibilities a sudden, and—to Anna who'd seen it countless times before—unsurprising transformation took place. The fight didn't disappear, too much adrenaline in the system for that, but instead did an abrupt about-face. "Don't you want me to show you how I found—it. All that. I mean, it could be important. What I touched and what all." The implication that Anna didn't live up to police procedure as seen on TV was clear.

"Would you like to come up with me?" Anna asked mildly. "Maybe tell me on the way?"

"Visitors might come," Shelly said stubbornly, but she was winding down, anger leaking out of her shoulders and neck. Anna waited patiently, no glances up the hill to the inn, no tightening of the mouth.

"Somebody might come," Shelly said. "They

shouldn't . . . I mean nobody should . . . like kids," she finished lamely. The last vestiges of warfare dribbled away. The yellow-brown eyes were clear, if bruised by what they had seen. From harridan in the inimitable style of Anna's grandma Sanderman, Shelly had settled back into a tractable, well-intentioned employee of the National Park Service.

"It'll be all right," Anna said. "You can come back down if we see anybody."

Shelly adjusted her summer straw Stetson more squarely on her head and, with tiny fingers, plucked the pleats on her breast pockets straight. The man about to grant them an audience was way beyond caring about a woman's personal appearance, but Anna didn't say anything. Everyone has her own way of girding for battle.

They walked in silence through the short breezeway. To either side were glassed-in bulletin boards with the usual park paraphernalia: maps, camping instructions, rules, warnings. This season on the Natchez Trace, visitors were told to be on the lookout for rabid raccoons and to wear bright colors while hiking. On either side of this federally controlled ribbon of land it was deer hunting season. Who could blame a good old boy for taking aim across park boundaries if he thought he spotted a deer?

Anna's pumps clicked officiously on the concrete, and she felt suddenly, overwhelmingly absurd teetering along in pointy-toed, high-heeled girl's shoes. As they stepped out of the shade and into the crystal sunlight, the noise shifted to a less offensive crunch on the gravel path.

The path curved gracefully along the bottom of a small hill. Ancient live oaks shaded the split rail fence separating the house from a field planted with cotton, a remnant of the twelve hundred acres of the original plantation. Lovingly refurbished by the park service to its 1820s self, the inn stood alone on a low knoll overlooking the field and the Trace, watery window glass watching Fords and Buicks where once had been soldiers of the American Revolution, Indians and traders from the Ohio Valley. Brick steps, built by the NPS for visitor convenience, led up the grassy slope.

The stand was built, as were all well-appointed dwellings in the old south, with an eye to shade and breezes. Stilts supported it several feet above ground level to aid in air circulation, and a deep porch, complete with a rocking chair, ran the length of the house. Three doors opened onto the porch. Two were closed, probably bolted from the inside if the last interpreter off duty the previous night had adhered to protocol. The one farthest to the left stood ajar as if someone had left in a hurry.

"Why don't you tell me exactly what you did," Anna said as they reached the bottom of the brick steps. Probably it wouldn't matter much, but she knew Shelly needed to tell her story and would probably feel more comfortable talking now that they were getting close.

"I got here just before eight," Shelly said. "And I opened the visitors center like I was supposed to. The visitors center door and both the bathroom doors were locked." Shelly was speaking slowly. Her voice wasn't as high-pitched as it had been when Anna arrived, but she would probably sound like a child all of her life. There was thought behind the park aide's words. She was working to remember details. A good witness, if she'd seen anything worth witnessing.

"I opened the cash register. Everything was just like it was supposed to be—you know, nothing missing or anything like that."

They were on the brick stairway now, and Anna's heels were clicking annoyingly again.

"At nine I walked up here, up to the house, to open it up. I opened Grandma Polly's room first. There on the end."

Anna knew which room was Grandma Polly's. One of the reasons Mt. Locust was so well preserved was that it had belonged to one family for many generations. Paulina Chamberlain came to Mt. Locust as a bride in 1801. When she died in 1849 she left it to her descendants. In the 1940s, another Chamberlain gave Mt. Locust to the Na-

tional Park Service and stayed on to serve as the first
ranger there. The last of the line, Eric Chamberlain, still
served, working as a GS-4 park aide. There was one open
plot in the family cemetery at the end of a tree-shaded lane
on the park boundary. When Eric died the cemetery would
be complete and Mt. Locust would lose by it.

"You opened Grandma Polly's room," Anna nudged
when Shelly failed to go on.

"It was locked like it's supposed to be so I wasn't thinking about anything, then I saw this thing on the bed. I
thought it was like a big fish, a landed walrus maybe.
That's stupid, isn't it?"

"Not stupid," Anna said. The human brain was an organ
designed to make sense of things. When faced with the
senseless, it scrambled madly through known images, desperate to make a match.

"What then?" Anna asked. They'd reached the top of the
brick steps and stood on a landing. The wooden stairs to
the porch were in front of them. Anna wanted Shelly to finish her recital before they went up. It would be easier to
clear her mind if her attention wasn't divided.

"I paged you."

"Did you go into Grandma Polly's room?"

"No. Yes. Sort of. I went in maybe a few steps. Till I saw
what it was."

"Did you touch anything?"

"Nothing." Shelly was emphatic about that.

"Did you check for a pulse?"

"No. God no. I mean this guy's *really* dead. Dead dead.
I wasn't going to touch him. No way. Gross."

"Okay," Anna said. "Were the other doors locked?"

"I don't know. I went down to the VC to call you. I guess
I should have checked."

"No. You did just exactly the right thing." Anna started
up the wooden stairs, Shelly trailing after.

"Want me to check them now?" the aide asked. No
longer alone, she was warming to the adventure aspect the
crime offered and was eager to be a part of it.

"No," Anna said. "Right now it's best if we touch and disturb as little as possible."

"Oh, right. Fingerprints."

The door hardware at Mt. Locust was so old and pitted with rust Anna doubted they would be able to lift any fingerprints, but she said nothing. Shelly had found a reason she could understand for leaving well enough alone. If it kept Anna from being interfered with, she was happy with it.

Anna's patrol car, with everything she'd need in the trunk, was parked in front of her house at Rocky Springs, fifteen miles north of Port Gibson. Before heading south, she'd stopped in the Port Gibson Ranger Station and scraped up a tape recorder, camera, gloves, measuring tape and notebook. The camera, long in storage, was dusty; its functioning suspect. Having set the grime-streaked rucksack she'd liberated from behind the seat of the fire truck to tote this hastily assembled investigation kit on a bench beneath a window, she pulled out two pairs of latex gloves, put one on and handed the other to Shelly.

"Let's take a look," she said. Mt. Locust was painted white, the paneled doors and shutters over the windows done in a bright cheery blue. Heels clacking on porch planks, Anna walked to the half-open door, Grandma Polly's room. Using her fingertips she gently pushed the door until it was completely open. A shaft of early sunlight chased the door's shadow, running across the worn wooden floor to illuminate the old bed, its mattress stuffed with Spanish moss, ropes netted beneath for support.

The sudden light in the gloom threw the object on the patchwork coverlet into glowing relief. Big fish. Landed walrus. The images were apt. "Gross," Anna murmured, unconsciously echoing Shelly Rabine's summation.

Lying on Grandma Polly's bed, drenched in autumn sunlight, was a fat white man. Very white. Fish-belly white. But for a pair of underpants, probably cotton, possibly Fruit of the Loom, he was naked. From her vantage point at the doorsill Anna could see the wide puffed bottoms of two splayed feet, heavy calves and meaty thighs, a great rise of belly as white as lard and folded in on itself near the navel. One arm and hand, so brown from the sun they looked as if they'd been borrowed from a different cadaver, stuck over the side of the bed, elbow locked, palm up. The face was obscured by the mounded belly and one sagging pec.

"You going to wait till somebody else gets here?"

Part of her brain registered both the disappointment and the understanding in Shelly's voice. The young woman thought Anna was afraid to face the dead by herself. In Anna's estimation, dead bodies were about the most trust-worthy humans on the planet. It wasn't squeamishness or fear that kept her in the doorway; before she contaminated the crime scene with her presence she wanted to take note of everything she could. Contamination, to her, not limited to the inevitable effluvia of her hair, skin and shoes, but to her mind as well. Once she stepped in the door she became part of the room. She would see it differently.

"Hand me the radio, Shelly. There in the bag." The part of the Natchez Trace Anna served as district ranger ran through four counties: Adams, Jefferson, Claiborne and Hinds. All were held in concurrent jurisdiction with local law enforcement. Investigations were worked by federal, state and county agencies. It was a system that worked well; cooperation was the rule rather than the exception. The other death Anna worked had been at Rocky Springs in Claiborne County, so Paul Davidson had shared that tragedy. Mt. Locust was in Adams County, where Anna had yet to meet the sheriff. That was about to change.

She called dispatch in Tupelo and requested they contact him and the coroner to ask them to come to Mt. Locust.

Handing the radio back to Shelly, who still held the rucksack in front of her like a little kid with a trick-or-treat basket, Anna said, "Camera please." Shelly traded radio for camera, looking serious and professional and happy to have something to do.

Camera to her eye, Anna began framing death; the first step in the compartmentalizing process, boxing off the dead from the living. The last box would be of wood and buried in the ground.

The stand was built in the French style of the early nineteenth century with enclosed rooms or *cabinets*. Bedrooms didn't open into the central taproom where the travelers ate, but onto the porch. In Polly's room a second door exited out the far side into a storage room with access to the back porch.

Anna clicked four pictures: as wide an angle of the room as she could get in tight quarters, showing the rear door, the bed and the window on the left-hand wall next to a shallow fireplace. The other three were close-ups of those areas. Probably a waste of film but it might be important later when wondering if things were open or closed, locked or unlocked, without having to rely on memory.

Lowering the camera, she looked carefully at the floor. It was of worn planks, with a single tied rag rug to soften it. Visitors were not allowed in this room. The public had to stand behind a waist-high, clear plastic barrier, slid into brackets on the doorframe where Anna stood. The floor was clean, swept, but not recently; a thin film of dust coated the planks. Dust had collected on the dressing table by the door and the rocker in the corner. A couple months' worth at a guess.

The sidelight provided by a low November sun was ideal for her purposes. Anna got down on hands and knees and put her cheek on the doorsill.

"What're you doing?" Shelly asked.

"Looking," Anna returned repressively. Between her nose and the rag rug, the dust was unmarked. Beyond the small rectangle of faded cotton, in the area from the storage room door to the bedside, the dust had been disturbed.

"Get on the radio, Shelly. Have dispatch get in touch with the sheriff. Tell him we got tracks in dust. Special paper, kind of a cross between Saran Wrap and tinfoil, will lift them. Several different brand names. Port Gibson District doesn't have any. Tell him to bring some if he's got it." Anna wasn't optimistic. She'd never worked in a park that kept that kind of stuff on hand. There was no reason a small town sheriff's department would. The technology of criminal investigation had far outstripped most law-enforcement budgets. Taxpayers weren't willing to cough up the funds to equip a town with maybe one homicide every four or five years, and most of those straightforward I-shot-the-son-of-a-bitch-and-here's-why situations, with the high-priced bells and whistles, much less the funding to train an ever-changing cadre of sheriffs' deputies to use them.

Of course, if things got dicey, the public would be up in arms because the combined genius of NASA and the CIA hadn't been brought to bear on whatever backyard slaying the media dictated they take an interest in.

Anna was rather glad that in most places in America crime hadn't reached levels where cutting-edge Buck Rogers goodies were factored into everyday standard operating procedures. In most of the country cops still took pictures, drew sketches and crawled around on their hands and knees with tweezers and envelopes.

Standing up, Anna said, "I'm going in," then nearly laughed out loud. She'd uttered the words with the intensity of Dirty Harry about to clear out a felon-infested warehouse on the New York City docks. Maybe she'd gotten a tad cynical and practiced at looking cool, but the sight of a dead body in suspicious circumstances still triggered an adrenaline rush. It was good to be alive. She reached into the bag Shelly held and took out a tape recorder.

"Uh-oh," Shelly said.

"No danger," Anna reassured her. "I'm just going to step inside."

"No. You got your dress all smeary." The genuine sympathy in the young woman's tone reminded Anna how pretty the dress was, and how expensive.

"It'll wash," she replied, hoping it was true. Stepping through the doorway, she shut Shelly, the spoiled dress and everything else from her mind and took in the sense of the room. Simplicity, the utilitarian nature of pioneer construction and furnishings, lent it a beauty that was rarely evident in late twentieth and early twenty-first century homes: four-poster bed beneath a sash window, a desk, a rocker, a bureau. Beneath the bed was a trunk. Two hooks on the wall above the bed served the needs of a closet for a way of life that required few changes of clothing. Candles in sconces and an oil lamp would provide the room with light. Had the body been an aged family member, laid out in burial garb by loving hands, Grandma Polly's bedroom would have retained its symmetry and peace. It was so steeped in history, death itself did not seem out of place. Nudity, modernity did.

Anna crossed the room and, standing on the bit of carpet so she wouldn't destroy the tracks in the dust nearer the bed, she looked over the body. "Moby Dick," she muttered irreverently as she stared down at the great white whale beached in her park. She clicked on the tape recorder, tested it, then began.

"White male, fifty to sixty years of age, maybe five-foot-ten inches tall, well over two hundred pounds. Hair gray and brown, thinning on top, cut short. Eyes blue." Eyes. Anna was not a big fan of the eyes of the dead. Never was it clearer that they were the windows of the soul than when, looking into them, one saw only emptiness, a place devoid of hope or humanity. Once she'd seen eyes like that on a living person, a boy of eleven in a psych ward she'd visited. He'd been mutilating the family pets. His parents finally brought him in when he'd tried the same thing on his little sister.

These dead eyes were rolled back slightly, as if their owner had been looking out the sash window above his head, trying to catch a last glimpse of the stars before he died. Flesh fell heavily in the bags beneath the eyes and in his jowls, pulling down his cheeks and lips till the tips of straight, white, clearly artificial crowns could be seen.

Her gaze moving methodically down the body, Anna continued her visual exploration. "No jewelry around his neck, no marks of strangulation. No visible wounds on head, shoulders or arms." Standing on tiptoe so she would see over the man's bulk, she checked his other side. "No defensive marks evident on hands or forearms." Her focus shifted down to the torso. Here things began to get interesting. She'd started at the top of the head because thoroughness in police work was worth a great deal more than inspiration. "Torso marked with bruise pattern," she said into the machine. "Bruising evident beneath the arms. Bruising and chafing in a band approximately four inches wide just below the sternum. Abdomen unmarked. Subject wearing white men's briefs. No blood or semen stains visible. On the inner thighs bruising and chafing, contusions having oozed blood."

"Major, *major* yuck," said a voice in Anna's ear. "Like, this is a sex crime! God. I think it'd be a crime for a guy like this to have sex at all."

"Spoken like a young, thin person," Anna said. Drawn by adventure and the macabre, Shelly had drifted in to stand behind Anna's left shoulder. Anna checked to see that she stood on the rug. During the busy season half a hundred visitors a day poked their heads in. Park aides had the run of the place. And soon the room would be populated with the sheriff's people, the coroner and whoever else got sent on the call. A few dark hairs or pale flecks of skin from Shelly Rabine weren't going to obfuscate any clues.

"Don't touch anything," Anna reminded her and left it at that.

"I know not to touch," Shelly said, slightly aggrieved. Everybody knew it and everybody, even seasoned professionals, had to be reminded. Other than on the body itself, maybe the patchwork coverlet and the tracked bit of floor, it didn't really matter. The unbroken veil of dust on planks and furniture made it clear there would be no recent fingerprints to be lifted.

"Maybe it was that auto-erotica thing or whatever you call it," Shelly suggested. "You know, where guys hang themselves while they jerk off."

"No ligature marks," Anna said. "And his underpants are still on."

"Oh. Where are his clothes? You'd think they'd be lying around somewhere."

"I doubt he was here alone. Whoever killed him or found him before we did probably took them."

"Why?"

Anna had no answer for that. It was too early for answers. She said nothing but traded Shelly the tape recorder for the camera and began taking photographs of the body and, as best as ambient light and mediocre equipment would allow, of the tracks in the dust on the floor.

When she finished and looked up, Shelly had moved away from the bed. No longer on the island of rug, she stood in front of Grandma Polly's writing desk. Anna felt a stab of annoyance that the younger woman had not obeyed her to the letter. Shelly's hands were clasped dutifully behind her back, carefully not touching anything, so Anna stifled her waspishness.

"What have you got?" she asked.

"Too weird. Come look."

On the writing table an old book lay open. On the right-hand page was a picture of Christ in the Garden of Gethsemane. The left side was covered in verse, and half of it had been circled in red felt-tip pen.

> *Sins against a holy god*
> *Sins against His righteous laws*
> *Sins against His love and blood*
> *Sins against His name and cause*

Great, Anna thought sourly.

"What do you figure?" Shelly asked. Either stress or proximity to religion was bringing out the park aide's drawl. Local girl, Anna remembered, from Vicksburg. First summer home from college after graduating from Ole Miss.

"Beats me," Anna said. "Could be a lot of things. Maybe means nothing. An impulse. Murderers are not the sort of folks known for controlling impulses."

"It'd of been night," Shelly said.

"Good point." Anna thought about that for a moment. Mt. Locust, true to its 1802 history, had no electricity. Whatever had transpired in Grandma Polly's room had been done by flashlight. The candles in the sconces had never been lit; the wicks were still white virgin cotton. The globe on the oil lamp was sheathed in a fine, unmarred layer of dust. It was unlikely, though not impossible, that whoever had been there had happened to see the verse. Maybe the picture. Only a religious person would know it was Christ in the Garden. Anna had needed to read the caption.

"Maybe the . . ." Shelly looked over her shoulder at the bed with its unsavory burden as if concerned its occupant would overhear them gossiping. ". . . the deceased," she continued self-consciously, "circled it himself. Like a sui-cide note."

"Nothing's impossible. Whoever did it had to have left a track in the dust. I missed it. Now it's been obliterated." Both women were standing on the bare wood.

"Oh, gosh, I know," Shelly said excitedly. "Baptists."

"Baptists?" Anna echoed stupidly.

"Yeah. It was done by Baptists. They're real serious about sins of the flesh. Not like Catholics or anything."

"They are?"

"Boy. You're sure not from around here. When you pro-file the killer are you going to make him Baptist?" Shelly asked hopefully.

"If I'm not mistaken, sixty percent of the state of Missis-sippi is Baptist," Anna said. She didn't want to go into the fact that garden-variety, one-corpse killers weren't pro-filed. "The sheriff should be getting here soon. Why don't you go down to the VC and wait for him."

Perhaps feeling contrite about stepping off the rug, or

having just had her fill of the vicarious thrill of unnatural death, Shelly Rabine handed Anna the rucksack she'd been holding and left without argument.

Anna took two close-ups of the picture of Christ and its accompanying verse.

"Damn," she whispered. Christians made her nervous, and here she had a corpse that appeared to have been bound and bruised by the Bible belt.

2

Taking camera and tape recorder with her, Anna walked around the stand to the back. An old grape arbor, leaves brown with the season, stood to one side. Behind the house remnants of a well—a circle of brick—were all that remained. Eric Chamberlain's kitchen garden had been put to bed for the winter. Beyond it lay a field, then the woods. Poison ivy stitched the tree line in scarlet. Beneath the pine and oak, grown through with roots, lay the bodies of slaves. Autumn had taken its toll on the leaves and the sign the NPS had erected showed through the branches. On it were the names of the dead identified so far. Two were familiar: Dinkins and Restin. Whether they were related to Anna's field ranger Barth Dinkins or Paul's deputy Lonnie Restin remained to be seen; the surnames were not uncommon in the local black community. Because of the habit of slaves taking—or being saddled with—the last name of their owners, tracing family history was difficult.

Barth was a curator by training and a historian by na-

ture. Sleuthing out the origins and descendents of the
Dinkins buried in the scrub was his pet project.

Anna pulled her attention from yesterday's dead to today's. Turning, she studied the back of the inn. Here, too,
was a covered porch, once used as an open-air bunkhouse
for travelers. To the left a small bedroom had housed generations of children. To the right was the storeroom that
opened both onto the porch and into Grandma Polly's
room. The storeroom door was open, the wood in the
frame splintered where it had been kicked in, modern lock
holding, ancient timbers shattering around it.

Anna took a couple photographs, bracketing for light.
The planks of the porch, shuffled over daily by tourists,
had collected enough in the way of dust to show obvious
tracks. A wide, clean line snaked from the top of the steps
in through the storeroom. Shelly's beached walrus had
been dragged in the back way. Dragged in dressed; Anna'd
noted no dust or splinters embedded in the corpse's ample
acreage of epidermis. She turned back to the porch rail and
studied the grass, the gravel path. No drag marks. Possibly
some on the steps but it was hard to tell. The walrus had
been killed or rendered unconscious, carried to the porch
then dumped, dragged to the bedroom and stripped down
to his undies.

The less-than-appetizing picture forming in Anna's
mind was blessedly fragmented by the sound of voices
moving up the gentle hill from the visitors center. Not
wanting to walk mindlessly over ground she hadn't
checked, she retraced her steps around Mt. Locust's south
side.

Led by the petite Shelly Rabine, three men crunched up
the gravel path beneath the live oaks. The sheriff, resplen-
dent in a uniform that looked as if it had been ironed by a
West Point cadet, walked beside the park aide. From the
old sweat stains on the man's hat and the scuffed boots a
heavy load of polish had failed to make shine, Anna
guessed the sheriff of Adams County wasn't usually so for-

mally turned out. Elections were coming. Lawmen all over Mississippi would be sprucing up.

Staying in the shadows a moment, she watched. The sheriff's name was Clintus Jones. Dispatch had given her that. Age was hard to tell. He was a black man with very black close-cropped hair, thin arched brows over wide-set dark eyes. His lips were full and precision cut. A mustache and goatee of incongruous white framed them. Jones wasn't tall, maybe a handspan over Rabine, but his bones were made for a big man: wide flat cheeks, broad shoulders and hips rounded into a barrel shape. "Under the spreading chestnut tree, the village smithy stands. The smith, a mighty man is he with large and sinewy hands." Anna whispered a line from a poem she'd presented to Mrs. White's third-grade class at Johnstonville Elementary School, and marveled that the words were still housed in her brain.

"Hey, Anna. The sheriff's got here," Shelly called.

Anna was annoyed, then impressed. Customarily, if she stood still in the shadows out of the natural line of sight she was invisible. She was mentally complimenting the young park aide on her sharp eyes when she remembered she was no longer in green and gray. Wearing a fire-engine red calf-length dress and high-heeled, red patent-leather pumps, she was as obvious as a cardinal in the winter woods.

"Hey," Anna replied, stepping into the clear and perfect sunshine. "Anna Pigeon, District Ranger." She stuck out her hand, and the sheriff took it carefully. Not the fishtail droop of a weak or reticent handshake, more the controlled delicacy of a bird dog trained to retrieve game without crushing it.

"Jones," the sheriff said and opened his fist to let her hand take flight. "This is my under-sheriff, André Gates." Gates was only African-American by the dictates of a culture that had once been proud of the premise that one teaspoon of black blood made a person black—and this was a bad thing—a form of insanity groups of northern white supremists were trying to keep alive. Gates was a product of what Anna hoped was intermarriage but was probably generations of rape. Regardless of how the man's gene pool had been filled, he'd turned out very pretty. Not as pretty as Harry Belafonte, but close. By the back tilt of his head and the set of his shoulders, she guessed he was also proud unto arrogance.

"André," Anna nodded politely.

The sheriff introduced the third man. "Gil Franklin."

White, portly and sweating through an expensive suit designed for harsher Novembers, the coroner cut Sheriff Jones off.

"Let's get on with it," Franklin said.

Anna half expected him to add the implied, "I haven't got all day," but he restrained himself. "This way, gentlemen," she said and took them up the porch steps to Grandma Polly's room.

Gil Franklin chuffed up the stairs with surprising speed. Either he had somewhere else to be or the thought of a dead body was a treat of the highest order. His leather-soled loafers clattered across the wood, drowning out the embarrassing click of Anna's heels.

"Gil, hold up a minute," Sheriff Jones hollered as the coroner steamed through the door, thrusting his considerable self into the small crime scene. Gil Franklin didn't hear or chose to ignore the request. Anna suspected the latter.

"Jesus, Mary 'n' Joseph," the sheriff muttered.

"I've photographed pretty much everything," Anna said.

"Glad somebody knows what they're doing." Jones's voice was mild but his black irises, set in slightly yellowed eyes, had gotten shiny, as if they'd grown hot enough to spark. Jones carried a lot of anger. That he had it under control only made it the more formidable.

"I'll check around back," André said. His smooth face showed nothing. Perhaps there was a hint of disdain in the flare of the nostril or in the curve of the lip. Perhaps Anna only imagined it because he looked too fine for everyday use.

"Gloves," the sheriff reminded him.

Gates nodded, a small tight movement that could be seen as either respect or insubordination, depending on what side of the bed one had gotten out of that morning.

"I'll be jiggered!" The words erupted from the direction the coroner had taken. Anna went to Polly's room, the sheriff at her shoulder.

The coroner had pulled on latex gloves but hadn't taken responsibility for his other extremities. His tasseled shoes were executing an odd little two-step in the tracks in the dust on the floor.

"What you got, Gil?" Jones asked.

"It's Doyce Barnette, Raymond's brother. I figured he'd get himself killed one day. Doyce never could tell 'come here' from 'sic 'em.' I figured he'd run his truck into a bridge abutment or fall off a roof. Now who'd bother to go and kill poor ol' Doyce?"

Despite the less-than-flattering eulogy, the coroner seemed genuinely upset. Anna liked him a shade better than she had.

Jones didn't say anything, but he pulled off his hat. Stepping neatly onto the rug, cognizant of the crime scene, he looked at the body. "Doyce all right. I better go on over after and break it to Raymond. A shame. There was never any harm in Doyce."

"That's a fact," the coroner said. "Rest of the family's mean as a whole nest of snakes, but I never heard anything but stupid against Doyce. I'm pronouncing him dead. I got to get out of here. I'm showing a house at ten-thirty." The moment of sentiment was over.

"What do you figure killed him?" the sheriff asked.

"I'm not saying, but you gotta figure he didn't come in here in his underdrawers and choke to death on a piece of venison. Homicide. Can't tell how long he's been dead. Less than twelve hours at a guesstimate." He prodded the dead man's jaw with a forefinger. "Hard as a rock. Full rigor. Closer than that I'm not going. The doctors with their doodads'll have to work it out. Let me know how the autopsy comes out." He left at a trot, the pitter-patter of his little feet retreating down the steps.

"Gil's a good enough coroner," Sheriff Jones said evenly. "He's just not big on the amenities." He took a pair of latex gloves from a leather snap pocket on his gun belt and pulled them on, careful to keep their powdery insides away from his spotless uniform. "You've got photos of the body, I take it?"

Anna said she did and Jones stepped carefully into the stir of dust Gil Franklin had left in the tracks on the planks by the bed and bent over the corpse. "Poor old Doyce. Let's see if you can tell us anything."

With delicacy and an innate respect, he began examining the body. Anna hovered nearby, feeling, in red frock and lipstick, like a ghoulish matron.

The marvels of modern science had made in-depth studies of the body on site passé. Too much fiddling by officers on scene was more likely to contaminate trace evidence than uncover a truth. The sheriff was looking for situational evidence, proof of cause and effect that would be lost when the body was moved from where it had been found.

"Quilt's rucked up," he said, pointing to the coverlet bunched under the locked and rigid knees.

"Dragged," Anna said and told him of the track on the back porch. "But not all the way. Carried to the inn, then dragged through it."

"Doyce wasn't just fluffy, he was fat. Well over two hundred pounds. Dead weight, what do you figure? Two, three strong men to carry him? Did you check for tire tracks? Maybe he got drove up out back."

"We'll look," Anna said.

John Brown Brown was coming down from headquarters in Tupelo, a three-hour drive if one broke the speed limit the whole way and didn't run into traffic in Jackson. The section of the Trace that would eventually link Anna's district on the southern end with the rest of the parkway was yet to be finished. At Clinton those northbound had to leave the false wilderness of the wooded two-lane road for the high-speed, commerce-choked freeways through Mississippi's capital city.

Chief Ranger Brown wanted to see the body in situ, but the day was warm and getting warmer. "Poor ol' Doyce," as Anna was coming to think of him, a title at least a hair more respectable than "the walrus," would be getting ripe fast.

"We use Stephen Hayne at the Mississippi Mortuary in Rankin County for autopsies," Anna said. "If that works for you, I'll get an ambulance sent down for poor—for Mr. Barnette."

The sheriff shot her a hard look, seeing if she mocked the dead. Evidently she appeared innocent of that trespass, and he softened. "Hayne is good." He stepped back from the bed and said, "Doggone it, this is looking ugly." His gaze wandered around the small Spartan room as if he hoped he'd find something to ameliorate the darkness of his thoughts. Nothing presented itself. "What do you make of the bruises, the chafing in the groin area, the state of semi-nudity?"

The sheriff was embarrassed. A possible sex crime, particularly one involving the male of the species, had caused his comfort level to collapse. Had he been ten years old, Anna suspected he'd have resorted to crude remarks and inane giggles to distance himself. A careful man, cloaked in the dignity of office, he'd opted instead for stilted formality and averted eyes.

Anna had a wicked desire to shock him just because she could. She contained her sophomoric urges. "The guy's obviously been restrained: straps, belts, ropes, whatever. My guess is straps. The bruise marks are wide and, but for the inner thighs, the skin's not broken. From the color of the bruising I'd guess the restraints were tight, brutally tight. No defensive marks or wounds. He must have agreed to the bondage. At least at first."

Jones's face was blank, his eyes fixed to the left and above Anna's right ear as if he listened to a siren singing on her shoulder. Either he was thinking deep thoughts or he'd had a small stroke.

Annoyed, Anna said sharply, "What do you know about Doyce Barnette?"

He didn't answer right away but the frozen look melted. Had Anna been a superstitious woman she might have said his soul came back into his body, such was the change from mindlessness to mindfulness in the man's eyes.

"Bondage," he said, shaking his head slowly. "Now that's a word we don't want to go throwing around down in this part of the country."

"Because of the whole slavery thing?" Anna asked, knowing she sounded about as sensitive and ethnically diverse as a hitching post.

Jones looked startled, then laughed. A big cackle, like that of a gargantuan hen with a whole clutch of new eggs, made the windows of Grandma Polly's room rattle with the ghosts of better times.

"No. No," he said, a rill of liquid merriment still running beneath the words. "We got the Internet, satellite TV and the Playboy Channel. New evils for the new millennia. Bondage means *bondage,* sadomasochism and the like. We start tossing that around amongst our conservative church-goers and poor ol'—and Doyce's family will take a heck of a beating. A heck of a beating," he repeated in case Anna didn't get it the first time. "And whatever Doyce got himself into, there's no need us going on about it now he's dead."

Anna must have looked unconvinced, though she was merely pondering the ramifications this omission might have on the investigation.

The sheriff went on to say, "His mother's still living, you

know. Ninety-three and still goes to church every Sunday and lives in the house where she was married."

"I don't feel any compunction to noise the details about as yet, sheriff," Anna said carefully.

Jones smiled. "Call me Clintus. This may be a long investigation."

"Clintus," Anna agreed, liking the man both for his laughter and his concern for old women.

"Speaking of conservative churchgoers, take a look at this." She led him to the antique writing desk and pointed at the verse circled in red ink.

"Sins against His righteous laws," Clintus read the second line aloud.

"You think maybe one of the righteous took against Doyce's extracurricular activities?" Anna asked.

"Ugly," the sheriff repeated and whistled long and low. "This couldn't have been circled some other time, maybe have nothing to do with Doyce and all?" he asked hopefully.

"I don't think so."

Both were silent for a moment, paying homage to confusion. Then Anna remembered the question that had gone unanswered. "You were going to tell me what you know about Doyce Barnette."

"I was, was I?" he returned but there was a twinkle, like a ripple in ink, in his dark eyes so Anna waited.

The room was growing crowded, the bloated corpse on the bed swelling in some non-corporeal way, pushing air from the confined space. Anna led the way out onto the porch and breathed easier for it. A bench, painted the same bright blue as the shutters and doors, was set under the window into the central room. She sat, not because she thought the story of Doyce Barnette would be a long one, but because she was paying the price of feminine allure: the snazzy red-and-black pumps were hurting her feet.

After first checking to make sure the paint would not flake off onto his uniform, Clintus Jones leaned against a post. The sun had climbed high enough so that the porch was shaded. A gentle breeze blew in from the southeast, dry and warm and sharp with the scent of pine. For an instant Anna was back in Colorado on an Indian summer day. The moment passed and, with it, the peculiar ache remembering the mountains always engendered.

"There's not a lot to know about Doyce," Clintus began. "I never had much dealings with the man either professionally or personally. We don't move in the same circles and, since I been with the sheriff's department, he's never run afoul of the law. But because this is a small town I can give you an idea—gossip I guess. No, more than that. Down here, with all of us living in the same spot more or less for umpty-ump generations, you get what you might call an ambient knowledge about folks. Nobody says. It's not written down. You just know your own folks." He looked at Anna to see if she was following his line of thought.

She tried to look intelligent. As for the knowing your own folks, she'd have to take his word. Anna lived a transient life, first in the theater with Zach, then in the National Park Service. People were from all over, most just passing through to someplace they thought would be better. Nobody had any "folks," just a series of acquaintances.

"Ambient knowledge," Anna echoed to get Clintus going again.

"Right. Doyce. His mama owns the old family homestead that backs up against the Trace that-a-way." He pointed west by northwest, indicating a line through Eric Chamberlain's kitchen garden and the trees beyond. "Big place. Nice. Lake. About three hundred acres. From the talk, there'd been near ten times that, but it got squandered and whittled down over the years. There's a house on the place, built right after the Civil War. Doyce lived there with his mama. There was some kind of disability paycheck he got and his brother helped them out some. Doyce never worked long as I've known. Likeable sort. Not real smart. Sucker to any modern-day carpetbagger with a get-rich-

quick scheme. Got along with his neighbors. Liked to hunt
and fish, played a little cards. Pretty much like a hundred
other Natchez boys," Clintus said. Anna raised her eyebrows, an oblique reference to the strap-marked, underwear clad body inside.

Clintus shrugged, a beefy heave of wide shoulders.
"Goes to show you what ambient knowledge is worth, I
guess."

The ambulance came. The body was removed. It was getting on noon. André Gates and the sheriff were waiting
for Anna in the parking lot. It had been decided she and
Clintus would break the bad news to Doyce's younger
brother, Raymond, and let him decide whether or not to tell
"Mama" she'd outlived one of her sons. A chatter of visitors, led by Shelly Rabine, was trickling up the path from
the visitors center, and still Anna was loathe to tear herself
away from the old stand.

Doyce Barnette's shade did not haunt the simple structure. Bizarre as his death was, the old stand had probably
known stranger. So many years and so many lives had
weathered the boards, a modern ghost apparently just
beaded up and rolled like rain off treated lumber.

There was no more to see, nor was Anna nagged by a
sense of having missed something. It was the Garden of
Gethsemane that kept her hovering around Polly's room.
The book itself had been gathered into evidence, a rectangle of dust-free oak left where it had lain open for so
long. She remained near the desk hoping for inspiration, if
not answers. The verse, circled in red ink was so ... so
what? Anna looked around the simple, honest room with
its spare utilitarian furnishings.

Cheesy. Circling the verse was superfluous, high
handed, melodramatic, de classé. Anna laughed aloud as
she pondered the crime of bad taste in conjunction with
murder. Personal human tragedy aside, though she'd not

admit it in polite society with over-population causing every aspect of the earth to groan under the collective weight of Homo sapiens, perhaps bad taste—or at least bad judgment—was the more destructive of the two.

Personal human tragedy aside. That was the rub. And, until she was one hundred percent certain she was not a member of the human race, she would care. At least enough to do her job.

"Those sheriffy guys are getting antsy," Shelly said, her head poking in the doorway. "Besides, I've got visitors."

Bad news could wait. Anna left Clintus and André in her office with placatory Coca-Colas from the machine in the maintenance shop while she drove the Rambler back to her house in Rocky Springs and exchanged it and her clothes for those more befitting an on-duty National Park Service law-enforcement ranger. In boots and gun and forest-green tie, Anna felt better able to face the world.

Taco, the loopy golden retriever she had inherited, leaped around on his three remaining legs with the same annoying energy he'd shown when he'd possessed the requisite four. Since he'd sacrificed the limb to save her life, Anna had felt she owed the great drooling beast and had taken to letting him patrol with her on the paper-thin pretext she was training him as a drug dog. The upside was, though he'd sniffed out nothing but a bit of beef jerky in a hitchhiker's front pocket, with Taco along compliance was a breeze. A three-legged ambassador from men's best friends tended to disarm hostile motorists. They still grumbled and argued over their speeding tickets but in a more subdued fashion. It was almost as if they didn't want to appear to be total assholes in front of the dog.

The downside was every time she put on her uniform, Taco thought he was going somewhere and became a grinning bounding idiot that filled her with guilt whenever she left him behind.

* * *

Clintus and Anna dropped André off at the sheriff's department in Natchez. He insisted he had work to do, but Anna suspected it was more that he didn't like riding three to a car with him in the cage in back. Appearing cool was probably fairly high on André Gates's priority list.

An hour and a half had been wasted while Anna had run north forty miles to change clothes. It was well after noon when they headed for Raymond Barnette's place of business. Clintus drove, leaving Anna free to study the town of Natchez.

The last city on the Trace, it had historically been the main port for goods rafted down the Mississippi River from the interior of the country. It was there the Kentucks and other traders exchanged their products for gold and started the long walk upriver and home. The trade goods were loaded on ships and taken downriver to the sea.

Modern-day Natchez was an unsettling mix of an affluent past and a struggling present. The interior of the town was crusted with antebellum mansions surrounded by live oaks that not so much towered over as embraced the property. New construction farther out along the highway degenerated into smaller, poorer homes, then the seemingly inevitable litter of Wendy's, Taco Bells and car dealerships. The directions they'd gotten from Clintus's secretary said Barnette's was situated between a Jiffy Lube and a Merchants and Planters Bank on the southern edge of the city limits.

Raymond Barnette was an undertaker by trade. According to Clintus, he was known behind his back by the nickname "Digger." Anna became familiar with his long face and toothy smile some miles before they pulled under the pillared portico at Barnette's Funeral Home. Driven into front lawns throughout suburban Natchez were color posters on wooden stakes sporting the grinning visage of the mortician. "Barnette for Sheriff. The last word in honesty," was lettered across the bottom of the cardboard, white on patriotic blue.

"The competition?" Anna asked as they passed a particularly prominent display.

Jones grunted. "He's put his signs out way early. Way early." He was silent for a minute, as if fighting the desire to say something bad about somebody. The bad won. "The last word is right. I think Digger's last honest word was in nineteen eighty-nine when he'd had a few too many and admitted he got along better with the dead than the living."

"Well, he ought to get along with his brother just fine now," Anna said callously.

Jones shot her a sideways look, but she thought a hint of humor glinted through his careful exterior. "It'd be a first," he admitted.

"Don't you have to have some kind of law-enforcement background to be a sheriff?" Anna asked.

"No. Purely an elected position. Law enforcement helps, but it isn't a requirement. Raymond was an MP in the army. He did an eight- or twelve-year hitch—I don't remember which—in the seventies. He's been leaning hard on that. 'A return to discipline.'"

As was his wont, Jones kept his voice even and cool, but Anna heard an echo of bitterness and remembered the sudden deep anger she'd seen at Mt. Locust. She wondered why, in all the chit-chat about notifying the deceased's family, he'd not bothered to tell her he was running against poor ol' Doyce's baby brother for the job of Adams County Sheriff. Vague, unfocussed suspicion flared, brought on more by a naturally cynical nature than by any untoward events. She doused it with logic. This was Mississippi. From Tennessee to Louisiana everybody pretty much knew everybody else's business. Clintus Jones might not have mentioned it simply because he assumed everybody already knew.

"That's it." Clintus pointed with his chin. An odd habit that had a military feel.

Like most funeral parlors Anna had seen, Barnette's was designed to look like an upscale home. A Mississippi na-

tive, Raymond had been unable to resist the antebellum
lure. White columns covered in plaster suggesting dead
Greek architects and Italian marble quarries fenced in the
two-story portico.

Either out of consideration or superstition, Clintus
didn't park his patrol car at the front doors in the shade of
the pillars, but pulled around back by a Dumpster, the contents of which Anna hoped never to become aquainted
with. The two of them walked back around to the front of
the building and let themselves in.

Oversized doors, with knobs higher than standard, always made Anna feel a little like the Lily Tomlin character
Edith Ann: too little for this world. Maybe that was the
point.

Within the doors was a predictable foyer, lush in pseudo
luxury with too many tasteful wall hangings. As befitted
the place's function, it was as chill and silent as a tomb and
smelled faintly of flowers. Not a pleasant smell, and Anna
wondered fleetingly why flowers in hospital rooms and funeral homes carried a different scent than bridal bouquets
and children's nosegays.

Hard-soled shoes on plastic parquet sounded from the
back of the building. Silence, ghost blooms and recent
events conspired, and Anna would not have been surprised
to see Vincent Price appear from the shadows.

It was the only slightly more reassuring countenance of
Raymond Barnette Anna had come to know from the
posters. The grinning visage was composed in that delicate
balance morticians master, somewhere between a welcoming greeting for those shopping for all eternity and a com-
passionate sympathy for those left behind.

As soon as Barnette saw who'd called him forth, the
professional mask crumbled. Even his gait changed, became looser, less formal.

"Why, hey, Sheriff Jones, what brings you here? Not
business, I hope? New recruit?" he said of Anna before
Clintus could respond to his first question.

Anna introduced herself and they shook hands. To her surprise his was warm, dry and firm. Contact with the dead had not robbed him of body heat.

"Actually, it is business," the sheriff said. He took off his hat and ran a hand over his hair, the fingers not mussing but gently patting it as if to assure him it hadn't been rearranged.

Because of the sheriff's careful observance of the amenities at Mt. Locust, Anna had wondered at his not removing his hat when they first came inside. She now suspected it was a subtle sign of disrespect.

At the word 'business' the undertaker's face altered slightly, not a return to professional empathy but veiled with a thin cast of wariness; that of a citizen wracking his brain for remembered indiscretions he'd believed had gone unwitnessed.

"It's your brother, Doyce," Clintus said. "I'm afraid we've got bad news. He's been killed."

A flicker of what might have been relief—or merely a changing of gears behind what Anna was coming to realize was an actor's countenance, capable of putting on one emotion after another without the inconvenience of feeling—briefly crossed Raymond Barnette's face. It was gone in a heartbeat and Barnette's features emerged in proper doleful arrangement.

"Yes," he said. "Gil called me from his cell phone. He's showing the old Shugrew place out past Mama's. A nice piece of property."

An odd detail to mention. Maybe it was callousness, maybe shock. Anna looked at Clintus. He'd taken on a slow burn.

"Gil called you?" he asked evenly.

Barnette picked up on the undercurrent. "Just a courtesy, sheriff. Gil and I go way back. He told me Doyce had passed. I was just now closing up shop to break the news to Mama. What was it? Gil said maybe heart attack. Doyce's never taken care of hisself—himself."

The correction triggered what might have been the first

honest emotion Anna had seen on Raymond Barnette's face: hatred. For himself, for his past, for what he thought he should be. A lapse in control that showed his lingual roots.

"It's a little more than that," Clintus told him. "Is there a place we can talk?"

"Surely. Surely." Barnette led them back to an office as formal and unused looking as the front foyer. Through that, behind a discreet door, was his working office, unadorned, cramped and cluttered with papers, coffee machine, copier, computer and other modern business paraphernalia.

All that differentiated it from any other business office were the salesmen's samples thumbtacked to the walls and littering the top of the four metal filing cabinets: tiny coffins, bits of wax shaped into a nose and what looked to be part of an ear, a color poster showing the before and after pictures of a corpse with a disfiguring facial wound carefully reconstructed with mortician's magic for an open-casket viewing.

Crowded in two narrow chairs, coffee offered and declined, Raymond settled behind his desk and Clintus told him how his brother had been found.

Details were omitted: the semi-nudity, the strap marks on the body. When the sheriff had finished, the three of them sat in silence for a minute or more. Anna passed the time watching Barnette's face. She could read nothing from his expression or lack thereof.

When he mentally came back into the room he said, "Mt. Locust? On the Trace there? What in God's name was that—was Doyce doing at Mt. Locust?"

"Well . . ." Clintus looked at Anna. She was no help. "It looks like it might be some kind of sex crime, Ray."

Barnette hardened, face and body, as if the muscles beneath the skin had suddenly turned to steel. He shot such a look of malevolent suspicion at the sheriff that Anna was startled.

"I don't know what it was, but it wasn't that," he said

coldly. "You go sayin' it was that and you got yourself a lawsuit on your hands."

The undertaker's careful diction had slipped again, but his meaning was clear enough. Neither Anna nor the sheriff responded. People in grief—if this was grief—said many things. Law enforcement officers learned not to engage.

"I got to break the news to Mama," Barnette said and stood to end the interview.

3

For reasons the sheriff chose not to divulge to Anna, they were going, uninvited, to be in attendance when Raymond told "Mama" that her firstborn was dead. During the twenty-minute drive through green and rolling hills north of Natchez, Anna covertly watched Clintus Jones. Anything that might have been there to read was locked beneath a mask of professional stoicism.

It crossed her mind that he went to the Barnette homestead merely to annoy a man he'd apparently never liked and who had recently become a rival. She might have believed it of another man, but Sheriff Jones just didn't seem the type. He had the anger, but it seemed reserved for moderately righteous causes.

"This'll be the Barnette's," the sheriff said, and he pointed to what once had been a classic avenue of oaks leading off the road to the right. There was neither sign nor mailbox, and Anna wondered if he had cause to know Doyce and his mama's home from previous visits or if it was merely the knowledge of all good small-town sheriffs of their constituency.

"Why go to Barnette's?" Anna asked.

"I don't know," Clintus confessed. "I got a funny feeling."

Anna had great respect for funny feelings. Undertaker Raymond Barnette's reaction to the news of his brother's death had left her out of balance as well.

Jones turned smoothly onto the gravel drive beneath the over-arching trees. The leaves of the live oaks never turned gold or scarlet or rained to the earth in autumn's annual celebration of death, but they did grow dry, the canopy thin-looking with coming winter. Many of the trees had been cut down, leaving gaps in a living sculpture that had been planted to endure centuries.

"Some kind of disease get the trees?" Anna asked.

"You might say that," the sheriff returned. "Hard times. Doyce and Ray's daddy died during the Depression. Their mama got on for a year or so with the help of the neighbors, but the neighbors were having hard times of their own. One day she sold half of 'em for lumber. Never planted new ones, never would let anybody dig out the stumps. Me, I wouldn't want to be reminded of the bad times every time I went to the mailbox. Takes all kinds, I guess."

Anna said nothing. She was thinking of a far-away day in high school in Red Bluff, California. She and Sister Judette had witnessed some form of aberrant behavior. To seem worldly, Anna had expressed the old cliché. The sister had shot her a sour look and retorted, "It doesn't take *that* many kinds."

The fractured avenue was short-lived, as though the original owner had the pretensions but lacked the acreage to carry them out with much aplomb. At the end of the corridor stood the homestead. It had never been a mansion—too small for that title—but once it had been a fine house. Two stories tall, it boasted a gracious front porch curving around a corner entrance. Rather than the long rocking-chair type, it was square, forming an outdoor room furnished with wicker sofas and chairs.

Clintus executed a Y-turn on the dirt in front of the house and backed the patrol car under the shade of a magnolia tree, the nose of the vehicle pointing back toward the road as if for a fast getaway. Ray Barnette's black Cadillac was nowhere to be seen.

"Looks like the hard times never left," Anna said.

"Never did, I guess. From what I've picked up over the years, Mrs. Barnette fell victim to about every get-rich-quick scheme that floated down the river and passed on the tendency to Doyce. Raymond's the only member of the family that ever did a lick of real work."

They'd reached the porch. An old fan was festooned with spider webs. The cushions on the furniture had faded to mottled gray-brown; stuffing extruded through rents in the rotting fabric. Leaves patterned the painted plank flooring. The roof was supported by squat pillars with peeling white paint, revealing the gray of weathered wood beneath.

This outdoor living space had not been used for a while. Anna and the sheriff stopped, neither wanting to be the first to try to breach the forbidding oak door that closed off the main house.

"Where the hell's Ray Barnette?" Anna asked. "He took out of the funeral home like a bat out of hell." They'd neither followed nor passed Barnette on the way, merely assumed he'd gone to "Mama's" as he said he would.

"Maybe he stopped for a cup of coffee," the sheriff said sourly. "We'll wait."

Anna eyed the wicker chairs but decided against sitting. The cushions looked as if they might have become a habitat for any number of crawly things.

Before a decision could be made on where to perch, the sound of shuffling steps and the turning of the door latch arrested their attention. Clintus shot Anna such a panic-stricken look she thought for a second he was going to bolt for his patrol car. She would have been right on his heels. By arriving before Raymond, they'd landed themselves in the midst of a potential social gaffe that even county and federal law-enforcement uniforms would not excuse.

"We'll chitchat till Ray shows," the sheriff stage-whispered and stood shoulder to shoulder with Anna, both looking as guilty as villains from a melodrama.

The door swung open. Clintus snatched off his Stetson. From out of the gloom of the high-ceilinged room an old woman materialized. Another midget: she was as tiny as Anna's maternal grandmother, no more than four foot ten. Her white hair was chopped off just below her ear lobes and held back on either side by pink plastic barrettes shaped like little butterflies. The childishness continued. The old lady wore a short, brightly patterned rayon dress Anna remembered seeing on the rack in the juniors department at Dillards.

What killed the quirky charm of the birdlike blue eyes and youthful attire was the double-barreled shotgun she pointed purposefully at their middles.

"Whoa," Anna breathed and, "easy now, lady," as she raised her hands in the universal I-mean-you-no-harm gesture.

"You git," the old woman shouted. "I'm tired of you sniffin' around prying into things, trying to steal my land. I see you here one more time you'll get a hide full of buckshot."

The threat was directed, not at Anna, but at Sheriff Jones. Again, Anna wondered at Clintus's familiarity with the place.

Without taking her eyes from Jones, the old woman said to Anna, "You get your boy outta here, now. I don't know what you're playin' at with these people but keep 'em away from me and mine."

Anna hazarded a look at Clintus. He appeared as genuinely baffled as she was.

"We'll be going now, ma'am," Anna said firmly. "You don't need that shotgun. Come on, Clintus." The two of them backed slowly toward the porch steps, the old woman following, nudging them along with short, sharp jabs of the shotgun barrel.

The crunch of tires on gravel arrested what Anna was sure was a ludicrous tableau.

"Mama, it's all right," Raymond called. He came up the steps behind Anna and the sheriff. "Mama's" aim never wavered and neither of them put their hands down.

"It's okay, Mama," Ray said soothingly. "No need for fireworks." He took the shotgun from his mother's wrinkled grasp. He tried to do it gently but the bony fingers held on till he gave the weapon a vicious twist. Anna flinched but Mama's trigger finger let go before the gun went off.

Disaster averted, Raymond put his arm around the tiny harridan in what looked to Anna like a parody of filial affection. "Mama, this is the sheriff," he said loudly. "*Sheriff Clintus Jones.*"

"Mama's eyesight isn't as good as it used to be," Raymond said with a smile that was meant to be ingratiating but, given the oversized front teeth, came off as mildly menacing.

"Let's go on inside, Mama." He herded his aging mother into the shadows behind the oak door and pulled it firmly shut behind them, leaving the sheriff and Anna marooned on the porch.

"Jeez Louise," Anna muttered as she shut herself in the sanctity of Clintus's patrol car. "Jeez Louise" was fairly unsatisfying but, since she'd moved to a region where "What church do you belong to?" was as common a question as "where do you live?" she'd consciously tried to cut down on taking the Lord's name in vain.

"You said it." Clintus whistled and shook his head. "What do you figure that was all about?"

Anna looked at him sharply. Mama Barnette had appeared to recognize and hate the sheriff. She'd accused him of, among other things, trying to steal her land. In memory the sequence of events was so Hatfields-and-McCoys via 1950s TV that Anna laughed.

"What?" Clintus demanded.

Antebellum dry rot, the decimated oak lane and the shotgun had conspired to dislocate Anna culturally and, for the moment, she felt a stranger in a strange land, unsure whether Mississippians had TV in the fifties and sixties, if the images that shaped the rest of the country would evoke an emotional connection in this part of the country.

"Nerves," Anna made a long story accessible.

"Jiminy Christmas," Clintus hooted, continuing the theme of ersatz profanity. "I felt like an extra in a bad episode of the Beverly Hillbillies."

Again Anna laughed, American pop culture restored and binding. For a few moments they sat without speaking. Absently she scratched at a fire ant bite on her wrist. She'd gotten it more than a week before, but the toxin of these minute monsters was persistent.

"What's Mama Barnette got against you?" she asked finally.

"Beats me," Clintus said with all apparent honesty. He shrugged appealingly and turned his hands up. His palms were wide and soft. Anna found strong men with pillowed hands particularly gentle-looking for some reason.

"She thought you were someone else," she said.

"That's my guess."

"Who?"

Again the sheriff said, "Beats me."

More silence. "We've got to go back in," Clintus said finally.

"I know." Anna felt like an idiot cowering in the car, facing the prospect of slinking back to the front door a second time. From the way the sheriff sat in a lump fiddling with a lacing on the leather steering wheel cover, she guessed he felt no better.

"I don't want to give her too much time with her number two son before we question her," he said. Anna nodded. Raymond the-last-word-in-honesty Barnette did not inspire confidence.

Clintus was the first to reach for the door handle. Anna had trailed him back into the shade of the neglected porch. As he stood before the door, presumably gathering his dignity for the coming interview, she enjoyed the timeless peace of a southern autumn.

Spring was a raucous season with the song of countless frogs and nesting birds creating complicated symphonies of new birth. By fall many of the birds had gone and the frogs, those who'd not given their leapy little lives that the birds might grow strong, had matured into middle-aged complacency and no longer sang.

This tucked-away place with its ancient oaks and magnolias hummed quietly. A moment of Indian summer, caught in amber by the perfect light and promising to last forever.

Not so the peace of the human animal. Clintus rapped on the door too sharply, overcompensating for the memory of their ignoble rout, and Anna was jerked back to petty mortality.

The wait before the knock was answered grew so long Anna began to ask that creepy question that comes to all law officers every now and then: *What will I do if they just won't play the game?* One can hardly batter down a grieving mother's door just to get an interview, and Anna couldn't picture herself or Clintus yelling, "We know you're in there. Come out and nobody will get hurt." Law and order, the day-to-day bread and butter stuff, was predicated on a cooperative citizenry. There are no policemen in an anarchy, only soldiers. Clintus knocked a second time. Another minute passed.

Ten minutes earlier she'd have been experiencing pure relief. Bringing tragic news to surviving relatives had never been one of her favorite parts of the job. Since the advent of the tardy son and the shotgun, her curiosity had been piqued. She wanted a go at the feisty old lady.

"Looks like we come back tomorrow," she said disappointedly.

"Wait," the sheriff replied. "Raymond's thinking, is my bet. Figuring the ramifications. How's answering versus not answering going to look in the local newspaper."

"Maybe he's hoping we'll bust the door down and find him protecting the privacy of his sainted mum."

Clintus laughed. "He'd love that." Local politics, for all that it seemed small-time to outsiders, carried much of the same low-down, mud-slinging, high-stakes ramifications as a bid for the presidency.

Anna promised herself never to run for office even if an adoring constituency begged her.

The sound of footsteps approaching announced the end of undertaker Barnette's cogitations. The heavy oak swung inward a foot or so, and Raymond extruded onto the porch pulling the door shut behind him. A mask of empathy was fitted over his features, but Anna sensed satisfied complacency beneath.

"How's your mama doing?" Clintus asked, southern manners at the fore.

Barnette shook his head in slow theatrical sadness. "It's a bad shock. I've called Doc Fingerhut. He's phoned in a prescription. Poor Mama is used to hard times. She'll weather." He tried a brave and understanding smile, but it was ruined by the oversized incisors.

"We need to ask her a few questions," Clintus pressed on. "See if she can shed any light on where your brother was last night, who he was with."

Barnette hesitated. Then, perhaps remembering he might hold the job of sheriff in the not-so-distant future, relented. "Don't be too long about it." Turning, he dug a set of keys out of his trouser pocket. He'd locked the front door behind him when he'd come out. Not since she'd lived in New York City had Anna seen such a paranoid display of personal security.

The inside of the house was so dark it took a moment for Anna's eyes to adjust. Blinds were drawn on the windows, then reinforced with heavy drapes, as if light was the enemy. Heavy furniture of antique design crouched in the gloom. Wallpaper was dark, a brown and pink background for pictures framed in dark wood, subjects indecipherable in the dim light.

Every available surface was cluttered with magazines, newspapers and cast-off clothing. Beer cans, half-eaten bags of chips and paper plates bearing crumbs finished the classic bachelor décor.

"Doyce lived downstairs," his brother explained as they threaded their way through the darkling mess. "Mama lives up."

Though the day was perfect, the temperature hovering in the low seventies with a slight breeze, the house was closed up tight. By the dusty fall of the heavy drapes, Anna doubted the windows had been opened in years. In place of the rich living air of the outdoors they were left with the chill flat touch of air-conditioning. It gave the Barnette ancestral home the same feel as Barnette's Funeral Home.

Remembering the dirty plates littering Doyce's lair, Anna looked on the bright side. Perhaps the air-conditioning kept the smells to a minimum.

Though the house was only two stories, the ceilings were close to fourteen feet high and to reach the upper floor they climbed two foreshortened flights. A window with a magnolia in stained glass shed green and yellow light on the landing where the stairs turned back on themselves. Below the window hung a flyspecked oil painting of the Last Supper.

Anna's knowledge of biblical history was sketchy at best but she seemed to remember the Last Supper was eaten somewhere in the vicinity of the Garden of Gesthemane.

"Sins against a holy God"; one of the lines circled in red at the murder scene. Anna shook off the thought. Probably half the homes in Adams County had religious images scattered across their walls. Besides, regardless of how tough old Mama Barnette was, she just wasn't big enough to lug around a piece of dead meat the size and heft of her older boy.

After the pizza crust and old gym socks ambience of the downstairs, Mama's realms were a heaven of order. The same overabundance of furniture prevailed, but above stairs it was at least clean and free of debris.

The upstairs consisted of three bedrooms and a bath clustered around a spacious landing at the top of the stairs. Two of the doors stood open and, by the light which filtered through the lace sheers, Anna noted the world Mama Barnette had preserved on the second floor. She glimpsed the bedroom to the right as they came up the last steps. The feel was prewar; not II or I, but Civil. A four-poster bed dominated the room. In lieu of a closet was a fine old armoire with mirrored doors.

"Mama's in here," Raymond said sharply, as if to pull Anna's prying eyes from the bedroom. He stood aside to the left of the landing and ushered them into another spacious high-ceilinged room. The second bedroom apparently served as Mrs. Barnette's sitting room. Careful arrangements of formal Victorian chairs flanked a small marble-topped table with carved legs bandied out from a pedestal. A high-backed cherry settee sat against the wall, and tufts of what may very well have been the horsehair of the original stuffing poked through the threadbare fabric. Crocheted doilies were pinned to the back and the arms in an attempt to hide the ravages of age.

Mrs. Barnette sat in a rocking chair by a fireplace. November had yet to get cold enough for fires and the opening was discreetly covered by a decorative paper fan.

Anna and the sheriff entered and stood awkwardly amid the fragile furniture, waiting to be received. Raymond scuttled over to his mother's chair. "This is the *sheriff*," he said in a loud voice. "The doctor's called in a prescription for you."

The old woman turned her round blue eyes up at her son. From where Anna stood, they appeared to be free of tears or any other discernable signs of grief.

"I know who he is," the old woman snapped. "I don't need no doctor's poisons. And I ain't deaf."

Raymond smiled. Anna thought it smacked more of an undertaker sizing up a customer for a coffin than the understanding of a devoted son.

Evidently it struck his mother the same way. "Stop grinning like an idiot," she ordered her younger son. "Your big teeth are hanging out."

Raymond did as he was told. His face clung doggedly to a mask of benevolence, but his eyes mirrored the pure nastiness of his mother's.

Blood will tell, Anna thought and glanced around her, an instinct to check for more vipers in the nest.

"We're real sorry about Doyce," Clintus began.

"Get on with it," Mrs. Barnette interrupted the condolences.

"Okay," he said. They'd not been invited to sit. As they stood like servants called on the carpet, Clintus started the interview. "We just need to ask you a couple of questions so we can figure out what happened."

"Ask them. Don't shuffle around all day scuffing up my good rug."

Anna heard Clintus sigh, before abandoning the delicacy he had thought the situation called for. "Do you know where Doyce was last night?"

"I don't. He got this bug to play poker all of a sudden." She said the word 'poker' the way a Carmelite nun might say 'sodomy.' "Friday nights he was off playing poker with his low-life friends. I don't know who they were and I don't want to know.

"He'd be out most of the night. He thought I wouldn't know but I heard him come in. I ain't deaf," she said again and glared at Raymond.

"He never mentioned who he played with?" Clintus tried. "Not even first names or anything?"

"I told you he didn't. I wouldn't have listened if he did. They were drinking and smoking and gambling. When that boy come in I could smell it on him all the way up here. That stink of sin coming right up the stairs.

"He was losing money, too. He lied about that but he was all right. Just throwing away all me and his daddy, God rest his soul, worked so hard for. The devil'd got hold Doyce and now he's dead."

Mrs. Barnette sounded as is she figured it served him

right but venting the anger had melted something in her wizened old heart and at the word 'dead' tears flooded her eyes and ran down in a zigzag pattern through the time-carved creases in her face.

"Mrs. Barnette, do you mind if we take a look around downstairs, see if we can find out who he was with?" Clintus asked.

Mrs. Barnette gave no indication she heard.

They'd gotten what they were going to out of the old woman. Clintus gave his condolences. Mrs. Barnette did not accept them, though Anna's she acknowledged with a sniff and a nod. When they left she was in her rocker staring straight ahead, tears running down her cheeks, her stony old face as unchanged by the tempest as the stones the rain falls on.

Raymond reluctantly supplied the permission they needed. Anna hoped he'd remain with his grieving mother but no such luck. The undertaker's lanky angulated form followed them downstairs like Edward Gorey's uninvited guest, his dark work suit melting in and out of the shadows on the landings.

Resolutely, she put him from her mind.

"You take Doyce's room," Clintus said, ignoring murmured instructions from their attendant mortician that the investigation could be better served in a myriad of other ways. "I'll see if the living room has anything to offer."

The part of the house Doyce lived in consisted of a spacious living room, a formal dining room, a kitchen and what had once been a library, a perfectly square room with built-in bookcases from the floor to two feet below the ceiling. The bookcases, painted dark green, took up two walls. A fireplace claimed the third and a bay window the fourth.

From the living room, Anna could hear the annoying rattle of Raymond Barnette's advice. Quietly, she closed the library door in the probably vain hope it would keep the man out.

The first order of business was light. Having threaded her way through the clutter to the bay window, she threw open the heavy drapes and was rewarded by a shower of dust. A spider, her web disarranged probably for the first time in generations, ran for cover. She was small and not overly alarming so Anna let her live.

The sheers were opened next. Though Anna did not handle them with undue violence one of them tore, the fabric so old it had become almost as fragile as the spider's web. The window shade was last. Finally, to Anna's relief, there was light.

It had been in her mind to throw wide the casement and let in the rejuvenating air of autumn, but one look at the paint-encrusted sill convinced her it wasn't worth the time and effort. She turned back to the room.

When the library had been forced into use as a bedroom no changes had been made, no closet added, a bed had just been jammed up against one of the built-ins. The books were long gone, and the cases were used to house an eclectic collection of the deceased's belongings.

The bed, a single that looked as if it had survived Doyce's childhood in the 1950s, was unmade. Blankets were tangled in a ball and the bottom sheet had come loose, exposing the mattress ticking. Adolescents were prone to crawling into nests of that sort rather than taking the trouble to make things neat. In an adult it spoke of a disregard or disrespect for one's self.

An unwelcome memory bloomed behind Anna's eyes. After Zach had died there'd come months she'd retired to just such a bed night after night. Usually fully dressed. Often too drunk to care. She shook off the image. It didn't surprise her Doyce lived as he did. From what little she'd seen, she didn't need a degree in psychiatry to know this was a seriously dysfunctional family.

The clothes scattered over the floor and the room's one chair told her little but that Doyce favored sweatpants, T-shirts and camo-patterned army fatigues. She supposed the former to be for at-home lounging and the latter for more formal occasions.

Half a dozen snapshots, unframed but propped up

against old sneakers and a half-empty box of rifle shells, showed Doyce in his finery. He and two other men, also in full camouflage dress, posed around the empty-eyed carcass of a deer.

The rifles were equipped with night scopes. The men had traces of blacking on their faces, aping commandos on night maneuvers. Anna shook her head. The stealth and technology men put behind stalking a timid herbivore with the cognitive capacity of an eighteen-month-old child mystified her.

She turned the photos over but luck was not with her; no names had been scrawled on the backs. Still, she slipped one in her pocket for future use. Chances were good at least one if not all of his hunting buddies would also be a poker-playing buddy.

The room offered up little else. Doyce's personal life was evidently centered on eating and sleeping. There were no books, only magazines, two on hunting. A third, imperfectly hidden behind a shoebox half full of loose change, matchbooks and spent shotgun cartridges, was a Penthouse from August 1998. The little things that tell of life and interests, checkbooks, letters, lists, pictures, gifts from friends and family, were missing.

The door pushed open and Raymond "Digger" Barnette shoved his long face into the room. "Are you about finished up?" he asked. "I need to get back up and see how Mama's doing."

"Finished," Anna said. She fished the snapshot of the hunters from her pocket. "Mind if I take this?"

Raymond looked at it for a long time as if seeking to see if there was anything objectionable in it. "Go ahead," he said grudgingly.

"I'll get it back to you," Anna promised.

"Keep it."

Anna buttoned the photo back in her pocket.

Clintus met her in the foyer. "Anything?" he asked as Raymond hovered around, trying to urge them out the door.

"Not much," Anna admitted. "You?"

"A phone message left last night at six-forty-nine. 'Hey Doyce, Herm, you up for it? Come on down,'" the sheriff recited, dropping into a heavy southern drawl that made Anna smile. "A place to start," he said. "There's just not that many Hermans in this part of the country."

Raymond saw them to the front door, then closed it behind them.

Anna trotted down the front steps and suppressed an urge to spread her arms like wings, turn her face to the sky and spin in the childhood dance celebrating life, air and the sun. The misery embedded in the house wasn't static. It lived and grew. Anna could feel it like a fungus on her skin. The touch of the sun burned it away.

Clintus didn't dance but he tilted his face to the light then rubbed it with both palms as if he washed in light. "I'd never been inside before," he said. "Man. If this had been a suicide I doubt I'd even of questioned it."

"There's not enough Prozac in the world to induce me to live like that," Anna said. She'd seen dumps before. Clintus would have, too. Places eaten away by poverty or neglect. Rooms and buildings ravaged by the violence of those who lived there, reflecting it back on the residents. Homes of people too mentally ill to care for themselves or their property. It wasn't the disarray downstairs or the absence of light and fresh air that had struck at Anna. The Barnette house was closed up, shut off in some way. Keeping in old pain and old pride. Shutting out a flow of life that, in normal circumstances, would bring new emotions, new interests, to replace those time had used up.

The place was a mausoleum. Anna was reminded of *Great Expectations,* of the old woman in her decaying wedding dress presiding over a feast long go eaten by mice and worms. The analogy wasn't quite right, but as Anna did not choose to think any more about it, it would have to stand until she came up with something better.

"Ish," she said as they fled for the second time to the

sheriff's patrol car. Clintus was in, and as Anna reached
for the door handle, she was stopped by a faint insistent
beeping.

Because of the bleak mental landscape the house had
engendered, a sudden picture of bombs, the kind favored
by filmmakers, with the last seconds ticking away before
the explosion, filled her mind.

Standing stock-still, she listened. The beeping came
from Raymond Barnette's Cadillac, a shining heap of Detroit iron painted, as befitted his calling, as funeral-black as
any hearse.

"Hang on a second," she said to Clintus through the
open window.

The undertaker's car was parked in the sun. Anna
crossed the weedy gravel turnaround. In his haste to get to
the house, Raymond had left the keys in the ignition and
the driver's door ajar. In an act of automatic kindness,
Anna started to close it for him to save his battery. On the
passenger seat was a sheaf of neatly stapled papers. Last
Will and Testament was blazoned across the top in oversized Gothic type.

Curiosity shouldered aside the good Samaritan. Anna
leaned in and snatched it up. "*Plain view,*" she whispered
to herself, quoting the rule that allowed law-enforcement
officers to use things that might be claimed as protected by
a citizen's right to privacy in evidence. Anything left in
sight for any eyes that happened by did not fall under the
privacy laws.

Kneeling on the driver's seat, she scanned the document.
Florence Littleton Barnette's estate consisted of the house
and property and little else: no stocks, bonds, mutual funds
or other real estate. The whole of it had been left to her
elder son, Doyce Felder Barnette. In the event that Doyce
should die before his mother, the estate would then go to
the younger son, Raymond Allan Barnette.

This, then, was why Raymond had been so long getting
to his mother's house with the tragic news. He'd stopped

off at his home or the lawyer's office to get a copy of the will.

Who better than a mortician to appreciate the notion that life is short, and one has to make hay while the sun shines?

4

Clintus, Anna and the pretty young under-sheriff, André, gathered in Anna's office on the outskirts of Port Gibson in deference to the Trace's chief ranger, John Brown Brown. Brown had made the drive from Tupelo to monitor the festivities and had been left to cool his heels in the district office for three hours. His usually equitable disposition had suffered in transit.

The doors at either end of the long, dingy office space were propped open and, in lieu of the grinding of the decrepit air conditioner that had sawed at Anna's nerves throughout the summer, the soothing sound of a breeze in the pin oaks and an occasional birdcall drifted in.

Chairs had been brought out of the tiny office Anna claimed as district ranger. The chief had taken one, Clintus Jones the other. Anna and André stood, leaning against the walls for comfort.

Anna's field rangers, Randy Thigpen and Barth Dinkins, their desks shoved together to form one large working surface, took their own chairs by right. Barth, just back from a morning at the dentist's, watched the proceedings with a half-frozen face that gave him a deceptively stupid look. Barth was African-American with short, black hair sprigged with white and smooth, dark skin. He'd been tee-tering on serious obesity when Anna had first come to Mis-sissippi. Since then he'd shed close to thirty pounds. He remained beefy and still soft but no longer fat. His eyes, a beautiful and startling feature, always had a mildly unset-tling effect on Anna. They were clear gray-green, the sclera white almost to pale blue. They gave her the same sense she had when being studied by a blue-eyed Samoyed, that there were forces she could not completely understand at work behind them.

Randy Thigpen wasn't scheduled to come on duty until 8 P.M., but as the murder had taken place during his shift the previous night, Anna'd asked him in early. Thigpen, a middle-aged man from New Jersey posing as a southern-fried good old redneck, had chosen to be a thorn in Anna's side since she'd been hired as district ranger, a job he be-lieved was owed to him.

Early on he'd sued her on the grounds of racism. Thig-pen was a white man, with reddish brown hair of which he was inordinately vain and a healthy bush of mustache, which was used to collect donut crumbs and hide his upper lip: both attested to Scots-Irish ancestry. He'd accused Anna of giving scheduling preference to Barth because he was black. It had been proved that during the time of Thig-pen's complaints, Anna had been following the schedule left in place by the previous district ranger and the lawsuit was dropped. Since then Thigpen had waged a war of petty insubordination. Today was no exception. Anna noted with the grim satisfaction one feels when an expected nastiness comes to pass that showing behind the open neck of Thig-pen's uniform shirt was a bright purple undershirt. Thigpen had been on the Trace for close to thirty years. He knew he was out of uniform, knew the chief ranger would notice, knew he'd mention it to Anna, a sign her district was lax in discipline.

Even before the advent of the purple underclothes, Anna suspected she'd lost some of John Brown Brown's good will. He had been instrumental in getting her the job on the Trace. Since he'd brought her on board there'd been two murders in one year. Two murders on the 450-odd-mile-long Trace was rare. Two in the sleepy Natchez-to-Jackson district was unheard of. Not since the bad old days when it was a wilderness footpath beset by robber bands had there been this much violence. From the sidelong glances the chief cast in her direction, Anna had the feeling he somehow held her responsible.

Randy caught Anna staring at the offending purple. He hadn't quite the audacity—or the courage—to smile, but she did not miss the slight tightening of his one visible lip and the glint in his pale blue eyes.

She took comfort in the fact that, unlike his compatriot, he'd not lost weight. At six feet tall he weighed in at close to three hundred pounds, most of it carried in a great gut. Surely he'd have a massive heart attack one day soon.

To give the devil his due, Randy was on his best behavior this afternoon. For once he'd abandoned his sneering, lounging demeanor. He sat upright in the wooden office chair, his heavy elbows planted on his desk amid the clutter of unrecorded speeding tickets and unfinished reports.

He followed the conversation with apparent interest, and when the chores were being divvied up, he actually volunteered. Clintus took on the task of tracking down the "Herm" who'd left a message on Doyce's answering machine. Failing to get that assignment, Randy asked to be the one to find and question the friends—if there were any—of the victim.

"Since the wife and I moved to Natchez in June we've tied in with the community," he said sanctimoniously. "I think the folks there trust me. The men'll talk to me." Even in this new and surprising persona of the good and helpful ranger, he couldn't resist shading the emphasis and sliding a look to Anna to suggest the locals wouldn't be so forthcoming with her.

"Works for me," she said, wondering what Thigpen was up to. Maybe it was just the thrill of being in on a major murder case. The previous spring circumstances and Thigpen's own goldbricking had allowed her to keep him on the fringes of the investigation of the murdered girl. Evidently he was determined not to be left out of the excitement this time around.

For hard leads they were pretty much down to Herm and the elusive poker party.

The autopsy might turn up something, as might the lab reports on the victim's underpants and the bedspread where the corpse had been deposited. Anna didn't envy the technician, given the coverlet. The patchwork quilt that had unwittingly become Doyce Barnette's penultimate resting place hadn't actually belonged to Grandma Polly herself, but the thing was probably sixty years old. Too frail to wash, it had been gathering whatever effluvia drifted by from half a century of visitors and park rangers. Searching for trace evidence was bound to become a microscopic archaeological dig.

Brown's sourness, Thigpen's cooperation; society as she knew it was out of balance. That or her attitude was still jaundiced from the interview with Mama Barnette. Whatever the cause, Anna was getting increasingly twitchy. Chief Ranger Brown fixated on the FBI. National Parks were federal lands. When capital crimes occurred, the Federal Bureau of Investigation could be given jurisdiction, either assisting or taking over from local talent.

Often, for reasons of their own, the Bureau was not interested and the park was left to solve its own problems. During her career with the Park Service, Anna had worked with the FBI three times. Naturally she'd heard the gossip about their high-handed, authority-stealing ways, but her experiences had been positive. Her discomfort stemmed not from the fact that Brown talked of calling in the Feds— this murder had the trappings of what could be a sex crime and, next to drugs and guns, the bureau seemed drawn to the bizarre—it was the way Brown was talking about it.

She couldn't tell whether he was motivated by lack of faith in her and her admittedly unpromising-looking crew or whether, because of the crime's potentially lurid aspects and the circled religious text, he was merely anxious to separate himself and the park service from it as much as possible.

"I'll call the agent in Jackson," she said to end the discussion.

"*I'll* call the agent in Jackson," Brown said, shutting her down in front of her rangers. He had the courtesy to look apologetic, but the satisfaction on Thigpen's face cancelled any comfort Anna might have taken from it.

In other circumstances in other parks, she would have wondered what she'd done to compromise herself in the chief ranger's eyes. On the Natchez Trace she wondered what Randy Thigpen said she'd done that brought about the change.

Days were growing short, clocks had long since been dialed back to daylight wasting time, and it was dark by the time the meeting broke up. Chief Ranger Brown headed back to Tupelo, preferring a late arrival home to a night in a motel by the freeway in Jackson.

Anna headed for her house in the Rocky Springs campground area.

The headlights of her patrol car cut along the tree trunks, firing a litter of leaves beneath. This fall had been bone-dry following a summer of drought, and the leaves were mostly dun-colored, but a few still sparked with crimson and flame orange. Two deer, caught in the high beams, stared at her with startled eyes. One was a doe, the other a young buck with polished antlers, either a two- or four-pointer. Anna could never remember whether one counted all the prongs or just those on one side.

She slowed to a crawl. Deer were silly creatures. It was impossible to tell which way they would break. Though it saddened her to see the carcasses, she never much blamed the drivers in car-deer collisions. As often as not the skittish deer seemed to throw themselves under one's wheels.

This time of year, danger threatened them from all sides. Cars on the Trace, and beyond the narrow ribbon of federally protected parkland, it was hunting season in the South.

Lacking the huge tracts of public lands of the west on which to hunt, Mississippians—or at least those who could afford it—joined hunting clubs. These clubs owned hundreds of thousands of acres in the state. The fancy ones boasted clubhouses, cabins and indoor plumbing. The simpler ones promised only male bonding and a chance to kill something.

The deer, for all their innocence and stupidity, seemed to have some sort of race memory. During hunting season, they crowded the safe zone of the Trace in staggering numbers. One night Anna had counted one hundred and twenty-three on the forty-mile stretch of road between Natchez and Port Gibson.

Disappointed hunters driving home from various hunting camps were often tempted beyond their ethics by this largesse. Poaching was an ongoing problem.

Turning into the familiar darkness of Rocky Springs, she allowed herself to think of home. Taco would be waiting with great leaps and slurps of canine welcome. Piedmont, an aging yellow tiger cat she'd rescued from a Texas flashflood when he was so little his eyes were still blue, would withstand the indignities of doggie exuberance to butt her legs with his striped skull and meow the day's disappointments.

Home is where the heart is. For a lot of years these furry creatures had been the main and stalwart keepers of Anna's heart. Regardless of this, the low brick house, built in the 1960s, too cold in the winter and too hot in the summer, had yet to feel like home. Though she had no plans to apply for work in other parks and tradition demanded one spend a least a year in a duty station that had come with a promotion, Anna couldn't shake the feeling she was just passing through.

Self-pity was cut short as she turned into her driveway. A familiar white Toyota pickup truck was parked behind her old Rambler American. The porch light was on. The lights she'd installed in the arachnid-choked carport blazed.

Father/Sheriff Paul Davidson had come to call.

Anna suffered a physical jolt, a sensation not unlike stepping off a step that isn't there in the dark. Paul: a complicated man enmeshed in complicated circumstances, who had appeared in the spring and upset the comfortable loneliness she had built up around herself since Zach died.

She drove into the "spider-port" and switched off the ignition. For a moment she sat behind the wheel trying to sort out her feelings. The attempt was unsuccessful. She climbed out of the patrol car, unsure whether she was exhilarated or deeply annoyed at this unexpected invasion. The thought of Paul with his slow smile and strong hands, waiting to hear her and hold her, carried her up the walk in an adolescent thrill. The sight of him, uninvited, in her front room, her personal cat on his lap, her private dog curled slavishly at his feet, transformed this volatile sensation into irritation.

"Hey," she said neutrally and, not meeting his eyes, busied herself with taking off her duty belt, a piece of wearing apparel heavier and more restrictive than any long-line girdle ever invented.

"Hey your own self." He stood in one fluid movement. Paul was fifty-one but he moved with a boy's natural grace and energy. Piedmont, boosted from lap to shoulder, curled shamelessly around Paul's neck. The cat studied Anna with knowing amber eyes and twitched the tip of his long ringed tail. The message was clear: she'd left his food bowl empty long after 5 P.M. She could be replaced.

Taco, having no dignity to stand on, rushed over belatedly to lick his welcome. Anna was unmoved.

"What brings you here?" she said to the sheriff and was appalled at how cold her words sounded. But he'd stolen the affections of her cat so she didn't retract them.

Had Davidson been snappish and peevish in return, Anna's day would have been perfect. She would have nailed herself back into the familiar isolation and been oddly comforted by it. He didn't. His smile of greeting turned to a look of concern.

"Bad day?" he asked kindly. "Here. Have a cat." He placed a purring Piedmont in her arms. Kindness, warmth and fur resolved Anna's conflicting emotions.

"Moderately sucky day," she admitted and leaned her forehead against his chest so he could hold both her and her cat.

With the exception of alcohol, a wonder drug Anna'd forsworn yet again when it had contributed to her getting beaten half to death, Paul provided everything she could have wished for: light, food, a kind ear and good conversation.

An illicit tryst between a married priest and the local widow lady would bloom far more salacious in the telling than in the transpiring. And, though they chose not to waste time worrying about it out loud, both Anna and Paul knew there would be the telling. Their relationship had been born under two microscopes: the gossipy insular world of the National Park Service and the gossipy insular world of Southern Mississippi.

The wonderful thing Anna'd come to know about both the service and the state was that they'd treat you like family. There was always someone to lend a hand or stand you a free lunch. The downside was they treated you like family: nosing in, giving unwanted advice, passing judgment, discussing your affairs ad nauseum.

After Anna had eaten they sat for a while at the dining table in the uncomfortable, ladder-backed rattan chairs Anna had inherited from her grandmother. Taco had the decency to lie at Anna's feet rather than at Paul's, and Piedmont came to sprawl companionably beside the salt and pepper shakers on the scarred cherry-wood tabletop.

The jarring ring of the telephone made both of them flinch. Paul looked suddenly young and guilty as if he was

afraid the bell tolled for him, that his wife was calling him
at his mistress's house. Anna swallowed the creeping nausea that image dragged up her throat and pushed away
from the table.

On the fourth ring she picked up the phone. "Rocky
Springs," she answered. Silence. "Hello?" Then a click.

"What was that?" Paul had risen from the table.

"A hanger-up," Anna said wearily. "It happens a lot, especially on the weekends. My number must be close to that
of a local pizza parlor."

Paul looked relieved and for the briefest of moments
Anna hated him for it. They sat again in the rickety ladder-
backed chairs. For Anna, at least, the mood had soured.

For a minute or more neither of them spoke. To talk
about "the relationship" with Paul's angry wife hovering at
the edges of their minds was too exhausting.

Anna broke the silence first, choosing to discuss what
they'd talked about on their first date: murder. Because
Paul was in law enforcement and because she trusted him,
but mostly because she needed to confide in someone, she
related the suggestive details of Doyce Barnette's corpse.

"I don't know the Barnette family," Paul said after a moment's consideration. "But of course I know of them."

"Of course," Anna said and was treated to Paul's slow
smile.

"From what I gathered, Doyce wasn't your sex-crime
type. At least not the S & M bondage sort. Doyce was a
southern boy. Hunting, fishing, football, that seems more
along his line."

"What's the sex-crime type?" Maybe she was just tired,
but Anna found herself bristling at the southerner's easy
assumption that the rest of the country was more deeply
steeped in sin than the Magnolia State.

Paul heard the acid in her words but chose to ignore it.
Anna was grateful. Though she felt prickly she had no
wish to be left alone.

"Our sex crimes tend to be family affairs," he went on
evenly. "Rape, incest, that sort of thing. Every society has

its aberrations, its sociopaths, deviants, what have you, but like it or not, culture does factor in. Down here we've got a close-knit church-based society. It breeds crimes of repression, but it's not fertile ground for deviancies that require group organization. There's no urban infrastructure in place to meet and greet with others of like interest."

He looked at Anna and laughed. Caught out, she wiped the sour look from her face and reached for his hand. Piedmont lazily put out a paw and snagged her sleeve, claiming her affection for himself.

"Sorry for the lecture," Paul said. "It's just this is something I've given a lot of thought to in my roles as sheriff and priest."

"The Internet's made an urban interface for the world," Anna said. "The perverts' Yellow Pages."

Paul said nothing. She'd just said it to say something. She didn't give it any credence. Doyce hadn't had a computer in his room. Even if he had it was hard to imagine any city trickster setting up a middle-aged fat man in rural Mississippi for trysting and death.

"Some other kind of bondage then," Anna said. Years before, in Idaho, she'd seen bruises sort of like those on Doyce's body when she'd worked a fire as an emergency medical technician. A smokejumper had been brought into the first-aid tent. He'd gotten caught up in a tree and hung there for several hours before he'd been found and cut down. The concept of Doyce being shoved from an airplane and dropping into Mt. Locust in his Fruit Of The Looms was too ludicrous to put into words so she kept her musings to herself.

Paul left soon after ten. The strain of being together without being together cost them both. As she watched his car drive off, the taillights the last to be swallowed by the darkness, she wasn't surprised that statistically the relationship that ended a marriage seldom survived. The emotions attendant on the dissolution were as caustic as battery acid, eating through what was once integral and whole.

The murmur of his engine faded. The night reknit itself.

Chill air smelling of downed leaves, campfires and a faint indefinable perfume that triggers nostalgia so sharp the ache overcomes the sweetness, brushed down from the rooftop to touch her face. Breathing deeply she hurt for everything that was and everything that wasn't in a past that became harder to remember every year.

A thin slice of moon beckoned from over the treetops. Anna looked to her house: warmth and light and the two loving spirits who did duty as her family. She was tired. The day had gone on so long Lonnie Restin's wedding seemed like a memory from another lifetime. Still she knew she wouldn't sleep, not even if the cat deigned to curl up on the pillow beside her and purr.

Still in uniform, Anna retrieved her gun and, ignoring Taco's most piteous pleas to come along, returned to her patrol car. It was Saturday night, America's night out. Surely she could catch somebody doing something. Then she'd come home to bed. Ruining someone else's evening was bound to have a soporific effect.

The campground was disappointingly quiet. Four groups were overnighting, all were either enjoying the last embers of their fires or tucked up snugly for the night.

Anna drove down the Trace. Going nowhere, really, just drawn, perhaps by the shade of poor ol' Doyce Barnette, toward the ancient inn at Mt. Locust.

Traffic was virtually nonexistent and the rich confusing draughts of air from a semi-tropical land shutting down for its short winter's sleep tugged at forgotten dreams. Anna wondered where the drunks and speeders were when you needed them.

North of Mt. Locust she finally got lucky. A flash of light at treeline caught her eye. Killing the headlights, she pulled to the side of the road. In the inky shadow of a huge pecan left behind when a frontier home had been re-claimed by the land, she turned off the ignition to listen. In the darkness she couldn't separate it from the black and jagged line of the woods, but she knew the hunting stand that had been built on the parklands was there. Most they tore down. This one had been left in hopes of catching the perpetrators using it to poach the public's protected deer.

Till coming to the South, Anna hadn't been acquainted with the phenomenon of hunting stands. They came in all shapes and sizes, from a couple of boards nailed into the crotch of a tree to the twenty-foot-high portable metal towers complete with chair, railing and gun rest sold at the local Wal-Mart come hunting season.

The point of the things was to get the hunter above the prey. Evidently deer seldom look up. It had been many generations since death had come from the trees.

Hunters with little sporting blood spread feed under the stands in the fall to accustom the deer to coming there to eat. Bone-lazy hunters with no sporting blood whatsoever would put the feed in automatic timing devices to habituate the deer to come at a certain time every day, no waiting involved.

The stand built in Anna's woods was of the least dishonest variety. No timer, no feeder, just a platform built about fifteen feet above the ground with a rudimentary ladder and a railing of two-by-fours. The platform was eight feet long, the length of a standard cut of lumber, and three wide. One end was nailed into the pecan tree, the other supported by stilts.

The meadow was dark, the trees beyond impenetrable, but Anna had looked at the stand every time she'd passed by for two months. She could have rebuilt the wretched thing without a plan.

No sounds came to her but those integral to the night. She'd not expected any. Men incapable of quiet in any other circumstances often managed silence when stalking their fellow creatures. Time passed. She waited without impatience. Over the years she'd come to like waiting as she'd come to like the night. There was power in darkness and focused inactivity.

Finally, the light showed, a flashlight carelessly handled. This flash was not at ground level but in the trees. A hunter had wandered into the trap he'd set for the unwitting deer.

"Gotcha," Anna whispered.

At the south end of the meadow, the stand overlooked a line of trees reaching to the road. The black shadows would cloak the patrol car, the woods would hide her.

Accustomed to working alone, she hesitated before reaching for the radio. She'd be a fool not to let dispatch know where she was, but a call to them was a call to Randy Thigpen. This was his shift and staking out the hunting stand was his idea. Anna bit the managerial bullet and picked up the mike.

"Five-eight-one, Five-eight-zero," she radioed first Thigpen's call number, then her own to identify herself. He answered immediately and Anna was surprised. First the willingness to work on the Barnette case, now timely response to a radio call. Maybe the man was turning over a new leaf.

Briefly she told him where she was and what she was up to.

"You're not on duty, are you?" came accusingly back over the radio.

This was more like the Thigpen Anna'd come to know and be wary of. "I am now," she said. "What's your location?"

A moment of that peculiar empty silence generated by dead phone lines and unanswered calls leaked from her radio, then Thigpen's voice dispelled it. Whatever attitude he'd assumed at first hearing Anna had intruded on his night shift evaporated. He sounded clear and businesslike and Anna was grateful.

"I'm at mile marker thirty-five. Give me twenty minutes. There's an old dirt road'll take me behind them. You come in from the Trace side."

Mile marker thirty-five was ten minutes or so north of where Anna had parked. "Ten-four," she said. The park service, along with many other organizations, had gone to clear speak for radio protocol, abandoning the ten codes but, for old-timers, the habit was hard to break. "No radios," Anna said. "We don't want to scare them off."

"No radios. Be careful you don't get yourself shot," Thigpen said. "These boys'll shoot at anything that moves."

The warning sounded heartfelt. Anna wondered if it was or if he was just playing to an audience of one in the dispatcher's office, three hours north in Tupelo.

Anna drove the half mile to the line of trees growing close to the road without headlights. That peculiar acuteness that one sees in a stalking cat's eyes and the line of a hunting dog's spine on the scent pervaded her. Her mind was clear, her eyes sharp, her skin alive to the messages carried by the cold sweet air.

Slipping from the car and pressing the door gently shut, she reminded herself that these were poachers she was going after, armed men, probably hunting in packs, fuelled with the night, the dream of blood and possibly a couple six-packs of beer. Too many months of lecturing noisy campers and chasing teenage lovers out of Deans Stand had dulled her edge.

An image of the pallid remains of Doyce Barnette served to bring on the keen bite of evil. Thus armed and cautioned, she slipped into the woods. A six-cell flashlight served as both light and, though strictly against regulations, a baton if need be.

In the high deserts of Mesa Verde, Colorado, and Guadelupe Mountains, Texas, where she'd spent a bulk of her professional life, Anna might have attempted this night hunt without a light. In dryer, higher climes one could actually come to know the woods. Not so in Mississippi. Here the forests were rich and deep and as changeable as the sea. The land was not forged of granite and lava. There were no rocky outcroppings or mountains to hold the earth in place. Waterways changed their courses. Rivers and streams, not under the iron hand of the Army Corps of Engineers, left their beds to form new ones. Windstorms and tornadoes downed trees or uprooted them from the soft loess, the region's powdery soil, and flung them into the boughs of their fellows. Ice storms shattered branches, crushed them into the ground beneath. Through this ongoing upheaval and change, life as tenacious and persevering as that of the people who lived in the south pressed on. Vines claimed the fallen trees; trees sprang up in the old streambeds. The dirt itself rotted underfoot, crumbling away at a touch.

Shielding the light as best she could, Anna picked her way through the tangle. In high summer she probably wouldn't have tried it. The chance of becoming lost even in this small bit of the world would have been too great. With leaves down and scraps of light leaking through from the stars and a fingernail moon, she trusted she could keep her bearings.

Despite her best efforts, walking in true silence was not an option. Ankle-deep leaves of oak, maple, locust, dogwood, ash and sweetgum crackled with each step.

Every few yards she stopped her crunching to listen. When she'd reached what she guessed was the halfway point she was rewarded. Voices, no words, just murmuring and one short, sharp shout of laughter quickly stifled, carried through the still air.

Not a lone hunter, then. Two, more probably three. Anna checked her watch. Twenty minutes had passed. Randy should be in place. She moved again, changing her pattern. If she could hear them, they could hear her. She walked in short erratic bursts, altering the length and timing of her steps so that the rustle of her passage might ape the natural sounds of the woodland creatures. Always, she kept trees between herself and the meadow over which the hunting stand stood sentinel.

When she'd worked in Texas the hunters there had what they called a "sound shot," perfectly acceptable to their way of thinking. A sound shot was where they merely blasted away blindly at a noise in the bushes. Anna had no intention of falling victim to a hunting accident should the tradition of the Texas "sound shot" include the entire South.

Twice more she halted her progress to listen but there

were no more murmurings. Either they'd recommitted
themselves to the business of hunting or they'd heard her
coming and were even now motoring away, popping the
top of a cold one and having a good laugh at the ranger's
expense.

Fifteen or so yards from the stand she checked her
watch. Thirty-two minutes had passed since she'd put in
the call to Randy Thigpen. Time enough.

For the length of ten breaths Anna was absolutely still. A
silence that felt unnatural in its totality descended. The
breeze that had stirred her so when she'd first left the house
in Rocky Springs had died. No leaves rustled overhead. No
nightbirds chattered. Frogs, asleep with the cold, kept their
own counsel. And no sound from the hunters. This close on
a windless night sound carried as surely as it would underwater. She should have been able to hear the scraping of a
boot on the wood, the shush of fabric, the click of a rifle
barrel rested on the railing.

Nothing.

They must have spotted the patrol car or heard her and
left. The thought brought with it a letdown. The fatigue of
an over-long day began to seep into her bones. Then she
smelled it: cigarette smoke. Somewhere in the hopeless
night, in the trees surrounding her, someone had lit up.
Whoever it was screened the flare of the match and cupped
the glow of the cigarette, someone who'd been hooked on
tobacco for so long he'd forgotten normal people didn't
breathe that kind of air on a regular basis.

Anna unsnapped the keeper on the holster of her Sig-
Sauer nine-millimeter. The slight snick of the snap letting
go was echoed by a shush from the trees, a shifting of
weight or a shuffling of feet. The sound came not from the
direction of the hunting stand but from the tangle of trees
behind her.

In that instant Anna went from the hunter to the hunted.
The excitement of the chase turned to cold, hard fear.

They had known she was coming. Instead of fleeing,
they'd laid an ambush and she'd walked right into it. In

other circumstances she would have cursed herself for a
fool, but hunters, for the most part, weren't given to felony
behaviors. Bluster, intransigence, even threats were common fare but not ambush and assault. The stakes weren't
high enough. To lie in wait for law enforcement was
freakish.

Fear accelerated; Anna could feel it reach her heart, up-
ping the beats. Thigpen. He smoked like the proverbial
chimney. He must have come in from the road and, finding
no one at the stand, come to meet her.

Without a light.

Not Thigpen.

Anna shifted the heavy flashlight to her left hand then
eased the semi-auto from its holster. Had she known where
the smoker and, she had to assume, his cohorts, were she
would have done the sensible thing and slunk away under
the cover of darkness. Till she figured out their whereabouts she didn't dare move.

Another rustle, then a man's voice shouted, "Now!" and
the night erupted in screaming light and sound.

Not a flash but a high-powered spotlight exploded from
the trees to Anna's right, blinding her with such violence
she threw up an arm as if warding off a blow. Other smaller
lights joined it. Anna felt as if half a hundred men charged
from the edges of a nightmare, but it might have been a
trick of her wounded night vision or the shattered edges of
fear.

Raucous voices clamored: "Hoo boy!" "We got us a
lady ranger!" "We're gonna have us some fun now."
Phrases right out of a cheesy remake of *Deliverance*
mobbed Anna and, even as part of her mind noted the
threadbare clichés, the words served their purpose. The terror of ten thousand years of abused women welled up from
a gender memory she'd not known lay buried in her
sinews.

The deafening report of a rifle fired at close range spun
her around. She dropped to one knee, her back to the rough

back of the tree she'd thought herself hidden behind. The Sig-Sauer had found its way into her hand, and she pointed it into the harsh glare of the spotlight.

Though she kept her pistol pointed at the spotlight, Anna resisted the natural instinct to stare into the light, try to see who was behind it. In a moment or two spill from the spotlight began to work for her. Flashlight beams danced lustfully and erratic as fireflies to the left of the spotlight. There were three men, possibly four. Two at least wore camouflage, pants, jackets and hats. Not the green and gray shapeless blobs of the military's all-purpose stuff but hunter camouflage: fabric printed with a litter of leaves and twigs. At first, in the glaring spot and moving beams of light, she thought her attackers were African-American, though they didn't sound black.

In polite society one wasn't allowed to say someone sounded black, looked Jewish or any of a hundred other racial, cultural or religious generalizations. Anna'd learned to take information regardless of the package it was presented in. Clichés were based on old regional truths and, in the south at least, a majority of blacks sounded black. The men that harassed her sounded white and as southern as grits. In the wild play of the lights, she could see monster faces, faces daubed with mud or grease or paint.

"Turn off the spotlight or I shoot it out," she shouted over the tumult.

Catcalls died. Anna could feel their insecurity. These were Saturday night hunters, crazed by darkness and power and playing at predators. By day they probably checked groceries at the Piggly-Wiggly or pumped gas. "Turn it off," Anna said again. Into the new-won silence came the sibilant sound of a whispered conference followed by a hooting laugh that sounded, to Anna's hyperextended ears, both relieved and exultant. A thick voice said, "You can't shoot us. We don't plan to hurt you none."

"Leastways it ain't gonna hurt *much*," came another voice. Laughter followed. Crude remarks. Boots pushing through duff. Mob courage was reasserting. Voices—only three—Anna's mind took note even as she fought down panic. Sexual remarks, sneering, inarticulate whoops melded into a cacophony of pack hatred. The lights began to converge on her.

"Stay back," Anna yelled. "I don't want to shoot anybody tonight."

"She ain't gonna shoot," said the speaker, the holder of the spotlight. "She can't. It's the law. We ain't threatening her life."

A whoop from the left and the lights moved closer. Taking careful aim, Anna pulled the trigger. Noise and light and breaking glass shattered as the spotlight exploded into a thousand pieces. A man screamed, high and wild like a hawk shot on the wing.

The ring around Anna fragmented. Lights spun, men shouted. Cloaked in chaos, Anna fled into the black of the woods behind her. Bat-blind from the spotlight, she stumbled and fell in a parody of countless film heroines destined to be run down by the villain.

The part of her mind that was never off-duty noted the yells of the men. "The bitch shot at me." "You said she couldn't..." "Shut the fuck up." "Fucking bitch." Then, with a baying of the hounds of hell, they came after her.

5

For a nightmare's eternity, Anna ran, fell, stumbled, noted without feeling the banging of her knees and elbows, the rip of thorny branches across her face and forearms. Her Sig-Sauer was still in her hand and she used it like a club, bashing through foliage that seemed sentient, closing around her trying to trap and hold. The six-cell flashlight had been dropped when she'd pulled her weapon, and she fought on in a darkness so complete she was choked with it.

Bit by bit her night vision returned and with it came a hopeful smattering of gray to her left: the meadow with its pooling of light from moon and stars.

Too far. The hounds were closing in. The pitch of their baying rose in the excitement of the chase. The cut of flashlight beams slashed green from a glut of oak hydrangea to her right. They'd not yet seen her, but only followed the racket she made.

Forcing down the panicked need for flight, she made herself stop. The crash of boots and the guttural yells

would cover small sounds. Quick as a burrowing fox, Anna
dove for the ground. Crushing herself into the scratchy embrace of a drying shrub, she pulled leaves and needles up
over her as best she could. Curled in a ball, elbows touching knees, shoulders hunched, she raised her gun up to eye
level and waited. A snake in the grass. Like a snake, her
blood grew cold, her eyes narrowed, and a snake's ethics
took over. If her pursuers came too close, she would strike.
If they passed by, she would let them live.

For half a minute, the crashing came on: three flashlights jabbing through the trunks and creepers. Anna
counted them by the lights. Their voices had melded into
one hurting cry of many notes. Lying as she was, coiled
half under a bush covered imperfectly with leaves, she felt
as exposed as if she stood naked on an empty stage.

She banished the urge to run and steadied the nine-
millimeter.

The advance of lights slowed, then stopped. The hulla-
baloo of sound lost volume and separated into voices.

"Listen," one said, a rasping pant. A man unused to having to chase down his prey.

"I don't hear anything."

"What're we chasin' now?" Another man spoke and a
part of Anna's mind registered a need to laugh at the sudden bewilderment in his voice, but this totally human response didn't make it past the cold and snaky heart of her.

"Shit."

"Listen."

"She's gone to ground." The rasping panting voice. He
was the leader then.

Gone to ground. They were hunters.

Anna'd forgotten that and she felt a chill. She'd never
been hunted by hunters before, men who prided themselves on knowing where the scared and helpless went to
hide. These men would not long be fooled by the dark and
a few hastily raked-together leaves.

"Let's go home," one said. Anna was pleased to hear the
fear she'd been suffering creep into his words.

Go home, she prayed silently.

"What now?" another asked. A time of quiet followed, broken only by the shuffling of feet and the crisp sounds dry winter scrub made near Anna's ears where crushed branches struggled to reassert themselves.

"Lights." Then in a whisper, hissed loud and commanding.

One by one the flashlights were switched off. A wave of fear and disorientation swept over Anna as the beacons pinpointing her pursuers vanished. She thought to scramble free of the bushes and run, but she knew she'd never make it. Had she had a tail with rattles, the clatter would have given her away. As it was, she waited in stillness, listening so hard she felt as if her ears grew out to wave around above her on stalks.

The hunters were conferring: murmurs, whispers, an occasional sharp and shining note of dissent but no words.

"Okay then," was shouted. "Fan out." Laughter followed, but it was hollow and nervous, not the full-throated baying glee of before. Something had changed. Perhaps the knowledge that one or more of them were going to die. At least that's what Anna hoped.

Flashlights were turned back on. Boots pushed through the undergrowth. A few mildly obscene catcalls were attempted, but they were half-hearted. The tenor had changed.

"Look both high and low," the leader said distinctly. "She coulda treed herself."

The lights separated and began moving more purposefully toward Anna's makeshift den.

This was it then. A cool and amoral calm settled over her. Breath and heart slowed perceptibly. Her mind cleared, leaving a cold, watchful place where heated thoughts had recently clamored. Time changed. It seemed she had leisure for idle contemplations.

Soon, she suspected, she would be taking a life. The thought bothered her not at all. The aftermath, the justification, the investigation, the paperwork that ensued when a ranger was forced to use her weapon was of greater concern than breaking whatever the hell commandment "thou shalt not kill" was.

Early on, before she'd run, one of the men had said she could not shoot them because they didn't intend to hurt her. Proper use of force was pounded into modern federal law enforcement. The rule was the officer could only go one level higher in the force continuum than his attacker. If the villain used fists, the officer could graduate to a baton. Only when the attacker evinced a clear and present danger to the life of the officer or the lives of others would the officer be justified in using deadly force. Why had these guys known that? Was one a policeman, a highway patrolman, sheriff's deputy?

Anna smiled a mean little smile. Her mind flashed back to her training at FLETC, the Federal Law Enforcement Training Center in Georgia. She'd been the only woman in a class of twenty-eight, the only woman and, by at least thirty pounds, the smallest. Mike Hurly, a man from the Tennessee Valley Authority, had been the biggest, close to six foot three and weighing in at two-ninety-three.

Instructor after instructor used Anna and Mike as examples of the sliding scale of lethal threat. Who could use fists and batons and pepper spray and bullets and when. Mike, being a monolith of a man, could not legally claim he feared for his life till his assailant at least pulled a knife.

The consensus was the diminutive Anna could pretty much kill anybody anytime if they were taller than an eight-year-old and threatened her with anything more substantial than a ripe banana and still legally claim she'd feared for her life.

Yelling stopped; lights spread out. Anna's brain focused sharply. In stillness more frightening than the shouting, she could hear each shuffling step, each grunt and muttered expletive. She fancied she could even hear them breathing, the serrated panting breaths of excited dogs. The stabbing of the lights, wild during the running, became purposeful, scraping high and low, raking through the woods to where she lay. The thick chest of the leader was thrown into faint silhouette by the man behind him, careless of his flashlight. Anna lined the two iridescent green dots on her gun sight, one to either side of center mass, and breathed in. As she exhaled she began a slow, even trigger pull.

Before her finger reached the point of no return, the black silence of the trees behind the stalkers was cut through with a shout. A familiar voice yelling. "Break it up. Barth go around to the left." A fourth light careened down on the backs of the hunters. "You there. Drop your weapons. Drop them." Hesitantly the men began to turn, not throwing down but at least lowering their rifles.

For the briefest of instants Anna thought she would fire anyway, kill because she could, because she wanted to. God or conscience or sanity stopped her, and she backed the pressure off the trigger.

Randy Thigpen had arrived. Anna'd given up on him, then forgotten he existed. Once before she'd called him for backup, and he'd quietly gone back to the ranger station and left her to deal as best she could. Randy'd come through. Barth, Anna knew, wasn't on duty. Randy was showing some imagination.

"Drop your weapons," he called again, and Anna whispered hallelujah.

The hunters stopped. Lights flashed. "Run," someone shouted and, with rebel yells that sounded, to Anna's jaded consciousness, more gleeful than disappointed, her attackers fled in all directions, the woods snapping and groaning with the violence of their passage. One of them laughed, high and wild, ending in a hoot. The crunching of their flight faded. Night's quiet flowed back into the woods. Still Anna did not move.

She felt as elemental as the dirt and leaf litter she'd cloaked herself in.

"Anna?" Randy called. She could see him now in the faint backwash of his light. The underside of the absurd mustache glowed orange and the dull gleam of his badge proclaimed him an honorable man. Still Anna stayed where she was, watching him come.

Finally he stopped not more than three feet from where she'd curled down into the forest floor. "Anna?"

In his face she read only concern, a deep fear for her safety. Mollified, she said, "I'm here."

Randy shrieked like a schoolgirl presented with a snake, stumbled sideways and fell on his most ample feature.

Uncoiling herself, Anna brushed the leaf litter from her trousers and hair. Her right hand still gripped the semi-automatic pistol.

Hit with the sudden loss of dignity, Randy's concern turned to irritation. "Jesus!" he said. "What the hell were you playing at? There were three of them armed with hunting rifles. What would you of done if they'd found you?"

"Killed them all."

By the weak and moving light Anna saw the muscles of his face freeze then twitch back to life again as his brain rejected—or assimilated—her violence.

"Jesus," he said again and, using a downed log for a lever, hoisted his considerable bulk into a standing position. "Don't they have such a thing as due process back wherever the hell you claim to come from? Those boys were just having some fun with you. They never meant you no harm."

"I was just going to have some fun with them," Anna said. The snake that had come to possess her soul had not yet fully let go.

Thigpen turned his light on her face. She didn't blink or look away. "Jesus," he called on his savior a third time. "You give me the creeps, you know that? Let's get out of here. I'll walk you to your car."

"No."

Randy stared at her a moment. "Okay," he said uncertainly. "Meet me at the Mt. Locust Ranger Station."

"Port Gibson." Anna needed the familiar around her, the

things of her everyday life to bring her back from the wild and dangerous place the snake had taken her. Thigpen must have gleaned something from her voice; he didn't argue.

"Port Gibson then."

Both waited. Neither moved. "You want my light?" he asked finally.

"No."

Anna stayed where she was and watched him go, a lumbering, overfed zoo bear, ill at ease in the forests of the night. When she could no longer see or hear him, she reholstered her weapon. The faint glow of the meadow beckoned, and she walked toward it. Adrenaline began to be reabsorbed. The scales of the snake fell from her eyes and she saw herself so small, so alone, so hunted. She noted without any recognition of fear that her knees were weak and her hands shaking.

By the time she reached her patrol car the fit had passed, leaving in its wake exhaustion so deep she wondered if she could drive the twenty minutes to the Port Gibson Ranger Station without falling asleep at the wheel. This day was not the longest Anna had ever lived through, but it was definitely in the running.

As she traveled the moonlit peace of the Trace, scraps of the last eighteen hours floated behind her eyes: herself in a red dress and high heels, the colored lights of dead saints dyeing her married priest/sheriff/lover's blond hair, Doyce Barnette, bruised and stripped and beached like an incongruous walrus on Grandma Polly's bed, Doyce's brother with his big teeth, his unctuous charm and his tiny model coffins, Mama Barnette carrying a shotgun and glaring with ancient evil eyes, men with daubed faces and raucous laughter chasing her through woods so choked with life that every step was an effort, the Garden of Gethsemane, the painting of the last supper on Mama's stair landing, Paul intoning "till death do us part." Mismatched images of violence and guns and God made the South a strange land and Anna a stranger in it.

* * *

She took her time driving back to Port Gibson, gathering her wits and cataloguing her injuries. Now that she had the time to listen, her body began to complain of the ill treatment: a scratched forearm, a bruised knee, a sore shoulder muscle. The flight through the woods hadn't been nearly as costly as she feared it might.

Randy reached the ranger station before she did. Lights were blazing. Anna pulled up beside his patrol car and got out. Her mad dash had sapped her strength. Muscles cooled, she found herself moving like a creaky old woman. Consciously she straightened up and loosened her gait. Feeling old and tired and frail was her privilege. Seeing her do so was not Ranger Thigpen's.

As if to point up her distress, Randy, older than she and fatter than Jabba the Hutt, was looking quite cool and dapper. He sat at his desk, facing the door she entered through, a bottle of Coke in his left hand, a cigarette in his right.

Despite years of federal and then, even in Mississippi, state laws banning smoking in public buildings, till Anna'd become district ranger the Port Gibson Ranger Station had been Thigpen's private smoking lounge. The walls and ceiling were yellow-gray with twenty years' accumulated residue. The only way to cleanse the building of the smell would be to raze it to the ground and build anew.

Her first day on duty the previous April, Anna had enforced the smoking ban. Since then Randy had played at compliance. He acted out the familiar scene again.

"Anna!" A grin, meant to be sheepish but merely sly, ferreted around beneath his mustache. "Caught me red-handed." Scooting his chair to the opposite door, he threw the butt out on the concrete where she'd have to wade through it and its pals. "Hard to remember after so long doing things our own way." Emphasis on the "our," chair rolled back to desk, triumphant look of innocence feigned.

Because she was new to management, because Thigpen had already sued her once, because she wanted to be fair and understanding, Anna'd put up with this scene half a dozen times. After it played itself through she sighed, dragging the tainted air deep and letting it go with the relaxed musculature of the seriously depressed. "Randy," she said wearily. He smiled. Anna smiled back. "If I ever catch you smoking in here again, I will put the goddamn cigarette out on your tongue." Perhaps she'd not shed her totem snake as completely as she thought.

Randy's smile quivered, cracked, ran and hid behind his mustache. Obnoxious retorts skittered through his brain; Anna could see them flittering like moths behind his pale blue eyes.

She waited, half hoping he'd say something stupid. Having been jeered, frightened and chased, she was in the mood to smack the hell out of somebody.

Thigpen wisely didn't give her cause. He rested a moment, then, true to form, went back on the offensive.

"Why didn't you wait for me?" he demanded. "You could of gotten yourself hurt out there playing at Navy Seals. Not that those old boys would have hurt you. They were just having a little fun. Running through the woods at night, you could've broken a leg or gotten yourself snake-bit."

Anna chose not to engage. With a satisfying ripping sound, she pulled her duty belt off its underbelt of Velcro and dropped it on Barth's desk. Thigpen winced and Anna was pleased. Settling into the chair facing his over the appalling clutter her field rangers stubbornly insisted on working in the midst of, she said, "You recognize anybody? Any voices, faces, anything? It's a good bet they were locals. Probably the men that built that stand in the first place."

"No," he said too quickly.

"You told Sheriff Jones you'd gotten to know everybody in Natchez. Who were those guys?"

Randy looked genuinely, sincerely hurt and confused. Proof, if Anna'd needed any, that he was hiding something. At an easy guess, Thigpen had done what he'd done once before, if only in part. He'd slowed his response time to her call for backup to the point she'd either have settled the matter before he arrived or it would have settled her. That was a firing offense and he knew it. He also knew, this time, there was no way she could prove it.

"I honestly don't know," he said. "I got a look sort of at one of 'em, but even if I had of seen him before, I wouldn't of recognized him. They had mud or something smeared on their faces."

Listening to him Anna felt only emptiness and fatigue. She glanced at her watch: quarter to twelve. The time surprised her. She had that gritty hollow feeling that comes just before sunrise. An absurd scene floated up from a distant past, one spent eating apples and reading novels in the crook of an old oak tree that grew in her parents' front yard: Scarlett O'Hara standing ragged and worn, clutching a fistful of Tara's good earth and swearing, "I'll think about it tomorrow. After all, tomorrow is another day."

Tomorrow was fourteen minutes away. Anna didn't want to start it in the presence of Randy Thigpen. Rising, she gathered up her gunbelt. "You're off duty in a minute and I've about had it. We'll talk tomorrow."

As the door was closing behind her, she heard Randy's light pleasant voice calling "goodnight" in an offensively cheerful cadence.

"Fuck you," Anna whispered. "Fuck you all." The "all" was catholic: Anna hadn't the energy to separate the saved from the damned.

6

Another exquisite Mississippi fall day greeted Anna. Air was dry and cool, sky as blue and deep as a poet could wish. The woods, so sentient with entangling evil the night before, sighed with peaceful dreams of the winter's sleep to come and breathed out a perfume delicate with sweet memories of a glorious spring.

Anna inhaled and tried to be appreciative. After the painfully long day before, she'd thought she would have slept like the dead but perhaps the analogy was too apt. She'd tossed and turned till Piedmont abandoned the bed for the Morris chair in the living room. She'd made so many trips to the bathroom that finally even the faithful Taco gave up escorting her down the long dark hallway. Nightmares plagued her, a confusion of images full of violence and failure. On waking, she remembered none of them, but they'd left her with all the symptoms of a hangover. It was nearly enough to drive her to drink. Paying the piper when the son-of-a-bitch never played rankled.

Standing at the foot of the crude stairs leading to the

hunting stand, she tried to unclutter a mind as full of junk as Fibber McGee and Molly's closet.

She'd parked her patrol car on the Trace in the same place she'd parked the previous night and backtracked, following her flight through the trees. After a few false leads, she'd found the place she'd gone to ground. Looking at the stirring and heaping of downed leaves and needles she'd used to camouflage herself brought back the specter of the snake. In her weakened state, her basic humanity precarious, she'd felt an icy touch remembering how close she'd been to taking another life and the keen and joyless pleasure with which she'd looked forward to doing so.

Tracking her hunters had been a piece of cake, even through the usually trackless fecundity of the Mississippi undergrowth. They'd pursued her with the delicate touch of a pack of all-terrain vehicles, smashing over rotting logs and crashing through thin dry branches. Unfortunately no one had been thoughtful enough to lose a unique button or drop an engraved cigarette lighter.

By the time she'd reached the tree where they'd first surprised her, she knew no more about them than she had the night before, beyond the fact that they were a mindless group of mean-spirited bozos. During hunting season that didn't narrow the field of play by much.

Her flashlight was where she'd left it so the search wasn't entirely fruitless. She scoured the area where the hunters had lain in wait. Scuffled duff, a few marks in the bark and the butt of three filter cigarettes was all she got for her trouble. The cigarette butts she retrieved and dropped in a baggie, not as evidence but as litter. An interchange such as she'd experienced didn't warrant the time and expense of high-tech lab work. No DNA would be lifted from the butts. Chances were good her hunters had no criminal records. As Thigpen had said, they were probably just "good old boys having a little fun."

Anna sneered at the thought. She'd cleaned up after that brand of American macho gang "fun" too many times: rape, vandalism, harassment, assault. Men and women in

the United States carried a terrific burden of anger against
the other gender for reasons Anna could never fathom.
Women took theirs out in psychological torture sometimes
aimed at men, more often at themselves. Men were more
hands-on: and the hands were too often on the smaller,
weaker sex.

"Not all men," Anna forced herself to say out loud. "Not
even most," the rational voice of her sister in her head
forced her to add. Some days it was harder than others to
remember that evil was still front page news. Goodness
and order were so much the norm they needn't be reported.

A dozen feet or so from the stand itself Anna found a
small excavation, a hole maybe a foot across, a couple
inches deep and still damp. There being no other reason for
its existence, she figured it was where the men had poured
out their canteens to mix the mud they'd smeared on their
faces.

The timing bothered her. The mud, the three cigarettes
at the ambush sight. They'd had time to plan and wait before she came. They must have seen her patrol car the moment she'd stopped. Clearly, they'd had all the time in the
world to stroll back to their vehicles and simply slip away
undetected. Instead they'd painted their faces and lain in
wait.

Spontaneous combustion of assholes was frightening
but usually soon over. Premeditated viciousness was apt to
recur until its goal, whatever it was, was achieved.

She shook off the musings, shrugged out of the night before, and came back to the sweet-smelling sunlight at the
foot of the stairs. Her last chance at evidence lay there. She
needed an open mind.

The steps, made of unpainted two-by-fours weathered to
gray, were clean. She climbed up, enjoying the childlike
feel of climbing into a treehouse in spite of her darkened
mood. The stand, a wooden platform with a simple rail
around it, was as clean as the steps. No clues. Few leaves.
Spotless.

"Damn," Anna muttered as she stared at the weathered

boards. The thing had been swept, not with a branch or anything else that one might imagine would be handy to a group out hunting deer and lady rangers, but swept with a broom. What had once been muddy boot prints was now a veil of dried dust neatly streaked with the fine stiff straw of a household broom. The maid had been in.

She climbed the last step onto the platform. There was no evidence, not even so much as a clue left behind to disturb. She might as well enjoy the view. Leaning her elbows on the railing, she looked out over the small meadow toward the Trace.

The hunting stand was well-placed, several yards back from the meadow's edge in the branches of an old pecan tree. Mixed hardwood, pine and the fast growing weed trees, mimosa, willow and popcorn, had crowded back around the pecan once its protectors were gone. Now it provided a leafy hidden bower.

With a clear shot to the meadow.

Anna had never grasped the lure of hunting. When she went to the trouble to travel to quiet, beautiful, isolated places, usually the last thing on her mind was killing anything.

She walked the length of the stand. The wood was weathered and splintery and the stand was in uneven repair. The steps were rickety and one side of the platform rotted through, but a piece of the railing had been recently repaired. Time had come to tear the stand down. Surely nobody would be using it now.

Surely.

For a moment she remained, thinking. Decision made, she backed down the rudimentary stairs. The stand would stay. The hunters had put so much time and effort into building it. They'd successfully terrorized and chased away the lady ranger. Maybe they'd be back. It was worth a try. Each ache of bruised muscle and sting of torn flesh earned the night before reminded her how thoroughly she wanted to catch the bastards.

* * *

At ten-thirty Anna met Sheriff Jones at the Mt. Locust Ranger Station. When she'd first come to the Trace, the office was housed in two grungy rooms in the maintenance building. Since then some of the seasonals positions were cut, housing reappropriated, and the ranger station moved to a house much like the one she lived in. The "new" office was located between the maintenance yard to the north and Mt. Locust to the south. From the luxury of a screened-in porch, the visitors center and the old stand were visible.

"You look beat," Clintus said kindly. "Bad night?"

Anna ran her fingers through her cropped hair then realized, far from smoothing it, she'd probably stood it all on end. As much white as brown had begun to show in recent years. She'd discovered that white hairs, like old women, did just as they pleased.

"Hard night," she agreed and told him of her nocturnal adventures with the local sportsmen.

Clintus listened with flattering attention and reacted with satisfying ire. He could identify with Anna's horror of "good old boys having a little fun." Validation and support were all Anna got, all she expected. He could no more guess the identity or track down her night-hunters than she could.

"I'll check old reports," he promised. "See if we've got anything on poachers over the past few years. Don't get your hopes up. Around here it's a kind of slap-the-wrist and wink crime. Left over from the days everybody hunted to lay in meat for the winter. Or maybe just not liking to be messed with by the government."

"I won't hold my breath," she said and they moved on to other matters. Anna hadn't given poor old Doyce a thought since she'd first spotted the hunters' light from the stand. It was a relief to return to a crime that engaged only her mind and left the rest of her in peace.

"I believe we've got our Herm," the sheriff said. Herm was the man who'd left a message on Doyce Barnette's an-

swering machine. Their visit to Mama and Doyce's homestead felt like it had happened when dinosaurs roamed the
earth, and Anna had to concentrate to bring the threads of
yesterday together.

"André nosed around and I made a few calls. It seems
Doyce used to pal around with Herman Thornton. He runs
an Army surplus place on the highway outside Natchez. He
and Doyce own a bass boat together. Fishing buddies.
Down in these parts that's a bond more lasting and meaningful than marriage."

"Have you talked with this guy?" Anna asked.

"Nope. Figured you'd want to be along."

Anna had liked Clintus Jones right off. If he kept up this
level of considerate professionalism, he could give Paul
Davidson a run for his money. Pure widow's reflex made
her look at his left hand. A dull gold band proclaimed him
a married man.

At least he wears one. The bitterness of the thought
jerked Anna upright in her chair. Anger, sorrow, hate, envy,
joy—those were emotions she could live with. Bitterness
was a trap. Mixed with self-pity it became a quagmire.
"Ugh," she said aloud and shook herself like Taco after a
bath.

"Beg pardon?" Jones murmured politely.

"Nothing." Anna swung her feet down from the third
chair. Because of the beauty of the day, they'd eschewed
the confines of the office, reeking with Thigpen's stale cigarette smoke, and adjourned to the screened-in porch. It
was furnished with three plastic chairs, the stackable kind,
left over from some bureaucratic endeavor or another.

Clintus rose as Anna did. Never let it be said Mrs. Jones
didn't raise her son right. "Shall we beard Herm in his
den?"

"He'll be at the surplus store," Clintus said stolidly. "I
drive." The sheriff had control issues, a hazard of law enforcement.

"No problem." Anna had spent so many years on foot
and horseback that, to her, driving was a chore.

Crashing through the woods from the direction of Mt. Locust stand arrested their attention. Anna felt a flash of fear, the sound momentarily putting her back into the night of the baying hunters.

Bearlike and almost growling, Barth Dinkins emerged from the trees onto the small swale of mowed weeds that served as a lawn.

"Hey, Barth," she called through the screen.

He hadn't seen them and his head swung up at her hail. He grunted, completing the image of the marauding bear.

"We got a problem," he said as he charged toward the porch.

"Yeah, tell me about it," Anna muttered. Barth didn't hear her. He was beyond listening. Anna'd never seen Barth angry before, and it transformed him. The softness was gone; the bland, amiable face hardened and his strange eyes, too light for his brown-skinned face, glittered like something from a grade-B science-fiction movie.

Banging open the screen door, he stepped onto the small porch. His energy sucked the air from the little enclosure. Anna found herself and the sheriff backed against the far wall.

"You're going to give yourself a stroke, Barth," she said mildly.

"Yeah... well..." He cast about as if for something to smash but settled for hurling himself into one of the recently vacated chairs. Once seated, the anger gushed out of him and he shrank back to his normal size.

"My sign," he said. "They just tore it all up. Broke it to bits. It's never over. It's just never fucking *over.*"

Not once in the months she'd known him had Anna heard Barth use foul language. From him it generated the disgust and vileness that over-use had robbed it of in the mouths of an increasingly foul-mouthed society.

Anna took the other chair, sat and waited. The sheriff remained where he was, watchful but not interfering.

Barth gathered his wits. He stared down at his broad hands, the nails neatly trimmed, the beds a rich purple.

"No call for me to be using that kind of language in front of a la—in front of you, Boss."

Both Barth and Randy had called Anna "boss" when she first arrived. They'd used it in sneering derision. After she and Barth had worked together on Danielle Posey's murder, Barth's way of saying it changed. Now, from him at least, it was a term of respect and acceptance.

"What sign?" she asked.

"Up at the slave graveyard. I was up there to do some measuring, see if I could suss out where more of the people might have been buried. I got there and the sign listing the names of the dead had been tore down. Not just tore down but tore up."

Anna waited but Barth had sunk into a place from which he didn't seem inclined to communicate. His reaction was extreme for a sign knocked over, a kind of vandalism not unusual in the parks. Barth Dinkins wasn't a man prone to emotional vapors. There was more to the story.

"Show us," Anna said. She shot a look at Clintus, an apology for cutting into his time with park matters. An almost imperceptible nod from the impeccably groomed head excused her.

Barth dragged his face up, and Anna was surprised to see what looked like shame in his eyes. "I guess," he said uncertainly.

Anna and the sheriff followed him back through the band of trees separating the makeshift ranger station from the visitors center and around the stand to Eric's vegetable garden. Shelly was on the back porch with a group of tourists, her childish voice telling a tale of bandits and bloodletting.

Wordlessly the three of them crossed the plowed land to the trees where the old slave cemetery had lain unmarked and ungrieved for so long. At first glance the damage didn't seem bad enough to warrant Barth's reaction. The sign was well made: two treated four-by-fours driven deep in the clay, one-by-sixes nailed across, the names of deceased they'd been able to identify burned into the slats.

Three more boards, still empty, awaited new discoveries. The boards with the wood-burned names had been hammered off and lay scattered around the sign.

Barth stopped, turned back and stared across the field toward Mt. Locust as if divorcing himself from the party.

"It doesn't look so bad," Anna said as she stepped around him. Then she stopped. "I take that back." The four boards lying at her feet had not merely been knocked loose, they'd been attacked, defiled. A maniac with hammer and hatchet had hacked and clawed at the names until they were barely legible. Hatred, deep and vicious, emanated up from the crazed cuts and dents. Not satisfied with mere destruction, whoever had ruined the sign had taken the time to defecate on one of the boards before leaving. Vaguely, Anna remembered her sister telling her that was the calling card of a psychotic, and she felt a shimmer of dis-ease though she was well-armed, well-attended and standing in the sunshine.

The shame she'd seen on Barth's face made sense now. This had been done to annihilate and degrade. *It's just never fucking over,* the mindless hatred of one people for another.

"I am so sorry," she said sincerely. An ice-cold glance from Barth and a stony lack of reaction from Clintus let her know her sympathy had come across as pity, but she couldn't take it back.

"Get maintenance to clean up the mess," she told Barth. "Call Tupelo and get new signs made. Then see if you can find out who did this." The last was just a sop and the three of them knew it. Unless vandals were caught in the act or stupid enough to scrawl their names, it was virtually impossible to trace them. Most often it was kids. This didn't look like kid stuff.

Clintus drove. Anna rolled her window down but even the crystal air seemed tainted with humanity's spiritual excrement. She didn't speak. Though she knew she was not personally responsible for the collective sins of the world, she couldn't shake a creeping shame for enslaving

Africans, decimating the American Indian tribes, annihilating the passenger pigeon, building strip malls on California's beaches and leaving behind unsightly junk on the face of the moon.

Clintus's single-minded attention to the rules of the road smacked of shame as well. Whoever had desecrated Mt. Locust's slave cemetery had had the power to embarrass across color, religious and gender barriers, an all-purpose slime.

Herman Thorton's Army surplus store, imaginatively named "Herm's Army Surplus Store," was on the outskirts of Natchez along Highway Sixty-five in the midst of a scattering of other unprofitable-looking business establishments. Herm occupied half of a low flat-roofed building. The other half had housed a dry cleaners, since out of business, the windows soaped to discourage vandals. Herm himself might have had a hand in the demise of Kris's Kleaners. His portion of the building was daubed and dabbed and smeared with green, gray and brown paint aping the design of jungle camouflage. "Herm's" was hand lettered in white across the unappealing mixture.

"I checked up on Thorton," Clintus said as he parked in front of the store. "No serious trouble with the law that I could find. He's been getting the court's attention for about seven years for nonpayment of alimony and child support, but it's never gotten so far as to come across my desk. He's been in and out of half a dozen businesses."

"Career in interior design didn't pan out, I take it," Anna said.

Clintus laughed. Both were glad to move away from the thoughts left behind by Barth's discovery.

"Opened his surplus store about three years ago—Oh, well, isn't that just peachy," Clintus said, his attention diverted to the left of the defunct cleaners.

At the corner of the building was a shiny black Cadillac.

"Raymond Barnette?"

"Looks like," the sheriff replied.

Suspicions pattered through Anna's mind on sharp little dik-dik hooves: Barnette colluding with Herm Thorton in the death of his brother, come to warn him, come for vengeance, come for information?

Clintus sighed deeply, staring over the steering wheel at the globby storefront. "It would look real good in the newspapers if he solved a murder case while running for sheriff, wouldn't it?" he said sourly.

That was a cynical twist Anna had not come up with. Given how skeptical she was concerning the innate goodness of the human race, she was surprised at herself.

The sheriff's cynicism was borne out. Pushing open the glass door of the shop, they could hear the undertaker's somber bell tones ringing forth from beyond the boots, guns and fishing rods.

"So Doyce was found dead there at that old historic Mt. Locust on the Trace. Found yesterday morning around nine. Looks like he was suffocated somehow. Maybe smothered or choked is my guess. I'm looking into it sort of in a semi-official capacity, being Doyce was related."

Anna stepped closer, the better to eavesdrop. In doing so, she trapped Clintus in the doorway at her shoulder.

"Well." She felt his breath stir her hair. "Now Herm knows everything we do. That's just dandy."

The sheriff's whisper carried the icy draft of the sudden anger she'd noticed he was prone to. She stepped quickly aside.

He shouldered his way through the enclosing racks of used military uniforms. Anna, trailing him, had a sudden picture of grim-faced commandos pushing through foreign jungles, AK-47s held at ready, hearts beating heroically, ready to kill for their way of life. Maybe she'd underestimated Herm. If he'd engineered this high and overhanging mass of green and gray materials to feed into the fantasies of men bored with their lives, bored with the paltry out-

come of their dreams, men like the s.o.b.s who had so gleefully hunted her, then Herm Thorton's decorating skills
were superb.

More likely, he was just a Doyce kind of guy: happier
when curled in a mess of his precious stuff. Despite the
implements of death and destruction with which Herm surrounded himself, he was a pleasant unprepossessing-
looking fellow. Whether because of the history Clintus had
given or because she actually could read it in the man's
face, Anna saw one of life's gentle losers. Hair thinning,
body gone to fat, nails chewed to the quick on what had
once been fine, almost delicate hands, he cowered behind
his glittering array of knives. Earlier on, in his twenties
and thirties, Herm might have raged against his fate,
bashed from one get-rich-quick scheme to the next. Acceptance had come somewhere along the line. He'd
crawled into this well-lined nest and hidden. Anna saw no
fight in the man.

No passion.

Remembering why they were there, she wondered if
committing a sex crime, one that resulted, intentionally or
not, in the death of the partner, required passion. Surely it
would. Perhaps a passion so cold and dark most would
blessedly never feel the icy spark of it, but passion
nevertheless.

At the moment Herm Thorton looked only beaten and
shaken and scared. A flash of anger seared through Anna;
not at Raymond for frightening this rabbit-man but at his
blundering in and doing it first. She was willing to bet
Herm Thorton was a man easy to break. It would have been
valuable to have seen his first, unprepared responses to
questions.

"Raymond!" the sheriff said sharply. Silence fell. Into it
Clintus dropped words like ice cubes. "What brings you
out here, Ray?"

Anna sidled between a display of camouflage duct tape
and a shelf of squashy hats in jungle, forest, desert and—

most useful in Mississippi—snow camo, and oozed out of the clutter to flank Barnette and Thorton.

At the rear of the shop, nestled in a thicket of fishing nets, battered oars and stacked boots, Herm stood behind a glass-topped counter inside of which the knives were displayed. Good knives from the look of them. But for a few of the firearms, probably the only items in the shop worth anything.

If the undertaker was put on the defensive by the sheriff's demeanor, he didn't show it. Leaning against the counter, casual in khakis and a pink Izod shirt, he smiled at Clintus, his teeth like aged ivory piano keys in the dusty light of the shop.

"Well, Sheriff, I've got a natural interest in what happened to my brother, now don't I?" he drawled. "Seeing as Herm here was the last person to see him alive, I wanted to have a word with him. That makes sense, doesn't it?"

Barnette's questions weren't meant to be answered and the sheriff didn't try. Looking beyond Raymond's insolent slouch, Clintus said, "That right, Mr. Thorton, you saw Doyce that night?"

"No!" Had Herm been an actual instead of a virtual mouse, he would have squeaked. Locked in the trappings of man, he just sort of gasped, then scurried from one end of the counter to the other. Finding the way out blocked by Anna, he scurried back nearer the known evil of Raymond Barnette.

"No," he repeated. "I never saw Doyce—"

"Heard him then," Barnette interrupted with a wave of the hand as if it were the same thing.

"No!" Herm said and this time he did squeak. "I never talked to him. I just left that message on his machine. That's all."

"Okay. Okay. The last one to talk to him." Barnette seemed fixated on this last-to theme.

"I didn't *talk* to him," Herm said desperately. "He wasn't

there. He didn't answer. I just left a message that's all. I swear."

Anna watched Thorton's disintegration with annoyance. It would be nigh unto impossible to read anything of value from Thorton's reactions now.

Pity the people of Natchez if they elect Barnette sheriff, Anna thought.

Clintus broke in. "Settle down, Mr. Thorton. Ray, we need to ask this gentleman a few questions. It won't take long—" This was to Herm, and he looked ever-so-slightly comforted by it. "But I know you're a busy man, and I don't want to waste your time."

Barnette lounged against the counter, making himself more comfortable. "I'm in no hurry, Sheriff. Got all the time in the world."

Anna could see Clintus coming to a boil. She didn't have all the time in the world, and she was sick of watching the unfolding drama of local politics. Stepping into the cramped playing area, she took stage.

"This is a federal murder investigation, Mr. Barnette," she said clearly. "We need to talk with Mr. Thorton. For the sake of all concerned, we'd like the privacy to do so."

Barnette stayed where he was.

"Go away," Anna said unequivocally.

No wriggle room left, Barnette smiled his oily smile and took an unhurried departure.

The second the door slammed on the undertaker's perfectly pressed trouser seat Herm Thorton began to babble. Anna couldn't tell if it was a gushing of relief because Barnette was gone or if he poured forth a wall of words to forestall any questions she or the sheriff might have.

"Raymond said poor ol' Doyce has passed," Herm gasped, his voice thinned from emphysema or fear. "He said it was murder. Somebody murdered Doyce. Why'd anybody go and do that? Nobody'd kill ol' Doyce. He was good people. He must of just ... Then he says I'm the last one to see him alive. I'm not. I didn't see Doyce alive..." Seeming to hear himself for the first time, Herm let his voice peter out. The desperate trancelike look cleared from his face, and he looked from Anna to Clintus. His mind finally engaged. "Not that I saw him dead," he amended. "No, sir. What I'm saying is—and what Mr. Barnette wouldn't hear—is that I never saw Doyce at all that night. I called him to remind him we were playing poker. But Doyce never showed up. That's all. That's all."

Herm's eyes flickered between Anna and Clintus. His delicate fingers patted a nervous little dance on the countertop. He wasn't merely nervous, he was downright scared.

Again Anna cursed Raymond Barnette. In playing detective, he'd muddied the waters. There was no way of knowing how Herm was normally, what scared him, guilt or the very natural terror of being treated as guilty of something by a dead man's brother. Especially if that brother buries people for a living.

Clintus said nothing and Anna admired his instincts. She didn't speak either. They stared impassively at Herm, waiting to see if Herm's nerves would shake loose something worth hearing.

They didn't. After a tense moment in which he began to skitter back and forth behind the counter in his small trapped animal persona, he started again to tell about the phone message.

The sheriff cut him off. "Where do y'all play poker?" he asked.

Thorton stopped the aimless movement and gave them a blank stare. His eyes were dull hazel, slightly bulging and looked to Anna to be full of tears.

"Whose house," Clintus clarified.

"Oh." The blankness cleared and Herm laughed, a rattling burst like the chatter of a chipmunk. He was relieved. He was on solid ground now. Anna wondered whether there'd been something to alarm him in the first half of the question or whether he was overjoyed at finally being asked something that related to reality as he knew it.

"Badger Lundstrom's," he said with his first sign of authority. "Bradford—we call him Badger. When he was a kid he badgered everybody near half to death. Still does." Again the chattering that passed for a laugh. "We play at Badger's house."

The phrase was so childlike Anna was hit with the image of aging boys still pretending, playing at soldiers and forts and cowboys and Indians.

"Who's 'we'?" she asked.

"Me, Badger, Martin Crowley and Doyce," Herm said promptly. Another question he was comfortable with. "But Doyce never showed up," he added.

"So you played three-handed poker all night?" the sheriff asked.

Anna wasn't well versed in the nuances of the game, but from Clintus's tone she deduced three-handed poker was not the ideal.

Thorton seemed thrown by the concept as well. The assuredness he'd so lately found deserted him. He skittered again, his small feet shuffling loudly across the rubber mat laid down behind the counter. This time he recovered more quickly. "Not all night. We couldn't really get going without Doyce. And we was kind of worried about where he was and all. We just chewed the fat for a while. Then went home."

"What time?" Clintus asked.

"Midnight." Herm was real clear on the time.

"You were worried about Doyce?" Anna asked.

"Real worried, yes, ma'am," Herm replied. The mixture of discomfort, unctuousness and sadness in his voice confused her.

"Did you call him again? Try and see where he was?"

Herm looked startled. A question he wasn't prepared for. "I didn't," he said finally. "One of the other boys might've."

The man was such a mishmash of emotions that there was little sense to his recital. Raymond Barnette had succeeded in getting him sufficiently stirred up with his "last seen alive" routine that the reactions Anna and Clintus were eliciting could be coming from anywhere in Herm's befuddled psyche. Anna gave up. For now. Maybe later, when the undertaker's influence had worn off, they'd be able to see the real Herm Thorton.

Clintus must have felt the same. He asked no more questions but requested and got the addresses and phone numbers of Badger Lundstrom and Martin Crowley.

Calmed by the knowledge the session was over and his interrogators were moving on to other victims, Herm hazarded a question of his own. "Ray said they found Doyce at that old inn there on the Trace. Was he just parked there in his car or what?"

The question sounded genuine. Herm didn't strike Anna as much of an actor—not enough ego, not enough control. She believed the man did not know where and how Doyce Barnette's body had been left.

"Something like that," she told him. They'd been so angry with the undertaker they'd let it splash over onto Herm Thorton. Anna took an even breath. Time to go back and ask the customary questions. "Do you know if Doyce had any enemies, anybody who'd want to hurt him?"

The question startled Herm, then offended him. "Doyce? No. There wasn't nobody didn't like Doyce. Oh, some folks had no use for him at all but that's not the same as not liking. There wasn't nothing not to like about Doyce."

"Was there anything to like?" Anna asked.

Herm had to think too long and it embarrassed him. "Doyce was just real easygoing. There just wasn't nobody minded having him around."

A cipher, Anna thought, one of those people who by choice or genetics is incapable of stirring up much emotion. A strange sentiment of her father's floated into her brain: "People either love me or hate me but, by God, they know I'm there." It sounded like no one knew or much cared if Doyce Barnette was "there."

Yet he'd been found stripped to his underdrawers, the victim of what, on the surface, appeared to be a crime born of man's darkest and most twisted passions; an unholy hybrid of sex and violence. *Stripped to his underdrawers.* Suddenly that struck Anna as odd. Why not naked? That scrap of squeamishness or prudery didn't fit.

Clintus was talking. Anna dragged herself back from her private musings.

"Did Doyce have any friends or acquaintances you know of that were unusual in any way? You know, somebody he might have known that wasn't one of the regular guys. Somebody he kept kind of secret?"

Clearly Herm Thorton thought that was a stupid question but now that he was no longer under attack he seemed to want desperately to cooperate. Either that or he dearly hoped he could come up with an answer that would steer the questions away from him and his.

Honesty prevailed—or powers of imagination failed— and Herm shook his head sadly. "Doyce's been here his whole life," he said. "He don't know anybody but the rest of us."

Herm was done. Anna and Clintus took their leave. As she opened the shop door, from behind the racks and shelves, she could hear the telltale peeping of a digital phone as the numbers were punched in. Herm was in a heck of a hurry to call someone. Undoubtedly Badger and/or Martin.

Not an unnatural reaction. As her grandmother used to say, "One little cloud is lonely." Her father, more earthy by nature, said, "What's the use of being given a load of manure if you don't spread it around?"

Clintus and Anna climbed into the sheriff's car. The big sedan—a Crown Vic like the one Anna drove for the NPS but a newer model—had the ancient luxury of a bench seat. Clintus buckled himself in, then leaned back and blew out a sigh. Like a teapot, Anna guessed, blowing off steam.

"Ray Barnette's beginning to get crosswise with me. So far he's stepped right between the first couple folks we wanted to talk with and just royally screwed things up," Clintus said.

"Friends and family are usually who gets you in the end. We need to take a close look at brother Ray," Anna said.

Clintus thought about it for a moment. It wouldn't be the first time it had crossed his mind. "Ray inherits his mama's place now. Place has to be worth something. Two, three hundred acres. Probably going for—what—maybe a thousand an acre plus whatever that old house is worth. A quarter of a million's motive enough in my book. If Doyce had been found with his skull bashed in or a bullet in his chest I'd've been putting Ray under the microscope. It's the bruises from the straps, the underwear. That sexual or whatever angle...I don't know. Doyce and Ray were brothers."

Homosexual, homicidal incest: it did seem a bit much. Anna couldn't say that she, personally, had seen worse but guaranteed somebody had. Any evil that could be conceived could be and usually was executed somewhere in the world. Man was the animal who created. Like the God in whose image he was supposedly made, he created his own heaven and his own hell.

"Raymond could have killed his brother, then set it up as a sex crime to throw us off," Anna offered.

"Those bruises were made while Doyce was still alive," the sheriff reminded her. "As easy going as Doyce was said to have been, I can't see him letting his brother truss him up like that for any reason I can think of."

"Right. Me neither."

"Darn it all to heck," Clintus said, and he slammed the flat of his hand against the steering wheel.

"Why don't you just swear," Anna said. "It'll make you feel better."

The sheriff shot her a look that told her he thought he just had.

"What?" she asked.

"Two things. Doggone it." He sighed and began again. "Two things. One, if Ray had done it, he'd've made sure it didn't look like anything obscene, or tried to at any rate. It gets out that this was some kind of perversion—even if it turned out to have nothing to do with Ray—he'd lose a lot of votes. Folks down here don't want to vote for somebody who's got bad blood in the family. Not just a spot of mental queerness—everybody's got a *loony* cousin wandering around the delta somewhere—but a serious kind of sickness like this would be. You know, what with the homosexual angle and all."

Anna waited but Clintus seemed uncomfortable with telling her what the second thing was. "And," she said to move him along.

"The second thing's a bit trickier. Politics. I go and noise it around that Ray's a suspect in his own brother's death, it could look like I was just trying to get rid of the competition. He just now got on the docket. There may be a couple other candidates running for sheriff, but at the moment, it's just him and me."

Anna admired his sense of honor. A lesser man might have jumped at a chance like this. "Tricky," she agreed. "I guess we go slow."

"Grab a burger then tackle Badger and Martin?" the sheriff said.

Anna looked at her watch. "Later. John Brown's FBI agent's due at the Port Gibson office in forty minutes. You ought to be in on that."

"I guess," Clintus admitted and put the car in gear.

7

The Federal Bureau of Investigation was waiting for them when they arrived at the Port Gibson Ranger Station. His car, painted shiny black and bristling with antennae, was parked out front. Alongside it were two NPS patrol cars. Barth was on duty, and it looked as if Randy had taken it upon himself to come on early so as not to miss out on any potential humiliation that Anna might be dealt.

He'll be wanting overtime for it, too, Anna thought sourly and wondered if she'd have the spine—or the mental energy—to deny it to him.

Barth Dinkins was on the phone. He looked up long enough to give Anna and Clintus a nod, then went back to his conversation. From the one-sided scraps Anna could hear, he was talking to Tupelo, arranging to have the names of the dead slaves re-created on a new sign.

Randy Thigpen's desk was empty. From Anna's office came the sounds of voices. Thigpen had commandeered her personal space as well as the attention of the FBI agent Brown had called in. Mississippi, one of the more sparsely populated states in the eastern half of the country, was getting downright claustrophobic. Everywhere Anna turned in this wretched investigation, it seemed there was a slithytove of good old boys plopped down between her and her immediate objective. The irritation that had tingled when she'd seen Randy's patrol car began to burn.

"Anna, Sheriff," Thigpen said expansively as they appeared in the office doorway, the good manager hosting his staff. "This is Special Agent Ronnie Dent out of Jackson."

Dent nodded. Neither man stood. There were only two chairs in the office and Thigpen was parked in Anna's. It was a small secretary's chair with an adjustable back. The back had been sprung when she'd taken over that spring, and Anna had gone to some time and trouble to bend it back into an ergonomically correct piece of furniture. Thigpen's fat ass was squashing it into worthlessness.

"Agent Dent." Anna said evenly. She introduced Clintus. Then, "Randy. Why don't you call and see if the autopsy report is ready?" It wouldn't be. Not till later in the afternoon, but Anna was damned if she was going to stand around on one foot then the other in her own office.

Thigpen reached for the phone on her desk. "Got that number?" he asked.

"Why don't you use the phone on your desk," she said. "Barth's got a directory, I think."

There was a brief battle of wills. Thigpen's eyes narrowed and his long mustache twitched as he tried to think of ways to maintain the high ground without doing anything overt that might get him fired or, at any rate, a reprimand from the big dogs in Tupelo.

"Ronnie, go ahead and bring Anna up to speed," he said finally, and levered his bulk out of the ruined chair.

"Randy," Anna stopped him. "Bring the sheriff a chair, if you would please."

He tried to think of a comeback but failed. For once Anna'd gotten the last word. She indulged in a moment of satisfaction knowing, with Thigpen around, it was bound to be short-lived.

When he'd cleared the doorway, Anna took possession of her chair. The back was so bent if she'd put her weight against it she would have toppled over backward. Balancing herself on the seat, she sized up Special Agent Ronnie Dent.

He was young, early thirties at a guess, and put Anna in mind of a brick: stocky, short, red hair, red face pocked with old acne scars. Because of his face Dent came across as a much bigger man than he was. With little alteration and still maintaining its humanness, it could have been a baboon's face, disproportionately wide and flat. Either through natural physiognomy or learned control, it was a face that gave nothing away.

Briefly, with occasional inserts from Sheriff Jones, Anna recounted what they knew of the killing of Doyce Barnette, including the unsatisfactory interview with Herm Thorton.

During the recital Randy returned and, finding the chairs occupied, leaned in the doorway. He filled it completely and Anna felt a twinge of claustrophobia closing her throat. Having Thigpen between herself and freedom was unsettling.

The instant she'd finished talking, Thigpen pushed his voice if not his person into the room. "Autopsy'll be done this afternoon or tomorrow," he said, speaking only to Special Agent Dent. "I doubt there'll be any surprises there. This thing's pretty much what we were talking about earlier. As straightforward a case of sadomasochism gone wrong as I've seen in my thirty years working this beat."

Anna only just avoided rolling her eyes. Thigpen had been on the Trace for thirty years, but she was willing to bet the closest thing to a sadomasochistic homicide he'd seen was the perverse way possums insisted on committing suicide under the wheels of speeding cars.

"Rape's about the only sex crime we get down here," Dent said, sounding mildly disgusted at southerners' lack of imagination. "If you can call that a sex crime."

Thigpen shot Anna a look of triumph as though Dent had scored one for the home team, but Anna knew what the

FBI agent meant. Rape was about violence, hate and dominance. Sex had little to do with it.

"Any ritual trappings about the corpse or the room you found it in?" Dent divided the question between Clintus and Thigpen. Anna'd been born female, she'd grown into a small woman and, in the past ten years, had slid into middle age. If ever there was a cloak of invisibility, time and circumstances were trying to weave her one. Once she would have fought it, clamored for her share of the attention. Now she merely used it, sitting quietly, watching the interplay, hoping to learn something.

"Like Satanism, you mean," Thigpen said.

"Yes." Dent sounded hopeful.

For a bit, Randy didn't say anything. Anna thought he looked disappointed. He'd not seen the corpse. Everything he knew was secondhand. She waited with interest to see if he'd refer the matter to her or the sheriff. He didn't. After a few seconds he brightened.

"There was a religious text circled," he offered.

Dent wasn't much impressed. "Just asking," he said. "Routine. We've gotten a lot of press attention over the Satan cult thing but they are like ghosts. Everybody seems to believe they exist but nobody can find any real evidence that they do."

He pushed himself up, choosing to be the one to end the meeting. At least he spoke directly to Anna. He might prefer dealing with men, but he knew where the seat of power lay in this office. That was enough for her.

"We'll run your murder through the mill, see if we get any hits on the MO, see if there's any known operators hereabouts, that sort of thing. You get any hard evidence, fingerprints, whatever, give me a call and I'll plug them into the system for you."

Your murder. You get. For you. Dent was semiofficially dumping the crime back into Anna's lap. Should something interesting turn up, the door was left open for him to snatch the case back. Anna was glad she was not an ambitious woman.

Once Dent had taken his departure Thigpen shifted gears. The change was sudden and relatively complete as if he'd remembered that he'd turned over a new leaf. He became friendly, interested and what, to the uninitiated, could have passed for open, honest and helpful.

Since she was in the office, had Clintus on tap and both her rangers in house, Anna decided to have an impromptu meeting to see if they'd learned anything. Barth was occupied with the vandalism of the Mt. Locust sign but Randy, during his last brief phase as a decent hardworking park ranger, had volunteered to seek out the friends and associates of Doyce Barnette. Randy spoke first. Anna let him. She didn't want to dampen any real enthusiasm the guy might have developed for the work he was paid to do.

Thigpen had been industrious. He'd compiled a list of people half a page long, single-spaced and, for a wonder, neatly typed. No addresses or phone numbers had been included and Anna had a cynical moment wondering if Thigpen had just made the whole thing up. The names of Badger Lundstrom, Martin Crowley and Herman Thorton were not listed.

"We'll need to divide the list up," Randy finished. "Interview the lot of 'em. Anna, why don't you take the first six and the sheriff and I'll split the last."

Anna let the suggestion slip by. "Clintus," she said.

The sheriff briefly outlined their interview with Herm Thorton.

"Talking to folks around town I didn't hear those names," Thigpen said when he'd finished. "If they were friends of the deceased, there's not much there. I doubt he saw them much."

"According to Mr. Thorton they played poker together every Friday night and some Saturdays," Anna said.

Randy looked annoyed. "Yeah ... well ..." Whatever he was going to say next, he apparently thought better of it. His face readjusted into the visage of the new and improved Ranger Thigpen. "Well, if you all think they are worth the time, I'd like to be in on it when you talk to them. Once they've been got out of the way I think we'll need to take a good close look at these fellas." He waggled the list he'd made as if to tempt them to do the right thing.

The sheriff had business to take care of. Probably getting the lunch Anna had denied him earlier. It was pushing three o'clock. It was decided they'd meet back at the Port Gibson office near 5 P.M., quitting time for Badger Lundstrom. Lundstrom was a scrap metal dealer. He and his twenty-six-year-old son lived a bachelor existence on the western edge of Port Gibson.

Randy wanted to talk about his list of names. Barth needed her to stop by his slave cemetery on the way to Natchez. A blinking light on the old phone machine that served the district office summoned Anna to the news that Chief Ranger Brown wanted to speak with her.

Anna had been a field ranger for more than ten years. She'd been a manager for seven months. The seven months seemed the longer of the two. With mumbled excuses and vague promises, she fled the office and her erstwhile assistants. She wanted to see Paul. Just see him, talk to him, hear his voice. A touch would be nice, but she could forgo that. It had been so long since she'd truly needed a man she felt the craving in a place deeper than hunger.

"Jesus," she murmured as she turned on the ignition. *Been so long.* Less than twenty-four hours had passed since she'd said good-bye to Paul Davidson on her doorstep in Rocky Springs. The fall equinox had come and gone two months before. Theoretically, the days were getting shorter. *Time is relative,* Anna reminded herself. For reasons of its own, it had chosen to do its petty pace thing this day.

For a minute she just sat. The aches and stings from her rush through the woods gathered in force and she felt old and tired and decrepit. Last night she'd been hunted. How could it be only last night? Eons seemed to have passed. Time was kaleidoscoping. Zach, the high deserts of Colorado, riding Gideon through the backcountry of Texas—

these things seemed to have happened only yesterday, yet
her strange adventures in Dixieland felt as if they'd taken
place in another life.

Memories of who she'd once been struck so acutely she
was moved to tears and had to fight to keep from sobbing
out loud. She missed her husband, her sister, the sound of
dry wind in the piñon pines.

"Get a grip," she ordered herself and jammed the Crown
Vic into reverse, not sure where she was going but knowing getting away from where she was was imperative.

The piercing shriek of a siren cut through the mental
storm, and Anna slammed on the brakes. In her preoccupation, she'd not looked behind her and had very nearly run
into another patrol car. This was why law enforcement was
trained to back into parking places, she reminded herself as
she shut the ignition down.

Sheriff Paul Davidson got out of his squad car. In the
perfect gold light of afternoon his blond hair gleamed.
Anna had not noticed before but now, liking the way his
uniform fit him, liking the way his thighs pulled the fabric
taut when he walked, she saw he'd lost weight. The divorce
he was fighting for was costing him. He'd grown leaner,
harder looking. It suited him and Anna wanted nothing so
much as to collapse in his arms and feel the strength of him
down the length of her body as once she'd craved the feel
of the earth against her bones.

"Hey," she said neutrally, shoving her feelings into a box
that got harder and harder to open again over the years.
"What brings you out here?"

A fleeting shadow of pain darkened his blue eyes at the
curtness of her greeting. Pain of Anna's own answered it,
but she didn't amend her words by so much as a smile. Un-
reasonable as it was, her sudden need for him and his in-
ability to answer it made her angry.

"I've got a couple little things, excuses mostly," he
replied in a drawl made genteel by four years at the University of Tennessee and three years in seminary in

Austin, Texas. "But my main-most reason was to see you, see how you're doing. Rumor has it, you've been stepping out on me."

For a moment Anna was aware of nothing but confusion and the perverse pleasure of having, however unwittingly, stirred this splendid man's heart. Then she remembered. "Last night," she said.

"If I'd've known you were going for a moonlight walk, I'd've hung around." Paul was smiling his slow gentle smile but there was an edge to his words. He was angry that Anna had been in danger, that she'd been hurt, made afraid, that he wasn't there to take care of her.

At least that was how Anna read it, and she was made weak by the glorious sensation that somebody cared whether she lived or died.

"If I'd known I was going to be accompanied on my evening constitutional, you would have been my first choice for an escort," she said and gave him the smile spite had been withholding.

"Tell me about it over a cup of coffee?"

"I was hoping for lunch," Anna said.

"Your car or mine?" Paul answered but Anna had seen the ghosts of the gossips haunting him before he'd answered. He was uncomfortable being seen with her, even in uniform.

"Coffee'd be better," she said. "I'm short on time."

Paul had the grace not to look relieved.

Barth had gone. Randy was still slothing about. He was on the phone when they walked in but hung up with a hurried "Call ya back," when he saw them. Probably talking to his mistress of many years. Once off the phone he seemed to Anna to be all eyes and ears. Either to avoid work, annoy Anna or to make himself feel important, Randy attached himself to Sheriff Davidson. He attempted classic man chat: sports, guns, dogs, internal combustion engines. Anna fought down the irritation that came with the belief that he was doing it on purpose to exclude her from the manly world of law enforcement. A tiny voice, whispered in her ear over twenty years before by a woman who didn't like Anna enough and liked Anna's husband Zach too much, came back. "Trust your paranoia."

"How do you take your coffee?" Anna cut through, choosing to pretend she didn't remember.

"Black."

Anna poured a cup of the disreputable-looking brew for herself and Paul and led the way into her office where, for once, she was grateful there were only two chairs. Undaunted by the lack of facilities, Randy lumbered after them and took up his old place in the doorway, three hundred pounds of lard Anna'd have to blast her way through to gain the outdoors.

The idea was beginning to appeal strongly to her when Thigpen was saved by the jarring bell of the office phone. She and Randy locked eyes as it rang a second time. On the third ring she said, "Would you get that for me, Randy? I need to have a word with Paul."

Reluctantly he pulled himself away only to reappear a minute later. "Tupelo," he said. "A motorist call in. Cell phone. Needs an assist up to Rocky. Dead battery it sounds like."

Again the staring contest. "Guess you'll be wanting me to take that," Thigpen grumbled. Anna said nothing. "Don't you be going to Lundstrom's without me. I want to be in on that."

"You'll want to wrap up the motorist assist in record time, then," Anna said.

Finally he had no choice but to go, and she expelled the breath she'd not known she'd been holding. "God, but I hate that man," she muttered.

Paul laughed. "Gee, I'd've never guessed. So." He nudged her knee gently with his booted foot and at once Anna was warmed and connected. Love was most assuredly blind but its other senses were remarkably acute.

"First, who told you about last night's escapade?" Anna's question wasn't to seek out idle gossipers. The hunting stand "prank," if one chose to call it that, was the sort that the participants would want to brag about. It had all the ingredients of a bar boast except for the sex, and she doubted the perpetrators would have any compunction about using their imaginations to add that element. Anna was hoping they would boast. Realistically it was about the only chance she had of nailing the bastards.

"Triletta told me."

Paul named a new clerk at the Port Gibson Sheriff's department. Anna remembered not the woman but the name. Tired of white men's hand-me-down names, many African-Americans in Mississippi had taken to naming their children or, if their own folks were conservative, themselves, with exotic-sounding syllables that pleased the ear and annoyed the hell out of the sense of spelling.

"The tooth," Paul said, tapping his front teeth to jog her memory.

"Ah." Triletta had capped a front tooth in gold with a diamond chip inset in an etching of a star. Another culturally based fashion. "Find out who she got the story from," Anna said.

"Will do. Now tell me."

Anna related her adventuring, enjoying the growing anger that burned in his eyes and tightened the muscles of his face.

"Randy Thigpen wasn't exactly Johnny-on-the-spot," he said when she'd finished.

"At least he showed up before somebody got hurt."

"I'll see what I can dig up on my end," he promised.

They sat without speaking for a while. Anna let herself simply enjoy the companionship, the sight of him against the green and gold and blue that leaked through her one fly-specked window.

At length he began to fidget, the small shifts and wriggles preparatory to leaving.

"What do you know about a Badger Lundstrom," Anna asked. The question was legitimate—Lundstrom lived in Paul's county—but Anna asked it to buy a few more minutes of Paul Davidson's time, and she hated herself for the pathetic need it evinced, if to no other judge and jury but the one in her head.

"Lundstrom."

"Owns a scrap metal yard," Anna said.

"Okay. Got him. He's a local boy. His folks and their folks all lived right here. Big man. Heavy drinker but never been in trouble for it—no DUIs, not the sort to get into brawls or anything, least not that's ever come to my attention. Used to be a big football star when he was in high school. To my way of thinking he never much got past that stage. Kind of a class-clown type, though he's got to be pushing forty if he isn't already there. Not a church-going man to my knowledge. Divorced some years, if I remember right." He thought a bit and Anna waited to see if anything more floated up from Mississippi's pool of communal history. In the country, where everybody knew everybody else's business, secrets kept were necessarily buried deep, covered in years, sometimes generations, of lies. The anonymity of the city could not be counted on to mask antisocial behaviors.

"That's all I got," he said finally. He glanced at his watch.

"It's a help," Anna said, then added, "I guess I'd best be getting back to work," to make up for keeping him longer than he'd intended to stay.

"Me, too." He stood, took his Stetson from the counter. Reaching out, he touched her hair lightly. "Call me when things happen. Call me at home, at night, at work. Don't shut me out. You need somebody to be there for you."

Anna said nothing. Not sure what she felt and afraid to trust anything to words.

"I need to be there for somebody," he amended.

Anna collected herself enough to say, "I'll call." She doubted she would, at least not when things were new and raw. Too needy. Perhaps not for him, but for her to have to witness in herself. Maybe she sensed if she ever let herself need somebody she'd fall into a bottomless pit of it.

Behind her the radio began babbling. Her number

wasn't mentioned and Anna ignored it. Paul drove away with a crunching of gravel and still she stood in the doorway, not mooning over her departed lover, merely bereft of the will to move, to act, to do.

The other door being pried open galvanized her into looking alive even if she did not feel it.

Thigpen barreled in on a waft of stale cigarette smoke.

"That was quick," Anna said, too distracted to keep a note of accusation from her voice.

"I radioed Frank up at Rocky. He's going to jump the battery. Problem solved," Thigpen said. Frank was the maintenance man at Rocky Springs campground. Anna hadn't known he had cables and was certain the little three-wheeled cart he drove lacked the guts to jump a car battery.

As if he read her thoughts, Thigpen added, "He's got the stuff in that old truck he drives."

Anna knew she'd probably get complaints from maintenance because one of her rangers was leveraging off his work onto their people, but there was little she could do about it at the moment.

"Problem solved," she agreed. She looked at her watch. Ninety minutes to kill before Clintus Jones returned. Scheduling duties awaited on the derelict computer in her office. She'd not yet begun the chore of writing up reports on the Barnette murder or the incident at the hunting platform. She'd pulled her gun. If every cop on television had to write up a detailed report every time they unholstered a weapon, primetime would be about paper shuffling. The NPS insisted a ranger have justification for first pulling the weapon; then if, God forbid, one actually pointed it at someone, a whole new set of explanations was required. That and civil litigation partially accounted for why police all over the nation were under fire in the media for looking the other way when crimes were being committed. Easier to let the perpetrators die of old age than justify every action taken in subduing them.

Thigpen was staring at her. She'd yet to move from the doorway. Anna looked at the dingy light leaking from her

office, then at the rich glow of the November afternoon
outdoors. Paperwork would have to wait. Her brain was
getting claustrophobic. Time had come to air it out.

"I'm going to head on down to that meadow," she made
a sudden decision. "Look around again. I should be back
before Clintus gets here but if I'm not, ask him to wait. It
shouldn't be more than a few minutes."

Randy Thigpen followed her as she stepped into her office to retrieve her hat and duty belt. Velcroing it on, Anna
was aware of the familiar pain on her hipbones where the
heavy belt bruised them. She needed to put on a little
weight, pad herself.

Thigpen was blocking her way out again. A flash of
anger so hot and irrational flared in Anna she was mildly
surprised her hair didn't catch on fire.

"What is it?" she asked.

"Mind if I ride along with you?"

*No more than I'd mind being staked out naked on a fire
ant nest,* Anna thought, but said nothing. Maybe she
needed food. Something was making her more vicious
than usual.

"I need to have a talk with you," Thigpen said. His voice
was somehow different, his stance less aggressive, the eternal sneer gone from his one visible lip.

Anna relented. This manager shit was killing her. In
good clean fieldwork one was not obligated to give second
and third chances. "Sure," she said. "I'll drive."

8

Randy was uncharacteristically quiet for the first few miles. Anna summoned calm and strength by concentrating only on the deep blue of the sky, the patchwork curtain of foliage that screened the Trace from the real world of Quick Stops, billboards, car dealers and fast food. The colors had peaked two weeks before. The first hard rain would strip the last of them from the branches. Having grown up in the high desert of eastern California, where hardwoods existed only in front yards and forests were of pine, Anna never tired of the falling of leaves in a true deciduous forest. Day after day, as though there were an endless supply, leaves rained down. A deluge of yellow, orange, rust and red. They fell slowly, erratically. Anna could catch them on their casual journey into oblivion.

Now, to either side of the narrow ribbon of asphalt the Crown Vic confined her to, she could see this peaceable storm whispering behind tree line. As always she was charmed, amazed and enjoyed the sense of reality and time being suspended.

"I need to have a talk with you," Randy repeated his earlier sentiments. Reality slapped back down, cold and smelly as a dead carp on a chopping block.

Randy waited for her to graciously invite him to share. Feeling petty, Anna didn't. Finally he gave up and began again.

"I know that we've had our differences," he said.

Mentally Anna rolled her eyes, sniffed and said, *"Gee, ya think?"* Corporally she merely drove, eyes on the road, the glamour of the changing forest lost to the tunnel vision of the highway.

"I guess maybe I owe you an apology. All I can say in my own defense is that I pretty much figured the district ranger position would go to me. I been here nearly thirty years. Got old driving this stretch of road. Been a GS-7 living like the poor folk most of that time. Finally the s.o.b.s make me a GS-9, then the district ranger leaves and, the way I look at it, they owed that spot to me."

Randy had segued smoothly from apology to whine to belligerence. The teensy-weensy spark of camaraderie and understanding that his first words had ignited behind Anna's breastbone was rapidly being extinguished.

Maybe Randy saw the faint light die. Maybe he heard the changing tone of his own voice. For whatever reason, he took a breath and changed tactics.

"Anyway, enough of that," he said. "They hired you and I guess they had to, you being a woman and all . . ."

"If this is an apology, it's downright crappy," Anna said without taking her eyes from the road.

Thigpen was quiet for a moment, then he laughed. It was the first truly sincere noise Anna'd heard him make and she found herself smiling. Though she hated to say or even think anything favorable about the man, he did have a lovely voice, light and clear and warm. His laugh was even better, a throaty chuckle Burl Ives would have been proud of.

"Okay, okay," Thigpen said. All traces of his borrowed southern accent vanished, and Anna heard the more natural iron and granite of his New Jersey upbringing ring under the words. "I'm a hidebound, opinionated, sexist pig," he said. "That's how I was brought up and when I die I'm going to be carried to my grave by six *men* in suits, and if the preacher who recites the Twenty-third Psalm over my grave isn't wearing pants, I'm going to sit right up in my coffin and raise holy hell."

Anna laughed, delighted as much by the sudden honesty as the image his words conjured up.

"But, given all that, the way I'm figuring it now is you've been a good district ranger. You're not some fast-track equal opportunity bimbo they're trying to get political points with. You've actually been around—learned your stuff. That killing this spring was a bad welcome to Mississippi and you took it in stride. Got yourself nearly killed going at it without proper backup," he had to add.

Anna was sorely tempted to remind him that the one time she did call him for backup he hid out in the ranger station at Port Gibson and left her to her fate.

He must have remembered the incident, too, because he hurried on before she could say anything. "Be that as it may, you pulled it off. That gave me—gave a lot of us—respect for you. You're not a whiner and you got guts."

The compliment sounded genuine and, while Anna didn't allow herself to be taken in by it, she did allow herself to feel a moment's pleasure in the accolade. Near as she could remember, it was the first positive thing Randy had had to say since she'd come to the Natchez Trace Parkway. She might as well enjoy it; it could be the last as well.

"I'm not trying to butter you up," Randy said. Which of course he was and Anna knew it. By the semi-finality in his tone she guessed she was about to find out why.

"I don't have long to retirement. Two months sixteen days—but who's counting?" He laughed again, alone this time. "And I'd like to leave with a good taste in my mouth. I'd like you and me to work together. Let me show you what I can do. I'm one hell of a ranger. I'm good at what I do. Since you came on board, I know I've been dogging it a little. Sulking maybe because you took my—took the job I wanted. Believe it or not, it's been harder on me than it has on you."

Anna doubted that. Goldbricking never got anyone beaten half to death, though there were times she was tempted to change that.

"I don't want to leave a thirty-year career feeling bad about myself, you know, leaving you thinking I couldn't cut it. What I'm saying is, I'm turning over a new leaf here. I want to be part of this investigation. Bring poor ol' Doyce's killer to justice. That'd be a good way to buy the gold watch. What do you say?"

Anna knew she should feel relief, even joy, at this unforeseen announcement. A tribute to her stellar attributes as a manager. But she didn't want to be pals with Thigpen. Over the months she'd come to take a perverse pleasure in hating the man. He'd hung her out to dry, refusing her backup for a dangerous car stop. He'd sued her on the grounds of racial discrimination. Turning the other cheek had served only to get her smacked upside the head. Again.

Shelving these uncharitable thoughts, she said, "Sounds good to me."

Thigpen wisely settled into silence. From the corner of her eye, Anna watched him. Beneath his groomed hedge of a mustache, he was smiling. Perhaps at the glow of doing right. It looked to Anna more like smugness. Thigpen had turned over a new leaf. Anna couldn't help wondering what was under the old leaf that he didn't want her to see.

They reached the meadow north of Mt. Locust where the illegal hunting stand was built, and Anna pulled the Crown Vic into the shade of another of the meadow's old pecans. Beneath its spreading branches, a black family, what looked like grandmother, mother and six children ranging in age from eight or nine to an infant snug and sleeping in a nest of blankets tucked into a wooden peach crate, gleaned pecans from the yellowing grass.

The women and children, the tree, the meadow unfurled behind them, a gentle rain of leaves from above, several caught in the coarse dark hair of the harvesters, presented a picture of such timelessness and peace Anna was hard-pressed to remember the night hunting with its guns and the baying of the human hounds. Yankees—herself before a lust to climb up one rung on the career ladder had up-rooted her from the mountains of Colorado—persisted in painting the South, most particularly Mississippi, in broad and simple strokes of Black versus White, the people as two dimensional as cartoon characters.

Mississippi was the most complex place Anna'd ever lived, in both culture and landscape. Worlds collided: swamp and forest, ever-changing sameness, past and present, affluence and poverty, African, Asian, Indian, sublime and ridiculous. A mix of people who'd lived and worked together for four hundred years and yet did not share a history.

"What are we looking for?" Thigpen asked, trying on his new role as helpful sidekick.

Anna put the car in park and switched off the ignition. "I'm not sure. I've been over the stand. There's nothing. It was swept down, literally, with a broom."

"You're kidding?"

"Not kidding."

"I wouldn't have credited any of those lamebrains with the sense to cover their tracks like that."

"Doesn't much matter," Anna said. "Chances are those guys are the brand of garden-variety jackasses who never get on any law-enforcement records. Their crimes are the sort that aren't reported except as jokes told over too many beers."

Thigpen laughed and Anna was annoyed. The picture did not amuse her in the least.

"I just wanted to take a look around the meadow," she told him. "See if they'd had any luck with the hunting—that is before I showed. Maybe they got careless and forgot to police that."

The meadow was small, not more than ten acres. In previous years it had been leased to local ranchers for cattle grazing. This year there'd been no takers and the meadow had rejuvenated itself. With the possible exception of sheep, raising cattle was one of the most devastating things humanity had done to the environment. Too many hooves, too many mouths—each feeding multiple fore-stomachs— on too small a piece of real estate, left the land looking as if it had been visited by a plague of half-ton locusts.

The South, with its miraculous powers of regeneration, fared far better than the fragile arid lands of the West. The meadow had sprung back with such fervor that if it wasn't leased the following spring it would have to be mowed as a fire hazard. This time of year it was thigh deep in coreopsis, an orange sunflower-like bloom a couple inches in diameter. Most of the flowers were blown, but for just an instant Anna was eight years old again, seeing the poppy field in Oz through Dorothy's eyes.

"Ought to mow this shit," Randy said, killing the moment. The two of them waded into the fading blooms.

Randy's new persona was more irritating than his old. Taking charge, he attempted to direct the search in odd sporadic bursts, first in one direction then another. Anna ignored him and walked a zigzag pattern, eyes on the ground. Shutting out his chatter, she narrowed mind and vision, noting only the yellow of the pollen the flowers painted across the dark fabric of her trousers, the clean acid scent of the crushed plant stems and the scraps of soil visible beneath the tangle of dusty green.

Randy, daunted by the heat—a pleasant seventy-five degrees in the sun—or his own fat, stuck to the meadow's edges. Half a dozen times he called Anna to come look at something. Twice she left what she was doing to comply. The first call was to inspect a cluster of frail bones and feathers several months old. The second was to show her a rusted and dented hubcap. Thigpen had trouble articulating why this relic of Detroit was of any concern to their present occupation. The next four calls she ignored, throwing Thigpen an "in a minute," so she wouldn't seem as rude as she felt.

Half an hour of careful searching and she found what she was looking for: the remains of a deer poached no more than a day or two earlier. The head, hooves, genitalia and a pile of guts were all that remained; leavings from a hurried field dressing of a young doe. Blood and meat were still fresh enough to attract flies. She worked out from the find in tight circles, seeking any trace of themselves that the hunters might have left behind.

Excited by success, Randy Thigpen plowed his way in from treeline, Ferdinand the Bull in a field of flowers, and commenced chattering and stomping around the edges in an erratic search destined to destroy rather than unearth anything left behind.

Anna didn't call him to order. This had been a wild goose chase at best, merely an excuse to get away from the office that backfired when Ranger Thigpen had insisted on accompanying her.

There were tracks, transformed by recovering leaves and stems, worthless from an identification point of view. Bloodstains where the kill had been shot showed brown a couple yards out in the direction of the stand. Nothing nifty in the way of a classic clue presented itself. In her years investigating crimes Anna had yet to find a silver lighter engraved with the perpetrator's initials or a matchbook that lead to an exclusive club. Wilderness work lacked the classic glamour.

Time ran out shortly before her patience did, and they headed back to Port Gibson. Anna was quiet but Randy was as juiced up as if they'd had a wondrous success. For the twenty miles to the ranger station he talked about his brilliance, insight and bravado, reliving and, Anna didn't doubt, rewriting war stories from his years on the Trace. By the time she turned in under the pin oaks protecting the district office, she felt she had truly come to understand the expression "bending your ear."

Clintus Jones was waiting, sitting quietly at Randy's desk across from Barth Dinkins. Barth had some of the battered and defiled boards from the vandalized sign on the

desk. From the cold looks and belated greeting she and
Randy received, Anna guessed the two black men had been
discussing the centuries of evils the white race had perpet-
uated on their people.

Customarily Anna wouldn't have blamed them. Racial
guilt or an innate understanding of the tenacity of psychological wounds would have allowed her to be kind. An
hour and a half with Randy Thigpen, reformed or not, had
successfully milked her of human kindness.

"Hey, Barth," she said shortly. "Ready to go find Badger
Lundstrom?" she asked Clintus. A shifting of gears
showed in his face as he emerged from a past where she
was the enemy to a present where she was a comrade in
arms. Anna was an adept reader of people but Clintus was
hard. It was his eyes, she realized as he pushed himself up
from Randy's long-suffering chair. They were beyond
brown, very nearly black. The pupils and the iris were so
close in hue they seemed focused inward, as though he saw
only in the dark, things cats and mediums see. The windows of the soul were effectively curtained.

Lundstrom was a scrap metal collector, buying anything
made of iron, steel, tin or aluminum, then reselling it to
be melted down. Being a long-time fan of Charles Dickens, Anna'd thought the Lundstrom homestead would
somewhat resemble Dickens's garbage sifter, who lived in
a shack surrounded by mountains of refuse.

From the look of the home Lundstrom had built on the
western edge of Port Gibson, there was a whole lot more
money in scrap metal than Anna would have thought. And
a whole lot more imagination in ex–high school football
players who, if Paul's assessment was correct, never grew
up.

The house was well kept but its architect had been interested more in speed than immortality. It was the yard that
caught Anna's fancy. November, near five o'clock, the sun
had set. The short fall dusk was composed of clear light,

directionless, that leached rather than lent color. Illuminated by this shadowless glow was a wide lawn, at least
three-quarters of an acre in size and sparsely dotted with
live oaks. There were none of the great piles of junk Anna
had envisioned but the lawn décor left no doubt as to both
Lundstrom's vocation and avocation.

Fantastic sculptures stalked through the evening light.
Prehistoric-sized creatures made of pot-bellied stoves,
caterpillar blades and television antennae pursued bipeds
welded together from shovels, stove pipes, tire rims and
oddly shaped machine parts that Anna did not recognize.
Something resembling a pterodactyl, wings forged from
the black panels of a cast-off satellite dish, swooped down
over a crouching bank of azaleas holding glossy leaves
close, blooms only vaguely remembered from the previous
spring.

"Wow," Anna said.

"Yeah, what a mess," Thigpen returned. Anna'd forgotten they'd had to bring him along and didn't appreciate being reminded.

"Looks like our poker-playing friend is a man of many
talents," Clintus observed.

Leaving the sheriff's car, they threaded their way up a
concrete walk inlaid with gears, the smallest no bigger
than a quarter, the largest easily a foot across. Anna had
fallen to the rear, letting the men take the lead. Without
quite knowing how it had happened, this investigation had
been coopted by others. That or Anna was out of the practice of sharing. Whatever the cause, she felt a wrongness.
Three uniformed law-enforcement officers descending on
a citizen en masse didn't strike her as the most effective
way of getting the relaxed cooperation that was required
for eliciting accurate memories and information. Innocent
or guilty, most people clammed up, even lied, when they
were frightened.

As the men reached for the front door, hidden in prema-
ture night beneath a peaked suggestion of a gabled roof,

one of the iron shadow monsters detached itself from a clump of oak hydrangeas and rushed toward Anna.

The animal, a pit bull, ran without sound, no barking, no growling.

"Dog," Anna said with much the same urgency she would have said "gun" to warn her fellows if a suspect suddenly produced one. Had she been alone, she would have pulled her Sig-Sauer. All cats were divine till proven otherwise; all dogs were suspect until cleared. Pit bulls got the least benefit of the doubt. Perhaps their rage was nurture not nature, but she'd taken against them when reports of them attacking and killing children had hit the newsstands.

"Elsie!" came a call from the house. "You leave that nice lady alone."

Elsie stopped so abruptly her hindquarters nearly caught up with her ears. Anna moved her hand away from the pepper spray on her belt. The old stuff, mace, hadn't worked well on non-human aggressors. The spray adopted over the last ten years, made from the essence of hot chili peppers, was much the same as the spray marketed to dissuade grizzly bears. Anna had never tried it on a dog but, theoretically, it would have worked.

The dog underwent a personality transformation at the sound of her master's voice and came to Anna wriggling and wagging like a joyful shih tzu. Anna was not impressed. To bond with Lundstrom she bent down and patted the beast. As Elsie groveled under her hand, Anna realized she'd left her weapon holstered, not because a charging pit bull was insufficient provocation but because, should the dog prove non-threatening, she didn't want to appear a coward and fool in front of her field ranger and live through weeks of nasty verbal digs that would be mined from the incident.

Bad form. The kind of peer group pressure that could get a woman killed. Straightening up, she promised herself she wouldn't grant Thigpen that kind of power.

"Elsie's a pussycat," Lundstrom was saying. He'd

emerged from the darkness of the vestigial porch. During her short walk through his garden gallery, night had sucked the remaining light into its belly and Anna could see the man no more clearly than she could when he'd first appeared.

Big was the impression she got. An ex–football player, Paul said. His silhouette looked it. Six foot, maybe six-one and built square. By the way he moved, Anna guessed he'd not let himself go to fat in middle age.

"What with the Smokey Bear hat and badge, I'm figuring you for Anna Pigeon, one of them rangers on the Trace." He stuck out his hand and Anna shook it. His skin was warm and dry, palm and fingers callused from years of working with his hands. It put her in mind of the hands of the ranchers and cowboys where she'd grown up.

Lundstrom totally ignored Clintus and Randy, though he'd had to walk past them to get to her, and Anna wondered why. "Ranger Pigeon, ya'll," he turned and belatedly acknowledged the others, "Why don't you come on in."

Dutifully the three of them trailed into his house. He'd not asked why they were there. He apparently recognized Anna and showed no interest whatsoever in the sheriff or Randy. The man was behaving as if Anna were a welcome and anticipated guest who'd brought along two strangers unannounced. He was as bizarre as his front yard, Anna thought. Then the obvious came to her. Herm Thorton would have called all the poker buddies. She was, if not welcome, most certainly anticipated. Lundstrom was possibly ignoring Clintus as a slight to his race, and Thigpen he hadn't expected.

Having solved at least one tiny puzzle out of the mess of puzzles that beset this case, Anna felt better.

The inside of Badger Lundstrom's house was clean— probably due to the ministrations of a cleaning woman— but had the cold unsettled look shared by a majority of bachelor abodes Anna had had cause to enter. The nesting instinct so pronounced in women seemed absent in men, at least straight men. No brightly colored runners graced

tabletops, no flowers stood in vases. The knickknacks
leaned toward the puerile: whoopee cushions, fake vomit
and a device Anna remembered seeing advertised in the
backs of comic books when she was a kid—a buzzer that
could be strapped to the palm to shock and amaze those
one shook hands with—as well as plastic dog poop, a coffee cup with a ceramic spider affixed inside, and a foam
rock looking real, weighing nothing.

Elsie's bed was a ragged blanket folded into one corner.
As docile as the pussycat her master vowed her to be, the
dog trotted over, circled twice and flopped down with an
audible sigh.

The one delight in the room was the collection of little
sculptures. The living room resembled a nursery for the gi-
ant creatures that guarded the lawn. Lizards, birds, dragons
and other beasts born of Lundstrom's idiosyncratic
mythology perched in places of honor on the mantle and
end tables.

"Sit yourselves down," Lundstrom was saying. In the
light of three torcheres Anna recognized from the electrical
appliances aisle at the Super Wal-Mart, she began to fill in
the man from the hulking silhouette that had greeted her on
the front walk.

He was handsome and somehow Anna was surprised.
He looked both like an artist and a scrap metal dealer:
craggy, hardened from years of work in all weathers. A
boyish sense of fun was in the crow's feet at the corners of
his eyes and the permanent smile that had etched two sets
of parentheses around his mouth. Like his skin and hands
life had hardened the lines, and Anna wondered if there
wasn't a touch of malicious enjoyment when he served up
coffee in his spider mug or put his fake vomit on somebody's laptop.

"Can I get anybody coffee or maybe something a little
stiffer? Adjust our attitudes?"

Lundstrom looked as if he could use a drink. Strain
showed through the jovial host routine. Nothing big: nervous flicking of the eyes, the smile held too long. Three

officers descending on house and home might have that effect. So would jonesing for a drink if one were an alcoholic.

Clintus and Thigpen accepted coffee. Anna abstained, not willing to sip while anticipating what sort of flora or fauna might come peering up from the bottom of the mug.

Introductions made, duties done, tumbler of something on the rocks, time came to get down to business. Left with nothing to busy himself with, Lundstrom's comfort level dropped. First he sat in a soft, low armchair, the fabric spotted from dinners in front of the television. Apparently feeling at a disadvantage, he stood again and went to lean on the mantel, soothing himself with swallows of booze and strokes down the rustic back of a saber-toothed cat, its body made from an oversized spring, a lug nut for a head.

Clintus was opening his mouth to speak when Randy cut in too loud, too fast, anxious to be in charge.

"Mr. Lundstrom—" he began.

Badger's head jerked around. "Randy," he said, then, for no reason Anna could see, he laughed nervously.

"Mr. Lundstrom," Thigpen plowed on firmly. "We're just here to ask a few routine questions to find out where Doyce Barnette was before he was killed. From Mr. Thorton we know he was supposed to meet you for a poker game around six. He never showed up. Nobody phoned him, just figuring he'd got caught up in something. You fellas played till around midnight then everybody went home. That 'bout it?"

It was all Anna could do not to drop her head in her hands and groan. Thirty years in law enforcement and Randy hadn't learned a damn thing about interviewing. He'd given Badger Lundstrom his story—if, indeed, he needed one, wrapped up and tied neatly with corroborating details. Clintus was looking as appalled as she felt, and a wave of embarrassment washed over her as if she and the National Park Service were personally responsible for Ranger Thigpen's ineptitude.

"That's pretty much it." Lundstrom took the testimony

Thigpen offered on the proverbial silver platter. There was no way of knowing if he was relieved at the gift or if it was simply the truth.

Either way, it served to make him more comfortable. He left off petting his cat statue and seated himself at the hearth, elbows on knees, his drink cradled loosely in his hands.

Anna asked him a dozen or more questions about the poker night. His story matched with Herm's in every detail, matched with the handy Cliffs Notes version Thigpen had so thoughtfully recited. Clintus came at him with the same questions phrased differently and got the same answers. Thigpen, seemingly satisfied with his brilliant introduction to the evening, remained quiet. Elsie eased out from her blanket nest and crept across the carpet on belly, elbows and knees so Randy could scratch behind her ears. Now there were two good things Anna knew of Thigpen: he wasn't a racist and he had a way with animals. Every little bit helped.

Poker night sufficiently rehashed, Clintus asked the standard question: "Do you know anyone who might've had a reason, or thought he did, to kill Doyce?"

Badger thought about that for a while. Anna could tell he wanted to give them names: a common reaction. Once the heat was off, people liked to talk, liked to be seen as someone with important information. To his credit, Lundstrom didn't give in to the temptation to make something up. For the first time since they'd begun talking about the killing of Doyce Barnette, Lundstrom's poker buddy, he looked saddened by the death of his friend.

"Just nobody. I didn't know Doyce all that well. We'd only been ... playing poker together a little while but he seemed a nice guy. Harmless, if you know what I mean. Shoot, half the time you hardly knew ol' Doyce was around."

Silence followed, a moment given over in honor of the dead, then Anna asked, "How'd you come to know Herm, Thornton and Doyce? They're Natchez boys?"

Badger twitched slightly as if he'd been bitten by a horsefly instead of asked what Anna'd thought to be an innocuous question. For just a moment confusion—or fear—tightened his weathered face.

"Thorton's in surplus. Bound to come across scrap metal in that line of work," Ranger Thigpen suggested helpfully.

Clintus shot Thigpen an angry look and again Anna suffered a pang of embarrassment on her field ranger's behalf.

"I bought stuff off him now and then. We weren't real social outside of that or anything." Maybe Thigpen had been right on the money. Maybe Badger was just taking the hint and running with it. "I was down, loading up an old caterpillar tread he'd run across, and he mentioned this Friday night poker game he and some guys were putting together. Well, my dance card wasn't what you'd call full up so I joined 'em."

Apparently there were to be no great revelations. Clintus thanked Badger, hands were shaken all around. The scrap metal dealer and his dog escorted them to the door. Rather than vanishing back into the house, the man and his best friend stood on the aborted porch as the rest of them headed down the curving walk to the sheriff's car. Southern tradition and Clintus's careful good manners dictated that Anna go first. She didn't mind. Lundstrom's size and bluff good cheer were mildly oppressive, and it was a relief to be in the chill night air. The moon had yet to rise but, free from the light pollution of the cities, stars shone vividly. Summer's golden tint was gone, replaced by a hint of ice blue she remembered from winter skies farther north.

Behind her she heard a final hostly remark that detained her companions. She kept walking, thinking of Taco and Piedmont and food, none of which she had seen hide nor hair of since leaving the house ten hours earlier.

Faint squeaks, metal on metal, cut through her preoccupation. The sound was so alien to the natural rhythm of the night her internal alarms went off. Instantly hyper-alert, her feet stopped moving. Her chin came up as a dog's would when scenting the air for danger. As inappropriate as it seemed, the noise had come not from the house or road, but from overhead. Feeling wild and alive with the sudden injection of adrenaline, Anna's eyes scanned the treetops.

Ahead and to her right a starless chunk of the perfect sky detached itself from the rest, a black hole, swallowing stars. For an instant she could not make sense of it. Another squeal of metal and she realized that the half ton of scrap iron forged into sharp beak, claws and wings of an ancient beast of prey was swooping down, plummeting from thirty feet up in the branches of a live oak to rip her to pieces with talons forged from the teeth of a derelict harrow.

Hurling herself forward, Anna struck grass and concrete walk, rolled once and came up on hands and knees crawling. A nightmare sense of moving in slow motion was upon her, and as she moved she waited for the first deadly bite of Badger Lundstrom's freak.

The sound of laughter caught her up short. On all fours like a dog, she looked over her shoulder. Badger was laughing so hard he'd had to rest his hands on his knees to bear up under the load of merriment. Thigpen joined him and held his big belly with both hands in an ugly parody of St. Nick. Clintus stood apart, halfway down the walk between Anna and the men on the porch. His face was lost in silhouette but he made no sound.

"Whoo-ee, that was a good one. You done good, little lady. Most folks just lie right down and die when old Spot there come for 'em. I do believe you'd've got clean away," Badger managed on gusts of unholy glee.

Anna got to her feet. Above where she'd stood when the sky began to fall the iron bird swung gently on three chains. These tied into a rope that fed into a pulley high in the branches. Against the drop of night, Anna couldn't see it but there would be another rope running to a second pulley above the porch where Lundstrom could operate it to abuse his visitors.

"Clever," Anna called and laughed good-naturedly.

"Clintus, Randy, we better hit the road before anything else comes to life." She waved good-bye to the practical joke-ster and led the way to the car.

"Jesus fucking Christ," she hissed, effectively shocking Clintus to stillness in the midst of buckling his seat belt. From the rear seat she heard a snort from Randy that might have been amusement. He had the good sense not to laugh in such close proximity to her.

"If I've so much as got a grass stain on my Class-A uni-form trousers I'm going to bust that son of a bitch for as-sault on a federal officer, reckless endangerment and littering."

She'd gotten more than grass stains. Her shoulder ached where it had struck the sidewalk. Humiliation or instinct kept her from admitting any weakness.

9

A 1940s vintage, candy-apple red pickup truck was parked in Anna's drive when she rolled into Rocky Springs just after seven o'clock. Tired, hungry, the residual humiliation of Spot the Pterodactyl's attack clinging to her like a bad smell, she was still not sorry to see she had a visitor. At least not this visitor.

Steve Stilwell, the district ranger from Ridgeland, just north of Jackson where the Trace resumed, stepped out from the shadows as she pulled in. Seeing Steve always cheered Anna. Though nearing fifty, he retained a boyish charm that had never soured. Grizzled hair, worn too long for the brass's taste in Tupelo, fell over an unwrinkled brow, and a devilish smile glowed from his neatly cropped beard.

"Hey, Steve. You're about the only company I wouldn't shoot on sight this evening."

"Rarified air," he said in mock ecstasy. "I am living in rarified air. Pity the poor mortals who are not *me*."

Before Anna was hired, Stilwell had the onerous duty of

running not only his own district but serving as acting district ranger in the Port Gibson/Natchez District. When Anna had first arrived, she'd found a note from him and five gallons of bottled water waiting in her kitchen. Once she'd tasted the Rocky Springs water, she understood the thoughtfulness of the gift. Not only did the water emerge a brownish color but it tasted as if cottonmouths had been eating, sleeping and giving birth to their young in it shortly before it arrived at her sink.

Feeling better than she had in a while, Anna ushered him inside. While Taco made a fool of himself in a bid for the Ridgeland ranger's attentions, she made herself a grilled cheese sandwich.

Fortified by food and seduced by good company, she spilled her romantic woes. Nursing a single malt scotch liberated from the glove box of his truck, Steve listened with flattering attention. Anna stuck to tea. Fortunately whiskey had never tempted her. She'd consumed the stuff on occasion to be sociable but had never gotten past the point where it tasted like something used to remove varnish from ships' decking. And the high had never been giggly or warm like the giddiness wine brought, but merely a dullness and a lowering of the I.Q.

When she finished recapping her soap-opera role in the Davidson vs. Davidson vs. Pigeon affair, he took a pull on his scotch, savored the burn on his tongue, swallowed and said, "There's a quote attributed to Marlon Brando that comes to mind. 'With women, I've got a long bamboo pole with a leather loop on the end of it. I slip the loop around their necks so they can't get away or come too close. Like catching snakes.'"

For a second Anna was stunned. She wanted to laugh it off, be strong and cynical and worldly. With nothing but a cheese sandwich shoring up her backbone she couldn't quite pull it off. "Oh, God, what a grisly image."

Unable to suppress a groan, she laid her head back against the cushion of her grandmother's morris chair. Concerned, Taco came over. A calculated swat from Piedmont stopped him from laying a sympathetic chin on her thigh.

"You're really stuck on Paul, aren't you?" Steve asked. His voice was devoid of the underlying playfulness that was both his charm and, Anna suspected, his defense against the world. This being sufficiently rare, she was inspired to open her eyes.

"Maybe." Hearing the surprise in her own voice she repeated the word, "Maybe."

"I worked with Paul a couple times when I was ADR down here. I don't think he's the Brando type," Steve said kindly.

Anna said nothing. She was afraid if she spoke he would know how deeply the thought that Paul Davidson was toying with her affections frightened her.

"But one never knows, does one?" Steve added, the playfulness back.

This time Anna could laugh and it felt good.

Steve finished his drink. "Time to saddle up."

Having dislodged the limp and grumbling form of Piedmont from her lap to drape him over her shoulder, Anna walked Stilwell to his truck. The evening was dead still and cool. Temperatures would be in the forties by morning. Moon not yet risen, the forest surrounding her house was perfect black, ending in a star-studded lace where leafless branches etched the margins of the sky. Invisible in the night, a creature skritched through the thick blanket of leaves beneath the trees.

Steve opened the door of his antique truck, the candy-apple red blood-black without the light of the sun. He didn't get in.

"Since you've been sufficiently unwise as to choose someone other than yours truly who, I might add, has no wife to speak of, upon whom to bestow your affections, I'll see what I can do. I worked down here for seven months. Got to know a lot of the locals."

He didn't sound like he was joking. At least not completely. "What're you planning?" Anna asked warily.

"Bribe a divorce lawyer? Hire Bubba to smash her knee caps?"

"Anna, you sting me to the heart. I'll be infinitely subtle. Toodle-oo."

Anna watched him drive off, wondering what new imbroglio she'd just tumbled herself into.

Monday and Tuesday were Anna's lieu days, and she was determined to take them. Despite the public's view, murder was one of the lesser evils. An officer could afford to take days off during a murder investigation. With the exception of serial killers who, fortunately, were rare as hens' teeth, unlike raging wildfires or rising flood waters, most murderers weren't an immediate danger to citizens. The garden-variety murderer killed whomever he or she thought needed to be dead and the matter was settled. Those willing to kill to solve their problems were sometimes of such a mindset that, should a second problem arise, they might turn to the same solution, but more often than not, it was a one-time thing.

Anna went into Clinton: she did her shopping, got her hair cut, and went to the movies—an activity viewed by most as social. She'd grown so accustomed to doing it alone over the years she'd come to prefer it that way. Despite his recent invitation to call anytime, she didn't call Paul Davidson and he didn't call her. In saner moments they agreed that, until the divorce issue was settled, less contact would be best. Constraint rankled and Anna cursed Steve Stilwell for putting the image of Brando's snake-catching into her mind.

By Tuesday she'd run out of things to do and sat in the sun on the cold cement of her kitchen step drinking coffee and wondering what people with real lives did when they weren't on the job. Insistent ringing rescued her before she'd had time to convert restlessness into self-pity.

"Rocky Springs," she answered. Anna's being on the phone was, for some critter-born reason, a signal for Taco and Piedmont to vie for her attention. Both arrived on schedule to butt, paw and vocalize their demands.

"What the heck is going on?" came an equally demanding voice snaking through the ether of the telephone lines.

Caught off guard, Anna shoved Taco away without the customary pat of apology. "May I ask who's calling?" she asked politely.

Fighting fire with fire was a technique almost guaranteed to fail in verbal confrontations. A lot of years of trial and error had trained Anna to grow calmer in direct inverse proportion to her adversary's excitement.

"This is Raymond Barnette, Doyce's brother," the voice came back a degree or two less hostile.

"What's the problem?"

"You read the papers this morning?"

Anna hadn't. Nobody wanted to deliver a daily to Rocky Springs. Not only was it too isolated to make it cost-effective, but commercial vehicles weren't allowed on the parkway: no semi-trucks or trailers, no Papa John's Pizza delivery, no newspaper boys.

"It's in all of them," Raymond went on, the hostility back full bore. "The Natchez paper, *The Clarion-Ledger* in Jackson. It's all over the front pages. Do you know what this could do to me in the election? I've got a mind to sue."

A lawsuit; one of the few things in life that could strike terror into Anna's heart while not actually threatening her person with sharp objects. "What's on the front pages?"

"Listen to this," he said and began to read. " 'The investigation of Doyce Barnette, found dead last Saturday morning in the old stand at Mt. Locust on the Natchez Trace Parkway nine miles north of the city of Natchez, has turned up new evidence. A source closely involved with the murder investigation, who asked not to be named, informed *The Clarion-Ledger* reporter Fowlard Yost that the body of the deceased was found in a condition indicating he was killed in the commission of a ritual sexual act. Though unable to release details of the finding due to the ongoing investigation, the Ledger's source went on to say Doyce Barnette appeared to have been involved in acts of bondage or possibly sadomasochism. A religious message, the contents of which were held back, again to protect the investigation, was left near the body. Our source declined to say what the official consensus was regarding the text and said only that it was Christian. Clintus Jones, the county sheriff heading up the investigation, declined comment, saying only that the investigation was continuing. District Ranger Anna Pigeon of the Natchez Trace could not be reached for comment.' "

Anna was at a loss for words. Knowing Barnette not only expected but deserved a response, she scrambled around and came up with one. "This information wasn't released by the National Park Service or the sheriff's department. A number of people saw Doyce's body. One of them could have called in the information, or it might even be someone they told."

"Who saw the body?" Raymond asked.

"I'll look into it," Anna promised.

"Who saw? I got a right to their names."

Barnette, faced with his brother's death, a shotgun-toting mother and, when found interrogating Herm Thorton, two annoyed officers of the law, had remained civil, moderately urbane and, in an indefinable way, cold. Faced with a situation that directly threatened his plans, Anna was seeing a new side of him. He was still cold, but rather than the chill of empty tombs Anna'd sensed before, he'd taken on an edge, a determination. Not for the first time she wondered if he'd killed his brother. Cain and Abel. It fit in with the quasi-religious theme suggested by the circling of the verses on Grandma Polly's writing desk.

Maybe he'd left Doyce in a public place to spread suspicion around and took his clothes to destroy trace evidence, never realizing it would look like a sex crime.

"I'll look into it and get back to you," Anna said.

"You're liable to find yourself in the middle of a lawsuit if you don't get this mess straightened out and quick," Barnette said.

"I'll call you when I know anything." The lawsuit threat was empty. The information leaked to the papers was information she and Clintus had decided to keep confidential, but all of it was true.

Anna decided to conduct her inquiries in civilian clothes partly because they were more comfortable and partly so she could pretend to herself she was giving up a chunk of her "Sunday" under duress. To corroborate her unofficial standing, she took Taco with her when she drove south.

The task carried with it absolutely no urgency and, on Anna's part at least, very little irritation. She and Clintus had kept the secret of how Doyce's body was found not so much to aid in the investigation but to protect the feelings of Doyce's family. Now that Anna had met Raymond and Mama Barnette she didn't much care whether their feelings were hurt or not.

Seeking the source of the leak was merely something to do. If it should turn out to be a malicious or self-serving act on the part of an employee in her district or local law enforcement, it would give her a heads-up on who to avoid. Proving who did it would be difficult and a waste of energy.

Even if the action was proven, the illegality of it would remain in question. Heads wouldn't roll. Hell wouldn't be paid. The juice wouldn't be worth the squeeze.

The coroner, Gil Franklin, was a possibility. He'd seen the body, then taken it upon himself to call Ray Barnette. Shelly Rabine, the little interpreter at Mt. Locust, had discovered the body. That lent her a cachet the newspapers would love. There was Clintus Jones of course. He was the only one Anna could think of off the top of her head that would get anything other than attention out of the disclosure. As Barnette said, linking his family to a sex crime wasn't going to bring in the Christian voters come election day. But since it was Clintus who suggested keeping the details under wraps in the first place, Anna crossed him off her list. André Gates, Clintus's pretty, haughty undersheriff, might have done it. Anna doubted he'd remain in his position long if Barnette was elected. If Raymond didn't oust him, he'd probably quit. André didn't strike her as the type to have patience with an arrogant and inept white boss-man. Randy Thigpen and Barth Dinkins knew the details. There was nothing in the telling for them but momentary attention and a sense of self-importance. Unfortunately that was enough to tempt some people over the line. But her field rangers were the only two who would suffer consequences if caught. The United States might fiercely protect the right of free speech, but her government agencies had all manner of rules against its exercise by their employees.

Anna doubted Barth would do it. He was honorable and preoccupied, his energies taken up by the desecration of the slave cemetery. She hoped Randy hadn't done it. He'd already proved an embarrassment. On the bright side, if he had, maybe she could get his fat ass fired. Anna smiled at the thought.

Thigpen and his weighty derrier would not be on duty till four. Anna decided to start with Shelly Rabine. Not only did she intimidate the little interpreter, she rather liked her—two factors that would ease the questioning process. Besides that, at Mt. Locust, Taco could get in a good run if he were so inclined. The poor dog had been sorely neglected since the murder of Doyce Barnette had begun usurping most of Anna's time.

Only one car was parked in the lot in front of the visitors center, a '91 burgundy Honda Accord that belonged to Rabine. Anna pulled her Rambler American in beside it and sat for a moment enjoying the phenomenal stillness. If she skewed her reality just a few degrees, it was easy to believe the world had come to a full stop; that, like the first entrant into the thorn-shrouded castle of Sleeping Beauty, she was the only living thing not frozen in thrall.

Not the only living thing. Taco was bounding and slavering to be set free. Hauled back to the mundane, Anna leaned across to open the passenger door. The three-legged Lab leapt out with a speed and agility many four-legged dogs would have envied.

Shelly had evidently seen the Rambler through the visitors center window. She came out and waited for them on the concrete apron in front of the little building. Taco, who had never laid eyes on Shelly before, rushed over to greet her like a long-lost sister. The dog must have weighed nearly as much as the child-sized park aide, but Shelly was unthreatened and allowed him to express his saliva-laden devotion much longer than Anna would have.

Watching Taco's ecstatic tongue lap at Shelly's thin cheeks, Anna felt a mild stab of guilt. Where dogs were concerned, she was never going to get the Owner of the Year Award.

"Hey, Anna," Shelly called in her wispy voice. "Anything new? It's been dead around here since Saturday."

If the pun had been intended, the young woman gave no sign of it but chattered on happily. "Not one single visitor yet this morning. The big excitement here was old Mack fussing about poltergeists moving his stuff."

Mack, Anna remembered, was the oldest and most senior of the maintenance men in her district, maybe on the Trace. He was secretive about his age but he had to be near eighty. He'd been forcibly retired from driving the tractors used to mow the edges of the parkway when his sight began to make him a danger to automobile traffic. That had been a decade or more before Anna's arrival. Since then, he'd putzed, pottered and gardened the Mt. Locust site with the possessive fussiness of the little-old-lady cliché.

"Find any more bodies or anything neat?" Shelly asked with innocent ghoulishness.

"No more bodies," Anna said. "Want to close up shop for a few minutes and walk with me? Taco needs some space."

Shelly was only too glad to abandon the tedium of her post. She locked up the VC, and because it was the way traffic naturally flowed, they wandered up the path toward the stand. Taco bounded ahead, apparently bent on showing that the district ranger's dog was gloriously and illegally off leash.

For the first time in weeks, the succession of clear blue and gold autumn days was broken. The sky was overcast, hinting at the possibility of much-needed rain. A fog so thin it was second cousin to mist fell like a scrim over the meadow, giving trees and fences the vague outlines of things dreamed and poorly recalled on waking.

"You just busman's holidaying or what?" Shelly asked. The mist and the stillness didn't seem to oppress her one bit, just as seeing a dead body hadn't had any dampening effect on her spirits that Anna had noticed.

"Well, kind of," Anna replied. "I was wondering, you being here every day all day, if you'd maybe noticed something—any little thing—that we might have overlooked." The best way to get people to talk was to get people to talk. Words, like water, flowed better en masse.

Flattered and delighted with the question, Shelly wrinkled her smooth brow in concentration. Watching her, Anna flashed back to when she was in her twenties, when she and Zach had lived in New York City, he struggling to find work as a director and she dabbling in the world of acting. Cast in a role older than herself, she'd sat in front of a poorly lit mirror, the silver backing peeling off at the edges, in a dressing room of a ramshackle, roach-infested theater near the Port Authority Bus Terminal. With like concentration she'd screwed her face into wrinkles and painstakingly painted lines where the flesh folded. Now the lines were always there, a roadmap to her past.

Shelly's best effort failed, and to her credit, she didn't invent anything to cover the fact. Not the action of someone starved for attention. Anna pursued her inquiry anyway.

"The way you found the body—you know, in his under-pants and all—was weird. Did anybody you told about it have a theory we might not have thought of?"

"I thought we were supposed to keep all that a secret," Shelly said. The affront in her voice was too genuine to be feigned, colored not with anger at being accused but disappointment that she'd been righteously withholding a terrific story that was hers by right while others were dining out on it.

Shelly wasn't the one who'd leaked the information to the newspapers. Anna decided to let the matter rest. "We were," she said. "But somebody screwed up. The details were in the morning's paper."

"I didn't tell them," Rabine said indignantly.

"I know," Anna said.

"I didn't."

"I believe you."

Shelly opened her mouth to protest her innocence again but chose to accept Anna at her word and said nothing. They reached the fork in the path below the inn. The wider trail led toward the bricked steps to the porch. Following Taco, they took the road less traveled and walked around the back to Eric Chamberlain's kitchen garden.

"Do you have any idea who might have told?" Anna asked.

"Shoot, no," Shelly said. "I don't even know those guys—the sheriff and that fat, tiny-footed guy."

"The coroner, Gil Franklin?"

"I guess. The only one besides you was Randy. And I only know him to say 'hi' to. It's not like law enforcement spends any time hanging around talking to lowly park aides."

The bitterness in her voice was not new to Anna. In most parks she'd worked there'd been friction, sometimes a little, sometimes a lot, between the various disciplines. Of late it had been exacerbated. Once they were all known as park rangers. For reasons that escaped Anna, the NPS had decided to remove interpreters, naturalists and historians who brought the park to life for the visitors, from that proud and time-honored group, forcing them to be referred to as park aides. If they wished, at some point, by jumping through administrative hoops, they could regain the title of park ranger.

The bureaucratic logic of pay scales, promotional series

and career development paths had been explained when the change took place, but the sense of disenfranchisement remained. Little boys and girls didn't dream of growing up to be aides. They dreamed of growing up to be rangers.

"Anyway," Shelly said, regaining the cheer that seemed her natural state. "Mississippi's like hometown central for stories. A good story'll spread like kudzu. Friday it's this deep dark secret and by Sunday morning half the preachers in the state are preaching a sermon about it. Down here we don't have to tell stories, we just sort of breathe them in and everybody everywhere knows."

Anna laughed. She couldn't argue with that. Southern secrets were kept from outsiders, but everybody else knew things by osmosis.

Taco was digging madly at the end of a row of corn plants, the leaves brown and papery. Anna shouted at him. He looked up, his tongue lolling out between muddy jaws. He then obediently left off what he was doing to come rub dirt and dog spit on her Levi's.

The interview was pretty much at an end. Chilly and gray, the day didn't tempt Anna to dawdle. Pushing away Taco's demonstrations of abiding love, she started to turn back.

"Barth's sure been working his tail off in the old slave cemetery," Shelly said quickly. "Wanna go and see?" Anna looked at the young woman. Her slightly protuberant eyes were further exaggerated by the wide hopeful stare. Rabine looked all of twelve years old and just as transparent. She didn't want to go back to standing behind the counter in a cramped visitors center waiting for visitors that never showed.

"You're as bad as Taco," Anna muttered.

Shelly said, "What?" and Anna was glad the park aide hadn't heard her impossibly grown-up condescension.

"Let's take a look," she said. Taco bounded off as if English was his second language and he understood every word. Seeing the childlike look of delight on Shelly's face,

Anna wouldn't have been surprised if she'd bounded off after him.

"Maybe I should go into law enforcement," Shelly said as she walked across the broken field between the garden and the edge of the woods, following the dog and leading Anna. "You guys get to do all the fun stuff, and you don't have to work. I mean *work* work," she added, glancing back over her shoulder to see if Anna had taken offense.

She hadn't. She knew what Shelly meant. It was one of the things she loved about being a law-enforcement ranger; the freedom to move, car to horse to hiking trail, not being tied to a minute-by-minute schedule or weighed down by a desk or a tour group that could not be deserted. And, the greatest freedom of all, freedom from supervision. By the nature of the work, field rangers made most of their own decisions.

Anna'd always felt a mild guilt about the disparity in pay and promotional opportunities between park inter- preters and park law enforcement, especially the seasonals. Interpreters were the backbone of the park service, yet by some twist in the power structure, they'd ended up near the bottom of the bureaucratic ladder.

"Hey. Barth cleaned it up good," Shelly said as she reached the edge of the cemetery. All that remained of the sign were the two upright four-by-fours. The broken and defiled boards were gone. "You know he had to do it all by himself. Mack's like a zillion years old, kind of entered the feather-duster stage of janitoring. Barth told Mack, though, and Mack told me what the vandals did. You know the . . . mess . . . they left. Major mondo caca."

"Well put," Anna said with a smile.

They stopped by the skeletal sign and stared into the trees. Fog robbed the trees of what scraps of autumn bril- liance they still clung to. Spanish moss, a favorite Yankee image of the South, hung gray and apparently lifeless from the branches of cedars more black than green. "Cemetery" or even "graveyard" didn't quite fit the picture. Unmarked, scattered, trees and shrubs choking the burial grounds, it put Anna in mind of that horrific crime scene where the evening news showed grim policemen carrying out body after body, excavated from shallow graves in serial killer John Wayne Gacy's backyard. Irrational fear grabbed her by the scruff of the neck and shook her. Feeling hunted, haunted, female, and frail, she stifled the urge to look over her shoulder, move closer to the slight figure of Shelly Rabine.

With an effort she shrugged off the image and the sudden hatred of slave owners it brought with it. Time had stolen the humanity of owner and slave alike. Before the Civil War, when the cemetery was in use, it wouldn't have looked anything like this forlorn scrap of land. Trees would have been cleared, wooden markers erected, probably flowers planted by loving hands. Without money for stones of granite and fences of wrought iron, the love of the living and the names of the dead had been reclaimed by the land.

Under strict mental discipline John Wayne Gacy's grisly garden receded from Anna's mind and with it the growing sense of creepiness.

Undaunted by human megrims, Taco loped gleefully into the mist. Because he was alive and happy and his glossy golden coat shone with color, Anna watched him. Half of him disappeared behind the dark gleaming leaves of an oak hydrangea. Supported by his one remaining hind leg, his feathery tail wagged in ecstasy and the dirt began to fly as he dug madly. Soft yellow-brown dirt of broken ground. In this sacred and yet profane place the land was settled, covered in duff, undisturbed for countless years.

"Taco's got something," Anna said, and remembering the last search the dog had accompanied her on when he'd led her to the corpse of a teenage girl, she moved into the dripping woods to investigate. Infected by Anna's unease or the soul-sucking silence of the place, Shelly followed without her usual running commentary.

"What the hell . . ." Anna took hold of the dog's collar. Taco had been burrowing in what looked to be a new grave.

Earth had been removed—clods of Mississippi's hard clay littered the duff near the grave—then replaced. An attempt had been made to restore the ground to the existing pattern of the forest floor, leaves and needles raked back to cover the gout of turned soil. The camouflage might have worked had time and rain been able to do their work before the dog did. As it was, scars of a recent disturbance showed.

"Give me a hand." Anna began clawing the leaf and needle litter from around Taco's dig.

"Oh, gross." Shelly didn't move from her place half a body length from the site. "You don't think . . ."

"We'll think later," Anna said curtly. "All we're doing now is looking."

Distaste overcome by courage or curiosity, Shelly dropped to her knees on the damp leaves and helped scrape away the duff.

"Go easy," Anna said when, caught up in the moment, the young woman began to exhibit the uninhibited fervor of the dog, flinging bits of woodland flotsam out behind her. "Could find something useful in this mess," she explained.

Shelly stopped all activity suddenly and sat back, her skinny little butt perched delicately on her pointy little heels. "Oh. Wow. Like a finger or an eyeball or something?"

Anna laughed at the wondrous hope in Shelly's voice. "I was thinking more along the lines of a dropped wallet with a driver's license in it."

"That'd be good, too." Shelly went back to work removing pine needles with the exaggerated care of an archaeologist.

Within minutes they had enough area cleared to see what had been done. In a tidy rectangle, corners shovel-sharp and precise, a piece of ground six-foot long and three-feet wide had been dug out and replaced. As neat a grave as Forest Lawn could hope for.

Hands dirty, both breathing hard as if they'd done a great deal more physical work than they had, the women stepped away. Anna seemed beset by media pictures this morning and for an instant she imagined muddy clawlike hands thrusting up out of the newly dug earth.

"Barth, maybe? Working on his project?" Shelly suggested.

"I don't think so."

"Do we get shovels?"

"Shovels and strong backs to wield them," Anna said. No use being a manager if one couldn't delegate at least a few of the more odious tasks.

10

Using the telephone in the visitors center so her conversation wouldn't be broadcast to all and sundry, Anna called the Port Gibson Ranger Station. Barth Dinkins answered. Barth had proved himself a good ranger with excellent instincts but preferred more scholarly—and sedentary—pursuits. Usually he could be counted upon to be sitting behind his desk.

Barth knew nothing about the new dig they'd discovered except that it hadn't been there Sunday, two days previously. Barth worked Sunday as did Anna and Randy. On Sundays law-enforcement rangers in all of America's National Parks got holiday pay. Everybody wanted that little boost to the paycheck. Sundays were a bad time to commit a crime on park land.

Agitated by news of further trespass on the grave sites, Barth wanted to rush to Mt. Locust. Anna managed to keep him on the phone long enough to give him a list of things she needed him to bring down.

Three other calls had to be made: one to Chief Ranger

Brown and, though Anna's lesser self argued against it, one to Randy Thigpen. If this disturbance related in any way to the death of Doyce Barnette, she owed it to Randy's new-leaf promise to include him. Brown wasn't in. She left a message with the deputy chief. Thigpen unfortunately was in and would join them as soon as he'd dressed. Her last call was to Clintus. The sheriff and his under-sheriff, André Gates, would join them.

Finally there was nothing left to do but wait. Anna and Taco returned to the slave cemetery. Shelly, against her will, was left behind in the empty VC, pouting.

Anna used the time before the heavy-footed troops arrived to make a delicate and minute search of the area around the newly dug grave. The chill damp of the fog worked its way through her clothes; the dead silence worked its way through her mind, until she felt as if she had inadvertently crossed the River Styx with her faithful hound and dwelt in the realms of the dead. On those rare occasions when she tried to picture life after death, it was never the sunny shores on the far side of the Jordan portrayed in Gospel music but a place very like this: cold, damp, gray, silent, eternal.

Oddly enough, an excellent place to look for clues. There were no distractions and the diffuse, netherworldly light illuminated without creating shadows.

A shuffle of shod feet across the duff alerted her to another refugee from the land of the living: Mack, the ancient maintenance man, bringing the light leaf rake she'd requested before leaving the VC. Anna glanced at the feet that announced his arrival. Shod wasn't quite the right word. The old man was wearing bedroom slippers. They were leather, roughly the right color—somewhere near cordovan—and had soles, but bedroom slippers all the same. She said nothing. Feet that had been in service as long as Mack's deserved a break from the rules.

Mack must have lied when he told Shelly he was pushing eighty. He was a hundred if he was a day. Maybe African-Americans really didn't visibly age the same way their Caucasian counterparts did. Youthful looks clung to them much longer. When true old age was reached, they slipped effortlessly into the sere, elemental look of antiquity. Mack had shrunk and dried up till he looked to be made of petrified mahogany.

He handed Anna the rake. "I'm going to want to put this back. You folks don't put things back like you ought to." Mission accomplished, he didn't leave. Anna suspected he'd wait as long as need be to retrieve his rake and carry it back to its proper resting place.

Mack didn't squat or sit or lean but stood with his bones piled carefully one on top of the other. Anna suspected he remained upright to defy the grave waiting at his feet. He was old enough to be on a first-name basis with Death. As he stood he talked.

"There's places like this all around these parts," he told Anna, his voice as papery and thin as the sound of the leaves underfoot. "They was marked one time but that's gone. Rotted down. Or kids kicking 'em down. Negro graveyards not even s'posed to have ghosts. Like that place in the yard where you bury old dogs. Not all, of course. Lots of family plots got slaves in 'em. Now of course we got churches, and they write down where you're at, and it gets put in the family Bible. Back then nobody owned the good book and couldn't't've written in it or read it if they did. So in the ground you went and ten years later it's like you never was."

"Now Barth, he's a good bloke—"

Anna, half listening, lulled by the whispering breeze of words, looked up sharply wondering how the English slang word "bloke" had found its way into Mack's vocabulary. Another layered Mississippi mystery she would never solve.

"Barth's going to bring these people home," Mack went on. Like so much of humanity, Mack believed in the power of names. To name a thing was to own, control and understand it. Could Barth name the dead, they'd exist again, returned to their rightful places in the universe.

Mentally she drew a line out from the southeast corner of the rectangle of disturbed earth, continuing the process of quartering an imaginary circle around the site. That done, she began her inspection. In the first quarter she found much stomping and signs of movement where the digger stood to work but nothing to illuminate who he was or what work he was doing.

"Barth was saying lots of folks what had no kind of church got recorded maybe by the cabinet maker as built the coffin," Mack said.

Three more quarters of the imaginary circle revealed no secrets. Anna finally put Mack's rake to use, neatly piling up the leaf and needle litter she, Shelly and Taco had removed from the grave itself. Later she would comb through it. That done, she began peeling back the forest's skirts around the grave. The cushion of litter had protected the earth, and she found no useable tracks. One mark was of interest, a forty-five degree angle cut into earth, softened and disturbed by the shovel, that indicated where the digger or diggers had set a box. There was just the one and it was faint. The impression hadn't been made by a box heavy enough to have contained any respectable corpse.

Voices cut through the silence that had reknit around her when Mack stopped talking. Shelly was bringing Sheriff Jones, André Gates, Randy and Barth to the site. The little interpreter had inadvertently added Guide to the Realms of the Dead to her job description this week. From her bright eyes and pink cheeks, Anna knew she loved the excitement. Law enforcement might be right for Shelly. Anna made a mental note to talk with her further about it.

The men carried shovels, which Mack eyed with proprietary disapproval.

Anna was glad three of the four men were black. She didn't give two hoots about what happened to her bones when they were no longer securely encased in a working skin but knew from long experience with the Navajo that people got exceedingly testy when the graves of their ancestors were defiled.

Barth pushed his way through the others, effectively barring their way, and looked down at the peeled earth with its rectangle of newly dug soil in the center. His eerie gray-green eyes glowed with a light alien to the shadowless woods. "I hadn't got this far out," he said accusingly. "I don't know where any of the graves are past that line." He nodded to a scrap of orange surveyor's tape tied around a young pine tree. A corresponding scrap was tied thirty feet away, the line between them falling three or four yards closer to the burial ground's entrance.

"By the look of this one, it isn't one of yours," Anna said soothingly.

Anger pinched Barth's well-shaped lips down at the corners. "Probably somebody chose here to bury a pig or a dog or garbage," he said. Though he tried to mask it with the hard edges of anger, Anna heard the hurt behind the words, the exhaustion at a lifetime of slights he hadn't earned. She turned away, ashamed to see the shame he carried for the sins others committed.

The men dug. Anna let them. Her days of insisting on backbreaking labor merely to prove a point were past. André Gates had removed his uniform shirt, as neatly pressed as the sheriff's, and hung it carefully on a branch. Anna noticed it had been tailored to fit close to the body. Then she took note of the body and dismissed the vanity. A man with a build like André Gates had a civic duty to share it with the world. After a few shovelfuls, face red, breathing heavily, Randy stopped, stepped back and lit a cigarette. Periodically, he gave the other three meaningless instruction to indicate he was not lazy but purely managerial.

The dig was short-lived. Three men, soft earth, they completed the excavation in a quarter of an hour and found nothing. The hole wasn't as deep as a proper grave, only two or three feet. The bottom was damp but hard-packed, the earth below obviously undisturbed for decades. When the last of the dirt was raked out and thrown on the pile, the five of them and Mack stood around staring into the pit for a few moments. Taco paced behind them, eyeing the soft dirt and emitting faint groans of canine frustration that he couldn't dig in it.

"I'll need those shovels cleaned and put back where you got 'em from," Mack said querulously.

No one else said anything. Anna broke the silence after a bit. "I guess we're done here," she said for lack of anything intelligent to add.

"Why dig yourself up such a spiffy hole and then not put anything in it?" Randy asked. He stubbed out his cigarette, then virtuously put the stinking butt in his shirt pocket.

"Must have taken something out," Clintus stated the obvious. As one they all looked at Barth, the accepted expert on the burial ground.

"I don't know who was buried here," he said. "I don't even know for sure this was a grave site. They might have been looking for something else."

Various possibilities were bandied about. When Union soldiers came, confederate families would sometimes bury silver, jewelry, things of value they didn't want pillaged. But Mt. Locust was never a silver and jewels kind of place. It was an inn for travelers. Food was served off wooden trenchers, then, when things were prosperous, cheap crockery. The "silver" would have been pewter at best.

"Maybe the slaves stole something. Hid it out here where the white folks wouldn't be poking around," Mack offered. Anna could tell he liked the idea and she said nothing to disabuse him of it, but stolen treasure would have been of no use to a people who couldn't fence it, a people who could be put to death or beaten for spilling the wine while serving at table, much less pilfering from the master.

"It's a grave," Barth said stolidly. "They been dug the same forever. Six by two-and-a-half feet. Around these parts they weren't all six feet deep. Water table is too high. Somebody dug a grave here. More likely dug up an old grave and took whoever was buried here."

"What was left anyway," Clintus added. André moved from the circle and pulled his shirt on, hiding his sculpted back and shoulders under the tailored polyester.

"Whoever smashed up the sign," Barth said. "Just dese-crating the grave."

Anna didn't think so. The earlier vandalism had shown violence, rage, disorganization. The defecating on the final mess smacked of psychosis. Had the same perpetrator dug up the grave, the remains would have been thrown around, skull smashed, finger bones snapped.

"Barth and I'll stay and sift needles and dirt, see if we missed anything. I guess you guys got dirty for nothing. Thanks for coming out," Anna said, breaking up the party.

As they stirred, she remembered her original mission. Since she had the primary players together in one place she said, "The local papers got hold of the details of how we found Doyce Barnette's body. Raymond is up in arms about it. Anybody know how it got leaked?" Nobody did. Or nobody admitted it. Anna considered the subject closed. She wasn't going any extra miles on Barnette's behalf.

Taco was banished. Clintus took him back to the VC to sulk with Shelly. Anna and Barth spent the next two hours sitting on the damp earth, the fog soaking into their clothes and their spirits, clawing through lumps of hard clay and pine needles. Their combined efforts produced a pile of what appeared to be rotted wood and three bones. The bones were tiny and old. No flesh remained on them, and they were so brittle with age they looked more like sticks than pieces of human skeleton. From the size and general shape, Anna guessed they were either from a foot or a hand.

When they finished, they set their finds aside and began shoveling dirt back into the hole.

"Somebody dug up a grave," Barth said. Despite the cold, his shirt was dark with sweat. Beads of moisture from the fog glistened in his close-cropped hair. His pale green-ish eyes shone with exertion or passion. "They dug it up and stole the body, coffin and all. It being so old, it must of fallen apart. These pieces we got were left behind."

"Looks that way." After crouching so long absorbed in the minutia of dirt clods and needle clumps, Anna was enjoying the sheer physicality of lifting and moving shovel-fuls of dirt.

"They just must've dumped the remains in a garbage bag all higgledy-piggledy and hauled them off," Barth went on. Sadness and outrage embittered the words. "Why would anybody want to do that?"

That's what Anna was wondering. The odds of anything valuable being buried with the body of a slave were negli-gible. On the million-to-one chance that had been the case and a historical treasurer hunter had discovered it, there would have been no need to take the body and what was left of the coffin as well. A vague possibility presented itself.

"Maybe the descendents of whoever was buried here wanted to reinter the remains in a churchyard or family gravesite and figured the park service wouldn't let them," Anna suggested. Like most other government agencies, the park service had been taught the importance of ancestor re-mains by the more outspoken Native American groups. If a person could even kind of sort of prove the remains were theirs, the parks would not only have turned them over but paid for removal out of the public coffers—but most people didn't know that.

Barth mulled over that thought for a while. He was a thorough man. Multitasking was a concept he would never embrace. The better to concentrate, he stopped working and leaned on his shovel. Anna kept on, enjoying the heat exertion generated, enjoying the mindless repetition and the pull on her muscles. Soil and duff fell in soft rhythmic thuds as the hole slowly filled.

Finally Barth shook his head and resumed shoveling. "Doesn't feel right," he said succinctly.

It didn't. Folks sufficiently concerned about ancestors, final resting places and being right in the eyes of their god tended to do things in the open. If it were politically moti-vated, as Anna suspected a number of such claims were, then it would have been done in loud voices on the steps of the capitol after the local television stations had been alerted.

"Some kind of creepy cult thing where they needed the bones of a black man?" Barth suggested. Anna looked up at him and thought she saw a flash of superstitious fear twist his face. Christianity, in its fundamental state, brought not only the Heavenly Host into the homes of its adherents but a counterbalancing army of The Fallen. The devil was part of a package deal. Barth didn't seem to be of that school of thought, but given a childhood in the 1950s in Mississippi, he very well could have been raised in a home that was.

Thinking of her field ranger's personal history, it occurred to Anna that he had grown up in the era of segregation. As a child he would have been denied white schools, drinking fountains, bathrooms. Certain stores, bars and restaurants would have had "Whites Only" signs in the window. Growing up in the West, these things were ancient history to Anna, the Civil Rights movement a vaguely remembered event that took place in black and white on a thirteen-inch TV screen. For Barth it was the warp and weave of his childhood. He would have been in high school when Rosa Parks refused to move to the back of the bus, when *Life* magazine's cover featured the picture of a little girl walking with such courage and dignity through a phalanx of National Guardsmen to be the first black child in an all-white school. When Mississippi was burning.

Anna had known these things in a bloodless history-quiz sort of way but had never given it much thought. Trying not to get caught doing it, she watched him as he scraped up the last heap of dirt, then began packing the excavation down with the flat of the shovel. From now on a part of her would look at him differently. The way one looked at World War II veterans, concentration camp survivors, astronauts and Peace Corp volunteers; those who lived through experiences that most people merely watched on television or read about in books.

Anna preferred to leave the psychoanalyzing to her sister, but the thoughts did help her understand Barth's odd

mixture of pride and anger, fear and shame. And his determination to make things right.

He finished smoothing the now-empty grave, looked up
and caught her watching him.

Erasing the probably offensive compassion from her
face, Anna said, "I doubt the remains were taken for any
dark reasons. At least not of the racial or metaphysical variety. My guess is the bones were taken so we wouldn't
find them. Because the bones would tell us something
somebody doesn't want us to know."

"Like there was another body in the grave, one not so
steeped in history?"

Anna hadn't thought of that.

11

Seven o'clock: Anna had been up for two hours and had her uniform on for half that. Sleep had been so filled with dreams of dead bodies and empty graves it contained little in the way of rest, and she was anxious to get back to work. Interviewing people about possible sex crimes and sorting moldy bones might not be the most captivating of pastimes but at least it was something to do.

Seven o'clock in Mississippi, eight o'clock in New York. It was late enough to legally call her sister, Molly. Her Park Avenue practice didn't open till ten but she was an early riser. Frederick Stanton, Anna's erstwhile lover, now Molly's husband, answered on the second ring.

In the thirteen months he'd been married to Molly, Frederick had been well trained in the Pigeon sisters' unique phone etiquette. After the briefest of in-law chitchat, he handed the phone over to Molly.

Connected to the world by the sound of her sister's voice, Anna unloaded the feelings she'd kept pent up in a skull that was coming to feel too small to house them. She didn't talk of the professional dramas that beset her: murder, vandalism, Thigpen's new leaf. That was business as usual, things she could discuss with Clintus, Barth or, in a pinch, even Randy Thigpen. Girl talk was what she needed. She told the story Molly'd heard a dozen times before: of Paul and the Mrs., frustrations, gossip, conflicted feelings. When she'd finished, there was silence, true silence, and Anna was grateful for it. Over the thirty years they'd been paying AT&T blood money for the privilege of staying close, most of the gaps in their conversations had been punctuated by the hush of cigarette smoke entering and exiting her sister's precious lungs. No more. Thigpen wasn't the only human being capable of change.

Because geography dictated that Anna and Molly's relationship be conducted primarily over the phone lines, Anna had learned to read her sister's silences the way others read body language. This one held a hint of exasperation and, even more alarming, a strong undercurrent of sympathy.

"Married is married," Molly said finally. "Statistically your chances of happiness are not good."

"Lies, damn lies, and statistics," Anna voiced a half-remembered quote from somewhere.

Molly laughed. A wonderful sound. The years of scotch whiskey and unfiltered Camels had given her voice a gravel quality that warmed the listener's soul like the embers of a dying fire. Molly was a top-notch psychiatrist, but Anna had always suspected it was her voice that prompted her patients to fork over the big bucks for a fifty-minute hour.

"He's getting a divorce," Anna said, hating herself for sounding hopeful, hating having to defend Paul Davidson.

"When?"

Anna said nothing.

Another silence ensued. Anna could feel sympathy and love leaking through the black distance and it made her squirm. Taco, sensing discomfort, came over to where she sat on the hall floor tethered to the wall by the phone cord and stuck his tongue in her free ear to comfort her.

"I understand that he's got a lot to lose," Molly said finally. "Respect as a man of God and votes as a man of the people. But the key word here is 'man.' As a man—at least one that you'd want—he's got to stand up for what he needs and take whatever hit is coming. If that need is you, that's what he'll do. If the need for community acceptance is greater, then he'll keep sneaking around in a guilty relationship.

"It's your call. Either you'll accept that or you'll move on."

Molly was right. Anna knew it; had known it before she'd called. She was behaving like a crazy person, doing the same thing over and over and expecting a different outcome each time. The only flaw in her sister's logic was the "moving on." Moving on to what? Anna had spent nearly a decade grieving for Zach, living in the widow's fantasy that death claimed a perfect love when, in reality, it merely intervened at a perfect moment in a humanly imperfect world.

It was a lonely fantasy but tremendously comforting. It excused Anna from taking part in the rigors of the mating dance and the emotional dangers inherent in opening up to another person. When she'd awakened from this dream, she'd found herself well into middle age. The landscape was no longer peopled by single men anxious, willing and able to enter into relationships. The men she met were as scarred as she, as weighted down with baggage. Paul was the first she had felt a true yearning to be with. Anna sensed she would not move on but go back to the aloneness she'd cultivated so assiduously.

"Do you think Paul's your last chance?" Molly said, reading her mind with annoying accuracy.

"No," Anna lied.

"He's not. This isn't the end of your rope. This isn't the time to tie a knot and hang on."

Again Molly was right, but Anna had no intention of admitting it. She changed the subject to mental illness—mental illness other than her own current delusion and denial.

Molly wasn't much help. Not because she hadn't thought and studied, but because the finite information did not exist. Unlike serial killers, there was no standard white-male-between-thirty-and-forty-five profile for those who deviated from the norm. In the sexual arena most things that could happen did, and fairly regularly. Old, fat redneck Mississippi boys were as likely to harbor a secret desire to wear silky ladies' underthings or to play with whips and chains as their more urbane Yankee brothers.

Since talk had turned to murder, Frederick was invited into the conversation. In his years with the FBI's Chicago office he'd run across his share of sex crimes. Like Anna, he thought good ol' Doyce's situation didn't quite fit the bill for cold-blooded murder.

The more likely scenario was sex games gone bad, the body moved to confuse the issue and save the other partic-ipant embarrassment and possible prosecution.

Anna hung up none the wiser but feeling better for hav-ing talked with like-minded people.

Overnight the Indian Summer bliss of the past two months had blown away on the tail end of a cold front pressing down from Canada, dumping snow on the Midwest and dropping temperatures as far south as the Gulf of Mexico. Anna drove to Port Gibson under a slate-gray sky that ap-peared to weigh as much as slate itself. Rain lashed out from the storm's underbelly, cutting sodden leaves from the trees. Red, ochre, green, shapes in soft rounds of oak and knife-edges of willow pasted themselves across the car's windshield.

It was a day to curl up by the fire with a good book. Since Anna had nothing but a decrepit oil stove from the early sixties and Thomas Gifford, her favorite author, had died, she was glad she had an office and job to go to.

But for the maintenance men, holed up in the me-chanic's workshop, Anna was alone.

Not quite sure what to do with herself, she sat in the

chair Thigpen had ruined and grew still, dumping the rag-tag shreds of her personal life so her mind could organize itself along more productive lines.

The phone rang. In the outer office that her field rangers shared she could hear the answering machine click on, followed by the insistent hum of the fax. Glad to be given direction, she went to the machine and watched the paper curl out.

This fax was the cheapest money could buy, ninety-six dollars in the electronics department at Wal-Mart. Sick of being the only ranger station on the Trace without one, Anna'd bought it and installed it herself.

The fax was from the medical examiner's office in Ridgeland, a northern suburb of Jackson. Anna took the pages as the machine cut them off and read them standing.

The revelations were few. Doyce's tox screen was clean. He wasn't on any drugs—or at least not the more common ones they tested for. His BAC was .04, a blood alcohol content commensurate with a couple of beers in a couple of hours, not drunk enough to be banned from driving.

Trace evidence had been gathered and sent on to the lab in Jackson. The obvious was noted in the report. Fibers, a cotton-poly blend, tan in color, had been found in the contusions in the groin area. Dirt was embedded in the corpse's heels, the back of the calves and the seat of the underpants. Three splinters, acquired after death, were lodged in the flesh, one in the right heel, two in the right buttock. They'd been driven in at an angle that confirmed the body had been dragged headfirst in a supine position over a surface of rough wood.

No injury marks were found on the body, no blunt trauma or cuts. Cause of death was listed as suffocation but there were no signs of strangulation or of anything being held over the nose and mouth.

There were no bodily fluids: no blood, no semen in the mouth or the rectum. The rectum showed no contusions or tearing. He'd not been sexually assaulted nor had he been

willingly engaged in any sexual act just prior to or after
death.

Bruising on the inner thighs, buttocks and chest were
clean and surrounded by chafing. Two darker bruised areas
indicated metal buckles, the kind with clasps and a sharp
tongue, had been used to secure the straps. The medical examiner's opinion was that the deceased had not been
beaten but had been hung in a harness of some kind. Due to
the man's obesity, his organs had been compressed while
hanging until he was suffocated by his own fat. There were
no defensive injuries on the hands or arms and no sign that
Doyce had fought his attacker. Chafing indicated that, once
in the harness and hung, he had struggled long and pitifully
until strength, air and, finally, life had abandoned him.
Time of death between 11 P.M. and 2 A.M.

Anna spread the report out on her desk. For reasons un-
known poor ol' Doyce had allowed someone to buckle him
into a harness, probably of leather or canvas webbing. He
had allowed this person to string him up.

Anna let that grisly picture dangle in her mind for a
while, wondering what sort of game could have been being
played. If sexual, it had not reached its natural climax unless the other party got his satisfaction merely from watching, which certainly wasn't out of the realm of possibility.

After Doyce drowned in his own blubber, he'd been
taken down, the harness removed, and carted to Mt. Locust
to be dumped on Grandma Polly's bed. From the fibers
found in the scrapes on Doyce's inner thighs, it was a good
bet the harness had been worn over his clothes. When he'd
been dangling to death he'd rubbed the fabric into his
flesh. Pants and underpants had been on at the time of
death. The sexual aspect of the crime was staged. Anna
was unsurprised.

Mt. Locust was a very public place, one guaranteed to
garner local media attention. Yet, at night, it was as dark,
deserted and private as one could want for acting out nefar-
ious activities. Ideal for setting a stage, the curtain to rise
promptly at 9 A.M. just as the sign in the visitors center

window said. An elaborate ruse to throw investigators off track? To merely louse up the investigation, the easiest thing to do would be to hide the body, tie it to a sack of bricks and dump it in one of the bayous. By the time it was found—if it was found—alligators, snapping turtles, fish and bacteria would have effectively devoured any clues. Anybody who watched television would know that much.

Whoever had moved the body had not been attempting to dispose of it but to advertise it.

Why, Anna couldn't guess. The Bible text had been circled. Was it a warning? Retribution?

The body had been put at the old inn for a reason. Dead wasn't enough. A message was being sent or a finger being pointed or something else Anna wasn't thinking of.

Trussed and buckled in a harness. If Doyce had not been willing, he might have been unconscious. Anna mulled that over for a bit and discarded it. Humans were pretty tough animals. To render one unconscious usually left signs. Even if chloroform was used there'd be some faint burning in the nasal passages, traces of the substance in the blood.

The other option was that Doyce had put himself in the harness for reasons of his own. He'd strung himself up, then couldn't get down and suffocated while trying. Sort of a new twist on the auto-erotica deaths that occasionally occurred when somebody tried to heighten the masturbatory experience by partially hanging himself during the event, lost consciousness and was found not only dead but looking extremely undignified.

If Doyce had hoisted himself on his own idiosyncratic petard, who had found him, stripped him and moved him? "Why" was the key. Anna didn't need to know what message the dead messenger was carrying, only to whom it was sent. If she could figure that out, she could work backward to the sender.

Anna stopped speculating and returned to the report, still warm from the fax machine and curling on the desktop like autumn leaves. Wishing she'd had the fiscal wherewithal to buy a better fax, one that used real paper, she found her place in the blurred text.

No defensive injuries: cuts, contusions or bruising on the hands or forearms that would indicate an attempt had been made to ward off blows. No bruising on upper arms or wrists indicating the victim had been held or bound.

Anna had been reading quickly, the information pretty much all of a piece with things she'd observed on scene. She stopped skimming and reread the second-to-last paragraph. The palms and fingers of the victim's hands had been contused. The nails, bitten to the quick, had traces of bark beneath what was left.

Tree bark. Contusions on palms and finger pads. Shortly before death, if not during the actual event, poor, fat ol' Doyce had been climbing trees.

Rectal tissues were healthy, no indication of prolonged homosexual activity. Anna thought about that for a moment. Doyce was evidently not gay and had not regularly or recently been involved in any rough-and-tumble sex games. Men in late middle age, whether closet homosexuals or closet masochists, were unlikely to suddenly find the nerve to act out their fantasies. That fit with her instincts but not with the way Doyce Barnette had died or the way the body was found.

She shoved the report to the side of the desk, not rejecting it as worthless, but shelving information that might become important at a later date.

A short stack of messages and reports had been dumped at her work station during her two days off. Needing to reconnect with the daily life of her job, she began going through them.

Clintus Jones called twice. The slip from Monday said he'd called; no message. Tuesday's told her Martin Crowley, the last of the three surviving poker players, had returned. Clintus would wait for her before questioning the man.

The rest of the messages were bits and pieces from

Barth's ongoing research regarding the slave cemetery. Barth was continuing to talk with local black families whose last names matched those of the few known inhabitants of the old cemetery. He'd included several synopses for Anna's edification. A Mrs. Jackson, eighty-seven, of Fayette, Mississippi, believed her grandmother to have been a slave at Mt. Locust. No records existed to verify the old woman's memory. She claimed her son, a machinist at the Packard plant in Clinton, had tracked down two old bills of sale, one of a man he believed to be his great-grandfather, to a plantation south of Natchez, the other from a cabinet maker who'd built coffins of cheap pine to house the mortal remains of human chattel for local slave owners. Barth had added a note that he'd be following up with the Jackson boy.

The second synopsis was of Barth's talk with the mother of Paul's deputy, Lonnie Restin. Anna read that with more interest simply because she knew and liked Lonnie. Family lore had it that they'd descended from a freedman who'd once been owned by the Mt. Locust plantation. According to the stories, he'd been freed prior to the Civil War for saving the plantation owner's son from drowning in the Big Black River. A lovely story and possibly true, but Anna was cynical. Not that a black man could and would save a drowning child, but because orphans—and the African-Americans were orphans in the very real sense that their ancestors, their history, had been lost to the evil of slavery—often made up romantic stories about their origins. A group of people, made up of disparate tribes and conflicting customs, had been put in the uncomfortable position of reinventing a culture that would not only unite them but provide a historical matrix allowing a sense of belonging—to a place in history, to a place in the world.

Barth was looking for a needle of fact in a haystack of memory and illusion. Wishing him luck, Anna put aside the report and dialed the Natchez Sheriff's Department.

* * *

Crowley worked graveyard shift, 11 P.M. to 7 A.M. In hopes of greater cooperation, or at least greater coherence, they let the man sleep till two o'clock.

The Crowley residence was on a back road that ran roughly parallel to the Trace between the Parkway and the Mississippi River, and then veered to the west and the town of Vicksburg.

Anna met Clintus in his office. Together they headed north, in the sheriff's car. Rain still fell in cold unpredictable gusts, the wind playful in a malicious kind of way, buffeting the unwary from different directions, coating windshields with leaves and lying in wait near bridges to send cars skittering with sudden unexpected blasts.

The AM radio station Clintus listened to switched back and forth between Christian music and an announcer with a pronounced drawl gleefully predicting dropping temperatures with sleet by evening. Anna preferred the dire predictions to born-again messages set to rhythms designed for sex, drugs and rock and roll.

On either side of the two-lane asphalt road, land melted away in soggy fields of stubble rising and falling as gently as the chest of a breathing child, the "hills" of Mississippi. Ditches ran full and creeks were beginning to back up at the culverts under the road. Leaves blew and fell, stuck and slid with the rain till there was little difference between earth and sky.

Given the swirling of this post-primordial soup, it took them three passes to locate the Crowley place. A black stroke of willow leaf had stuck to the mailbox, neatly transforming 603 to 1603.

Set on several acres of land, the house was a small suburban-style tract house and looked to have been lifted out of a development. An attempt had been made to force a suburban lawn to frame it, but city grass was no match for rural weeds and its edges disappeared raggedly into the flooded fields.

Martin Crowley came to the door before Clintus knocked. He was clad in plaid pajama bottoms and a University of Southern Mississippi T-shirt emblazoned with USM's mascot, a dull-witted eagle.

Crowley was small and compact, with hair as blond as a child's. Anna put him in his late thirties. Though his face was prematurely aged, he was fit with the tidy matched musculature that told of hours spent working out with weights.

"Have trouble finding the place? I saw you drive by a couple times," he said. Anna glanced at the one window that looked out over the road. The blinds were down and closed. He'd been watching, waiting for them, worried enough to spend ten minutes peeking out from behind the blind slats. Crowley didn't appear nervous or concerned by their visit, but he didn't stand aside or invite them in, apparently intending to have the interview on the truncated porch.

"Mind if we come in?" Clintus asked politely. "No sense in standing in the door heating the whole outside."

Crowley couldn't think of a reason to refuse, but Anna could tell he was trying.

"I guess you better," he said finally and stepped back.

The interior of the Crowley home was reminiscent of a packrat's lair. The small living room was crammed with furniture that looked as if generations of kids and dogs had jumped up and down on it. Three of the four corners were dominated by cheap glossy knickknack cabinets filled with Avon's collectibles in perfume bottles and glass figurines of empty-faced women in flowing pastel gowns. One wall was decorated with dead fish mounted on wooden plaques. The opposite wall sported collector plates, united by a *Gone With the Wind* theme; a his and hers display of bad taste and matrimonial equity.

Martin dropped into a well-used Barcalounger and picked up a coffee cup from the stand at his elbow. The television, turned to *Divorce Court* or some equally irritating show, grated on.

Uninvited, Anna sat down, or perched rather, on the edge

of a sofa whose blue-and-white striped, low-rent elegance failed to hide the depredations of animals and foodstuffs.

Clintus, mindful of his sartorial perfection, looked around helplessly and Anna stifled a laugh. Stoically sacrificing the purity of his trouser seat to the greater cause of justice, he finally sat on a glider.

On the television, the room's only light source, an overweight white woman with improbably red hair whined on about a two-thousand-dollar car loan her ex had left her with.

"This about Doyce Barnette?" Crowley asked.

Clintus began, "As you probably know, Mr. Barnette was found dead at—"

"I read the papers," Martin snapped as if Clintus had accused him of illiteracy.

The vehemence of Martin's declaration created a momentary silence. Clintus recovered first. "Yes. Well then you know about as much as we do. You played poker with Doyce the night he was killed, that right?"

"Right."

"How did he seem?" Anna asked innocently. "Was he different than usual? You know, distracted or anything?"

"He . . ." Crowley's eyes narrowed momentarily. He ran a work-scarred hand through his hair, leaving blond spikes in its path. "He never showed up," he said. "I meant I was supposed to play poker, but Doyce never showed. He never showed up." Crowley shut his mouth in a hard line exhibiting no more lips than a snake. The casual coldness of a man forced to entertain the Law in his pajamas had been replaced by the hostility of a man under attack.

Anna and Clintus went through their questions, coming at Martin Crowley from every angle they could think of. His answers were short and pat. He'd been coached; he exhibited none of the vague memories of a man trying to recall an evening that had been unmemorable at the time. Common mythology would have it that the truth was easy to remember and lies tended to morph with the retelling. The opposite was true. A group of honest men, questioned about a social evening that was merely one of many like evenings, would argue endlessly about who showed up in what order, whether they ate ham or pastrami, who won the pot. Memories were not stored in a linear fashion, ordered by some cerebral Dewey decimal system. They were dumped in a vast mental junk drawer and had to be pawed through and sorted out.

Not so with Thorton, Lundstrom and Crowley. Their poker evening was meticulously scripted. The three of them had been up to something that night, but as yet, there was nothing to indicate it had been the killing of Doyce Barnette. Try as she might, Anna's imagination—or her stomach—was not strong enough to picture the timid purveyor of Army surplus goods, the practical-joking scrap metal dealer and this hard-bodied bass fisherman in a homosexual orgy with bondage trappings.

It was more conceivable that they'd gone to Jackson to frequent the titty bars and wanted to keep it from their local church vestry. Or, in Crowley's case, his wife.

Eventually the investigation might turn up a fact that could be used as a pry bar to leverage one of them out of their story. So far it hadn't, and both Anna and Clintus realized they would get nothing worthwhile from Martin Crowley.

They were winding it up with the usual handing out of business cards to be used if anything was suddenly remembered, when the door opened on a gust of rain-laden wind and female energy. Mrs. Martin Crowley was home.

"Ooh-ee! A gully-washer. I liked to drown just getting from the car to the door. I must look like a drowned rat." She took off her coat, exposing a trim body clad in tights and a black miniskirt hugging a nicely shaped behind. Giving the coat a shake, she spattered them with icy droplets. "Can't keep big hair on a day like this. Mine must be flat as a squashed cockroach. And I like it big. If it doesn't touch the roof of the car when you sit in the driver's seat, then you just aren't half trying." She tossed the coat over the arm of a chair and crossed behind the Barcalounger to plant a kiss on her husband's head, leaving traces of hot-pink lipstick on his yellow hair. "Hi, killer, why didn't you tell me you were entertaining today. I'd've swamped the place out. Hah!" she smiled into Anna's eyes, and Anna found herself smiling back. "Like I'd've really done it. I just say that so's you all will think my mamma raised me right."

Anna laughed. Crowley's wife was an irresistible rebel force, embracing all that was southern, reveling in it, revering it and laughing at it in the same breath. Anna wished she'd met her under circumstances other than the investigation of her husband for suspected homicide. By the way she'd kissed "killer" it was a good bet the Mrs. would have another trait of southern women: fierce loyalty and a willingness to defend her man tooth and lacquered acrylic nail.

"Isn't this a picture of southern hospitality," she said, perching on the arm of Martin's chair, ruffling his hair and exposing a lot of attractive leg. "Martin here in his pjs sipping hot coffee while y'all faint away from lack of something to drink. What can I fix you? Coffee, tea? We got bourbon if you're not Baptist. If you are, we never touch the stuff."

Clintus was smiling. Anna laughed aloud and was sorely tempted to take her up on her offer for the simple reason Mrs. Crowley was a woman with whom Anna wouldn't mind hoisting a few. Had she not been in uniform and not thought bourbon such a vile brew she'd have succumbed.

"Nothing," Clintus said and started to rise. "We were just—"

"Coffee," Anna said suddenly, cutting the sheriff off. She wasn't sure what she hoped to gain by presuming on the Crowley hospitality a bit longer. It was just a feeling, a hunch that now was not the time to leave. "I could use a good cup of coffee right about now," she said to cement the decision. Both Clintus Jones and Martin shot her a hard look but Mrs. Crowley seemed genuinely pleased. Anna doubted it was she, personally, that brought the sparkle into Mrs. Crowley's eyes but people in general, washed and unwashed, proper and im-.

"I can't promise good, but I can promise coffee." Having brushed a bit more bright lipstick on her husband's head, she stood and clattered into the kitchen, the heels of her leather boots at least four inches high. Without them and the "big" hair—dark brown and worn short over the ears in a modernized version of what the girls in Anna's class at Mercy High School had referred to as the Bubble—Mrs. Crowley couldn't have been more than five feet tall.

"I'll help." Anna escaped the living room, following in the energy trail of Mrs. Crowley's social comet, clearing the swinging door to the back part of the house before the sheriff could register a protest.

The kitchen was in the same disarray as the living area. The counter was covered with dishes, the dining table with catalogues, junk mail and used coffee cups. A shelf, built at eye level, ran around three sides of the room. Scarlett and Rhett, usually portrayed as Vivien Leigh and Clark Gable, were further immortalized on yet more limited-edition, mail-order, collectors-series plates.

"I'm Anna Pigeon," Anna said, introductions having gone by the wayside in the living room.

"Jerri, Jerri Lee as in 'Great Balls of Fire.' Daddy's hero till he found out Lewis had married his thirteen-year-old cousin. By then it was too late to change my name. I'd learned to spell it." Jerri lit a long, thin, brown cigarette as she bustled for coffee-making paraphernalia. She smoked more like the affected than the addicted, and it added to her hardball brand of belle charm.

Filter found, coffee spooned and the coffeemaker dripping companionably with the sound of the rain against the windows, Jerri slowed down. The chatter stopped. She leaned against the counter and took a drag on her cigarette. "Now Anna, why don't you tell me what this visit is all about." Jerri Crowley wasn't more than thirty-five, tiny, dressed and made up like a high-class tart with good taste, but there was little doubt of the intelligence behind the heavily mascaraed eyes.

Since she looked like a girl who'd learned to smell a lie at an early age, Anna opted for the truth.

"A man was found dead at Mt. Locust, Doyce Barnette. He was supposed to meet your husband and two other men to play poker the night he was killed. They say he never showed up. We're trying to backtrack, find out where he was. We figured Martin might know."

"*They say* he never showed up." Jerri went straight to the heart of the matter.

"So far it's all we've got to work with," Anna admitted.

Jerri thought through two drags on her cigarette, then stubbed it out less than half smoked, her porcelain nails cutting through the thin paper as she ground the butt against the glass of the ashtray.

"I don't know Doyce Barnette. Don't know his people, nothing. Martin didn't meet him till that poker night got set up. Herm Thorton invited him in. Martin bought a bass boat from Herm. Got a real good price on it. I guess they been card playing for about a month now. Maybe not that long. Martin's not a big gambler. He joined up with some guys last year, but the group piddled out after a couple months. Without a ball game of some kind to take up the slack in the conversation, men don't seem to have a lot to talk about.

"Martin never lost any money to those guys. Never won any either far as I could tell. And if Martin would've won or lost, I'd know. Not a penny comes through this house but what I pinch it. We got two boys and both are going to college if I have to drive them to school every day till they're twenty-one.

"What I'm saying is, Martin's got no reason to feel one way or another about this Doyce guy. And when you don't give a hoot, you got no reason to scrape up the energy to lie."

They drank their coffee standing in the kitchen, fannies braced against the edge of the counter in the time-honored tradition of American women. They talked of inconsequential things: how Anna'd come to Mississippi, where Jerri got her boots, if it was possible to get a decent haircut without driving all the way into northeast Jackson. They laughed a lot the way women do when relaxed, the kind of laughter that, if it were to be examined afterward, would be found not to come from a comedic arrangement of words but from an undercurrent of shared experience that provided unspoken punchlines to everyday events. While thoroughly enjoying herself, Anna was aware of two cold facts.

If the easy camaraderie was false, she was at risk of being manipulated should she let her guard down. Jerri Lee Crowley was intelligent and creative enough to feign any level of friendship if she felt it necessary to protect "Killer."

If the connections with Jerri were genuine, Anna was at risk of compromising the investigation of Martin Crowley by the conscious or subconscious motive of trying to save his wife's feelings.

Murder not only made strange bedfellows but distinctly uneasy ones.

This flawed but pleasurable kitchen idyll was interrupted after about ten minutes. The pressure of being left alone together had gotten to Clintus and Martin.

Martin stuck his head in the kitchen, looking mildly desperate. "You growing those coffee beans or what?"

Jerri smiled. "You want a refill, darlin'?"

"These people've got to go, Jer, and I got things to do."

In the well-mannered homes of the South, his comment was tantamount to being tossed out on one's ear. Anna left her coffee and followed Martin to the living room. Despite the freezing rain, Jerri walked with Anna and Clintus to the edge of the abbreviated porch. Her white Lexus was parked crookedly near the sheriff's car. Jerri saw Anna looking at it and said, "Bought it used off one of those rental car dealers. Don't I just feel like the Queen of Sheba driving around town?

"Oh!" she said suddenly, startling Anna. Over her shoulder she called, "I forgot, what with the company and all, your stuff's back from the butcher, baby."

Ignoring the rain, Jerri trotted out to the Lexus, apparently oblivious to the cold. "Hang on a minute," she said to Anna as she and Clintus reached the patrol car. "I've got a treat for you." Having opened the trunk, she grabbed out a small paper package wrapped in butcher from a pile of like parcels in varying sizes. "Genuine homegrown venison." She cocked her arm to toss it like a football.

Martin, rudely flopped in his chair as they'd left the house, was now on the porch barefoot in his pajamas.

"Jerri, you leave that be! Hear me now. Let it alone." The venom in his voice was uncharacteristic after the displays of obvious affection between him and his wife. Jerri didn't seem accustomed to it either. She faltered, but he'd yelled too late to reverse the order from her brain, and she threw anyway, wide and wild.

Instinctively, Anna dove for it and, sacrificing the knee of one trouser leg to the icy mud of the drive, managed to catch it before it hit the ground.

For a long moment, made longer by cold and awkwardness, the four of them waited for the mood to change. Anna was comfortable in polite society, and she was more or less comfortable in a fight. Nobody was comfortable in a domestic altercation: motives were too tangled, emotions ran too deep. The good guys and the bad guys kept exchanging hats.

Jerri didn't have the look of a woman accustomed to verbal violence. Dripping, beginning to shiver, she wore the stunned face of a favored child slapped down for behaviors that once earned only praise.

The rigidity born of anger or fear—Anna couldn't even guess—left Martin's face. "Sorry, baby. That ven...the uh steaks...I was planning to, to give them to the Catholic Charity in Port Gibson."

The excuse was so lame, so patently made up on the spot that Anna, who an instant before could think of nothing she wanted less than a bloody hunk of flesh that had once been a magical woodland creature, was now determined to keep her venison at all costs.

"Thanks a million, Jerri. They won't miss one tiny steak," she called gaily and, hugging her dripping prize, ducked into the sheriff's car and slammed the door.

"You a big venison fan?" Clintus asked as they drove away.

In the side mirror Anna could see Martin Crowley, still on the porch, watching the car leave. Jerri had darted inside.

"Martin didn't want me to have it," Anna said.

"And you know why?"

"Probably poached," Anna said.

"Martin's been around long enough he'd know we can't prove nothing without catching him red-handed."

"I know. There's something more," Anna said. "And I want to find out what."

12

At Port Gibson the sheriff dropped her at the ranger station and headed to Natchez to catch up on work he'd let pile up while chasing the National Park Service's murderer. Anna stayed in the office just long enough to reassure Barth that finding Mrs. Jackson's son and hunting down old records of cabinet makers was a worthy use of the taxpayer's money, and to read her messages.

The last was from Paul Davidson. Anna stared at it too long. "What's wrong?" Barth asked finally. "Feeling up to your back pockets in southern sheriffs?"

That was precisely what Anna was feeling. A woman with a lick of sense would have fallen for a veterinarian, a high-school teacher, dog catcher, anything but a local priest and sheriff. And she would have made damn sure he was single before she did it.

Predictable as most women in a like situation, she called him back. Paul said he needed to see her. *Needed:* his word. Again, appallingly predictable, she said sure. Then he did something that surprised her. He invited her to his

house for dinner. She'd been there before, but not after
dark, not since they'd become lovers. Paul's home was in
one of the many fine old houses that still existed in Mississippi. Even tiny towns on the back roads boasted a few.
Most were not the antebellum mansions one thought of
when envisioning southern architecture, but aped that graciousness and were better for it. Ceilings were high, nine,
ten, fourteen feet, doorways wide, windows generous,
floors of hardwood and banisters curved. Too many of the
old homes, fallen on hard times, were beyond saving.
Paul's had been rescued structurally but pillaged by bad
taste in the 1970s. As a new owner, Paul—or more probably Mrs. Davidson—had struck back. Evidently the marriage ended before the renovations. Scars remained where
partitions had been knocked out. Wallpaper was steamed
off and never replaced, carpet pulled up but the battered
oak floors remained unsanded and unsealed. Mrs. Davidson had moved to Jackson and put ten thousand dollars
down on a new condominium. Paul kept the house, living
there, a tidy but indifferent tenant. Paul and, she had to admit, she herself preferred the spurious privacy of Rocky
Springs.

Personal and managerial duties completed, Anna left
Barth to his historical sleuthing and drove south, following
Sheriff Jones toward Natchez. On a miserable Wednesday
afternoon in November there was virtually no traffic.
Come the weekend, hunters and football fans, traveling to
or from Alcorn State in Lorman to attend games, would
people the asphalt. Today she had it to herself. Even in the
relentless gray rain, she found the natural world to her liking. Had she been in a wet backpack on a muddy moun-
tainside, she might not have been so sanguine, but
protected by Detroit iron with radio, heater and the com-
forts of home, she enjoyed the subtle play of muted colors,
the tracks of raindrops on the side windows, naked
branches etched stark and ink-black across a gray rice-
paper sky. She reveled in being warm and dry yet still an
integral part of a cold, wet day.

Once she reached her destination, the meadow with the illegal deer stand, she had to get a whole lot more integral and a whole lot less warm and dry.

She'd anticipated a quick trip through the weeds to where she'd located the remains of the field-dressed doe she and Randy had found. Instead she spent just under an hour once more gridding the small meadow in a painstaking foot search. The poached doe's head, feet and entrails had disappeared. Coyotes possibly, black vultures, foxes, even wandering dogs; Mississippians used hunting dogs a good deal during deer and turkey season. Finding a beagle wearing a collar with a phone number on it was a common occurrence. People would pick them up and call the owners. Things got sorted out.

A quarter of an hour more disabused Anna of the scavenger theory. The rain would have washed away blood and drag marks, but something of the butchered doe would have remained: a bone, a hoof, a scrap of hide. Creatures that dine with tooth, beak and claw simply were not that tidy, yet there wasn't a single piece of the poached deer left behind.

The maid who'd so carefully swept the stand had apparently returned.

Another forty minutes of icy rain running under her collar, soaking through the leather of her boots, and Anna got lucky. Whoever had cleaned up had been too lazy to haul the stuff off. It was buried under the branches of a feral azalea bush on the southern edge of the meadow.

Without help, Anna never would have seen the scraps, but a little dirt never stopped a determined predator. The burial had been unearthed, the tasty pieces of treasure consumed, the inedible parts strewn around. Anna claimed a partially gnawed head with a nice bit of skin and a few tags of flesh remaining under the jawline. Wrapping her find in a clean oil rag, she trotted back to the car.

It was nearly seven o'clock and rain still fell from a sky so low the car's high beams snagged its underside. Winter and weather had stolen what light the day might have left.

Anna was soaked, her hair pasted to her skull, sodden wool trousers dragging at her knees. Even with the Crown Vic's heater turned to maximum, she couldn't shake off the chill but was pleased with the day's work.

The idea to search the meadow had been planted by Martin's unsouthern attitude about sharing the kill. She'd said nothing to Clintus. It wasn't that she was afraid she'd look a fool if it didn't pan out—she'd looked a fool more than once in her chosen profession. Most people feared that above all things, but Anna had come to know it wouldn't kill her. Besides, this idea had thunked home in her brainpan with the solid feel of truth. The problem had been words. Truth did not need to be articulated. Evidence did. Now that she had the evidence, she'd have no trouble finding the words to share it.

Her find in the trunk, she was feeling pleased with herself. Tonight, dinner with Paul. A bath, a little perfume, lipstick, who knew? Maybe she'd get lucky again.

The car's heater finally pumped out enough hot air to penetrate Anna's wet clothes. The luxury of heat, coupled with the visions of priest/sheriffs she had dancing in her head, was putting her to sleep.

Headlights appeared in the rearview mirror, and Anna came out of her waking dream. Visibility was nil, the road was slick with rain and dead leaves; it was not a night to be asleep at the wheel. The FM radio was turned to Public Radio Mississippi. Anna turned up the volume on "All Things Considered" to help keep her mind from drifting.

The headlights drew closer. She glanced at her speedometer: fifty miles per hour on the nose. Fifty was the posted speed limit on the parkway. On a dry sunny day it seemed too slow for cars and citizens engineered for the fast lane. On this classic dark and stormy night it was, if anything, a tad too fast for the existing conditions.

The idiot was speeding. Anna was in no mood to stand in the rain again to give some bozo a traffic ticket.

Lights bore down, high beams lancing from her rearview mirror. She flipped it to its nighttime angle and cursed the rudeness and incompetence of the driver. Even southerners, with their ingrained manners, became cads when given the anonymous opportunities the highway afforded.

Anna slowed to let him pass. Forty-five, forty: the car remained on her tail so close she could read the Ford logo on the grill in the reflected red glow from her brake lights.

"What the hell . . ." Braking gently, Anna came to a full stop. The car—truck, a pickup, the color unclear in the rain and darkness—stopped ten or fifteen yards behind her.

For a moment she sat, motor running, and waited to see what would happen next: a motorist assist, maybe, somebody needing help, a drunk so lost to the booze he just followed the lights in front, and when they stopped, he stopped. It could even be a good Samaritan of great heart and little brain, thinking it was Anna who was in need of help.

She watched her mirrors, waiting for the other driver to make the first move. Opening the side window, ignoring the rain blowing in, she listened. Over the hum of the Crown Vic's engine she heard the pickup idling, punctuated by the faint chronic cough of an exhaust system that had seen better days.

"What do you want?" Anna whispered. The situation was sufficiently bizarre that she was beginning to get nervous. Having picked up the mike, she radioed dispatch in Tupelo.

"Three hundred, five-eight-zero, I've got a vehicle stop at mile marker—" Anna'd been driving in a daze. She had no idea precisely where she was. Each mile of the 450-odd miles of the Natchez Trace was neatly marked with four-by-four posts pounded into the ground about bumper high. Though beautiful, much of the Trace had a green hypnotic sameness that, without numerical divisions, would have made finding specific locations a nightmare. The meadow with the deerstand was between mile markers twenty-three and twenty-four. At a guess, she'd been driving under ten minutes. "Mile marker thirty," she hazarded. "A late model truck possibly mid- to late seventies, Ford. No license number as yet." Narrowing her eyes, as if squinting could help penetrate the mixture of running darkness and stark light, Anna studied the rearview mirror. "The truck's got some kind of grill or homemade bumper welded on the front. Maybe to support a winch. Looks to be made of angle iron."

Not for the first time Anna wondered at the wisdom of Mississippi's Department of Motor Vehicles in requiring tags to be displayed only at the rear of the vehicle. The space on the front that car manufacturers provided for license plates was used for all manner of strange announcements, "Jesus is Lord" being among the favorites, followed by the rebel flag. Mud obscured the front plate of the truck behind her, but it looked like the masked mascot for the Bandits, Jackson's hockey team.

Car and truck were stopped in the middle of the traffic lane. In wet weather, to pull off the road was to be stuck in mud. To reduce the hazard somewhat, Anna eased two wheels off the asphalt and turned on her overhead blue lights. The truck didn't move, not to pass, not to park.

Anna unbuckled her seat belt. Satan or Samaritan, the driver of the truck clearly had no intention of braving the elements to declare himself.

Again she picked up the radio mike. "Five-seven-nine, five-eight-zero." Five-seven-nine was Barth Dinkins's call number. He answered immediately and Anna blessed him for it. "Barth, this isn't a routine traffic stop." She told him the situation and approximately where she thought she was located.

"I'm two miles south of Port Gibson headed toward Natchez. I should be there in five minutes or so." Anna thanked him and signed off.

For another half a minute she sat in silence listening to the rain and the sporadic racing of the truck's engine as the driver gunned it. Probably trying to keep it running at idle.

The utter wrongness of things was abrading Anna's nerves. Her senses were sharpening, growing more acute as adrenaline dripped into her system. She could drive on, see if the truck would continue to follow. She could sit out the slow minutes till Barth arrived. Or she could go out in the rain and do her job. Safety was important, her own safety first as befit a sensible law-enforcement officer. Face was also a factor. Not foolhardy bravado but, being female in a male profession, one that still had a strong undercurrent of cowboy machismo; saving face was important if she wanted to be a successful manager. Men would follow a woman who did not willingly enter into pissing contests. They would not follow one who would not lead once the contest had been declared.

"Damn," she whispered. "And I was just getting dry." She took the baton from under the seat. Patrol cars came from the factory with most of the niceties of civilian cars intact. One of the first modifications made was to disconnect the wires that automatically turned on the overhead light when the doors were opened. That small edge would do Anna no good this night. With the truck's beams spotlighting her, she was exposed and vulnerable. Since she'd pulled to the side of the road, its headlights no longer hit her square but were angled, highlighting the driver's side door. The passenger side was left in darkness.

Anna was a small woman, barely five foot four. The headrests might cover the fact she was no longer in the seat. Crawling on her belly, she slunk quickly across the front seat, shoving open the door on the passenger side, slipped out on her knees and quietly closed the door. Slick as an otter, she slid down the bank into pure darkness under the trees crowding the shallow ditch.

A moment later she was standing, threading the baton through a loop on her duty belt. Should this degree of stealth prove unnecessary, all it would cost her was the five bucks to get her trousers dry-cleaned. Wading through ankle-deep water, she walked up the ditch, wanting to approach this mystery driver from an unexpected—and protected—direction.

The pickup's engine was given gas once more, revving

up till it screamed with unaccustomed power. With an un-expectedness that startled a squawk from Anna, the truck leaped forward, smashing into the trunk of the patrol car. Glittering light, fragmented by raindrops, exploded into shards as her taillights and both headlights of the truck shattered. Brakes set, the Crown Vic skidded ahead, slew-ing sideways, putting the driver's side door at a right angle to the road. Blinded by its own assault, the truck was slammed into reverse.

The collision had been vicious but in no way deadly. Anna expected the driver of the truck to turn tail and run, his point, whatever the hell it might be, made.

Gears ground, engine screamed, the truck picked up speed and smashed into the driver's side of the patrol car, buckling the door inward. The side mirror rolled across two lanes of black asphalt like a severed head as the Crown Vic was bulldozed sideways.

Again the truck backed off, gathered RPMs and was launched. This time the entire side of the patrol car, weak-ened by the other blow, caved in. The truck's tires spun a moment, the smell of heated rubber mixed with the wet night air. Then the tires gained purchase and the iron grill bit into the side of the patrol car and began pushing. Metal screeching against metal. Fifty feet from where the cars had stopped was a stone bridge over one of the many creeks that crossed the Trace. Building up speed, the truck smashed the car into the stone railing with such force the roof of the Crown Vic burst upward. Whoever the driver was had not seen Anna get out; she was sure of it. Though the car had been knocked broadside, without headlights there was no way to tell that she was no longer inside. This was not harassment but attempted murder.

When there was no give left in the twisted metal that had once been Anna's car, the truck's backup lights flashed on. Its grill was imbedded in the Crown Vic. Shrieks of tearing metal accompanied the hiss of tires spinning and the whine of an overworked engine.

A lesser explosion, the sound of the crash played backward, and the truck was free of the wreckage. For a moment Anna thought it would charge again, though for what reason—excepting blind rage—she couldn't fathom, or turn and speed away reckless and blind, behind the curtain of night.

Neither happened. Bent, malevolent, headlights broken, taillights streaming red, the truck waited. *Bubba's nightmare of Christine,* Anna thought and for an instant believed the truck itself, like Stephen King's sentient automobile, had fomented the assault.

Hunkered like a beast of prey over its kill, it was watching, waiting to see if Anna was dead. *The driver is waiting,* Anna told herself. *A man, not a machine.*

Aided by rivers of bloodred running from the taillights, a sense of the surreal caught Anna in a soft grip creating a sense of ghostliness, of watching her own brutal death from a distance.

Her brain scuttled through half a dozen reactions. She noted with detachment that first and foremost her feelings were hurt. Shock at the violent need someone had to see her dead was next. Then anger came; hot, welcome, reattaching her to the world. In a singularly unwraithlike act, she pulled her nine-millimeter from its holster. Stillness, eerily deep after the hellish cacophony of crashes, poured down with the incessant rain. She was shaking so badly she couldn't hold the semi-auto at arm's length. Attempting to move forward she discovered she'd fallen to her knees. Icy water had filled her boots. She felt as numb as the corpse the anonymous driver thought he'd made of her.

Anna forced herself to her feet, stumbled, found her balance and began wading up the ditch toward the crouching vehicle.

"Come on, you son-of-a-bitch," she muttered. "Come on, goddamn it. Get out, admire your handiwork." As if in answer to her heretic's prayer, she heard the crack of a door being forced open past warped metal.

Her brain ordered her legs to run and they tried, but

numbed with cold and boots full of water, she moved with nightmare slowness.

From the north came the familiar whoop of a siren. An instant later the flashing blue lights of Barth's patrol car were visible.

Metal barked again. The truck's door slammed. The pickup came to life, backing rapidly away from the wreckage.

"Damn." Anna cursed Barth's timing and wiped the water from her eyes. The pickup roared backward, wheels milling heavy spray from the road, taillights riddling the night with watered reds.

It passed not twenty feet from where Anna stood. No license plate. Burgundy. She raised her sidearm and fired. Protocol on acceptable levels of force would not allow her to try and kill anyone, much as she ached to do so. She aimed at the tires, hoping to cripple the vehicle sufficiently so she could lay ungentle hands on the driver.

On the range, Anna was a dead shot, top honors. At night, shaking, in a ditch full of frigid water, she was no better than the average schmo. Maybe she hit a tire, maybe she didn't. The truck never slowed. Still traveling backward, it grew smaller till darkness or a bend in the road took it from sight.

Impotent with fury, she stared at the black place that swallowed her killer. The sound of her name being shouted called her back to herself.

Barth had arrived. In the pulse of blue lights she watched him run to the twisted mess that had been her patrol car, yelling her name, pulling at a door fused shut by the truck's impact, peering frantically through the shattered safety glass.

Wearily she slogged out of the ditch and walked down the center of the Trace.

"Anna!" Barth shouted again, then snatched his radio from his belt.

"I'm here."

The big man squealed and Anna laughed. It was grossly

ill-mannered but she couldn't help herself. The laughter carried her on a wave of mild hysteria that part of her mind watched with thin-lipped disapproval.

On the heels of the scream Barth did a classic triple take, looking from her to the car and back to her again. Though it was perfectly executed comedy, the genuine concern in his face dried up her laughter.

"I'm okay, Barth. I wasn't in the car."

"You weren't in the car," he repeated stupidly, his usually fine mind slowed by the drama.

"No."

"Thank God," he said simply.

Anna wasn't in the mood to thank anybody.

13

Much as it galled, Anna was forced to let the assault truck and its driver go unpursued. Her vehicle was totaled, the wreckage blocking the southbound traffic lane. Until it was towed she and Barth had to remain, lest some unwary traveler plow into the mess and kill himself. The best she could do was to radio the Natchez and Port Gibson sheriffs' departments and the state troopers to put out an all points bulletin for an old Ford pickup, probably burgundy, driving without headlights and sporting a home-grown cast-iron grill probably with bits of National Park Service ranger patrol vehicle stuck between its teeth.

The troopers or sheriffs might turn up something, but Anna doubted it. The Trace, fairly straight and decidedly narrow, harbored hundreds of small, half overgrown dirt tracks that provided access and egress to those who knew the country. Even in winter the growth was thick enough to hide a whole battalion of pickup trucks.

After setting flares at intervals fifty yards to the north of

the wreck, there was nothing more for them to do, and
Anna and Barth retreated to the shelter of his patrol car.
Trying to drive out a chill that had soaked more than bone
deep, Anna cranked his heater up high. Her trousers, even
her hair, steamed as the super-heated air struck them.
Rivulets of water ran from her boots and trouser legs to
pool on the seat and floor mat. The windows were as
fogged as those of a pair of teenagers at Lover's Lane, and
Barth was dripping more with sweat than any residual rain.
If Anna noticed she was broiling her compatriot, she was
too distracted to care.

To assuage her need for the hunt, she listed the things
she wanted done at the open of business the following day.
Barth, his paternal—or survival—instincts in good condition, said little and wrote everything she said in a small
notebook. A lesser man would have had to show her his
knowledge. Barth let her unwind in her own way.

"We'll need to call the local body shops to be on the
lookout for a truck with damage to the front end, and
wrecking yards to watch for anybody looking to cannibal-
ize headlight assemblies," she said. "Probably dead ends.
By the looks of it, the truck was a junker. Any repairs'll be
done by the owner if at all.

"We'll run a check in Adams, Jefferson, Claiborne and
Hinds counties. See if they got a record of anybody with a
truck of that description registered." Anna laughed and let
her head drop back against the headrest, wringing a stream
of cold water down into her collar.

"What?" Barth said, sounding alarmed.

His dark face was a strange color, the green of the dash
lights reflecting off the sweat on his forehead and chin.
Personal concern focused in his eyes and tightened up the
muscles of his cheeks. She'd never before noticed how seriously he took his caretaking duties. It wasn't a new side
of him, she realized. She'd seen it the previous spring
when he'd come and taken her out of the hospital in Jackson. It had been there all along; she'd just never bothered

to notice it, never asked him if he had kids, liked to teach, wanted to study emergency medicine or disaster relief.

Managerial shit, Anna told herself and made a promise to be better.

"What?" Barth asked again.

"How many hits you figure we'll get from the departments of motor vehicles if they run a search for old trucks in this part of the country?"

Barth laughed with her. "More than we got the manpower to follow up on."

They didn't speak for a bit, both listening to the rain and their own thoughts, watching for the arrival of the tow truck.

"Scratch the DMV search," Anna said after a while. "The truck had no plates. Probably isn't registered. Maybe hasn't been registered in years. The only way we're going to find it is luck. By now it's hid out back of some barn with a black tarp over it weighed down with old tires."

Barth didn't risk a remark but conscientiously drew a line through the last item on the list. Silence returned, mellowing with the passage of time. "Want to tell me what happened?" he asked.

Anna'd given him the short version when he'd arrived: "Bastard rammed me. I wasn't in the car." Now she told him how the events had unfolded.

"You couldn't see who it was?"

"Nothing," Anna said. "The guy's dash lights were out or masked and with the night and the rain..."

"Maybe it wasn't a guy. Could've been a woman."

"It could have been," Anna said.

A woman. The thought jarred as she thought of the one woman who might want her dead: Mrs. Paul Davidson. Nausea formed a hollow in the pit of her stomach at the tawdriness of dying because of an adulterous affair with another woman's husband. No honor in that. Anna'd only met Mrs. Davidson once when the woman had engineered a "chance" encounter at Rocky Springs to drop a fragment of information Paul had neglected to mention: that he was a married man, three years of separation notwithstanding.

It should have painted an incongruous picture: the petite and carefully coiffed Mrs. D in her pumps and hose behind the wheel of a killing truck, but it didn't. *Projection,* Anna said to herself. Maybe she could see it so clearly because there'd been too many times over the past months when she had wished Paul's wife would come to a timely end.

Not liking the person that made her, Anna forced the sheriff's wife out of her mind. Immediately it was replaced by an image of old wizened Mama Barnette behind the wheel, her head barely higher than the dash, fingers crooked with age and arthritis clamped on the steering wheel like claws. Anna laughed. "It could've been," she said again. "Fords are an equal-opportunity weapon."

"Do you think he was trying to kill you?" Barth asked, reverting to the masculine pronoun. "I mean kill *you* specifically?"

Anna thought about that. The attack felt personal but that didn't mean it was. In the dark the driver of the pickup might not have known who was in the driver's seat of the patrol car. He had the advantage of high beams but, rain filming her rear window, they couldn't have provided much more than a watery silhouette.

"One of us," Anna said. "You, me, Randy. It's common knowledge there's just the three of us for ninety miles of road. One of us or the park service in general. I suppose it could have been a Unabomber thing. You know—one lunatic against the federal government."

"Randy and I've been here a long time," Barth said speculatively. "Nobody's ever tried to kill us."

Anna shot him a sideways glance to see if there was an intentional cut under the words. His face was guileless; the sweat came from the sauna she'd insisted on, not guilt. Still it hurt. "Mama Barnette brought a double-barreled shotgun to the door thinking Clintus was you," she said peevishly. "What was that about beside murderous intent?"

"Shoot," Barth said, oblivious of the pun. "That old

woman wants to kill half the county. Folks think she's still
fighting the Civil War, trying to get back to the glory days
when her people were rich and genteel plantation owners
with darkies to empty their chamber pots. If she's taken on
a personal hate for me, it's because I've been asking questions: her, her neighbors, looking up old records, research-
ing the Mt. Locust graveyard. The Barnettes were nothing
but poor dirt farmers, most of them living worse than
slaves. At least slaves had enough to eat. There was no
money in that family till old lady Barnette's great-
grandfather moved into town and apprenticed himself to a
carpenter."

"Would she want to kill you for knowing that?" Anna
asked. She was serious. In another part of the country that
would never pass muster as a motive for murder. In the
South—even the "new" South—Anna wasn't so sure.

Both of them looked through the steaming windshield at
the crushed and twisted metal of the car Anna'd been driving. Had she not slithered out the right-hand door into the
mud, she'd still be inside it, shrapnel from the driver's door
where her left lung and heart once resided.

"Mrs. Barnette's meaner 'n a snake," Barth said. "Kind
of that mindless, ugly, old mean, like a cottonmouth."

"How about Raymond?" Anna asked. "I keep feeling he
factors into things somehow, but he's got an alibi for the
night his brother died. Vestry dinner."

"You think this is something to do with Doyce's murder?"

Anna didn't answer because she had no answers. It just
made more sense than a sudden crime spree on one of the
quietest sections of the Natchez Trace Parkway.

The car was towed. Reports, verbal and written, as to how
she'd managed to destroy a government vehicle had been
postponed till the following day.

Anna showered, melting away the chill in her bones.
She dressed with the obsessive care of an adolescent on

prom night, donning a soft green velvet dress that flattered her boyish figure. Her short hair she fluffed to accentuate the white streaks at the temples. Then, in a last-minute reversion to type, she threw the graceful ensemble onto the floor and pulled on Levi's, moccasins and an old lambswool sweater that had belonged to her husband, Zach. When she left, Piedmont was curling up on the soft forest-green velvet, improving its color and texture with a wealth of orange cat hair.

By 8:15 her Rambler was parked in Paul Davidson's driveway, and she was standing on the porch of his Port Gibson home. Rain still fell, as did the temperature. The roads would be covered in black ice before the night was over.

For some reason Anna was loath to ring the doorbell. Paul had invited her to dinner, to his home. In a small town, her car in his driveway at eight o'clock on a weeknight was tantamount to a public avowal of...*of what?* A relationship? Friendship? Assignation? Given his situation, the priesthood in the balance, possible jeopardy to the upcoming election for county sheriff that was going on throughout the state, inviting her to his home smacked of a final decision.

Finality: that was what kept her standing in the dark listening to the rain blow against the side of the house.

A plethora of emotions cold and damp as the gusts of rain-laden wind blustered through Anna. She was beset by a sudden longing to return to the safe familiarity of the loneliness that worked so well for her.

"Not good," she said, paying lip service to mental health more as a tribute to her sister than anything else.

She reached for the bell.

Paul beat her to it. The door opened to warmth and light. He folded her into an embrace that banished loneliness so completely that Anna groaned aloud and felt unwelcome womanly tears flood her eyes.

"Doggone it, Anna, I was worried half to death. Why didn't you call?"

His arm, still strong around her waist, brought her inside and closed out the night and the storm. "I've been half out of my mind. If I hadn't known you'd never forgive me for it, I'd've driven out there myself."

Anna let herself fall into a kiss that hit her like warm brandy on an empty stomach.

"I'm not all that late," she managed when her lips were free from more pleasant duties. "How did you know?"

Paul hadn't let her go and her words were muffled against the flannel of the shirt he wore. He held her like he never would, and Anna felt no compunction to wriggle away.

"I leave my radio on tuned to the park's frequency when you're on late," he admitted.

Radio.

Anna pulled back, breaking the comforting circle of his arms. Anyone who had a scanner and the park's frequency would have known it was her in that car: not Barth, not Randy, not an anonymous government representative. As was required by NPS regulations, she'd called in her location at the deer-stand meadow and called in again when she left. Not only her identity but where she was had been broadcast.

The attack was personal. Somebody had wanted to see her crushed and broken. Had Barth been a few minutes later, that person would have stepped from the safety of the truck and into the sights of her Sig-Sauer. She never thought she'd be cursing one of her rangers for responding too promptly to a backup call, but she did now.

"What is it?" Paul asked. "Are you okay?"

Anna told him: how cold she'd been, how scared, how angry, the noise the collisions made, the disorienting play of light and water. As she talked, Anna felt a growing understanding of the women she'd met during her career who had loused up schemes for both the law abiding and the law breakers by blabbing to "the boyfriend." At the time, these incidents had left her with a baffled contempt for the blabbers. Now, tonight, she experienced the heady liquor of sharing. That, coupled with the dangerous stuff of trust, could elicit secrets from just about any woman on the quick side of the River Styx.

During her recitation, they ate bowls full of curried chicken stew, the entire chicken, sans guts, brains and feathers, tossed in the pot for twelve hours, bones still to be picked out as they turned up in one's spoon. There was salad from a bag and good bakery bread.

From the dining table in the kitchen, they moved to the fireplace. Like many in the Deep South it was propane with fake logs, the two or three weeks of true winter not meriting the dirty business of cutting, hauling and storing wood.

Shoes off, feet on the stuffed arm of a couch with down pillows, her head on Paul's lap, she finished her tale as the grandfather clock at the base of the stairs was striking ten.

Paul asked questions as she went along, fueling the story, and Anna was content to be warm, lying in a man's lap, hearing a mellow bell marking the passage of time. After eleven strokes, when the gong fell quiet, there was a sweet aftertaste of sound soaking into the antique wood of the clock and the house. Then it, too, was gone and the sonorous rhythm of the pendulum and the tick of the seconds drifted back into the room.

"I've got my own story to tell," Paul said after a while. Warmth and the sound of the wind had sent Anna drifting peacefully. His words jolted her back. Suddenly no longer comfortable lying on her back, throat and soft white underbelly exposed, Anna struggled upright and propped an elbow on the back of the sofa. The down-filled cushions she'd enjoyed a few minutes earlier were now too soft, too yielding, like quicksand ready to trap and hold.

Paul turned slightly to see her face. "I had a long talk with Amanda last night." Amanda was his wife. For reasons Anna chose not to examine but which probably stemmed from vestigial adolescence, she never called or even thought of her by her first name. When forced to refer to her, Anna used "Mrs. Davidson." As an exercise in dignity and discipline, she always said it with neutral respect.

Hearing Paul say "Amanda" was jarring. Without appearing to do so, Anna took note of where she'd kicked off her moccasins and dropped her jacket in case she was leaving anytime soon. Perhaps Paul had said the name with a tinge of bitterness. Anna found herself hoping so. Paul never spoke unkindly about his estranged wife. At first Anna'd found that admirable. Lately it was beginning to get on her nerves.

These thoughts and others bandied about inside her skull. More than enough time elapsed for paranoia to be planted, sprout and flower; Paul had lapsed into a brown study. Much as she wanted to, Anna wasn't going to kick down the door. Or even lure him out from behind it with careful questions or listening sounds.

"She was different somehow," Paul said finally. "Softer in some ways. More malicious in others. It made me think."

Anna waited with feigned patience for these thoughts to turn into words.

"Amanda said a lot of negative things about you." Paul looked at her and smiled dryly. "No surprise there. We've been careful, but women have a way of divining these things."

"Why don't we call it off," she said, wanting to bring down the sword and slash open the Gideon's knot they'd made of their lives.

"No! That's not where this is going." Paul slid across the sofa and took Anna's hands in his. She was so strung out from the car crash and the conversation, it was all she could do not to snatch them away and run.

"I hated hearing her. I hated you being attacked, if only verbally. I hated myself for being a coward. That's why I invited you over. Half the people in my congregation are divorced. Half the men in the sheriff's department. And I've been cowering behind some mistaken propriety out of fear of who was going to throw the first stone. I told myself I was obeying God's law, that I was protecting you. I'm too old for that bullshit. I care about you too much. I'm trying to get a divorce I should have gotten three years ago. I'm courting the lady ranger. That's my life at present. That's what's important to me."

Having braced herself for the brush-off, Anna was unsure how to feel. Faced with the prospect of bringing their relationship out into the open, she was suddenly shy of her own privacy, her own reputation.

"What did she say about me?" Anna asked. She knew the question sounded self-centered and she knew she wouldn't want to hear the answer. She was playing for time.

"That's the second part of the equation," Paul said. He dropped her hands and stared into the fire. "And there is an equation. That's how Amanda's mind works: tit for tat, quid pro quo. I've never known her to do something without a reason, usually one that moved her in a direction she wanted to go. Her snipes weren't her usual stuff: bad hair, ugly clothes, loose morals."

The bad hair and ugly clothes stung. Anna resisted the urge to smooth the hair over her ears and tug Zach's decrepit sweater into more flattering lines. She consoled herself with the thought that it wasn't what one wore but how one wore it that counted.

"These were professional jibes," Paul went on. "Amanda wouldn't tell me who—she was secretive to the point of smugness about her source—but she's been talking to somebody in the Park Service who evidently has it in for you. Then she hinted that, for the right settlement, she might let the divorce go through uncontested. She's got something up her sleeve."

"Randy Thigpen?" Anna said. He was the only employee of the Natchez Trace who'd gone out of his way to be a major pain in the ass, but it was hard to see where a man of his style or lack thereof would connect with the fastidious Mrs. Davidson.

"Thigpen was my first choice, too," Paul said. "But I don't think it's him. Amanda didn't say it wasn't, but she implied it was somebody higher up, maybe one of the big dogs from Tupelo. She made it sound as if you were on the verge of getting fired." Paul looked at Anna questioningly. Firelight warmed the side of his face and touched his hair with flame orange.

"I don't think so," Anna replied carefully. In the nine months she'd worked the Trace she'd been part of two murder investigations, been sued for reverse discrimination and, now, totaled an expensive patrol car. Other than that, things had gone swimmingly. Her midyear review had been excellent in all categories. As far as she knew no one had it in for her up north. Chief Ranger John Brown Brown had been a bit testy of late but he continued to back her decisions. Still, an attack aimed at her professionally frightened her.

Out of anger she spoke unfairly: "So you decided to drag our relationship out of the closet—what? To defend me?"

Paul winced as if she'd slapped him. Anna was sorry, but for reasons she was unsure of couldn't bring herself to back down. She stared at him, hostility clear in her face.

"No," he said simply. "I did it for me. I honor you, but I did it for me. I don't want to be party to a deceit that goes against all I hold sacred. Love is one of the things I hold sacred."

Even Anna at her crankiest was not proof against that.

14

It was nearly three in the morning when Anna left Paul's. He invited her to stay the night. As tempting as it was to wake up in his arms, murmur sleepily of domestic things, watch him shave and dress, Anna opted for the rain, the Rambler and home. She'd reached an age—or a philosophical plane—where the temptation of her own bed, real sleep and waking with her own cat were tough to beat.

During the twenty-minute drive, Anna tried to keep the warm sweetness of the evening wrapped around her but her mind was as tired as her body and the demons found their way in. Who in Tupelo would verbally tear her down? Who in a beat-up Ford truck had tried to kill her? Was her job as well as her life in danger? *There are other jobs,* she thought, trying to comfort herself. It didn't work. Rangering suited her. The work had found her nearly a year after Zach died. She'd gone west, her car packed with little besides her father's old pearl-handled derringer and a case of cheap Yugoslavian red wine. In Utah she'd pulled off the road and driven into the rough sage-pocked hills. There

were no people, no houses. With luck, nobody would find
the body.

Because the gods didn't want her company, the body
had been found. Anna'd inadvertently driven off road on
National Park Service land. A ranger, Ellen Rictman,
stumbled on her when she was two bottles down.

Ellen had talked to her for seven hours. By the end of the
night Anna had passed out. When she woke up Ellen was
gone. A note was pinned to Anna's collar. When she could
focus, she read it. "Ask for me at Arches," it read. "I promise to work you to death if that's your desire."

That summer Anna worked as a volunteer repairing
trails and fence line in 110-degree heat. Her sister sent her
enough money for food and the rental of a fifteen-foot
house trailer in Moab. By fall she'd found a way to live
without her husband.

People often joked about being married to their jobs. In
Anna's case, it wasn't all that funny.

"It is not necessary that you think so much," Anna
quoted a Chinese psychiatrist her sister admired. Settling
in to the Zen of the rain and headlights on the road, by the
time she reached her bed at Rocky Springs she was ready
for sleep.

In spite of the fact that Anna got less than five hours sleep,
she woke refreshed and full of good cheer. The sky had
not cleared but the rain had stopped and the weatherman
promised temperatures in the high forties or low fifties.
Cold for Mississippi. Used to winters at seven thousand
feet in southwestern Colorado, Anna still considered fifty
to be downright balmy for late November. As she got out
of her car at the ranger station she realized she was
whistling a happy little tune and stopped abruptly. In Port
Gibson it was a good bet her Rambler, parked in the sheriff's drive until the wee hours of the morning, had not gone
unnoticed, and in small towns everywhere, what was noticed was remarked upon.

She had no wish to personify the cliché by being aggressively cheerful the morning after. She needn't have worried. The antidote to happiness was hunkered down at his desk eating an Egg McMuffin with sausage and cheese. Another waited in a bag at his elbow in case the first should call for backup.

Randy looked up from his steadfast munching as she let herself in. For a moment he stared at her, his face locked in an expression Anna couldn't fathom: a witch's brew of irritation, disappointment, rage, weariness, and maybe a touch of admiration. The mix made Anna feel as if he looked not at her, but at the memory of a bad time he was sorry had ended. Alcohol or insomnia puffed the soft tissue around his pale eyes, turning the red rims slightly out. His heavy jowls were shaven but he'd missed places, and rough stubble, darker than his hair, showed like the beginnings of mold on a blancmange.

"I've got a bone to pick with you," he said as she closed the door. He leaned back, his chair groaning in protest, and smoothed his mustache with thumb and forefinger. Some crumbs were brushed off onto his shirt front, others driven deeper into the course sandy thicket.

Anna pulled out Barth's chair and sat down. "Pick away," she said. In her office nothing waited but paperwork, reports in quintuplicate that would generate a flood of questions from headquarters that, as yet, she had no answers for. A set-to with Randy Thigpen was just the thing to get her blood circulating, put her in fighting trim.

"I thought I was in on the investigation. I've been in on it since the beginning," Thigpen said belligerently.

After that first peculiar look, he'd ceased making eye contact and gazed intently at the McDonald's bag. "I've been working my tail off on this and now you go and shut me out. What have I done?"

What Randy had done was louse up one interview and produce a list of names that were so patently worthless Anna and Clintus had agreed to waste no time on them and quietly consigned them to the wastebasket.

Thigpen wasn't done. The loose skin under his eyes quivered with barely contained emotion. Anger, Anna suspected. It was what he was good at. She waited.

Randy finally reached the bone of contention he wanted to pick and began gnawing on it. "You interviewed Martin Crowley without me," he said, undecided between sullenness and outright aggression.

"It was your day off," Anna replied mildly.

His gaze finally came up from his breakfast and his eyes locked on hers.

"You could have waited."

She'd've been more impressed if he'd said, "I could have come in on my day off." His statement deserved no reply and she made none.

Avoiding anything so provocative as prolonged eye contact, she studied her field ranger. Try as she might, it was hard to picture the fastidious Mrs. Davidson taking him to her bosom as a confidant. Still, Randy was the only park service employee she could think of who had anything to gain—and one could never underestimate the allure of petty revenge as a perceived gain—by trashing her professional reputation. Paul said his wife suggested her information had come from higher up, maybe Tupelo. Nobody at headquarters knew Anna well enough personally to hate her or to be able to dish the dirt on her with any accuracy. Barth did. Like Randy, he worked with her most days. That thought was so repugnant she shoved it under the rubble in the back of her mind. She and Barth had had their problems when she'd first come on board, but she liked to believe they'd reached a place of mutual respect bordering on friendship.

The coffee pot announced it was done by a strangled gurgle. Doors slamming and muted voices let her know that the maintenance men had arrived at the shop attached to their offices.

She waited a little longer. When it was clear Thigpen had nothing else to add, she said, "Would you like a report on the Crowley interview?"

"I guess." After the fuss he'd made he sounded singularly uninterested. As she began to tell him, he unwrapped his emergency backup breakfast and started stuffing it under his brush of mustache. Watching the greasy muffin crumbs lodge in the stiff hairs, Anna found herself hoping he'd spent the weekend in Bovina with his mistress of long standing. The man's poor wife deserved a break.

"Crowley's a dead end," Randy said when she'd finished. "That whole poker thing's been a waste of time; Doyce never showed. Obviously he went elsewhere with somebody and got himself killed. You and Sheriff Jones have got us barking up the wrong tree."

"What else have we got?" Anna asked reasonably.

"The list," Randy said. "We never started checking out that list of names I came up with."

"Good point. Why don't you get on that today. You're our local man in Natchez."

Thigpen glared at her as if he'd been trapped, which he had. "What're you going to do today?" The question sounded like an accusation.

Anna got up. The conversation was over as far as she was concerned. She wanted to end it while she still retained a bit of the glow from the previous night. "Don't know yet," she said. "The day's still young."

"You don't have a car," Thigpen's voice pursued her into her office.

"I'll think of something."

"You better ride with me."

"I may just do that," Anna lied. She wanted to close her door on the conversation but knew to do so would send a message of retreat so she left it open, the fumes of sausage fat leaking in along with Randy's ill will. He wouldn't be going anywhere soon, and he would probably make sure, if he could, that she didn't go anywhere without him. Maybe he was afraid she'd catch Doyce's murderer all by herself and the blaze of glory he hoped to retire in in seventy-three days would be snatched from his legacy.

As the weather continued nasty, and no new leads presented, she wasn't averse to remaining in a warm dry office catching up on the paperwork.

The first order of business was dealing with the aftermath of having her car totaled. For convenience and safety, the wreck had been towed to the ranger station at Mt. Locust. National Park Service cars, like many pieces of government equipment, were leased from the Government Services Administration. GSA, which had a yard in Jackson, Mississippi, would send someone down for the car and dispose of it as they saw fit.

Anna placed a call to them and another to the chief ranger's secretary in Tupelo to keep John Brown Brown apprised of the incident and set the wheels in motion to get another vehicle. The next thirty minutes were dedicated to writing the "accident" report. The forms for accidents, incidents and criminal incidents were different. There was no question that this fell into the third category. Nothing about the destruction of her Crown Vic had been accidental.

By half past nine the necessary forms were completed and a car had been found for her. A new one would be ordered from GSA, but it would be a week or ten days before it was delivered. Till then she would drive a patrol car from the Kosciusko District north of Steve Stilwell's on the other side of Jackson. The district ranger there had a position yet to be filled. Until it was, there was an extra vehicle. It would be driven down to Port Gibson later that day.

She drew up the schedules for the upcoming two weeks. Aware that she was taking the coward's way out, she meticulously gave Randy everything he wanted: late shift Fridays and Saturdays, Sundays so he could get time and a half, and Tuesdays and Wednesdays off. With barely ten weeks left to deal with the man, she didn't want to give him any excuse to make more mischief for her. Seventy-three days. Anna smiled. Randy wasn't the only one counting the days till his retirement. Thanksgiving, a week away, made scheduling a bit trickier. Barth would want to be home with his family. Randy would want to be home with the turkey. That left only her to work the holiday.

Anna preferred it that way. Ever since Zach had died and she'd joined the park service, she'd managed to work every Christmas, Thanksgiving, New Year's and Valentine's Day. If one couldn't be snuggled in with one's own family, arresting someone else's was the next best thing.

When it was completed, Anna printed the schedule and went into the outer office to use the copy machine. Randy, looking mildly guilty, probably annoyed at himself for being caught actually working, stood near the copier tamping a stack of fresh copies into alignment.

"In the middle of something?" Anna asked politely.

"Done," he said. "It's all yours." Turning a vast acreage of backside to her, he crossed to his desk and secreted the pile of papers in a side drawer.

Anna opened the copier. "Forgot your original." Randy grunted like a stuck hog.

She pulled out the page he'd been reproducing to hand it to him. When she turned it over Randy's face was staring up at her in black and white. Emblazoned underneath was RANDALL THIGPEN FOR SHERIFF. EXPERIENCE COUNTS.

"What's this?" she asked.

Randy looked sheepish for a second, then whatever guilt he felt hardened into a self-righteous mask of entitlement.

He stepped away from the desk and took the paper from Anna's hand to put it in the drawer with two or three hundred other like flyers printed at government expense, on a government machine, on the taxpayers' time.

"I intend to pay for it, a nickel a page like at Office Depot. I just had no time to get into town to do it."

He lied. He'd been with the service long enough to know there was no system in place for collecting the nickels of pilfering employees. Not only that, but government employees were forbidden to run for elected office. The potential for conflict of interest was too great, as was the possibility of undue influence being used for leverage.

Anna waited for Randy to say something. When he finally did, she was surprised at his demeanor. It wasn't exactly contrite, but he was striving manfully for humility,

and though his natural truculence poked through the thin
places, he was nearly succeeding.

"I know it's against regulations technically. But I'm going to be shed of this place in a couple months so there'd
be no big overlap."

He was right and he was wrong.

"I'm fifty-six," he went on when she said nothing. "If I
miss this election I'll be sixty before the chance rolls
around again. I know I'm not in the best of shape. I'll probably be an old man at sixty."

Listening to him, Anna realized she was hearing his real
voice for the first time. The overlays he used to hide behind, intimidate and blend in had fallen away. The adopted
Southern accent was gone, leaving a trace of his childhood
in Jersey. Bluster, bravado and heartiness were stripped
away. At long last Randy Thigpen pared down to the bare
bones of his truths: he was fat, he wasn't getting any
younger and he wanted to be the sheriff of Adams County
in his retirement.

Honesty, Anna could respect, even—or perhaps especially—from the likes of Randall Thigpen. "You got any
leave time built up?" With leave time tacked on he could
retire early.

"No."

"Sick leave?"

"Tons."

"We'll work something out. Till then keep this stuff out
of my sight and use the copier at the Piggly Wiggly if you
have to."

Thigpen smiled. This too was genuine and, because of
that, damn rare. It was charming. For a moment Anna allowed herself to almost like the man.

As if in payment for the favor, Randy asked, "What happened last night? I mean, I got the gist of it through the
grapevine this morning but no details."

This was the first interest he had shown in her near-death
experience. A normal coworker would have been hovering
around the coffeepot when she walked in, waiting for the

news. Rangers loved stories, especially their own. Randy had either subverted this natural urge for tribal gossip to his own need to gripe about being left out of the Crowley interview and run copies of his campaign poster, or he genuinely didn't care enough about her continued existence even to the extent of mild curiosity. Indifference was colder even than hatred.

"Glad you asked," she said honestly and told him how the destruction of her vehicle had come about. He laughed a little more than she would have liked but almost made up for it by appearing impressed by her clever snaking out in the dark on the passenger side, a fortuitous bit of paranoia that had saved her skin.

Randy'd seesawed from anger when she first arrived because he'd missed the Crowley interview to nearly honest humility when caught making campaign posters. Now that her story was told, he'd returned to the role he'd chosen for himself earlier in the week; the new leaf was again in evidence.

Anna watched for a moment, waiting to see if any more emotional about-faces were in the offing, but Thigpen had stabilized in the helpful ranger mode.

The act of having a simple conversation with Randy was tiring. Muscles used only by middle managers and tightrope walkers were constantly taxed. The need to be alone, or at least away from Randy, became paramount. With a sigh she tried to disguise as a yawn, Anna stood, retrieved her duty belt and headed resolutely for the door into the garage where the pumper truck was housed.

"Need a lift to Mt. Locust?"

"I thought I'd take the pumper truck," Anna said. "It's time it was given a run. This is as good an excuse as any."

"I took it out for a run the other day." Randy rose reaching for his duty belt. "Everything's just peachy. I'll take you on down to Mt. Locust. I'd kinda like to see the wreck by the light of day."

Had Anna been a betting woman she would have put a month's salary on the fact that Randy hadn't taken the pumper truck out "the other day"—or any day since she'd come to the Trace. That sort of routine activity wasn't logged so there was no way to prove it. To call him on the lie would only cause him to lie again. Why, Anna couldn't guess. Maybe he found her company too irresistible to pass up.

"I'm not going to Mt. Locust." Anna changed plans instantly. "Thought I'd go on down to Natchez, have another talk with Raymond Barnette."

Randy lost interest. "I don't have time to go all the way to Natchez," he said and returned to the R & R catalogue, his sudden helpfulness evaporating.

Anna'd hoped he'd say that but wondered what had killed his stated desire. Driving the pumper truck into the gloomy day, she contemplated why interviewing Raymond Barnette was of so little interest to Thigpen. He'd been avid about the interviews of the poker players and the physical examination of the meadow. He'd been pointedly indifferent to the incident where her car was crushed and, now, totally unconcerned about participating in further congress with the undertaker. Was he merely being capricious or did he know something she didn't? And if so, what?

Most of the way to Natchez she pondered those questions

She also spent mental time on the odious fact that someone had tried to kill her. The night, the rain, then Paul's revelation and the intimate and most welcome celebration that followed had conspired to make the assault on her patrol vehicle seem almost a dream. Till she found herself driving with one eye on the rearview mirror, starting to sweat every time a pickup truck appeared there, she hadn't been fully aware of the impact the attack had on her.

Just past the bridge where the incident occurred, she pulled two of the pumper truck's wheels off the road and parked.

Maintenance had done a thorough job of cleaning up the site. Anna found two pieces of red plastic, probably from the Crown Vic's taillights, and a piece of chrome from a shattered headlight. That she kept. It was a long shot but it might help to get a positive ID on the truck if they ever found it. Before day's end she would track down the guys who'd cleared the road and go through any other debris they'd swept up.

Rain and wind had cleaned away what maintenance had missed. The only evidence remaining that anything had occurred was the scarring on the stone blocks of the bridge rail. For a minute or more Anna stood in the cold, the air so heavy with moisture that droplets formed on her hair and eyelashes, with one hand on the slick surface of the rock, allowing the stone to remember for her. Memories rushed back: crying metal, ice water filling her boots, the sense of watching her own earthly death from a place removed. No revelations came. Either she was deeply hated by an individual, or she'd gotten close enough to something in the murder investigation that it made it worth that individual's while to take the risk of removing her.

Had anyone hated her sufficiently to go into the berserker rage in an old Ford truck, Anna believed she would have sensed it, read it in his or her face at a previous encounter, therefore she must be on to something.

"Damn," she whispered and took her hand away from the stone. Had the would-be murderer known how totally in the dark she was, he could have saved himself the time and the taxpayers a car.

When she reached Barnette's Funeral Home, Ray's black Cadillac was parked out front. There were no other customers. Funeral homes weren't big shopping draws, even this close to Christmas.

Anna let herself into the ornate foyer. The place was still and cold as befit the nature of the business. Raymond was not in the chapel or showroom. Following the circuitous route he'd led her and Clintus on the first time they'd visited, she made her way back to his office. That, too, was empty. Opportunity presenting itself, Anna looked through the papers on his desk. Bills for casket fittings, a funeral

scheduled for Saturday, catalogues of awnings, black arm-
bands and florists were collected into neat piles. Nothing
indicated he was other than what he said he was: a mildly
grieving younger brother. Because he stood to inherit a
valuable piece of property and because he was a genuinely
creepy individual, Anna rather liked him as a suspect in the
murder of his brother. Clintus did, too, though, given they
were rivals for the coveted position of Adams County
Sheriff, he'd never been so crass as to say it out loud. He
had, however, discreetly checked to see if Raymond had an
alibi for the night Doyce was killed. He had: a meeting
with seven men and two women at a vestry dinner. According to Clintus Jones, the dinner meeting had gone from
seven-thirty to past midnight, effectively letting Raymond
off the hook.

One of the windowless walls of the undertaker's office
held a collection of old photographs. During her first visit,
Anna'd been so taken with the commercial macabre of tiny
coffins and ads for embalming fluids that she'd not noticed
it. There were seven pictures displayed with pride, if being
separated from the necessary minutia of the undertaker's
trade was any indication. The oldest had the sepia tones of
daguerreotypes or tintypes.

Anna loved old photographs, and having come to see
Barnette more or less to escape the company of Mr. Thigpen, she was in no rush to find him. The collection
chronicled the history of Barnette's Funeral Home over at
least a hundred and fifty years. The earliest photo was of
greatest interest. Most pictures she'd seen that pre-dated
the Civil War were formal portraits of unsmiling people
dressed in their best and posed in front of painted back-
drops. This was unrehearsed, as if the photographer exper-
imented with a more modern concept of capturing real life
on celluloid. Two men stood in a carpenter's workshop.
One was black, the other white. They were shoulder to
shoulder, both in overalls, the black man's torn out at the
knees. Behind them was an exquisite armoire. Three tables
and a bentwood rocking chair, not yet completed, were

scattered around them. Neither man was smiling, intimidated probably by the momentous event of having their picture taken, but by the way they stood—close, casual, comfortable—Anna guessed they were friends, that they'd worked together long and well.

She took the photograph from the wall and looked at the back. "Papa Doyce and Unk Restin 1861 Natchez" was written in a crabbed and fading hand.

She replaced the picture with care and studied the others. The closer they came to the present, the less interesting they became. The last, in glossy color, of a slightly younger Raymond Barnette, leaning on a younger version of his black Cadillac and grinning at the camera, she gave barely a glance.

On a waist-high filing cabinet that ran beneath the photographs was a stack of color posters: Barnette for Sheriff. Including Randy Thigpen, there were at least three hats in the ring. Anna knew Barnette had high hopes. Some of them were undoubtedly pinned on the fact that he was white and Clintus Jones was black.

Except for a handful of hard-core, old-style racists, Anna doubted it would do him much good. Of the fifty or sixty percent of Adams County who were not African-American, Barnette's association with a brother, not only murdered, but branded a sexual deviant by the story leaked to the papers, would rob him of their vote. Once that story had come out, Ray Barnette's campaign was dead in the water, though he'd chosen to stay in the race.

Thigpen might be another matter. Anna was the first to admit he had a plethora of faults, but racism was not one of them. The African-American community would know that. In order to survive and prosper, most had developed good intuitions along those lines. Another factor might win Randy a few votes: older blacks sometimes preferred "the Boss" to be a white man. There was a sense of security in the familiar that helped shield them from a younger generation of African-Americans whom they feared and could not understand. Randy's career as a park ranger would also lend him an unearned reputation for having a history in law enforcement. That could turn the election in his favor.

It crossed Anna's mind to give Clintus a helping hand by lousing up Randy's plan. Since she'd more or less given her word that she'd help, she abandoned the idea as soon as it came to mind.

Snooping having availed her nothing, she resumed her search for the funeral parlor's proprietor. Clichés of the dead dogged her as she wandered down the hall past a bloodlessly non-denominational chapel: silent as the grave, cold as a tomb, dead still. The next door opened into the showroom. Ornate caskets lined with tufted crepe and polished to a satin finish, their hinged Dutch-door lids half open as if inviting one inside, lay in state on dark wooden tables. The air smelled faintly of varnish.

Anna had never bothered to write a will. With the exception of a couple of good Navajo rugs, she had nothing of value to leave anyone. Looking into these empty houses of the dead, she promised herself she'd write one if for no other reason than to demand her remains be cremated and let free to blow on the prevailing winds.

Farther back in the mazelike bowels of Barnette's establishment she came to a door that, unlike the others, had no pretense of somber elegance but was of metal, scratched and dented by good hard use.

Pushing it open, she stepped into the only part of the building that felt alive: a carpentry shop. The air was warmed and dried by an old woodstove. Classical music full of strings gentled her nerves. The smell of newly cut wood and coffee reminded her of life and industry.

Raymond Barnette stood at a lathe in the middle of the far wall. His back was to her. He whistled tunelessly, relaxed in the mistaken assumption that he was alone. Anna had been well trained in shop etiquette. One never startled a man working with machinery. Careful to make no sound, she studied Barnette while he completed his task: rounding off the edges of an oddly shaped piece of hardwood.

He wore faded Levi's, an old sweatshirt and boating

moccasins stomped into slipperlike shapelessness. It was the first time Anna had seen him that he wasn't dressed in his meet-the-public clothes. He looked smaller, nicer, more approachable.

Having finished his task, he switched the lathe off. Anna cleared her throat to announce herself in the least alarming manner.

"Ranger Pigeon," he said, recognizing her, then spoiled the kinder gentler thoughts she'd been having of him by smiling with all his big white teeth.

The better to eat you with, my dear. The words of the Big Bad Wolf came unbidden to Anna's mind and she knew why she'd come to see him. She wanted to know whether he owned an old Ford truck with a cowcatcher welded to the front bumper. Perhaps he hadn't killed his brother, but there was something about the man with his toothy ways and his closeness with the dead that led her to believe he might be willing to kill as long as he didn't have to actually lay hands on a live body in the process.

To his credit, he didn't seem either surprised or disappointed to see her alive, but she put little credence in that. During their brief acquaintance, she'd seen him don then doff half a dozen emotions in minutes without blinking an eye at his own duplicity. If he had a police scanner, he could have heard her call clear of the scene of the wreck the previous night and had time to prepare his face for when they should meet again.

"What brings you here?" he asked as he slipped the piece of wood he'd been working on out of sight behind a canvas-draped sawhorse. Till he did that, Anna'd been singularly uninterested in his woodworking project. Now she wanted to see it. "Good news, I hope," he added.

The words jarred. When one's only sibling was ignobly and irretrievably dead, what good news could one possibly expect? "We've no new leads as to who might have killed Doyce, if that's what you mean."

"Too bad." He didn't sound particularly aggrieved. Niceties concluded, he looked at her expectantly.

Anna told the first easy lie that came to mind. "I know in your capacity as a concerned family member and possibly the next sheriff of Adams County you've been doing a little investigating of your own. I was down to meet with Clintus and thought I'd drop by, see if you've come up with anything we might have overlooked."

The mixture of girlish—if aging—respect and a plea for assistance worked its customary magic. As the words were soaked up, Ray's lugubrious features rearranged themselves into avuncular condescension.

"Coffee?" he offered. "It's cold enough to freeze a grave digger's hind pockets today." He grinned at his topical humor, and Anna dutifully grinned back. She was afraid they'd retire to his claustrophobic little office for the proposed coffee klatch, but he had a pot on a hotplate by the lathe.

"Hope you take it black," he said.

"Black is good." Anna couldn't stomach the stuff without a healthy dollop of heavy whipping cream, but she wasn't here to drink; this symbolic breaking of bread might help her find out what he knew. Coffee attended to, Ray slung one buttock onto a table and Anna perched on a sawhorse.

"Like you said, I've done a bit of nosing around on my own," Barnette said importantly. Anna could almost see his chest swelling under the imagined sheriff's badge. He rambled on for a while. Listening expression in place, wide eyes, furrowed brow, chin tilted down, Anna let him. He'd done little and learned less, but after ten minutes or so he'd softened himself up with love of his own voice sufficiently that she could ask the questions she'd come to ask.

"Do you know of anybody who owns an old Ford pickup truck? Burgundy or dark red probably, with a heavy iron grill custom-welded to the front?"

Barnette laughed. His laughter sounded hollow but it always did; the sound of a man aping his fellows but never getting the joke. No change came into his face that Anna could detect, no infinitesimal twitch of surprise, guilt or recognition, not even the faint glimmer of smugness that occasionally gave away smart criminals who took pride in their work.

"Old trucks with heavy grills are not exactly rare as hens' teeth in these parts," he replied. "Oh, you see those SUVs everywhere, but they're just for show. Mostly moms hauling kids and guys with desk jobs pretending they're big game hunters come the weekend. Anybody around here really wants to haul something's got himself an old truck."

"Anybody special sell used trucks around Natchez?" Anna asked.

"Sells? Sure. Everybody. They sell them, trade them for work, a used deep freeze, a load of lumber. But pink slips and taxes? With a truck that old I'd say not. After a while they get passed on like old clothes." Barnette bared his ominous teeth once again, happy to have given Anna information that showed she didn't know a whole hell of a lot. Other than that, it was totally useless.

"You're probably right. Keep your ears open and give me a call if you hear anything," Anna said. No harm in keeping up the fiction that they were working together. She eased her rump off the sawhorse. She'd learned what she'd come for. Unless her instincts deceived her, which wasn't out of the realm of possibility, Barnette had nothing to do with the assault truck. "Thanks for the coffee."

On the way to the door she passed the lathe and remembered the undertaker's surreptitious stowing of the wood he'd been working. She stopped and turned. "This is a nice shop," she said. "You work in wood?"

"Not as much as I'd like to. Business is too good." Anna waited for the "people are just dying to trade with me" joke, but mercifully it never came.

"What're you working on now? That was—what?—oak you were finishing?"

"Just keeping my hand in. My great-great-granddaddy Doyce started out as a cabinetmaker. Had pieces in some of the finest homes in Natchez."

"Would that be Papa Doyce, the guy in the picture in your office?" Anna asked. "I went in there looking for you and got to admiring your pictures."

Ray's cheeks quivered and the ease in body and face he'd had when lecturing on the economics of old trucks leaked away.

Anna didn't make too much of it. Maybe he worried she'd found incriminating evidence. More likely he was just alarmed at having anyone unattended in his private office. She would have felt the same way.

"Papa Doyce," Ray said, his proper business face back on. "He started the business in eighteen fifty-six. My brother was named for him." While speaking, the undertaker was making the moves of an impatient host trying to get a guest to leave. Anna stood her ground.

"I'd love to see what you were working on. I used to do a little woodworking myself."

"It's just something to keep my hand in." Ray touched her elbow to expedite her departure.

"Still, I'd love to see it." Anna leaned against the lathe, settling in for the long haul.

Barnette had two choices. He could make a scene by continuing to refuse a simple request or he could acquiesce. He was enough of a politician to give in with what would have passed for graciousness had Anna not been close enough to see the strain in his smile and the fury behind his controlled movements. He took the plank from its impromptu hiding place.

Angry as Barnette might have been, there was no slamming about of things. He handled the wood with the care of the true craftsman, lifting it then laying it on the lathe's table.

It was not as Anna had first thought, a single plank of fine oak, but several pieces of lumber glued almost seamlessly together and sanded to a fine sheen that showcased the subtle tight grain of the wood. The piece was three feet or less in length, but the shape was unmistakable. Disparate images of children, rotted wood and mouldering bones clashed in Anna's skull. Maybe one mystery was solved. Maybe another was born. Unsure, she cleared her mind.

"A child's coffin?" she said.

The undertaker blinked once as if she'd spoken a language foreign to him, then his eyes cleared and he said yes, smiling in a way he probably truly believed was reassuring.

"You do beautiful work." Anna had a deep love for natural wood in its many incarnations: living trees, sturdy cabins, fine furniture, logs for the fire in winter.

Either the sincerity of her words or the flattery dispelled the undertaker's anger. His long fingers stroked the edges, newly made from the lathe, with pride and pure sensual pleasure.

"Do you make many coffins?" Anna asked, remembering the glossy ornate boxes in the showroom.

Warmed by the genuine interest in her voice, Raymond's facial muscles thawed, his smile became less ghoulish. "Not anymore. Nobody wants to pay for handwork anymore, and I don't have the time like I used to, but every now and then I'll get a special order."

"Somebody ordered this?"

Again the hitch in his features, so fleeting Anna wasn't sure she really saw anything. "People get a little crazy when a child dies," he said. "That's when they call me. They seem comforted to know their loved one will find a home made with care by somebody they know."

For all his oily ways and toothy deceptions, Raymond Barnette was serious about his work. Anna didn't doubt that he cared deeply about the housing of humanity's mortal remains.

"Do you want to see the coffin I picked out for Doyce?" he asked brightly. "It's top of the line."

An image of an upholstered box with a satellite dish to collect Monday night football and a cup holder for poor ol' Doyce's Budweiser filtered through Anna's brain, disturbing her composure. "Some other time," she said. "I'd better be getting on with my day."

What that day was to comprise, other than avoiding Thigpen and awaiting delivery of her "new" patrol car, Anna wasn't sure. Because she was in Natchez, she headed in the direction of the sheriff's office. As she drove she reviewed her interaction with Raymond Barnette, playing it back in her mind as if it were a videotape she could start and stop at will. This habit of review had stood her in good stead over the years. Try as one might, it was impossible to keep emotions from clouding one's perception when in the company of others. Fear, intimidation—those were easy to spot and so to see past. It was subtle feelings that obscured details: self-consciousness, embarrassment, the desire to appear more powerful and professional. It was easy to get so wrapped up in one's own performance that the nuances of one's fellow actors slipped by unnoticed.

Mental viewing, after physical distance was attained, lent clarity. Critiquing her scene with the undertaker, what struck her most forcefully was his reluctance and discomfiture regarding his woodworking project. Once she pressured him into letting her see his work it was obvious he took pride in his skill, in the skill of his ancestors. Why then hide it and fuss over showing her? What was there in the crafting of a child's coffin to be wary or ashamed of?

One solution had already occured to Anna, and she dearly hoped it was the right one. But she wasn't willing to bet the life of a child on it.

What child had died recently?

This was not her jurisdiction and, arguably, none of her business. Even with an imagination as fertile as her own, Anna would be hard-pressed to articulate how it related to the incidents on the Trace. Still, she would find out. In the local parlance there was "probably no cheese down that hole." Nevertheless, she would follow it till she reached the end. If it proved a waste of her time it would serve to even up her karmic balance. Her motives were far from pure; she would dearly love to pin something on the unctuous mortician. And, unlike the murky unpredictable malice that had lain over the Trace for the past couple of weeks, finding death stats was easy; there was a clear path to follow. Both considerations factored in, but mostly Anna felt uncomfortable turning her back, humming the American mantra "not my problem," on any situation that included Raymond Barnette, a child and a coffin if there was anything the teensiest bit shady about it. Raymond's evasion and anger provided more than the requisite teensy bit.

Investigation that required only a mind and a telephone was the sort of thing Barth Dinkins did well. Anna would start him working on it. Long habit had her reaching for the truck's radio. An unbidden memory of her patrol car smashing into the bridge railing stopped her hand. The more she thought about it, the less keen she was to share her concerns over the radio. She turned the pumper truck around and headed back up the Trace toward Port Gibson.

Barth was behind his desk at the district office, half-glasses sliding down his low-bridged nose, the clear gray-green eyes alight in his dark face.

"I was wondering if you could help me with some legwork," Anna said upon entering. "It requires no actual legs, mostly wheedling legally available information out of bureaucrats." Barth sat behind a stack of photocopies; old land deeds, birth, death and marriage certificates from the look of them. Anna ripped her gun belt from the Velcro underneath and dropped it on Randy's desk.

No New York City socialite took off her spike heels with a greater sense of relief than Anna divesting herself of her duty belt. Permanent discolorations marred the skin over the pelvic bones from constant bruising. She'd once complained to her district ranger in Mesa Verde and been told to fatten up. Despite the south's penchant for deep-fried food and plenty of it, she had failed to gain the necessary poundage.

"What you got?" Barth said amiably and pushed his papers aside to let her know she had his full attention.

Anna related the tale of the tiny coffin. Barth's strange eyes seemed to iridesce, become opalescent. The pupils were shrinking to pinpoints. The man was an enigma to

her. They worked together most days; respect and a form
of friendship had grown between them, but nothing approaching intimacy. Anna'd never been invited to his
home, and he'd managed to wriggle out of the invitations
she'd extended to him and his wife. The two rangers never
spoke of personal concerns. They knew no one in common
who wasn't park service. Barth was black, Anna white. She
was his boss. He was a married man and she a single
woman. Too many hurdles to overcome.

"No problem. My work can wait." A child, a coffin cap-
tured his attention. Like most big men, Barth had little understanding of anyone preying on the helpless.

Anna thanked him, divided up the phone chores, then
sequestered herself in her office. For three hours, including
a break for lunch, she talked on the phone. She called city
clerks, county clerks, county coroners for Adams, Jefferson and Claiborne and all the hospitals. By the size of the
coffin Barnette had been crafting so lovingly, the recipient
had to be under three or four years of age. Anna framed her
questions accordingly.

Because of the pressing nature of embalming and inter-
ment, she set her time frame to include the previous ten
days. Bodies were seldom kept that long, but she wanted to
make sure she didn't miss any possibilities.

By midafternoon she knew there had been no children
recently dead from foul play, accident, domestic abuse or
disease. None of the hospital doctors had signed death certificates. None of the three coroners had been called to declare a small citizen dead. No child, no infant had died in
any of the counties contacted since September.

Barth had fared no better in finding small dead people.
Wanting to lean back and prop her feet on her desk, the ap-
propriate position for deep and meaningful thought, Anna
cursed Randy soundly for ruining her chair. If she leaned
back past center she would achieve, not comfort, but a
comic moment; her backside hitting the floor providing the
laugh.

Remaining upright, she considered the lack of information so laboriously accumulated. Sixty-three days without the death of a single child should have been cause for celebration, but Anna wasn't happy. If no child had died why had his or her parents commissioned an expensive oak coffin? Had any parent really ordered the coffin? And, the question that bothered her most, was a live child slated to fill that coffin either by somebody in conspiracy with Barnette or with Barnette simply an innocent working in good faith?

It was possible, Anna supposed, that the parents or guardians of a terminally ill child might commission a coffin against the inevitable moment of death. Possible, but she doubted it. On the two blessedly rare occasions she'd had to deal with parents of dying children, denial was what kept them functioning. Somehow, some way, a miracle was going to happen, God or modern medicine was going to step in. Their child would not be allowed to die.

The mindset of a mother who would order a coffin for her living infant was unfathomable.

If no one had ordered it and no child had died, why in hell was Barnette making it? More to the point, why did he tell her it had been ordered for a deceased child? Unless there were sinister overtones she was missing, he'd lied to her.

She listed out the scene: she'd seen Barnette working at the lathe. He discovered he was being watched and made haste to hide what he was working on. When she'd asked to see it he refused. She insisted. He acquiesced but was angry. She asked what it was for. Barnette became uncomfortable. Then he told her it had been ordered. After that he was comfortable, talkative.

The lie had let him off the hook.

If not for a child, why was he making a tiny coffin? There were plenty of legitimate reasons: a prototype, a model, for practice, even just for fun. Everybody was wired differently.

Had any of those been the case he would have had no reason to lie. Had he chosen one of those lies, Anna would never have caught him. In the fear of the moment, he'd said the first thing that came into his head. Unfortunately for him it was also the one thing she could trace, prove to disprove.

Anna decided to shelve the unanswerable questions and mark the one answer she'd found in her mental column: Raymond Barnette had lied to her.

15

Near four o'clock, the light going fast as if the rain that had begun in the afternoon washed it from the sky, Anna's replacement car, along with Ranger Steve Stilwell, showed up at the district office. Both were a welcome sight. Given that her world now consisted almost entirely of a road, she'd not felt quite dressed driving the pumper truck. Steve asked for a lift back to Ridgeland and she was glad of an excuse to visit with him, play hooky from office politics for a couple hours.

Stilwell, his soft stick-straight hair in its usual disarray and needing a cut, seemed pleased with himself and life more than usual. He listened kindly to her tale of the wreck and was properly incensed at the perpetrator.

Strains of classical music soft on the radio, rain and darkness making the warm privacy of the moving car intimate, Anna and Steve whiled away the drive to Ridgeland in pleasant fantasies of the violent revenge they would wreak upon Anna's growing number of attackers should they meet them in an alley one dark night.

Because the attack was committed with a battered pickup and conducted with bubbalike vehemence, Stilwell leaned toward the perp being one—or two, Anna couldn't swear there hadn't been a passenger—of the hunters who had chased her the night she and Randy stalked the illegal deer stand, and having nothing whatsoever to do with the murder of Doyce Barnette.

Coming from Steve, the theory sounded good, and Anna rather liked the idea that only one group in Dixie wanted her dead, but she couldn't buy it. The hunters had merely been opportunistic. They'd achieved what they wanted: her humiliation and escaping scot-free with their poached meat. They had nothing to gain and everything to lose by a second attack on her. Even if they believed she was able to identify and prosecute them for the poaching, in Mississippi the penalty for poaching deer was not sufficient to motivate murder.

All through the maze of speculation and retribution that they wandered, Stilwell maintained an undercurrent of gleeful superiority. Anna sensed, because he so clearly meant her to, that he knew something she didn't. Because he was so smug about it, she suspected it had nothing to do with murder and mayhem but was personal.

Rather than reassuring her, that increased her sense of disquiet. She wasted a lot of energy wondering what he was up to. By the hints he dropped she could tell he wanted her to try and wheedle it out of him. Her curiosity was such she would have dedicated herself to cajolery if she'd believed it would work, but Stilwell was having way too good a time to tell his secret. She chose not to give him the satisfaction of watching her fail.

As they neared North Jackson with its plethora of trendy eateries on County Line Road, Anna's stomach reminded her it was nearing suppertime. Once the idea was conceived it took over. A nice dinner in good company would be an excellent way to cleanse her soul of the niggling loneliness and insecurity that had been dogging her the past week. "Want to get a bite to eat?" she asked.

"Can't," Steve said. "I've got a hot date."

He didn't even have the decency to sound disappointed.

"On a weeknight?" she asked with some asperity, then had to smile because she heard her mother in her own words.

"When sweeping a woman off her dainty little feet, the key is consistency and, above all, persistence. Women can't resist perseverance. Taps into two of their driving forces: guilt and vanity."

Steve was so pleased with himself and so right Anna wanted to punch him. Seat belts and the spurious dignity of middle age kept her from it.

"Who is the lucky lady?"

"Wouldn't you like to know," Steve said delightedly.

She would but would never lower herself to ask.

He suffered through the silence for less than a minute. "A mutual friend," he said finally, trying to tease her back into the game.

Anna said nothing. The only mutual friends they had were large, armed men. "You're gay and at long last throwing wide the closet door?"

Congratulating herself on social heroics, Anna turned down his offer of a consolation prize consisting of a drink of single malt scotch served in a coffee mug.

Partway down Interstate Two-twenty, the freeway that, until the fifteen-mile stretch of scenic parkway between Clinton and Ridgeland was completed, connected the northern portion of the Trace to the southern end, she remembered the dead deer parts she'd been ferrying when the killer truck appeared in her rearview mirror. They were the sole reason she'd been on the road the previous night. The excitement of the crash with its aftermath of report writing had pushed it from her mind.

General Services Administration had a center in Jackson. The wrecked Crown Vic would have been picked up from where she and Barth had dumped it at the Mt. Locust Ranger Station and towed there. Turning off at Medgar Evers Boulevard she wound her way into the city, reaching the GSA yard at quarter of six. Luck was with her; one employee, already working late and mildly disgruntled that he would have to stay later, pointed to where her vehicle had been unloaded. Deciding his duties did not require him to both stay late and get wet, he remained in his office as Anna squished across the yard toward the far corner of the lot. Cyclone fencing eight feet high and topped with razor wire secured an assortment of government equipment, some new, some discarded.

At the sight of her car, mangled and crushed into a wad of metal, she realized she could never have survived and was overtaken by an unwelcome frisson of pure terror. The jolt of fear was so strong she stopped and stood in the rain, willing it to pass. Occasionally law-enforcement officers lost their nerve, had to retire or go into another line of work. Experiencing the paralysis of overwhelming fear for her mortal self, Anna fully understood the phenomenon.

She'd pushed or badgered another human being to the point they wanted to pulverize her in a fist of steel. For a moment she thought about that. Pulling out the punkiness of adolescence, she shook herself. "Fuck 'em if they can't take a joke." Arrogance and indifference; it was an old garment but it still fit.

The glare of the mercury vapor lights ringing the yard was such that Anna didn't need her flashlight. Fog clung to fences, trees and car bodies picking up and reflecting back the orangy light till she felt as if she walked inside a pumpkin.

The mirror on the passenger side was the only part of the Crown Vic that had escaped damage. Using a chunk of twisted metal picked up from the ground, she smashed the intact mirror just for the hell of it. Seven years bad luck; Anna was unmoved. She hadn't enough faith to be superstitious. Turning to more practical destruction, she bashed what remained of the safety glass from the window on the passenger side. Breaking glass was fun; watching the crystals shatter and fall glittering red-gold from a hundred facets mesmerizing. If rangering didn't work out, maybe she could get hired on at a wrecking yard.

The car's door was bent beyond opening, the metal folded inward in front of the handle. The back of the seat had been crushed until it was inches from the dashboard. The glove box had sprung open, but Anna's spare flashlight and sunglasses were still inside. Taking pains not to cut herself, she retrieved them.

To the rear of the car the trunk was open, probably popped during the crash, though she didn't remember it. The field testing kit for illegal drugs was intact. The briefcase containing her investigative paraphernalia was there, as were the road flares, though they'd been thrown from their box and scattered throughout the now peculiarly shaped trunk. Everything had been put at sixes and sevens by the repeated impacts but nothing appeared to be missing. Except the package of venison Jerri Crowley had given her and the maggot-infested doe's head she'd picked up in the meadow.

It was possible those packages, the last items tossed into the trunk, on top and unsecured, had been thrown clear of the vehicle during the crash. Possible. Anna turned on the flashlight she'd taken from the glove box and, nose inches from the metal, examined the trunk's lock. With the damage inflicted by the truck's grill it was hard to be sure, but there appeared to be several clean vertical scratches where the trunk might have been pried open after the fact. The Crown Vic spent eighteen hours unsecured outside the Mt. Locust Ranger Station. The place was deserted at night; time and privacy for a bit of car-clouting wouldn't be hard to come by. Anyone listening to the park's frequency would have known that was where the car was being towed. A good little ranger, Anna had called the information in to Tupelo at the time.

Squatting on her heels, she rocked back, staring into the crooked maw of the trunk. Stilwell believed the truck assault was engineered by her poachers. Maybe he wasn't as far off the mark as she'd thought. Who but the illegal hunters would have any interest in stealing the remnants of a butchered deer?

Before meat and bone were taken, Anna'd had only a casual interest in the deer; interest based on nothing but a hunch and a guess. Given the effort to deprive her of said items, her interest heightened.

The venison steak, neatly wrapped in white butcher paper, was gone without a trace. Where the deer's head had rested on the floor there remained a stain—brain effluvia—and what looked to be two bits of flesh and three disappointed maggots.

Using her pocket knife, Anna carefully cut the carpet in a neat square around the area and slipped the carpet, maggots and all, into a paper sack from the evidence collection equipment she'd salvaged.

That done, she loaded up the items she'd chosen to keep and plodded back through the rain to tell the GSA man he could lock up and go home to his supper.

The Crowley homestead was more or less on her way to Rocky Springs. Martin Crowley, she remembered, worked the night shift at Packard. Jerri would be home by herself. Leaving the black and peaceful lanes of the Trace, Anna followed the back roads that would take her by the Crowley place.

Rain turned to mist, mist to fog. White tendrils, putting her in mind of graveyards and Victorian novels, snaked across the road in the low places. Discretion suggested she slow to a crawl but commuters, hurrying home from work, drove like lunatics despite the lack of visibility. She was afraid if she slowed to a safe speed, she'd be rear-ended, and she'd had enough of that sort of action to last a while.

Jerri answered the door at the first knock. Usually when
Anna called on lone women after dark they were relieved
to see it was her, a small member of their own gender and
therefore no threat in the way of bodily harm or fates
worse than death.

The sight of Anna in her diminutive and female aspect
didn't have that calming effect on Mrs. Crowley. Since Anna'd last seen her, their budding friendship had been
nipped.

"Mrs. Crowley?" Anna said, no longer comfortable with
using Jerri's Christian name.

"Ranger Pigeon," Jerri returned formally. "What brings
you here after working hours?"

Since Anna was in uniform, fully armed with a radio
crackling at her belt, Jerri pointedly referred to her own
working hours. Because she was born southern and raised
right, the censure was delivered obliquely with the overlay
of sugar that never quite masks the taste of the medicine.

An invitation to come in out of the rain and the cold was
not forthcoming. Anna decided to force the issue. "Mind if
I come in and sit a while? It's been a long day." She smiled
in her best Catholic school manner and adopted what she
hoped was a harmless appealing look.

"Martin's at work," Jerri said.

Anna said nothing and did her best to look pathetic and
bedraggled. It wasn't a stretch for even a novice actor. Her
adventures at the wrecking yard had left her clothes damp
and rumpled, her hair alternately plastered to her head and
curling rebelliously where it had dried in the air from the
heater.

Southern hospitality triumphed over self-preservation.

"Come on in." Jerri opened the door the rest of the way.
Anna stepped inside thinking that Ted Bundy would have
had a field day in Mississippi.

"Can I get you a cup of coffee?" Jerri asked. Now that
Anna's muddy boots had crossed her threshold, hostess duties kicked in.

Anna accepted and perched on the edge of the well-worn sofa, watching Jerri leave through the kitchen door. At home, no husband or company expected, Jerri still dressed to the teeth. Hair was high, makeup immaculate. In place of skirt and boots she wore tight new Levi's and red high-heeled mules with a scrap of jaunty boa accenting the toes.

The living room was in the same state of total disarray as it had been on Anna's previous visit. The carpet and furniture showed the depredations of kids as well as dogs. Anna wondered where the little beasts were.

Jerri reappeared with a single mug of coffee. She'd remembered Anna liked cream but she wasn't going to drink with her.

"Do you have kids?" Anna asked as she accepted the coffee. People liked to talk about their kids; Anna was striving for common ground.

"Two boys. I told you before," Jerri replied. Her tone sent the message that this was to be business only. To see how firm this stance was, Anna tried again. "Do you have a dog?" She nodded at a chew toy left in front of the fireplace.

"Outside." Jerri didn't sit but leaned her elbows on the back of her husband's Barcalounger. "Killer" she'd called him when she kissed his hair. How apt was the nickname? Anna wondered as she sipped her coffee.

"What can I do you for?" Jerri asked, her southern drawl now made of edges instead of curves.

"Actually I've come to beg a favor," Anna said.

Jerri didn't help by asking what that might be. Drumming porcelain nails silently against the fabric of the chair back, she waited.

Anna wasn't going to charm this woman against her will. Women were harder than men. They saw more, trusted less. Anna decided to get on with it. "That venison steak you gave me the other day was delicious. I've never had venison before." The last part, at least, was true. "I was hoping I could talk you out of another." Asking for food. An almost sacred request. Jerri was proof against it.

"All gone," she said. "Sorry. If Martin ever gets another deer we'll set a couple good cuts aside for you."

"To Catholic Charities in Port Gibson?"

"I don't know where he took it."

"From the grousing I hear hunting's not been all that great this year. When did Martin get lucky?"

"A week or so ago. I don't remember."

"Do you know where he got it? I could pass the information on to guys looking for a good place."

"He belongs to a hunting club."

That killed that line of inquiry. Hunt clubs were private property. The rights to hunt on them were jealously guarded and often expensive.

"Which club?" Anna asked.

"I don't know."

Jerri wasn't going to know anything and her bone-deep sense of hospitality was wearing thin.

Anna decided to leave before she was thrown out.

Jerri didn't stand in the doorway, porch light on, and watch Anna safely to her car, as was the genteel and lovely custom of these environs. She saw Anna as far as the door, probably to make sure she was really leaving, then shut it firmly a nanosecond after Anna's rear end vacated the airspace.

Halfway down the walkway to her car, feeling her way toward the whiter blob in the utter black of a rainy night in the country, Anna heard the unmistakable jingle of tags rattling on a dog's collar underscored by the delicate slurping sound of paws hurrying through flooded grass. Her experiences with Mississippi canines had been as mixed as that with the voting citizens.

Stopping, she eased her Mag-Lite from its leather holder and switched it on. Nothing yet moved within range. Never good to run from creatures born and bred for the chase. Till the dog—if it was a dog and not a collared alligator, raccoon or some other form of Crowley eccentricity—proved itself amiable, Anna took the pepper spray from her belt and waited. The jingle and splash was joined by a noise humans make only when indulging in a particularly sensual yawn, a cross between a whine and groan made in the back of the throat.

This same utterance from a dog invariably offered obsequious friendship and an invitation to play. Thus announcing himself, the animal wagged into the narrow beam of her flash. Putting away the pepper spray, Anna laughed, the unashamed friendliness of the puppy tickling her. It wasn't a big dog and, if behavior was any indication, not more than six or seven months old. The fur was moplike and curly, the eyes round and bright and black.

"Hey, buddy," Anna said, squatting on her heels. "You look like Benji's understudy. Where did you come from?"

Taken to unimaginable heights of ecstasy by the sound of her voice, the little creature wiggled all over, from blunt snout to feathery tail.

"What have you got there?" she asked in a voice only furry creatures ever heard her use. The puppy had a disreputable object in his mouth that he was alternately banging against her leg and dancing away with in an invitation to what, with a puppy, could evolve into an endless and soggy game of fetch.

He wriggled close again, into the circle of the flashlight, and Anna saw what it was: the hoof and anklebone of a deer. A treat Martin had probably saved for him from his most recent kill, a part of which had been stolen from the trunk of the ruined patrol car. The kill that Jerri had refused to give Anna another sample of.

"Come here, come on boy," Anna cajoled. The puppy pranced closer and she grabbed the hoof. There followed an undignified tug-of-war, Anna kneeling in the water on the front walk, the puppy growling happily and digging muddy paws into the brown winter grass.

Being the larger and more determined animal, Anna won. The puppy scampered off into the dark and barked, urging Anna to throw it.

Ignoring his importuning, she examined it under the light of her flash. Bits of hide and fragments of rotting flesh still adhered to the bone. It would suffice.

The puppy woofed again. "Sorry, little fella," Anna apologized. "I need this." Feeling more guilty than a sane person ought to, she carried her ill-gotten gains to the car.

The frustration of this investigation had brought her to new lows. Not only was she harassing women in the night, she was stealing from puppies.

16

Anna finished her day. She didn't follow her usual widowed habit of sitting with her cat on her lap reading a book; she chatted on the phone. Not with her sister. With her boyfriend.

She and Paul had entered into that time, usually sadly foreshortened, where the littles of the other's life are endlessly fascinating. Compassion flowed for the smallest affronts to the lover's safety or mental well-being. Jokes brought laughter even if they weren't funny but simply because they were shared. The phone was clung to, pressed to the ear, not because there was anything more to say but because the connection was too delicious to be broken.

Anna was old enough and cynical enough to step outside herself and see the meaningless babble for what it was. She was happy enough and young enough to watch this reversion to adolescence with a tolerant smile and a certain pride that Zach's death had left enough of her heart behind that she was still capable of it.

Before she went to bed, a touch of healthy paranoia

pushed its way into the euphoria induced by twenty minutes of Paul Davidson whispering in her ear. Walking Taco
through the campground—his constitutional, her duty—
she carried her service weapon in the pocket of her raincoat.

Back at her house she took the hoof she'd wrested from
the puppy's jaw and the evidence bag with its body fluids
and maggots from the trunk of her car and put it in her refrigerator for safe keeping.

Before bed, she locked her doors and windows.

The phone ringing dragged her out of a pleasant dream a
few minutes after midnight. Dislodging Piedmont from
her chest and receiving a claw in the shoulder for her dis-
service, she stumbled for the phone in the hall. All America
had cordless phones and cellulars. The National Park Service, consistently behind the technological curve, had yet
to graduate from a black phone tethered to a wall jack. As
soon as she answered the caller hung up.

Naked, cold and thoroughly awake, she stood in the
dark, Taco, ever helpful, licking the backs of her knees.
The calls, the hanging up, had been going on for several
weeks. Anna'd written it off to the vagaries of late-night di-
alers. The truck incident fresh in mind, she wondered if the
calls were not separate meaningless incidents but a way of
discerning her whereabouts.

Thinking back, she was pretty sure the mystery calls
came on or near the weekends. Tonight was Thursday
night. Anna worked late Sunday and Wednesday. Barth had
night shift Monday and Tuesday. Friday and Saturday had
been claimed by Randy. Thursdays were a hole in the
schedule.

Doyce Barnette had been killed and his body dumped at
Mt. Locust on a Saturday night. Had she received a call
that night? Anna couldn't remember. Was someone calling,
making sure the rangers were snugged up safe in their beds
so they could murder old fat men with impunity? Unlikely.

Poachers? That was closer to the mark. Locals might know Thursday nights were uncovered. They might also know Randy Thigpen worked Fridays and Saturdays and that he could be counted on to be warm and dry in the district office making personal phone calls and reading paperback novels rather than patrolling the roads. Randy had recently moved to Natchez. He wanted to be sheriff, wanted to be a big man around town. It wasn't beyond the realm of possibility that he would turn a blind eye to his future constituents' misdemeanors in the hope of currying favor.

Taco tried his best to get Anna to trip over him while she rechecked the locks. Before she went back to sleep, she put her nine-millimeter on the nightstand.

The following morning two messages awaited her on the office answering machine. Both were from Sheriff Jones. Anna rang him at his office. The dispatcher said he was out but she was to tell Anna when she called that they'd had a break in the hunt for the burgundy pickup. A 1978 Ford matching that description was registered to a Quantus Elfman in Natchez. Clintus and André had driven out to the Elfman farm to question the man.

Anna thanked her and rang off. For a minute or more she considered calling Randy. He wasn't on the schedule till 4 P.M., but she didn't relish him jumping down her throat again because the investigation went on even when he was off duty. In the end she decided not to. Giving in was the coward's way out and, much as she wished it didn't, that rankled more than the scene she could expect from her field ranger.

The next order of business was calling Kate Kendall of the United States Geological Survey, in Glacier/Waterton National Peace Park on the border of Montana and Canada. The previous summer Anna had had the privilege of working with Kate on a groundbreaking DNA project used to identify and study the grizzly bear population in the park.

From Kate she got the information she needed and the address of the lab at the University of Idaho where the DNA samples for animals were analyzed. Kate assured her that the fluids and maggots from the deer skull and the hoof and ankle bone she'd taken from the Crowley's dog should be sufficient for the extraction of samples.

Telling no one what she was doing, Anna packaged the body parts and FedExed them to the lab. Analysis would cost one hundred fourteen dollars. She paid for it out of her own pocket. Though Anna's salary wasn't as high as many thought it should be, she had been able to set quite a bit aside. When one had no life, one had relatively few expenses. If all went well, that could change. Already she was planning a clothes shopping trip to the mall on her next lieu day. One of romance's hidden costs. The lab expenditure had not been cleared with Tupelo, and she would probably have a fight on her hands when she tried to get reimbursed. It was her hope that, when the time came, the evidence would have proved sufficiently useful to make it worth the government's while.

Having left the FedEx office—actually a counter near the pharmacy in the back of Port Gibson Drug and Sundries that provided money orders and faxes, collected gas and water bills and cashed employment checks as well as handling Federal Express packages—Anna turned her car toward Natchez. The storm that crouched over the South was being pushed out by a high-pressure zone from the Northwest. Anna could see a line of blue-black arcing across the sky in a textbook example of an approaching front. Temperatures were dropping fast. According to the weatherman on the radio it would be in the twenties by midnight with a chance of sleet or snow. Anna didn't much like the cold but the prospect of snow was exciting. Since coming to Mississippi, she found she missed waking up in the morning and finding the world miraculously transformed into a clean and glittering place as cold and untouched as her own warped vision of heaven: a wonderful place to visit...

The unsettled weather helped her think. Steve Stilwell linking the assault on her to the poachers, then finding a person or persons had jimmied the smashed trunk and stolen the deer meat and skull, forged the first link in the chain of evidence suggesting the two were connected. If made by the poachers, the attempt on her life by the truck shed a different light on the mad-dog pursuit of her through the woods. It suggested that Randy had been wrong; they weren't good old boys having a little fun. They wanted her dead. Had the chase through the woods been the only incident, Anna would have thought little of it; opportunism, deadly but not sustained, an impulse to the kill requiring little in the way of planning or motive. When linked to the truck battering her car, the woodland chase lost any vestige of a one-time insanity. For two attempts to be made there had to be a motive greater than getting nailed for poaching. Putting the poachers together with the death of Doyce unloosed images she'd filed away as useless: the strange details of the autopsy report, the deer stand so beautifully swept and neatly repaired. One glaring anomaly bothered her: the place and the way the body had been "disposed" of, laid out in a public place with shameful implications underlined by the circling of a religious text pointing toward depths of depravity deeper even than those suggested by the semi-nudity.

At the roadside parallel to the meadow where the deer stand was built, Anna pulled over. Letting the engine idle so she could continue to enjoy the heat, she took the folder with Doyce Barnette's autopsy report from her briefcase and began rereading it.

The connection, tenuous at best, was there. No motive could be discerned, but if Anna uncovered the "how" of the crime, the "who" and "why" should follow, particularly if more than one individual was involved. Honor among thieves was pretty much a myth.

Anna changed shoes, trading her uniform boots for sneakers, took a length of sturdy yellow rope from the trunk and trudged the now familiar route across the meadow. Wind, growing ever colder, found the chinks in her Gore-Tex armor and poked icy fingers under her collar. Still, it was good to be out of doors and on her own. Nature could be benign, dramatic, deadly—any of a seemingly endless array of faces—but all of them were beautiful.

Black with rain, skeletal without their summer dress of leaves, branches raked at the dark sky, beckoning the winds that drove the front. The meadow grasses, too sodden and cold to move, lay in tawny shades, the brown of oak leaves lacing the edges near the woods. The air was not yet cold enough to be odorless, and on the gusting wind, Anna smelled the life sleeping beneath the ground and a faint breath of woodsmoke from where some soul kept the home fires burning.

The deer stand was as bleak and lifeless as the branches overhead. The new wood where the railing had been repaired was rapidly graying to match the rest. There'd been so much precipitation in the last week that for a moment Anna despaired. The minute traces she hoped to find might have been washed away.

Though she'd visited the place recently, the stand was higher than Anna remembered, close to twenty feet from platform to ground, twenty-four from the top of the railing. The old pecan it was built against was such a grand tree it dwarfed things merely human and confused the sense of scale.

Anna dropped the rope and the scurvy World War II knapsack she used to house her field investigation tools. From the sack she took an oversized magnifying glass worthy of Sherlock Holmes that she'd cannibalized from her Oxford English Dictionary set.

Wishing she had more light to work by, she set about examining first the tree and then the bottom of an angled two-by-four attached to the pecan by tenpenny nails driven into the flesh of the living plant to support the platform. The bark and the dead wood of the two-by-four were blackened and swollen from days of rain. Either water had erased the traces she sought or they'd never been there in the first place. After fifteen minutes of hoping and straining her eyes in the strange half-light preceding the storm, she gave up and carried knapsack and rope around to the stairs at the rear of the stand.

Deer stands, like duck blinds, icefishing huts and other structures used only a few weeks each year, received little attention in the way of upkeep and repair. The third step on the narrow stair hung by a nail. Three boards had rotted through on one side of the platform. A four-foot length of warping one-by-twelve had been thrown over them to provide a walkway. The railing on the north and backside of the stand was broken.

Anna gave this a cursory glance. What she was interested in was the thing that didn't fit. "What's wrong with this picture?" she muttered to herself, remembering the puzzles she and Molly had so enjoyed in the children's section of the Sunday paper.

The ill-fitting piece of this rain-soaked puzzle was the new construction on the southeast corner where the deer stand was affixed to the pecan. That portion of railing had been repaired. Two-by-fours nailed in securely, those they replaced taken away. On previous visits, her orderly mind had written it off as general upkeep. She hadn't bothered to question why this love and attention had been lavished only on one sector of the entire structure. Desperate events of the last week finally beginning to interrelate, she saw the repairs in a new and more sinister light.

The girth of the tree was greater than two men could girdle and still touch hands. Anna's plan to anchor one end of the yellow nylon to that particular immovable object was foiled.

The branches overhead were too high to reach. She probably could have thrown the rope over one that looked sturdy enough to hold a person ten times her size, but she was loathe to mark anything she could not examine first.

Accepting what was necessary, she looped the line around two of the uprights supporting the railing on the theory that should one give way the other would hold.

The encumbrance of a gun belt did not fit into her plans, but Anna was hesitant to take it off. In times of stress, guns were terrific tranquilizers. When feeling threatened Anna'd been known to sleep with her personal weapon, an old .357 revolver, literally under her pillow. Some nights a Colt was a better soporific even than a purring cat.

Reluctantly, she pulled the Velcro loose and laid the heavy belt on the platform near the edge. Remembering as she worked—it had been a while since she'd done any technical climbing, Mississippi was not the land of mountaineers—she wove herself an emergency harness from the line, looped the remainder around her middle and climbed gingerly over the waist-high rail.

Twenty feet was a long way when it fell away beneath one's feet. Consoling herself with the thought that the leaf carpet below was so waterlogged if the railing gave way she'd land with a splash rather than a thud, she leaned back. Letting the rope take her weight, she fed line out, lowering herself, one foot seeking purchase on the tangle of lumber haphazardly nailed from tree to platform, the other resting lightly on the bark of the pecan.

Both hands occupied with belaying, she'd been forced to leave her magnifying glass on the platform with her gun.

Nose inches from the tree, she studied each swollen scrap and shingle of bark as she descended an inch at a time. The nylon line cut into the backs of her thighs. Her feet grew cold from a lack of blood, then numb. She was only vaguely aware of the discomfort, her whole attention absorbed in the nicks and swirls in front of her eyes.

About halfway down she found what she was looking for, or thought she did. The scattering of tiny marks was almost obscured by the encroachment of the water. In and of themselves they'd never be used as evidence. They'd grown so faint Anna doubted it would be worth her time to try and photograph them. In another few days they would disappear completely.

Fortunately forensic science had evolved to the point

that things invisible to the naked eye could be used effectively to prove or disprove guilt.

Belaying rope in her teeth, she fished her Swiss Army knife and a plastic Baggie from the breast pocket of her shirt.

"You oughtn't be out here by yourself. You might could get hurt."

The voice, so unexpected, coming from above startled Anna. She squawked and nearly lost her bite on the rope.

Acutely aware of how vulnerable she'd made herself, dangling alone and unarmed on the edge of a deserted wood, her legs too numb to carry her away even if she did reach the ground, adrenaline dumped in her system. It was converted, not into energy, but into liquid fear wreaking unique havoc in her bowels and brain.

Forcing, if not calm then at least deliberation, she tucked the knife and Baggie in her belt and took the belaying rope from between her teeth. Thus freed, she could finally look up. Two great cordovan-shod feet were planted at the edge of the platform five feet above her head. The left, she noted, was on the tail end of her gun belt.

Her eyes traveled rapidly up the green and gray to the face hanging over the rail.

"Hey, Barth," she managed. "You scared the bejesus out of me. Why the hell are you creeping around like some kind of felon on little cat's feet?" Relief had not quite come. Anna replaced it with anger.

"I didn't do nothing on little cat feet," he said, mildly offended. "I came right across the meadow thinking you would hear me coming, then climbed on up the steps. You just weren't paying attention."

That was true. Anna had allowed herself to get tunnel vision, hypnotized by the patterns in the bark and the sweet musty smell of success.

Barth's pervasive normalcy at last brought on the relief. Anger faded. Without it, Anna felt the cut of the ropes, the cold, the numbness.

"What're you doing hanging like that?" Barth asked. "I've been trying to raise you on the radio from Mt. Locust. When you didn't answer I headed up to Port Gibson to see if you were hiding out in the office. I saw your car parked by the road."

"I'm..." Anna thought about what she was doing. Putting it into cohesive sentences, even in her own mind, it sounded far-fetched. "I had an idea. Needed to get some bark samples."

"Why didn't you get 'em from the bottom of the tree?" Barth asked reasonably.

"Just give me a hand, would you?" Anna grumbled.

Barth lay down on the wet platform and reached. By stretching, Anna was able to hand him the rope she used to belay herself. "Hold it till I tell you, then feed it out slowly."

"No problem."

Anna retrieved her knife and Baggie and scraped a half a teaspoon of bark into the plastic. Probably a sample from the bottom of the tree would have been fine. Since she'd had to hang midway to look she might as well take it from the source.

Her return to earth was ignominious. Technical climbing wasn't like riding a bicycle; one did forget. She'd made an error in tying her harness and the ropes had tightened as she put her weight on them. Though Barth lowered her with great care, her legs were so numb they wouldn't hold her and she ended up crumpled in wet leaves massaging her backside for several minutes before they could depart.

During the hour or so since she'd come to the stand, the temperature had continued to drop. On the outer edges of her hearing, Anna could discern the faintest crackle as she moved: leaves, wet with the incessant drizzle, were forming thin sheets of ice.

"You gonna keep up with the secret squirrel stuff or you gonna tell me why you were hanging there like a spider poking at that poor old tree?" Barth said as they recrossed the meadow to where their cars were parked.

"Steve had mentioned . . . I got to thinking about a couple things in the autopsy report and . . ."

"And what?"

Anna wanted to tell him, as a show of good faith if nothing else, but at the moment her ideas were not fully baked and she did not like exposing them to others in their half-baked state. "I got to think it through some more," she said.

Barth grunted.

"Why'd you stop by? Not just to visit, though I'm honored," Anna changed the subject. "You were trying to reach me on the radio?"

"I was down to Mt. Locust. Tupelo ponied my new sign down and I figured it was as good a day as any to get it up."

Barth sounded mature and manly, but Anna knew, where matters of the heart were concerned, few ever truly aged. Barth had come out in the teeth of an encroaching storm on what was arguably the nastiest day Anna'd seen in Mississippi to do hard manual labor—not his favorite discipline—because he just couldn't wait. The professional equivalent of getting up at 5 A.M. Christmas morning or wearing the new dress home from the store. Anna liked him for it. Passion she found admirable, even when it was misplaced, and Barth's wasn't. For a moment she thought of her other field ranger, Randy Thigpen. When she'd first arrived, he and Barth had appeared thick as thieves. As Barth warmed toward her, the friendship between the two men cooled. Neither seemed to miss it. Anna suspected it had been a marriage of convenience. They weren't so much compatible as the only game in town.

Thigpen had no passion for his job, his family, his wife. He even seemed lackadaisical about his mistress, if Anna correctly read the strained calls from a woman who left neither name nor message. Randy wanted things, but he wanted without caring. His lawsuit against her and the federal government, his desire to be part of this investigation, neither because he felt passionately about an unfairness, of capturing the murderer of an apparently harmless man.

With Randy motives were murky, driven more by an internal anger than a need to see the right thing done.

Anna glanced sideways at Barth, liking him better because of the comparison. "So what did you need me for? To make sure the boards on your sign are hung straight?"

"I'd better show you."

"The secret is different when it's on the other squirrel?"

"Something like that."

The short drive to Mt. Locust wasn't enough to thaw out. By the time they reached the slave cemetery, Anna was as cold as if she'd been hanging around the old deer stand. The sky was no longer cut across by the front but dark and threatening from horizon to horizon. A freezing wind whipped what few leaves remained on the trees into frenzied flight.

Anna dug her hands deeper into her pockets, annoyed that Mississippi's usually mild weather had lulled her into a false sense of security. Her good leather gloves were still packed in her grandmother's cedar chest.

The new sign, identical to the old, was up. The names of those identified had been burned into the cypress wood: Jackson, Restin, White, Pittman.

"Looks good," Anna said, wondering what of import Barth had dragged her down here to see.

"Thanks," Barth said. "But that's not what I wanted to show you. Come on." He led the way into the skeletal clutches of the winter woods, talking as he went.

"I'd finished up the sign and was packing my tools when I got to hearing this strange sound. Like muffled chopping. I got curious and poked on back through the trees." He stopped and pointed. Anna stood beside him and dutifully looked where he indicated. "See that blue triangle thing there nailed to the tree? No, past those bushes about six feet up."

Anna saw it. "Those mark the Trace's property line," she said.

"Right. Past here we're on old lady Barnette's land. That's where the noise was coming from." He walked on, Anna trailing him. The storm, early darkness, bony branches raking an inhospitable sky, Anna was getting creepy fantasies of Mama Barnette, cleaver in hand, springing out from behind a tree in the style of Alfred Hitchcock's *Psycho*.

"There." Barth stopped.

Anna stood close to his right side, letting his considerable self block the wind. Three yards in front of them, at the base of a young pin oak, was a neatly made child-sized grave. Dirt had been mounded carefully in the tradition of older burial sites.

"Did you ever turn up a dead or missing child?" Anna asked.

"No. Nothing."

"Did you see the digger?"

"It was Ray Barnette. I'm betting that little coffin you saw him making is at the bottom of that hole."

Anna wouldn't take the bet. "Did you see him?" she repeated.

"He was gone when I got here. But it was him. Who else could it be? The old lady's pretty spry but I doubt she could do this kind of work. We got to get a warrant. Dig it up."

"On what grounds?" Anna asked, genuinely hoping he'd thought of some. "A man has a right to bury things on his own property. Could be a dead cat for all we know."

"It's not a dead cat," Barth said stubbornly.

"We'll talk to him," Anna said.

"He'll lie."

Of course he'd lie unless it really was a dead cat, in which case they wouldn't believe him and in consequence suffer the same frustration.

"We could just dig it up, see for ourselves, and go from there," Barth said.

Anna was sorely tempted, she was guessing it was bones, old bones, but the thought of tainting the evidence and possibly letting a child-murderer—if indeed that's what they had on their hands—go free because of police incompetence kept her honest.

"Can't do that," she said.

"I know."

On the walk back Barth speculated about what was buried at the lonely grave site: an aborted fetus from an indiscretion, a child stillborn to a family too poor to go to a doctor, an illegitimate child born alive only to be dispatched to an unmarked grave, the polished oak casket a sop to conscience. Children were usually reported missing eventually. Infants were another story. If the mom said it was born dead, who'd argue?

"I'm thinking it's not a kid, Barth."

Barth wasn't reassured. "When'll we talk to Mr. Barnette?" he pressed. The forlorn little grave was weighing on his mind.

Anna looked at her watch. It was a few minutes after noon. The time surprised her. So dark had the day grown, it felt closer to sunset. "Have you had lunch?" she asked. He hadn't. "I need to stop in at the ranger station for a minute and make a call. We can get something to eat, then track down our undertaker."

"Are you going to ask him straight out what he buried back there?"

Anna noted the pronoun "we" had been replaced with "you." Being the boss had its moments, but not many of them. Part of her yearned to apply for one of the coveted backcountry positions in Rocky Mountains, Big Bend or Glacier. Jobs where the ranger lived alone in a primitive cabin much of the time, monitoring the health and well-being of the wild places. A backcountry job would entail a demotion and a cut in pay. Money and status in government work was directly related to how many other people one managed. Managing mule deer and chipmunks didn't count.

Then there was Paul.

Since the advent of the southern sheriff, being alone had begun to feel lonely. Anna was troubled by that. Alone had been comforting for a long time. She'd come to rely on it. In a very real way love, or whatever it was she felt for Paul Davidson, was eroding that one safe place.

"Well, are you going to ask?"

They'd arrived at the Mt. Locust office. Anna stood in the doorway. She'd been so lost in thought she'd traveled the last fifty yards like a sleepwalker. It took her a second to remember what they'd been talking about.

"That would be my first instinct," she said. "'Hey, we saw you burying that kid's coffin. What was in it?' But with Raymond I don't know. He's a cold fish and he's arrogant. It might be better to come at the thing obliquely. Give it some thought while I make my call."

Barth closed the door and leaned against it, determined to make this a short stop.

Anna called the medical examiner's office in Ridgeland. The ME had gone to lunch. His secretary, brown-bagging it at her desk, obligingly took the message and read it back to Anna: "Ranger Pigeon says to run a nitrate test on Doyce Barnette's hands."

"That's it," Anna said, then to Barth, "You drive."

"Why're you having them run the hands for traces of powder?" Barth asked. "He was not only unarmed, the poor guy was undressed."

"He wasn't killed at Mt. Locust, just dumped there. We don't know about earlier. Maybe he was armed and dressed, the stripping done after the murder to remove clues or suggest exactly what it suggested: sexual high jinks leading to a well-deserved end."

"He may have been dressed but if he was armed why is he dead? The coroner said he suffocated. Self-defense? The victim tries to shoot somebody and they suffocate him to save themselves?"

The edgy tone and harsh words were so out of character for Barth that Anna was taken aback. As he buckled himself in, she watched him covertly. Strain showed around his eyes and in the tense crimp of the well-shaped lips.

Now she knew two things about Ranger Dinkins. He

was passionate about the history and dignity of African-Americans and he was passionate about children.

Maybe that was why Anna admired people with passion. A person's passion told a lot about who they were. Those without passions seemed to have a hollow place inside. One never knew what grew in that darkness.

17

Anna was glad to be free of the ranger station. The office, seldom used, was cold and smelled of dust and stale cigarette smoke. "Any bright ideas?" she asked as they drove out. "I visited Raymond yesterday. Me showing up again without a plausible excuse is going to put him on his guard. If he isn't already."

Barth said nothing. Both thought for a while. Cold sapped Anna's energy. Heat now would be worse; it would make a nap inevitable.

"I saw some pictures in Barnette's office at the funeral home," she said at last. "Old photos. Barnette's was a cabinet-making shop before it evolved into a mortuary. Didn't you say something once about cabinetmakers banging together cheap coffins for the slaves of the outlying plantations? We could ask him if he has any records that could help with the history of your slave cemetery."

"Our slave cemetery."

"Right."

"A while back I tried to talk to old Mrs. Barnette. Being

as her property abuts there at Mt. Locust, I thought there might be at least old family stories or some such. She wasn't what you'd call forthcoming."

Anna laughed at the big man's delicacy. "She met Sheriff Jones and me at the front door with a double-barreled shotgun because she thought Clintus was you. Unless he took off right after he buried whatever, our boy Raymond is still at home with Mama. If we want to talk to him that's where we've got to go."

Barth looked torn. From previous experience, Anna knew he did not choose to meet hatred with hatred when faced with white racists. Perhaps his anger went so deep he was afraid to let it out for fear of what he would do. He didn't talk about it either. Like many abuse victims, he carried the shame of the abuser, taking their malfeasance as an indication of personal worthlessness.

"I'll be with you," Anna said, keeping any trace of offensive sympathy or understanding from her voice. "I'll be Melanie to your Scarlett."

Barth laughed at that and his face was transformed. Fleetingly Anna was saddened at the many walls of culture and society that would always stand between them, shutting them away from any true friendship.

"Now there's a picture," he said. "The Old South will be spinning in her grave."

"I hear if you put a knife under de bed it cuts da pain," Anna said, mimicking the actress who brought Prissy to life in the film version of *Gone With the Wind*. The instant the words were out of her mouth, she froze inside waiting for the iron doors to slam shut behind Barth's remarkable eyes at her aping Hollywood version of black speech. A second fear, that angered her even as she dismissed it, bolted through her innards. In the current cultural climate she could be brought up on civil charges for racial slurs in the workplace. Yet another of the many walls barring them from connection.

Barth laughed again. She'd underestimated the man.

"We've got nothing to lose," he said.

"Except the skin the buckshot blows off."

The Barnette home looked particularly grim in the blowing rain. Without the golden fall sunshine to ameliorate the depredations of age and neglect, it took on the aspect of the classic haunted house: dark, forbidding, shutters loose, paint peeling.

Raymond's black Cadillac, no longer shiny but splattered with rain and mud, was parked in the gravel drive. His was the only vehicle there. That had been the case on her earlier visit as well. Mama Barnette was old enough; chances were good she no longer drove. But where was Doyce's automobile? Given the plethora of hunting accoutrements in his room it was plausible he owned a pickup truck. An old burgundy with a cowcatcher welded to the front bumper was not beyond the realm of possibility.

Could Raymond have been behind the wheel the night Anna's Crown Vic was totaled? Why? She'd not yet seen the tiny coffin. Had he killed his brother and believed, erroneously, that she was getting close? But why put the body, stripped to its underpants, in an historic inn? Doyce's unseemly appearance at Mt. Locust had effectively ended Raymond's chances of getting elected sheriff of Adams County.

Anna unzipped her Gore-Tex parka so she'd have easier access to the gun at her hip.

Barth twisted the handle of the antique mechanical doorbell and its tinny bicycle-bell ring jinkled behind the heavy door.

Enough time passed that Anna grew certain there would be no answer. Little doubt existed that both mother and son were on the property.

"Could be Raymond's still out poking around the woods." Barth offered. "The old lady mighn't always hear a doorbell anymore up there in her rooms to the back."

Anna looked out from under the rain-blackened eaves protecting the porch. Needle-sharp teeth of ice were forming where the water dripped from the roof. In imperfect sheets, it had begun coating the windshields of the cars.

"Raymond's a pansy," Anna said apropos of nothing but a gut feeling. "He's not going to stay out in this any longer than he has to. Ring again."

Barth gave the butterfly-shaped brass a vicious twist and produced another short spate of jangling within. A minute or more elapsed. Time was said to be relative and nowhere was that more true than when waiting on a doorstep.

At length footsteps were heard crossing the hardwood floor and the door was pulled open. Days of rain had swelled the wood, and it screeched as it pulled loose from the frame. Anna started at the noise but managed not to screech herself.

Her nerves, she realized, were stretched a little thin what with the weather and the attempts on her life.

Raymond materialized in the black gash created by the open door. He was dapper as ever in gray gabardine trousers and a long-sleeved blue-and-white pinstriped shirt. Damp hair and wet loafers, mud streaked across the left toe, missed when the shoes were wiped clean, were the only indications he'd recently been wielding a shovel in the dank and lonely wood. Well, that and his smile.

Most of his teeth showed, the incisors as square and white as Chiclets. Either Anna's imagination was as inflamed as her nerves or his eyeteeth actually were longer and pointier than the average member of the living community.

Despite its sinister appearance, the smile seemed real, downright festive and celebratory. Anna wondered what it was he'd buried that had so freed his spirit. He was a man with a weight off his shoulders.

"Come in, come in," he urged them expansively. "Not even good weather for ducks. The roads will be one big sheet of ice by tonight. A lot of car accidents, no doubt about that."

Barth drew himself up in haughty disapproval, but Anna didn't begrudge the undertaker counting his chickens before they died. She'd done it herself a time or two when search-and-rescue work was slow and she needed the overtime. Nothing personal, but people who enjoy their jobs like opportunities to work.

"Mama's got tea upstairs. I brought over Claudia—she does for Mama. Mostly keeps her company. Let's see if she'll brew up a couple more cups."

Anna wanted a cup of hot tea and, after the welcome she'd received the first time she'd come calling, was pleased to be let in so graciously.

Barth Dinkins was not so easily won over. He followed Anna up the stairway. When it doubled back on the landing, illuminated on better days by the stained-glass window above the painting of the last supper, he walked like a man who suspects ambush. Should they be so fortunate as to receive the promised tea, she doubted Barth would drink his.

"Mama, we got company," Raymond called as he reached the top of the stairs. Had the tones not been so habitually funereal, Anna might have said he called gaily. The Barnettes were a strange family. "Claudia, put the kettle on," he followed up.

Anna followed him into his mother's over-stuffed and over-heated sitting room. A fire burned in the grate and a radiator murmured and hissed in the corner. Mrs. Barnette, looking tiny, ancient and not nearly as glad to see them as her son, sat in the rocker by the hearth, a hand-knit shawl over her shoulders, her feet in fluffy pink slippers so worn the fake fur was matted and mangy. The room was ninety degrees or better. To Anna if felt grand, like the first blissful submersion into a hot tub. Without waiting for an invitation to take off her coat and stay awhile, she shrugged out of the saturated Gore-Tex to better enjoy the heat.

"Claudia, take Ranger Pigeon's coat," Raymond said. A plump middle-aged black woman wearing a hot pink running suit and tennis shoes had entered from the second room of however many rooms Mrs. Barnette's "suite" comprised.

Claudia patted the old woman's shoulder reassuringly as she passed and smiled at Anna. "It's gonna be a cold one

tonight. This go in the dryer? I'll see if I can't at least warm
it up some."

Anna didn't know what a dryer would do to Gore-Tex
but, since it had failed to keep her dry, she didn't much
care.

Claudia offered the same service to Barth but he refused,
preferring discomfort to accepting what he clearly viewed
as tainted hospitality. Claudia shrugged round pink shoulders, gave Anna a wry grin that women of all races use to
communicate a shared amusement regarding the stronger
sex and left the room.

Raymond went to his mother and leaning over her chair
said loudly. "Mama, this is Ranger Pigeon and Barth
Dinkins."

Anna couldn't help but notice the undertaker failed to
give Barth his title. Undoubtedly Barth noticed as well.
Anna chose not to look at him to find out. Slight or over-
sight? Barth had had half a lifetime to become paranoid
over that decision.

"They've come to pay you a call," Raymond finished.

"I know who they are," Mama snapped. "Stop your hol-
lering and hovering."

Looking like he wanted to strangle the old woman and
smiling idiotically in an attempt to disguise it, Raymond
did as he was told.

"Sit. Sit," he said, again the generous host. Having
scanned the crowded room and not seen the shotgun, Anna
accepted the invitation, choosing a tatty glider that was,
despite appearances, incredibly comfortable. Barth remained at his post inside the door, sweltering in his coat.

Company arranged, Raymond folded down till his immaculate butt settled on a low footstool, the once ornate
embroidery worn and colorless from decades of use.
"Now, what brings you two out on a day like this?"

The winter grave, purposefully lost in the woods, was a
complicated issue so Anna started with the question foremost in her mind. Forgetting the southern tradition of start-

ing with the niceties, she said, "Did your brother Doyce have a vehicle?"

Whatever questions Barnette had been preparing for, this was not among them. For an instant he was nonplussed. "Vehicle?" he said as if the word were foreign to him.

"Car, truck, motorcycle, John Deere," Anna said to jog his brain.

"What does she want?" his mother demanded shrilly.

"She wants to know what kind of car Doyce had," Raymond said loudly.

"I'm not deaf," the woman snarled.

Raymond gritted his big teeth.

"A truck. Doycie had a truck," Mama Barnette said. "What else would he have? Damn fool."

Anna wasn't certain whether the last referred to her, Raymond or the deceased. Probably all three. The woman's malice was apparently universal in nature.

"What kind of truck?" Anna asked Raymond.

"Why . . . a Chevy I think, older model. It wasn't worth anything." If he harbored any maniacal memories regarding his brother's pickup, he was disguising them brilliantly. Anna pressed on, adhering to the theory of leaving no stone unturned. One never knew what might crawl out from under the most innocent-looking rock.

"Where is it?"

Her tone, harsh because she was tired and because the Barnettes and their creepy house made her uneasy, was wearing away Raymond's good cheer.

"Why?" he demanded. "It's at my place. I used it to haul wood. That's not illegal far as I know."

Realizing she'd alienated him to no purpose, Anna schooled herself to be nice. "No. No. Nothing like that. Sorry if I sounded officious. Occupational hazard." She smiled at him and he smiled back. An image of hostile dogs baring their fangs at one another filtered through Anna's mind. "We just need to know where it was the morning after your brother was killed."

"Here," Barnette said promptly.

"I didn't notice it when we came to tell Mrs. Barnette of the ... incident." Anna was being delicate in the face of the deceased's mother, more out of habit than necessity, she suspected. Mama Barnette, crouched in her chair, eyes sharp, turning her head this way and that, trying to make her failing ears catch every word, seemed more a preying falcon than a grieving mom.

"Doyce kept it parked out back. Mostly we come and go through the kitchen. Nobody much uses the front door except strangers. I came and got it that night, and seeing as Doyce wasn't going to be needing it ..."

Raymond must have realized he was sounding callous. He stopped talking altogether and for a half minute—a long silence in a small room choked with heat and people—the only sound was the pop of the fire and the hiss of the radiator.

Claudia plowed into the awkwardness with a tray of cups and a pot of tea, bringing normalcy with her in a welcome cloud.

When the clattering and sugaring had been accomplished, Anna asked, "Is the truck at your place?"

"Yeah. There in the drive."

Anna and Barth would check it out but she doubted it was the truck they were seeking.

"Why the interest in Doyce's truck?"

Anna's brain shifted gears effortlessly. Even if the truck had not been used in an attempted murder, it was of interest.

"If Doyce didn't drive himself the night he was killed, then somebody must have come by here and picked him up. Mrs. Barnette, did you hear or see anyone come to the house that night?" Anna pitched her voice louder but kept the tone conversational. It was the voice she used with people who were hard of hearing but who grew angry if anyone else noticed it.

"I keep to myself," the woman said. "What Doyce did was his business."

"Mama's apartments being at the back of the house like

they are, she can't much see or hear folks coming to the front," Raymond explained.

"I see and hear just fine," his mother reproved him. "Doyce parks right out back, there," she pointed a bent and knobby forefinger at a heavily draped window opposite where Anna sat. "I'd of heard if he drove in or out and he did no such thing."

"Did anybody else drive in or out?" Anna asked.

"If they did they didn't come to the back. Everybody who knows us, everybody welcome in our house, knows to come to the back."

Anna had been put in her place and acknowledged it with a nod. The information wasn't without value. If Doyce had not taken his truck and his killer or killers had come to the front of the house to fetch him they were, by Mrs. Barnette's definition, not friends. Yet he knew them and trusted them enough to leave the house and go with them.

"That's helpful, Mrs. Barnette. Thank you."

Barth cleared his throat. Anna's interest in the smashing of the car that she wasn't in was well and good, but he wanted her to move on. Barnette air was not healthy for a black man. Anna didn't wonder why he didn't speak for himself. Barth Dinkins as a man was interested in the treatment of African-Americans, socially, politically, historically. Barth Dinkins as a law-enforcement ranger was interested in results. Anna guessed Raymond might not be as racist as his mother, but the only way a black man would get a satisfactory response out of either of them would be with a baseball bat and maybe not then.

They'd agreed to come at Barnette obliquely regarding the little grave. Anna sipped the excellent tea as she thought about that.

Old people like to talk about the past. Why this was so, she wasn't old enough to understand, only that it was. "Mrs. Barnette," she began. "Raymond was showing me a picture of one of your ancestors. Papa Doyce. The photo was taken in eighteen sixty-one if I remember right. Eighteen sixty-one?" she looked to the undertaker for confirmation of this unimportant detail simply to include him in the conversation. After all, he was the one the chitchat was designed to lull into a false sense of security.

In that she'd failed utterly, though she couldn't imagine why. He was still perched on the low footstool, his teacup and saucer balanced on knobby knees, but the unexpected bonhomie with which he had ushered them in vanished. Fear replaced it, not of Anna but of his diminutive mother.

Mrs. Barnette's sporadic deafness had not saved him. She'd heard every word Anna'd said and was not pleased.

"I didn't show her the picture, Mama. She went into my office when I was in the shop." Raymond's defense was that of a frightened schoolboy.

Mama Barnette stood up, leaning on the arm of her rocker, glaring at her younger son. Her free arm was raised, arthritis making a claw of the hand. Anna watched in fascination, wondering if she was going to strike Raymond.

The hand lowered harmlessly, and she settled her frail bones back into the cushions of her chair. Plucking the shawl she'd dislodged back into place, she muttered what sounded like "no more brains than a coon."

Since the paternity of the Barnette line was not Anna's eventual goal, she shifted the conversation away from Papa Doyce. "Actually, what I was most interested in," she said brightly as if the bizarre vignette of family dysfunction had not transpired, "was the other fella. In that old photograph there were two men. Papa—your ancestor—and a colored man." Anna hoped Barth would forgive her the now politically incorrect term. She used it intentionally to soothe the old woman. African-American undoubtedly struck her as impossibly uppity. Like Barth, Anna wanted results.

Mother and son glared at her with fixed expressions. Anna was getting the same vibes she'd gotten when she did a night rotation in the psych ward for her emergency medical technician's certification. "Keep an eye on Kenny," a nurse had warned as she went off duty. "When his eyes stop moving and he just sits, he's usually getting ready to have a psychotic break." Kenny was straitjacketed and in a padded cell by 4 A.M. Anna had a loose tooth and the beefy orderly who'd finally been able to restrain him had a savage-looking black eye.

"The colored man in the picture; his name was Unk. Unk something." The brightness of Anna's tone was tarnishing rapidly and she faltered to a stop. "Unk's an odd name," she said just to say something.

"Short for 'uncle'" Barth volunteered.

"Ah," Anna said, "Restin. That was it, Unk Restin. Anyway Ranger Dinkins here has been doing historical research on—"

Mrs. Barnette came out of her chair a second time, the deep well of anger in her overflowing—erupting. The soft mouth, rubbery without dentures, pulled back, exposing bluish gums. Flecks of spittle glistened at the corners.

"Get out. You get out." Mrs. Barnette hissed rather than shouted, vocal cords and lungs papery with age. "Bringing niggers, comin' into my house. You're a disgrace."

Anna had risen but not yet moved. The woman, so small and wrinkled, hair thinning over a baby-pink scalp, struck her as the alpha and omega of human evil; the crone and the babe united in hatred. Like the apocryphal mouse with the cobra, Anna was mesmerized and couldn't make her escape.

Mrs. Barnette tottered forward, the mangy pink slippers shuffling across the carpet like newly resurrected creatures from a B horror movie. "Out. Out." The spit at the corners of her mouth speckled the air with each explosive utterance.

"Take it easy." Anna raised her hands to calm and, if need be, defend. "No offense meant. Thanks for the tea." She backed away until she was stopped by the solid bulk of her field ranger standing in the doorway. "Barth, we'd better be going." From behind her came a grunt of what she assumed was assent, and the reassuring wall of flesh at her back moved away.

Mama Barnette stopped advancing. Shaking with the

burden of her years and her rage, she glared at them, the flames of the open fireplace painting a rosy hell behind her.

"Sorry to have upset you," Anna said, then turned and followed Barth, already halfway down the stairs. When she left, Raymond was still sitting, knees as high as his elbows, on the footstool, cup and saucer in hand. Perhaps the Barnette men chose to deal with the dead because, as children, the living they'd known were too difficult to have relationships with.

Cold struck Anna the moment she escaped out onto the porch. Drizzle had turned to sleet and was icing everything on which it fell. After the over-heated, rebreathed air of the upstairs room it felt grand, but too long out and it would chill to the bone.

"You were wise to hang on to your coat," Anna said.

"Instinct," Barth said. For a second Anna thought he was going to offer her his jacket but professionalism overcame southern gallantry and he didn't.

"Jesus, that woman. Why didn't the slaves rise up and do some real damage?"

Barth chose to answer her question seriously. "I've thought about that. Slaves weren't a people. We were from different tribes, different parts of Africa. No common language. No common history. And each plantation was its own little world. The owner the dictator. Slaves couldn't communicate with each other. Revolution has got to have either leaders and communication or a whole bunch of mad people all together, like a mob. American slaves had none of that." He said nothing for a minute, then added, "Just me thinking. No big scholarly study or anything."

"Works for me. Let's get out of here."

"You want to go back and get your coat?"

"I'd rather die of pneumonia."

"Ranger Pigeon." The call stopped Anna just as she was about to duck into the sane space of Barth's patrol vehicle. Claudia trotted out from the shelter of the front porch, exposing her pink sweat suit and unprotected head to the inclement weather. Rolled tight under her arm, safe and dry, was Anna's rain jacket.

"Your wrap," Claudia said and handed the garment over.

"Why didn't you put it over your head, for heaven's sake?" Anna laughed.

"I didn't want it getting all nasty in case you might could be having to sit in it for a while."

"Hop in," Anna said on impulse. "I'd like to ask you a couple questions if I may."

Claudia glanced back at the house, then over to Barth who, either because of good breeding or good training, chose not to get into the car until Anna did. Good backup was tough to provide from a sitting position.

Anna couldn't tell if Claudia was concerned about her employer or didn't want anything to do with law enforcement. In Mississippi, as in the rest of the country, cops whether in green and gray or blue were not the first people to whom an African-American would turn in times of trouble or reach a hand out to help when asked to assist in an investigation.

"Please," Anna said. Barth's car was equipped with a cage, a dense wire screen separating the backseat from the front to both incarcerate criminals and protect the arresting officer. Anna closed her own door and opened the rear door. She slid in first to show Claudia it wasn't a trap. "Come on," she said. "You're getting soaked."

Claudia hesitated a moment and Anna thought they'd lost her. A decision was made and the woman bundled herself in beside Anna. In a nervous reflex, when she heard the door latch, she reached for the handle.

"They're disabled," Anna explained. "But I think we can trust Barth to let us out when we're ready." She smiled reassuringly and Claudia settled. "Thanks for bringing me my coat. I didn't have the nerve to go back for it."

Claudia laughed at the admission of cowardice. "I heard. When that old woman gets the wind up, she's a holy terror."

"Do you know what set her off?"

"The Missus has a big old well of nastiness. She's been some worse just lately. A few days back when I come over she'd wore herself out somehow. Clothes were muddy, she was all over scrapes and her old hands was so sore she couldn't hardly lift a cup. She'd been rampaging but wouldn't say as to what. Since, she's been just hardly fit to live with. When she gets on a tear, it could be most anything. Her main most hatefulness gets let out when she gets on the subject of blacks—" she shot an apologetic glance toward Barth. His face was impassive, unreadable. "African-Americans," she corrected herself. Claudia was older than she looked. Closer to fifty than the mid-thirties where Anna had pegged her on first meeting.

"She's just about scared to death with all this talk the government's been doing about reparations. Seems ya'll are going to come smashing in with jack boots and parcel out her things to the black folk. Everybody knows it's just politicians talking. Nobody's going to do anything."

Anna couldn't argue that. She changed the subject. "Have you been here all day?"

"I come in around nine most days and leave after I get the old lady's supper around six. Today I was running late. I been here since twenty-three minutes after. She's got nothing better to do than watch that clock over her door. Days she needs to bark at somebody, I think she sets it ahead on purpose so's she can fuss about me being late."

Anna wouldn't have put any wicked pettiness past Mama Barnette. "Were you here when Raymond came over?"

"Yes, ma'am. Mr. Barnette came in after eleven. I heard him rattling around downstairs and Miz Barnette sent me down to fetch him but he'd gone out again, didn't come back for near an hour."

"Did you see where he went?"

"He was walking out to the shed behind the house. I waited on him, thinking he was coming right back. He went in and come out with a shovel, then he takes off toward the woods."

"Was he carrying anything besides the shovel?" Anna asked.

"He had a big old box under his arm. Must've been pretty heavy. He kept hitching it up on his hip like."

"Did he have the box when he came back?"

"I wouldn't know that. I was back upstairs tending to Mrs. Barnette and didn't know he'd got back till he come upstairs."

Anna's eyes met Barth's. They'd learned nothing new but the confirmation was useful. Raymond had indeed buried something, probably a child's coffin, in the woods.

"Does Mrs. Barnette—or Doyce—have any pets. Cat? Dog? Anything like that?" Anna asked.

"Not since I've known her, which is twelve years now. She doesn't hold with animals in the house. Says she wasn't raised to live with livestock."

"Does Raymond keep pets at his house, do you know?"

"No, ma'am. I do for him every other Thursday. He's not even got fish in a tank."

Not a dead pet theory; Anna figured that but needed to cover all the bases.

"We were talking about an old picture. Real old, eighteen hundreds," Barth joined the conversation. "I've never seen it but Anna says it was of the ancestor that started the business, a Papa Doyce. There was an African-American man beside him in the picture named Unk Restin. That's what we were talking about when Mrs. Barnette got riled up. You know anything about that? Seen any pictures around the house or anything?"

"No," Claudia said. "There's no pictures of colored folk anywhere . . . wait there . . ." She pushed her thoughts back a few years. "We—Mrs. Barnette and me—were cleaning out the closet in the spare bedroom a while back. There was boxes of old pictures just thrown together loose. She showed me a picture then. There was this black man working beside another man on a wood thing, maybe a table or something they were building. Miss Barnette showed it to me and said, 'My husband's daddy was taught to call him uncle. Just makes me want to spit. A nigger uncle, can you beat that? And him as greedy and uppity as they come.' She tore up that picture, then had me throw the whole lot into the incinerator out back." She looked at Barth, then at Anna, for approval. "That was all," she said. "Might not even have been the same man as you're talking about."

18

On the drive back to Mt. Locust Ranger Station to get Anna's car, she and Barth chewed over the eventful tea party. Barth drove, his square, clean hands neatly in the ten and two positions on the steering wheel. Anna talked. "Papa Doyce and Unk Restin have something to do with the gigantic chip Mama Barnette carries on her shoulder. Papa Doyce, white. 'Uncle' Restin, black. They inspired or triggered the old bat's racism."

"Maybe she comes from African-American stock. If she is a descendent of the Unk Restin in the picture she'd be what? An octoroon if everybody married white on white from then on," Barth said. "Maybe Mrs. Barnette's spent her life 'passing' and thinks we're going to find out."

"Who'd care? Ancient history."

Barth looked at her from the corners of his pale eyes. In the shadowless light of the winter afternoon they were more gray than green and as transparent as water.

"What?" Anna asked when he just smiled and shook his head.

"Everybody'd care. You still got your head in Yankee sand if you don't know that yet. Down here—shoot, clear throughout most of the South: Georgia, Alabama, South Carolina—being of mixed blood's not exotic. Black mixed with white, now that's nothing. You get one Nigerian, one purely African man down here at seminary school or something and you can see there's not a drop of pure African blood in Mississippi. That Nigerian'll be black like a radial tire is black. Around that man we're just a rainbow in browns. Black mixed with white's a fact of life, an *improvement*." The word was sour in his mouth. "Even with us. Look at our heroes. They look like white folks in bad wigs. Only the sports stars look black and a lot of those guys get admired for being strong or mean." Bitterness got the best of Barth on the last word, and he took a short break to regain the control he used to survive in government service, in law enforcement. When he spoke again he'd leached so much emotion from his words he sounded like a scholar on the lecture circuit.

"What's no way acceptable is white mixed with black. A chemist wouldn't admit any difference but Miss Barnette's lady friends would. She'd no longer be okay, nobody'd be afraid of her anymore. She could still have friends—white friends—but not with anybody she'd want to be friends with.

"Ancient history just happened this morning for a lot of these old folks," Barth finished. He pressed his lips tightly together. "Sorry," he said.

"No. No. You're right." The apology made an awkwardness between them. Anna wondered if he was embarrassed because he'd shown his feelings, because hers might not be the same, or because he was annoyed at himself for wasting energy and air on something he could not change.

"See if you can't trace this Unk Restin. If he was a worker when Barnette's was a carpentry or cabinet-making shop there may be labor bills submitted for his work—"

A thought occured to Anna. She'd had it before but it

had been lost in a pile of higher priorities. "See if he might be linked to Lonnie and his family."

"I already talked to Lonnie Restin's ma," Barth said. "They can't trace themselves back more than a couple generations. Trouble is lots of times every slave on a plantation went and took the master's name. Then you get a passel of unrelated folks, black and white, with the same last name."

"Do what you can," Anna said.

"I will," Barth said. "There'll be something: birth, death, sale. If he could read or write he may've signed chits for supplies."

Anna shut up. Barth knew more about tracking individuals through time than she did.

"Barnette's was a cabinetmaker's. They might have old records of building slave coffins. Doggone it." Barth twisted his hands on the wheel, wringing the metaphorical neck of an evil thought. "I wish Raymond Barnette wasn't sneaking around in the trees burying little kids' coffins. It'd be a whole lot easier if he'd cooperate on this thing."

"You don't think the one could have anything to do with the other?" Anna asked. Barth's ramblings had shifted pieces of information around in her brain. The pieces weren't exactly falling together, but several of them were beginning to align.

"You mean the kid's coffin and the slave cemetery? I don't see how."

"Raymond Barnette inherits land that butts up against the Trace. There's a cemetery on the Trace. Raymond Barnette is an undertaker. A grave is robbed. He builds a little coffin and buries it. There ought to be a through line there somewhere."

"What is it?" Barth said with the open excitement of a child awaiting a fabulous secret.

Anna had to disappoint him. "Beats me. I was hoping you'd be able to see a pattern. Undertakers, grave robbers, coffin builders, grave diggers. Not a lot of people doing that sort of work these days."

"You going to add murderer to that list? Within a hundred yards of the slave cemetery the suffocated brother of your undertaker–coffin builder gets plopped down in the bed of the lady who owned the slaves buried out back," Barth said.

Anna's list of potentially related incidents hadn't yet encompassed homicide, but Barth was right. Like everybody else in Mississippi: old dead, recent dead and could-be dead were probably blood relations or at least knew one another.

"Raymond stood to inherit that property if his big brother was out of the way," Barth said.

"There's that," Anna said. "Is the property worth anything?"

"Three hundred acres, some of it good farmland. Might be worth three, four hundred grand. There's oil in these parts. He might could think the land's worth drilling."

Oil wells. That upped the ante. Most of the oil wells in the Natchez area were tapped out. The wells that still produced weren't making any Texas-style millionaires.

"Oil or not, that land's big with Mama Barnette. Maybe Doyce was going to sell it or some such and she got his little brother to do away with him. Raymond looks to be about scared to death of his ma."

"She could just change her will," Anna said. "Leave the place to Raymond. That'd be easier than murder, surely."

"Maybe she just wanted him out of the house. Fifty and still at home. Maybe it was getting on her nerves."

Anna laughed. "If Raymond did it, even at his mother's instigation, why strip the body and put it in a public place? Raymond knew right off any whiff of sexual deviation would kill his shot at being a sheriff. He seemed genuinely mad when it was leaked to the papers."

Barth had no answer to that.

They'd exhausted speculation and rode the rest of the way back to Mt. Locust in companionable silence.

* * *

Sleet turned back to rain, then to drizzle and finally resolved itself in a fine mist that hovered like gray gauze
between the observer and the observed. The denuded trees
with their blackened trunks and branches could have been
the inspiration for T. S. Eliot's last dingdong of doom.

Nothing but paperwork awaited at the ranger station.
Enough remained of the day that Anna decided to hand
carry her bark samples to the lab in Jackson and see what,
if any, information could be gleaned from them.

At the forensic lab she completed the necessary forms and
pushed them and her Baggie of bark scrapings across the
counter. The business day was coming to a close. She'd
hoped to stop by the medical examiner's office in Ridgeland,
but by the time she'd get there they'd be closed. She borrowed an office phone and called. The ME had left for the
day. His assistant checked the files. The tests for gunpowder
residue had been run on Doyce Barnette's hands. There were
indications he had fired a gun shortly before death.

On a whim, she headed up Interstate Fifty-five to drop in
on Steve Stilwell. After the surreal life she'd been living,
murderous trucks by night and raging old ladies by day, his
particular brand of insouciance struck her as the perfect
grounding to a saner world.

The Ridgeland Ranger Station, a few cramped rooms in
a long, low building that formed one side of a gravel yard,
was as crowded and dingy as that in Port Gibson. Two
desks filled the tiny front room. Four more were squashed
into the room behind. Walls, desktops and the few bookcases were cluttered with papers and other debris. It was
Anna's contention that future archaeologists would be able
to unearth the history of the National Park Service in microcosm via digging through a single ranger's office.

A handsome young ranger named King informed Anna
that Steve had gone off duty. She'd missed him by a half an
hour. "Try his quarters," King suggested.

The Ridgeland ranger's quarters were behind the ranger station in a wooded lot. Rangers planning on homesteading—staying in one park and, very possibly, one job—for a majority of their careers, bought real houses and lived like real people. Those like Anna and Steve, just passing through in order to take advantage of promotions, rented government housing.

Steve lived in a low, cheaply built, ranch-style house, new in the 1960s. Too many tenants and too little care had rendered it sad and shabby. In the mist and the dying light, it looked downright depressing.

Anna parked in the short drive behind Stilwell's patrol car. Her approach to the house was heralded by a frenzy of deep-throated barks and the ominous sound of a large maddened beast hurling itself against the door of the screened-in porch.

Rutger, an eighty-five pound German shepherd, was a failed experiment. Stilwell had purchased the puppy with great plans to train it in search and rescue with a minor in drug sniffing.

Either from neglect or inclination, Rutger had grown into a great hulking lump of pure orneriness, willing to bite all comers. Eventually Steve would have to get rid of him. Till then the dog lived the life of a convicted felon. On fine days he was tied to a run in the backyard. In inclement weather he was incarcerated on the back porch. From the crashing of dog flesh against wood, Anna doubted it would hold him much longer without structural reinforcement.

Despite the racket, Steve didn't come to the door. Anna knocked loudly, setting off another round of furious canine assaults from the porch at the side of the house. At Anna's second knock, Steve finally opened the door.

"Hey," he said cheerfully. "Look what the cat dragged in."

The warmth of the house drifted around him, carrying the scent of newly washed hair and good cologne. "Come in." Steve stood aside and gestured grandly. "Sorry I didn't hear you at first. I was gilding the lily."

Anna started. Men had so many euphemisms for mastur-bation mere woman could not keep up with them. Then she laughed. Steve was dolled up, hair clean and soft, beard trimmed. A fine broadcloth oxford shirt in rich burgundy was worn with pleated gray wool trousers.

"You even ironed your shirt," Anna said admiringly.

"Women can't resist a man who irons," Steve said. "It provides a hint of domesticity but doesn't commit you to a lifetime of it. The language of chores is like the language of flowers. Very subtle."

"I was hoping for dinner," Anna said. "But I've got a feeling this onslaught of personal beauty is not for me."

"It could have been," Steve said airily. "But you chose the inferior man and now it's too late. Your window of op-portunity is closed. And all this masculine appeal is for you in a way. The sacrifices I make on your behalf..." He waved Anna toward a couch. The furniture was worn, mostly hand-me-downs from the previous tenant. Stilwell could afford better but nomads traveled light.

"We've got time for a drink but that's about it. Duty calls," he checked his wristwatch, "in seventeen minutes." He sighed dramatically. "As it happens, I may yet be hoist on my own petard. A petard lifted, I might add, for you." Again she suspected him of double entendre. With Stilwell one could never be sure.

He wanted Anna to cross-examine him. That's what the alluring hints were designed for. The game required at least two players. Anna chose to play disinterested. For a moment Steve waited, his eyebrows lifted invitingly. Anna wished she'd fallen in love with Steve. Chances are the ride would have been short but a whole hell of a lot of fun.

He laughed and she knew she'd gained a point in what-ever game it was he was playing. During the remainder of their short visit she told him of the paltry pieces of infor-mation they'd turned up on the murder investigation.

"Corpse had a gun," Steve mused, clinking imaginary ice cubes. He took his whiskey neat: no water, no ice, but tended to shake the glass as if he sloshed the liquid over the cubes. A move he'd undoubtedly picked up from the movies thirty years before. The affectation had become habit at some point. Now, like a number of his other mannerisms, it merely added to his eclectic charm, the whimsical gentleman aspect of his complex persona. "So. He has a gun. He uses it. Yet he ends up ignobly dead. What do you figure? Either he shoots and misses or shoots and connects, in which case you should have a report of a gunshot wound showing up at a local hospital or a second corpse washing up in a bayou."

"Or he's shooting before the murder is committed."

"As in hunting?"

"As in hunting," Anna said.

"As in having to do with your pursuing poachers."

"Exactly."

"It fits better with the assault by the Ford truck. If it was done by the poachers—or at least one of them—killing to cover the crime of illegally taking the king's deer didn't make much sense. Covering up a murder's a different story.

"If Doyce had a gun, doesn't that suggest he would have tried to defend himself? According to what you said there was no indication of defensive wounds in the autopsy, that he'd been alive and probably compliant when he got strapped into whatever bruised him up."

"Two possibilities," Anna said. "Either the gun powder residue on his hands has nothing to do with the murder at all but only indicates he was shooting shortly before his death. Or he wasn't playing poker but out poaching with the boys and got himself killed, either by the boys or afterward by somebody else that he willingly played leather games with. Could be he was coerced into the leather games at gunpoint and nobody laid a hand on him till after he was dead."

Stilwell shook his head. "If I had a gun and an unholy urge I sure wouldn't waste them on a fat, middle-aged guy." Neither would Anna.

"Where does Brother Raymond fit into this scenario?" Steve asked.

"He doesn't," Anna admitted. "He's got an alibi both for the time of the murder and the evening the poachers chased me. And, far as I know, he's not a hunter."

"I guess working with the dead the thrill of the kill could get blunted. No more mystery: meat is meat."

"I don't know about the mystery but I doubt he'd agree with you on the meat issue. I believe Mr. Barnette takes his responsibilities to the deceased very seriously."

"As in building a fine wooden coffin for whoever he buried in the backyard?"

"Something like that."

Their allotted time was up. With an annoying air of secrecy about the event he'd been primping for, Steve walked Anna to her patrol car, then climbed into his glorious old truck.

The ice storm the forecasters had predicted with ill-concealed glee had backed off and Anna drove the fifty miles back to Rocky Springs without incident.

Again, shortly after midnight, her sleep was interrupted by the ringing of the phone. Again the caller hung up. Again Anna slept behind locked doors.

19

For three hours the following morning Anna was held hostage by the phone in her office. Waiting, biding one's time in the lee of a rock or undercover of a tree, until the unwary prey wandered by, had always been easy for Anna. The Zen of the huntress had survived eons of civilization and flowered in her soul. That morning, waiting in an office for unnamed bureaucrats and technicians to get around to phoning her was pure torture. She'd cast the toxic bread of this investigation upon the system's waters and could do little till it returned: lab reports to tell her if Martin Crowley's venison was from the same animal she'd found in the meadow by the deer stand, if the bark shaving from the tree she'd so assiduously scraped matched the bark found beneath Doyce Barnette's fingernails, what Clintus Jones had tracked down on the lead regarding the owner of the Ford truck that had battered her patrol car into tinfoil.

When Paul Davidson called, she was thrilled. It would kill time and, girlishly, she wanted to hear his voice. For a while they exchanged the inconsequentialities of their lives, basking in the joy of sharing. To her delight and, on the undeniably cynical level of Anna's middle-aged mind, mild embarrassment, she heard herself saying "I miss you" and reveling in Paul saying it back after only thirty-six hours of separation.

"My wife came over last night," Paul said guardedly when a lull came into the conversation. "We had a good talk."

The doors that had been pushed open a crack around Anna's well-defended heart started to close. Hearing him say "my wife" with what sounded like real warmth hurt, physically, a sharp pinch beneath her sternum. Hating herself for it, Anna wondered if the "good talk" had been had between the sheets.

"Oh?" she said and was pleased that fear did not chill her voice.

"She drove down to get some of her things that were stored in our garage."

Our garage. His and his wife's. Again the pinch. Anna didn't trust herself to speak lest she reveal her emotions. Time and self-preservation had taught her not to show weakness. She let the silence speak for her.

"You've definitely got an enemy in the park service," Paul said. "That worries me a little."

So. The "good talk" had been composed at least in part of evil rumors in which Ranger Anna Pigeon was prominently figured. Curiosity and an odd component of self-loathing—mostly for her own vulnerability—urged Anna to ask what had been said. She resisted it.

"What was the bottom line?" she asked. Cold infected the reasonable tone she'd hoped for.

"Oh. Could you hold a sec?"

Before Anna could scream, "No, goddamn it. Talk to me," she heard vague mutterings as he spoke with someone else in the room. Had he called her from the office or home? Was he sitting in the kitchen of *their* house, talking on *their* phone with the Mrs. pottering domestically about? "Damn," Anna whispered.

Paul came back. "Anna, I've got to go. Can I see you tonight? We need to talk."

"We are talking," she said.

"I mean in person, face to face."

Anna wanted to say she was busy, leaving town, anything to avoid it. *Take the hit,* she told herself. "Sure. What time?"

"Seven okay?"

"Seven it is."

He hung up hurriedly, anxious to get on with whatever or whoever was interrupting the call.

Anna sat at her desk, in her miserable chair, and stared at the fragments of the puzzle she'd been so intent on solving ten minutes before. Now it seemed meaningless, the joy in her work sucked away by other concerns. "Getting a life is highly overrated," she muttered.

When Barth showed up with a plan and the task to go with it, she jumped at the chance to get out of the office and actually *do* something.

Barth didn't need her assistance nor did he seem to particularly want it, but Anna volunteered as a helper and followed him out to his car. The ice storm that had failed to materialize the previous night had not passed over but merely backed off. The day was in the mid- to high thirties with the low dark skies and intermittent rain squalls of the day before. Barth drove the forty odd miles to Natchez. Anna was content to sit in the passenger seat, warmed by the heater, mildly irritated by the Christian music on the radio, and cogitate.

There were many things her mind could have amused itself with, but she had unwittingly passed a psychological point of no return in her relationship with Paul Davidson. She was old enough to keep the obvious signs under wraps. Except with her sister Molly, who, as a psychiatrist with doctor/patient privilege could surely never be called to testify against her, Anna never, ever gave in to the temptation to chatter on and on about The Boyfriend. She hadn't gotten a face-lift, lost weight or started wearing new eye-catching outfits to work. Once, she'd regressed to the point of writing Anna Davidson on a sheet of scratch paper to see what it looked like. No one had caught her and she had destroyed the evidence. It had been merely a whimsical reflex predating high school. First married at high tide of the feminist movement, Anna had kept her own last name. At the time it had seemed terribly important. For better or worse, richer or poorer, it was the name she would die with. It had defined her for too many years ever to be abandoned. And, in a strange way, to change it would be an insult to Zach. She'd refused to take his last name, how could she take another man's?

Of the foolishnesses that besieged her sex in matters of the heart, the one she had been unable to avoid was thinking too much about the object of desire. As the gray and black patterns swept by the car windows and rain streaked the side window in horizontal squiggles, Anna found herself reliving their phone conversation and growing more depressed by the minute. She focused on the last painful aspect.

"I've heard from a reputable source that somebody—probably somebody on the Trace—is spreading rumors about me," she said to Barth, sounding more defiant and belligerent than she felt.

Barth snorted softly as he was jerked out of his own reverie. "Well, it's not me, if that's what you been thinking."

"No, not you." Anna dismissed the idea without apology. Sufficiently self-absorbed, she didn't note the fact that she'd offended him. "Maybe Randy," she said. "But I don't even think it's him. There's been a feel of conspiracy about this, like from higher up." As she talked, Anna stared out the window. Trees, flooding meadows, creeks, flashed beyond the glass with a hypnotic sameness.

"You mean like some sort of conspiracy in the brass up to Tupelo to stir up a scandal or something about you down around here for some secret reason?" Barth asked.

"Yeah."

"Boss, you're getting creepy on me here. Maybe you should go get that psycho stuff they keep harping on."

"Critical Incident Stress Debriefing?"

"That's it. Sounds like you're in need of some serious debriefing. Maybe because of the car and all. Whatever, I wouldn't go talking conspiracy to anybody but me."

Anna saw her reflection in the window smile. With Barth, finally, she felt among friends. Professionally speaking, this duty station had been the loneliest she'd ever known. She was the boss, the only woman and, until Barth had chosen to let her in, hated outsider to the very men she had to work with every day.

With an effort, she pulled her gaze from the passing scenery and shook herself free of the fog that had formed in her skull. "Nope. Not that kind of conspiracy," she said. "I've not quite been driven round the bend yet."

Barth's face, hardened into mask of concern, softened a little at the intentionally sane and cheery note she struck.

"This is something I've heard filtering down from an un-expected source in Jackson," she said. "No big deal."

"Sheriff Davidson's wife?" Barth asked bluntly, and Anna was reminded that, in a National Park, no one had any secrets.

"Yeah," she admitted. Denying it was useless and silence was worse.

"What did you expect?"

Though buried in respect and what Anna hoped was friendship, she heard the condemnation in Barth's voice. Christian music bleated its saccharine rock, and Anna damned herself for opening such a personal can of worms. Though Paul and his wife had been apart for three years, though half the people sitting in the pews come Sunday morning were divorced, though their own fucking Bible said let he who is without sin cast the first stone . . .

"Whoo!" Anna said, blowing out the anger that had flamed up and crowned in the forest of her thoughts. "Pay no attention to me, Barth. The phone keeps wrecking my sleep. It's given me a jaundiced view of life this morning."

They didn't go to Barnette's Funeral Home. After the debacle of the previous day, there was little chance Raymond would be forthcoming on any subject except, perhaps, the planning of their own funerals. Barth had been giving thought to what Claudia told them. For that Anna was grateful. Her mind had been co-opted by the Sturm und Drang of her love life, and she'd been less than helpful.

First they went to the historical society, then to the library, then to the land assayers office and the county clerk. At Barth's suggestion they researched not the names he'd uncovered at the Mt. Locust cemetery, but the history of the Barnette family as told by the paper trail left behind. Since the Barnettes were white and owned land, records had been kept of their official interactions.

The earliest was a land grant of 2,300 acres to Joseph Doyce Barnette in 1743. What service he had performed to receive such a boon was not mentioned. The tract of land included the 300 acres now owned by Mama Barnette and an additional 1,900 acres stretching north and west.

Sifting through old newspaper reports of slave sales, weddings, social events, local elections, bills of lading, birth, death and marriage certificates, they patched together a history of sorts.

Joseph Doyce, born 1717, died 1799, had been prosperous. He bought and sold both slaves and cotton. He had given and been invited to balls and soirees of sufficient interest to be remarked upon in the society pages. During his long life, Joseph had seven children and two wives. Three of the children and both wives died young of a malady described only as "fever."

His land was left *in toto* to his eldest surviving son, Matthew Doyce Barnette. Whether hard times or profligacy afflicted Matthew, the dry pieces of paper they pored over didn't say. The records listed only the facts. Of the original 2,300 acres, 1,500 had been sold over a period of seven years. Matthew had also sold twenty-one slaves. How many had been owned originally and how many had been retained to manage the remaining 800 acres was not

recorded. Matthew Doyce Barnette died in a carriage accident at the age of forty-eight. The depleted plantation was
left to his only child, a son, Harold Doyce Barnette, aged
six, to be held in trust for him by his mother, Martha Gain-
street Barnette, till he reached twenty-one years of age or
married.

Anna and Barth could find little during the years Martha
held the land for her son. No record existed of her remarry-
ing, her name was not included in the society pages. Evidently with the change in fortunes, the Barnette family had
fallen from grace. Four formal complaints from creditors
had been lodged against her. Martha had held on to the
land, but in 1815 she had put five more slaves on the auc-
tion block.

The record of Harold coming into the property in the fall
of 1827 preceded that of Martha's death by three months.
Her duty done, she had evidently given up.

Harold Doyce Barnette was, historically speaking, an
invisible man after that. Search as they might there was no
record of his marrying, buying, selling, running for office,
getting arrested or even dying. That he must have done at
least some of these things was attested to by a record of his
will and the transfer of the land to his son in 1851. The son
was Doyce Altman Barnette.

"Papa Doyce, what do you bet?" Anna said when they'd
reached this point in the dusty saga. Her head was full of
dead people, her body cramped from sitting in an assortment of cold rooms throughout the day. Other than that she
felt fine. For the first time she understood the lure that
dragged historians back into the years. There was the thrill
and occasional satisfaction of any good investigation, but
the triumphs and atrocities were of only intellectual interest. The historian got no blood or vomit on her hands and,
most attractive, was under no obligation to change the future, to keep injustice or injury from happening to the living. There were no living. The dead had become merely
the stuff of ratified fiction.

Outside the day darkened, grew colder, rain fell. None

of it touched Anna and Barth. They were locked in the storms of previous centuries, those that could not, in reality, touch them.

Papa Doyce brought the Barnette family back onto the public radar. It was he who had started the cabinet-making business. Raymond's boast of his great-great-grandfather making fine furniture for the quality folk was not empty. Bills of sale to named gentry were recorded, and orders for expensive rare woods had been placed regularly by Barnette's Cabinetry. He'd even been written up in the newspaper when a wealthy Natchez matriarch commissioned him to build a bedroom suite as a gift to her soon-to-be married daughter and son-in-law.

In the article Anna found what Barth had known must be in the records somewhere. "I got it," she said, feeling a rush of intense satisfaction. "Listen: 'The suite, including bed, chest of drawers and armoire, made by local artisan Doyce Altman Barnette and his freedman Lanford Restin, will be open for viewing with the other wedding gifts for the public's enjoyment from ten A.M. till noon at the home of Mrs. Ronald Vincent Coleman, prior to the nuptials on June seventh, eighteen sixty-four.'"

"Unk Restin was a freedman," Barth said and laughed, taking pleasure in the good fortune of a man dead long before he was born. "Restin was one of the names in the Mt. Locust cemetery I could in nowise trace. If Unk Restin is that Restin or an ancestor, it makes sense. I was looking for slaves."

"Which plot is Restin's?" Anna asked.

"We don't know. Nothing was marked. I uncovered only the names of the dead from family histories. The exact location of the graves is lost."

The two of them fortified themselves with stale Oreos and unbelievably bad coffee from a vending machine and continued the search. Because Lanford "Unk" Restin was a freedman he had been given at least nominal status of personhood and entered recorded history, no longer living and dying with the anonymity of slaves and other livestock.

Late in the afternoon Barth startled Anna by an explosion of sound. "Holy smoke. This is it." The big man positively crowed.

Glad to stop wading through microfiche of barely legible newspapers, Anna quit working. "Well, out with it," she demanded when Barth held on to his information too long, reveling in his discovery all by his lonesome.

"Papa Doyce Barnette deeded three hundred and two acres to his freedman Lanford Restin April twenty-second of the year eighteen hundred and sixty-three."

"Where?" Anna asked. The crumpled feelings hours in the chair had left her with were gone. This information could very well have an impact on the living and, for all the pleasure she was taking in sleuthing the dead, the living were more in her jurisdiction.

"Where" was tricky. They traveled through the bowels of the Adams County Courthouse, guided by a succession of three helpful women who worked in this troglodyte habitat among ceiling-high racks of rolled, folded, filed, misfiled and ever-changing documentation. Zoning laws, county lines, city limits, property lines, dredging of canals, bayous, river beds; the human demarcations overlaying the natural topography and each other dating back 200 years were drawn in blue ink on yellowing paper.

Anna and Barth compared descriptions, property lines and maps of rivers and bayous no longer accurate because their subject matter, like all living things, constantly changed. Finally, with help and luck, they were able to conclude with fair certainty that the 300 acres deeded by Papa Doyce to his freedman, partner and probably friend, was taken from the acreage on the southern and easternmost borders of the 800 acres that remained of the original 2,300 in Joseph Barnette's land grant. Over a century ago Papa Doyce had given away the land Raymond and his mother were so proprietary about and given it to a black man: Lanford "Unk" Restin.

At some point in time the Barnettes had lost Papa Doyce's 500-acre parcel and reacquired Lanford Restin's

300 acres. "What do you bet if they bought it back, it was for peanuts?" Barth said. The words were soured by the potential truth in them, but his tone was cheerful. From the brightness of his gray-green eyes and the almost lascivious way he cracked his knuckles before opening or unrolling a cobwebby old sheet of paper, Anna could tell this was his idea of a really good time.

Day-to-day road patrol—speeding tickets, DUIs, visitor assists—tended to eat up Trace rangers' time and it was work that wasted Barth's talents. Had he been willing to move, he'd have found a home at a higher pay scale in one of the historical parks with curator duties. Barth was a Mississippi boy, born and raised. His family was here. Nothing short of revolution or the much touted power of wild horses would ever drag him from his home in Jefferson County.

Anna made a mental note to see if something local could be worked out. Half a dozen tiny historical graveyards existed on the ninety-mile stretch of parkway in her district. Most were being eaten away by time, neglect and vandals. She'd see if he could start with them, she decided.

They stayed until all but one of the helpful ladies had gone home for the day and the lady remaining was beginning to show signs of bad temper.

Several years after Lanford "Unk" Restin was deeded the property backing Mt. Locust, civil war racked the South. Written records of daily life suffered from the storm. Both Unk and Papa Doyce were killed. Not, as one might expect, with one in blue and one in gray. They'd both died fighting a house fire that apparently had nothing to do with the war. The paper said only that local businessman and landowner, Doyce Altman Barnette, along with his freedman, had burned to death when the roof unexpectedly collapsed while they tried to rescue two servants trapped on the second floor. Papa Doyce was survived by a wife and two sons. Of Lanford Restin, it merely said he'd chosen to be buried "back with his people."

Records surfaced of the sale of the acreage Barnette had

retained after he deeded the 300 acres to Restin. It had
been auctioned off in 1871 to cover bad debts. More recent
records from the 1900s existed telling of births, deaths,
taxes and building permits for the Barnette family on both
the 300 acres Mama still dwelt on and the cabinet shop
turned funeral parlor. Nowhere could they find any indication that Lanford Restin had sold, willed or given up his
land. Apparently it had been quietly reacquired by the Barnette descendents without legal documentation.

Darkness had fallen by the time they were ushered out
the door. Darkness, made palpable in sleeting rain, coated
trees and roads, but Anna and Barth were sufficiently
pleased with their day's work that it failed to dampen their
spirits.

Ten miles south of Port Gibson, dispatch in Tupelo
called for five-eight-zero, Anna's number. The dispatcher's
voice, usually a template for aural calm, had a ragged edge
to it. "What now?" Anna muttered irritably. She didn't appreciate the present interfering with what had been such a
successful day in the past.

"Five-eight-zero," she said into the mike.

"Where have you been? We've been trying to reach you
all day." The totally human demand from such a professional source alarmed Barth as it did Anna. He turned up
the volume on the radio as if it weren't already loud
enough. A frisson of guilt passed unmarked between Anna
and her field ranger. At some point in the afternoon the incessant chatter from the radios on their belts had become
distracting as well as annoying to those in whose offices
they toiled. They had turned them off and forgotten to turn
them on again.

"What's up?" Anna asked, wasting no time or pride on
public explanations.

"Sheriff Jones of Adams County's been trying to reach
you."

"I'll call him," Anna said. "Anything else I missed?"

"Not much. Pretty quiet. We should get some motor

vehicle accidents up here. The roads are already starting to ice over."

There was a good chance they'd get a motor vehicle accident or two in the Port Gibson–Natchez district as well. Anna hoped inclement weather would keep the traffic light. Though hunters, she'd noticed, seemed even more determined than the post office to ignore rain, sleet and dark of night.

"What time did Sheriff Jones call?" Anna asked.

"He *started* calling about an hour ago. Hang on. First call came in at three-fifty-eight P.M. Just over an hour."

"Thanks," Anna said, signed off with her call number, changed the radio to the frequency used by the Adams County Sheriff's Department and radioed Clintus.

"Clintus, Anna. I had my radio off."

"Where are you?"

Anna told him.

"I tracked down that matter I left a message for you about," he said.

"The truck?"

A moment's silence then. "Call me on a landline as soon as you get to the office."

"Will do," Anna said.

"What's all that about?" Barth asked. "He sounded about half-mad at you over something. You been stepping on the local talent's toes?"

"I don't think so," Anna said. "I don't know what the deal is."

Lights were on and Randy's patrol car was parked in front of the ranger station when they pulled in. A weekend night, Randy was on his requested four-to-midnight shift.

Barth rolled to a stop and Anna got out. He drove away, heading for the rear gate and the shortest route home. On her handheld radio Anna heard him calling out of service.

She turned and walked through the sleet toward the little porchlike area that fronted the ranger station. A thin sheen of ice had formed over the concrete, and she fought for balance as her boots hit it. The door opened and Randy appeared in the flesh, never a pretty sight.

"Hey," he said cheerfully. "Clintus just called. He traced that truck you had problems with to Badger Lundstrom. Wants us to meet him there. I'm to fill you in on the way. André and three other deputies'll be there. I guess Clintus isn't taking any chances."

Randy skirted his vehicle and headed for Anna's patrol car. She watched him for a moment, feeling the irritation that interaction with Ranger Thigpen invariably inspired prickling under her collar. Regardless of how many leaves the man turned over she doubted he would ever change perceptibly.

Giving in to the inevitable, she shrugged. "Guess I'm driving," she announced to an invisible and sympathetic audience.

Having dug the keys from her pocket, she slid in behind the wheel and started the ignition. Letting the engine warm, she pulled up the mike to let Tupelo know where they were headed.

Randy's hand whipped out. He switched the radio off as Anna was depressing the mike key. "Sorry," he said. "Didn't mean to cut you off like that. It's just I forgot to tell you. Clintus said to maintain radio silence. He got that from you I guess, thinking the truck driver must've been monitoring our frequency to get your location so exact."

Anger at having somebody—anybody—but especially Randy Thigpen screwing with her machinery hit Anna in a blast of sudden internal heat. Intellectually she accepted his reasoning. Clintus, when he called ten minutes earlier, had made it clear that he did not wish to discuss the Badger Lundstrom situation over the airwaves. That which ran deeper and more primitive than intellect stayed hot as new lava, and Anna chose not to respond verbally lest she expose her basic animal nature. She put the mike back on its hook, buckled her seat belt and drove sedately out the gate. Repetitious, habitual actions brought down her emotional temperature. The extent of her irritation was a clue to how tired and on edge the day—indeed the week—had left her. Not a good mind-set to carry into a potentially dangerous situation. Consciously she brought herself into the present, relaxed her body, breathed, opened her mind and let the dusty clutter of the day drift out of the corners. When she'd gained the level of calm and maturity she sought she said, "What's the plan?"

Without asking, she'd turned south when she left the ranger station, heading toward Lundstrom's residence on the outskirts of Natchez.

"Through the Adams County DMV Clintus tracked down a guy—a soybean farmer by the name of Quantas Elfman—who'd bought that truck," Randy said.

"Right. He was going to check it out," Anna said.

"Took him a while, but he did it. This Elfman sold it to a man runs a feed store in Utica about seven years ago. The feed-store owner traded it for two loads of metal pipe last winter."

"Badger Lundstrom provided the pipe," Anna finished for him.

"Yep. According to our feed guy Lundstrom had bought it along with a lot of other scrap an oil man was unloading when his business went belly up. Not that it matters where he got it," Randy said. "Clintus said André's already got Lundstrom's place staked out. Lundstrom's home. Clintus was leaving with the other deputies right after he called here."

"I'd been thinking Lundstrom for the driver of that truck made sense," Anna said.

"How so?"

It was a fair question, but the smirk beneath the words suggested Randy didn't believe her, that he thought she'd chosen to pretend previous knowledge where she had none.

Pride pricked her into sharing the suspicions she'd been keeping to herself the past twenty-four hours. "It's my guess Doyce, Badger, Herm, and Martin never played a hand of poker together. Their 'poker nights' were spent poaching from that stand by Mt. Locust. I got two samples of deer flesh, one from our meadow, one from Martin Crowley's dog. I'm betting when the DNA tests are done they'll prove to have come from the same animal."

"One man poaching a doe on federal park lands is a far cry from attempted murder," Randy said.

"There was bark under Doyce Barnette's fingernails, bark from a pecan tree. The stand is nailed to a pecan tree. And I got results back yesterday that the corpse had gunpowder residue on his hands."

"What? You figure Doyce was out hunting when he was killed? He wasn't shot."

"No," Anna said. "Cause of death was suffocation. Doyce and the boys are out hunting, illegally, up in a tree stand easily twenty feet above the ground. The stand's beat to shit but for one corner and there the railing's new, two-by-fours, spit and polish."

"So it got busted and they fixed it. I'm missing something here."

"What do guys wear in tree stands while they're hunting?"

"I give up," Randy said and laughed. "Boxers or briefs?"

Anna laughed with him, then she said, "Safety harnesses. Doyce falls or is pushed through the old rickety railing. He hangs in his harness, claws at the tree. Guy that fat, if he hangs long enough he drowns in his own fat."

"Okay, so Doyce falls. That's an accident. Why not just call nine-one-one?"

"Maybe it wasn't an accident."

"He could've been by himself."

"Not likely. And he didn't move his own corpse."

"Why not just leave him where he died?"

"Covering up that they were poaching?" Anna phrased it like a question because it was a question in her mind. Poaching deer in Mississippi was not a serious enough infraction of the law to inspire three ordinarily law-abiding men to go to such lengths to cover it up.

"Then what do you figure? The hunters get scared we're

figuring it out that they had something to do with Doyce's accident and try and scare us off with that hootin' an hollerin' show. That fails. Lundstrom goes after you in a pickup truck," Randy summed up for her. "Why'd they put poor ol' Doyce on Grandma Polly's bed in his underpants?"

"I haven't worked that out yet," Anna admitted.

They drove in silence for a while. Anna concentrated on the road. Over the bridges it was icy, she could feel the Crown Vic wanting to fishtail.

Miles passed in darkness. Sleet, sluggish and black, slid in tarry trails along the side windows. They passed the meadow with the deer stand. Randy, staring out his window, stirred from his lumpish quiet to ask, "Why would Badger Lundstrom leave Doyce hang till he suffocated? Why not cut him down?"

"Why did he loose a two-ton iron pterodactyl over my head?" Anna returned. "Because he thought it would be funny. Maybe this time the joke went too far."

Randy laughed unexpectedly. "You've got to admit your scuttling away from that thing was pretty funny. Too bad it was dark. You'd of been something to see by the light of day."

By the light of day. The phrase jarred Anna on a deep and disquieting level. Suddenly it became of utmost importance that she remember where she'd heard it recently. She almost asked Randy, but a voice she seldom heard but always listened to warned her not to. The ice water that was flooding the world came into Anna's body.

Backing her foot off the accelerator, she let her mind shift up from the asphalt and open to memory. Another mile past to the sharp stinging song of tires on wet pavement before the image came to her. It was the morning after her car had been demolished. Randy had come into the office. They'd spoken of the damage they'd noted to the car body. Then Randy had said he would like to see it in the light of day.

He'd seen the wreck.

He'd not seen it by the light of day.

Randy had a park radio. He'd known where she was and what she was up to. All at once the pieces fell together.

Badger Lundstrom had not been driving the truck, or, if he had, he'd not been alone. And they were not going to his house now. There'd been no last minute call from Clintus.

Anna had been a fool. The price for that would be high.

20

Randy was blathering on in his mellifluous voice, but she no longer heard the words. The obvious, or what should have been obvious had she not been so blind, so stupid, was slamming into her mind, being transmuted into ice water and pumped throughout her body till her bowels quivered and her extremities were numbed.

Randy demanding weekend nights. Her phone ringing after midnight on Fridays and Saturdays since...? Since hunting season had started, she realized. There was little public land in Mississippi. Hunting was done in privately owned clubs. Clubs were expensive. Badger, Martin, Herm, and Doyce were men of limited means. Randy had accommodated them, running a hunting club of his own that met on Friday and Saturday nights when no one patrolled the parkway but him. On those nights Randy must have rung Anna at home, making sure she was safely tucked in her bed and out of the way before the festivities began.

He'd not been late when she'd called for backup the

night the hunters had ambushed her. He'd been early,
maybe at the stand itself when she radioed. That's why
they had been lying in wait when she arrived. The new leaf,
the anger when she interviewed Crowley without him;
Randy had wanted to be in on the investigation to control
it, divert it, feed answers to his cohorts.

Anna felt an utter fool. She deserved to be smacked upside the head for it. She did not deserve to die for it. Unfortunately, for fools in law enforcement, death was too often
the penalty for even minor lapses.

Slowly, she came back to herself. Only seconds had
passed. She was still behind the wheel, conning the car
over the slick road. Randy was still talking. Her mind
cleared of self-recrimination and chain of circumstantial
evidence. For now she needed to get away from Randy.
Summon help if she could. Options clicked through her
brain and were discarded. If she reached for the radio, sped
up, slowed down or did anything out of the ordinary Randy
would realize she knew. So long as he thought her ignorant
she was safe. At least until he led her to wherever it was
this journey was to end. She was armed but so was he and
he had every advantage. Wearing a long jacket buckled
down over her gun belt, tricked into driving, Anna was
rather neatly trussed up and helpless. Randy, she noted in a
sideways glance, was coatless. His right hand, out of sight
behind his paunch, undoubtedly rested on the butt of his
service weapon. Randy was a smart man. His plan was
probably simple. She would disappear, her body buried in
the mire of the woods. A great hue and cry would be
raised, a search would begin, run, in her absence, by
Ranger Thigpen. Her car would be found, left in a place far
from where the body was buried. The search would center
on the location of the vehicle while her bones moldered to
dust in an unnamed grave miles away.

They approached Mt. Locust. Anna noted the rain-dark
sign in the spill of the headlights. She needed to take control of their geography. It was a lesson girls were taught in
defense classes: regardless of what is promised, never let

the villain take you to a second location. If she could get free of the car, the seat belt, while keeping Randy off the scent, there was a chance she could escape. Randy was quick for a fat man but not so quick as Anna.

"I need to stop in here a minute," she said. "I left my camera at the Mt. Locust Ranger Station."

"I've got mine with me," Randy said easily. The lie was well made but, without coat or bag, unless he carried it in his hip pocket, utterly transparent. He realized it and for an instant their eyes locked, the pale blue of his glittering in the phosphorescent green of the dash lights, then going black as he moved his head a fraction of an inch.

"That's okay," Anna said. "I may as well get mine. I have to go to the bathroom anyway." Her voice was natural, light even, but it was no good. The moment their eyes met information had been passed.

In a move so quick Anna realized his gun had not been holstered but waited ready in his hand, he shifted it neatly to his left hand and pressed it to her temple. She heard the hammer draw back and the unmistakable click as the cylinder of a wheel gun rotated a bullet into place. Randy, too clever by half, carried not his service weapon—a nine-millimeter Sig-Sauer semi-automatic like she wore—but a revolver probably unregistered and untraceable.

She'd underestimated Thigpen. He was a rotten ranger because he chose to be, not because he was incapable of the moves. His right hand lifted cuffs from his shirt pocket. Anna's hands, neatly aligned on the top curve of the steering wheel, were smoothly cuffed together. The entire action was over in seconds. Quick as it was, it was not quicker than thought. Ideas scattered up in Anna's mind thick and loud as a flock of blackbirds: moving her hands so she could not be cuffed, trying for the door handle, stepping on the gas or the brake to unseat Randy, even crashing the Crown Vic into the trees on the chance that, in the mess of airbags and broken glass, she could get away.

She did none of these things for the simple reason that she believed with every ounce of her being that Randy would not hesitate to pull the trigger if she deviated in any way from his dictates. No matter what she tried, his heaving finger on a two-pound trigger-pull would be faster.

Anna was not particularly afraid to die—a fact she hid from others as it seemed to set her apart, make her an object of suspicion. But to have one's brains blown out at close range, seat belt fastened, hands cuffed, weapon still holstered, and to have it done by Thigpen—that would surely condemn her to a special kind of hell. Maybe working as a lap dancer at aluminum-siding sales conventions.

The ratcheting sound as the cuffs were tightened stopped the skittering of her brain. The gun was still hard at her temple. Randy's right hand, closed over hers on the steering wheel, clamping so tightly she could feel the blood being pressed from her fingers as they were crushed between his and the hard plastic.

"Do what I tell you," Randy said shortly. Either nerves or the exertion of moving quickly had set him to panting. The smell of stale cigarettes on his breath was intense.

"Why don't you eat a mint or something," she heard herself say irritably. "You smell like a rancid ashtray." Part of her was scared stiff, another part, evidently the part controlling the vocal cords, really didn't give a damn. Disassociation; she'd heard Molly mention it. Was that what she was doing?

"Randy, you are such a piece of shit. If you kill me, I swear to God I'll never live it down. You wrecked my office chair, smashed my car up, what the fuck do you think you're doing now?" Again with the mouth. The saner Anna shook her head, feeling the barrel of the gun grind half an inch across the flesh of her temple.

"There's something wrong with you," Randy growled. Emotion edged his voice. Fear maybe. Excitement. Probably a mixture of both.

"Oh, man," Anna said and was shocked at the exasperation and contempt she heard in the words. "You've never killed anybody before, have you?" It sounded as though she sneered at overripe virginity. "If this is going to be like

Paul Newman and what's her name in *Torn Curtain* with
you flopping me around sticking my head in the oven and
whatnot, just give me the gun and I'll shoot myself." If she
didn't focus, and soon, this split personality business was
going to get both personas killed.

From the corner of her eye she could see beads of sweat
forming on his forehead. "Shut up," he said. Her verbal
sniping had unbalanced him; she could hear the dangerous
teetering when he spoke. Instinct and reason reunited behind her eyes, and Anna realized she'd needed to shake
him but hadn't realized she had the balls to do it. Balls had
been found, the terrified mother lifting the tractor off her
infant in microcosm.

"Turn right to Emerald Mound," he said. Randy's hand
over hers, they'd traveled several miles south of Mt. Locust. Emerald Mound, the finest Indian mound Anna had
ever seen, was on Trace property at the end of a narrow un-
lighted road. Several ramshackle homes edged the lane. If
the residents happened to be looking out their windows on
such a night as this, seeing a park service car checking the
mound would arouse no comment.

Anna did as she was told. "Turn out the headlights,"
Randy said. She did that, too.

In less than a minute they were at the mound.

"Pull off." Anna did. Randy dropped her hand long
enough to switch off the ignition, then grabbed it again.
She'd known Randy was a big man. She'd not realized he
was huge. His hand covered hers to the wrist. His bulk, behind the barrel of a gun, filled the Crown Vic's cab. The
terror she'd kept separated from by mental alchemy broke
through taking an old familiar form: claustrophobia. Suddenly she could see herself snapping, struggling, clawing
for air, a loud noise, then her brains mixed with the window glass on the dirt outside. Even then none would ven-
ture out of their snug homes. It was hunting season. The
sound of gunshots was commonplace.

"Here's where we get out." Randy's voice cut through
the panic rising in her chest. "This is the end of the line."

Inches from her ear Anna heard the hammer of his revolver falling gently, slowly. Terrible calm came then, a
sense of utter timelessness. An explosion, a bullet to the
brain did not follow. Randy was decocking the pistol. Life
clamored back, and Anna was almost sorry. Almost. "It
doesn't have to be the end of the line," she said. "So far
you're not in much trouble. Poaching's no big deal.
What'll you get? A slap on the wrist. Two months and
you're retired. Don't screw it up."

She sounded as desperate as she felt. Randy liked that;
she could see it in his face no more than a foot from her
own. He wanted more of it. Her humiliation was a balm to
his withered soul. That was good. She had something to offer in trade.

"You didn't kill anybody. You weren't even there, were
you? What? Did they call you in to save their own skins?
Get you to move the body?"

Randy's lower lip tightened, and Anna lost the teensy-
weensy opening her obvious fear had bought her. Gun
pressed hard to her temple, he reached behind him with his
other hand and opened the passenger door. Not for a second did his eyes leave her.

There would be a moment when he opened her door. He
was heavy. She could get out more quickly. If she could
keep her feet under her, she could get to cover. Randy
wouldn't want to carry the body far. He was lazy, out of
shape and knew better than to get blood on his uniform.
He'd want her to walk to her place of execution. Anna's
mind raced. The farther he took her from cars, road, houses
the less time she had to live.

The moment was not given her. Grabbing the cuff chain
between her wrists, he snapped her seat belt free and
lurched backward, dragging her face down onto the seat.
An elbow cracked into the dash, Anna's head struck the radio on the floor. Her boot twisted as her legs wrenched,
awkwardly trying to follow her body. She registered these
assaults but felt nothing. Helpless as a rag doll she flopped
and slid. Fight and she died now. Allow the inevitable and

she died later. Later was good. Randy grunted. Cigarette
breath washed over her, then a welcome gust of cold air.
He got his feet on the ground, pushed his butt over them
and hauled on the chain. Anna felt herself slide. Then she
was jerked to a sudden halt. The cuffs cut hard into the underside of her wrists, but her body wouldn't move. Pain
sharpened and maddened.

"Don't fuck with me," Randy hissed.

"Or what? You'll kill me?"

Randy put his considerable weight behind the next yank.
Cuffs cut deeper, Anna's arms were stretched in their sock-
ets and she cried out.

"Shoulder strap, you dickhead."

When he'd cuffed her Anna'd been wearing her seat belt.
He'd inadvertently cuffed her hands, one on either side of
the shoulder belt that effectively kept her tied to the car.

Anna pushed her head up to look at him. There was little
light. Nothing from the dead dash, nothing from the sleet-
weeping skies. She sensed rather than saw his fear. Something had gone awry. He would kill her now, get it over
with. She lay absolutely still, legs twisted under the steering wheel, upper body pulled across the seat. Over the
beating of her heart other sounds came to the strained
peace of the cab: Randy panting, sleet—almost hail—
striking the roof of the car, a tiny snick of metal releasing.
Randy had recocked the pistol.

"No. No. Please don't kill me. I'll do anything," she
whimpered. "Please. Oh, God. Don't hurt me."

"You just had to have a man's job didn't you?" Randy
sneered. Her sniveling was soothing him, taking the edge
off his panic. Anna kept it up. The act came easily, and she
despised the ring of sincerity her groveling conveyed. She
didn't want to die trussed up like a prize pig on the front
seat of her own patrol car, become the poster girl for why
women shouldn't be allowed on the front lines. If Randy
killed her she half hoped her body would never be found
and he would never be suspected. It would be too humiliat-
ing to have it known she was bested by a dink like Thigpen.

"Please, please," she whined.

"Nobody wanted you here," Thigpen said. "Things were fine till you horned in." He brought the pistol close to Anna's head. She cringed smaller. Another inch and she would strike out like an adder, bury her teeth in his wrist. If nothing else, maybe the son of a bitch would get rabies and die.

Two shots fired in quick succession near her face. So close, the muzzle flash struck her eyes like lightning and the thunder of the reports left her deaf and disoriented. Blind and dazed, she felt herself being delivered from the suffocating confines of the car and onto the cold wet earth. Randy had shot twice through the webbing of the shoulder strap and dragged her free.

Before Anna recovered from the shock of having two rounds fired from a .357 less than a foot from her face, she felt herself lifted by the scruff of the neck like a half-drowned kitten. Randy had the hood and collar of her coat clamped in one huge hand and was yanking her to her feet. He was talking; Anna could hear the sound distortion past the ringing in her ears, but couldn't make out the words. Sparks of white and red light blurred her vision; retinal ghosts from the muzzle flash.

Noise separated, began to resolve into sense.

"Stand up," Randy was urging, yelling without volume.

As her mind blew clear of the stench and clamor of cordite, Anna toyed with the idea of playing possum, making Randy carry her to whatever dense thicket he had in mind for dumping purposes. There'd be no hole, he was too lazy to dig and damned if she'd dig her own for the meager privilege of a few more minutes topside.

"Stand up." He shook her with the violence of a terrier onto a rat. She decided to comply. Perhaps it would be tactically wise to tire him with her dead weight, but she didn't like the idea of being manhandled any more than she already had been. And, too, he might decide it was too much work and dispatch her prematurely.

It took a couple tries but Anna got her feet under her.

Her legs felt rubbery at the knees and for a second she didn't know if they would support her weight.

The flares dazzling her eyes were fading but nothing took their place. At first Anna thought powder burn had blinded her or a freak of the explosion so close had caused the same effect. The pale cruiser swam into vision, and she knew her eyes were all right. It was the night that was blind. Seldom were nights truly dark. Starlight, light pollution from distant cities, the moon, brought shape and form out of the black.

At the pullout for Emerald Mound there were none of these.

"Stand up," he hissed. "I'm not screwing around with you much longer." He shook her again.

Pain rattled from ear to ear and her flimsy purchase on the vertical was compromised. "Enough already," she snapped. "I'm standing. What now?"

Anger had brought back Anna's butch side. Hearing it she backed off, slumped her shoulders forward and dropped her chin. Snuffling through mud, snot or whatever else had worked its way into her nose while she sprawled on the ground, she repeated. "What're you going to do? Look Randy, I'll never tell anybody. Swear to God. Just let me go."

"What we're going to do is get rid of your gun." Randy had hold of her coat with one hand, a six-shooter in the other. She could feel him hesitate, not wanting to let go of her, not willing to holster his own weapon to reach for hers. Schooling her body not to signal readiness, she waited.

"You get it," he said at last, and her hope of striking out at him died. "You do it slow. You even wiggle or twitch wrong and I kill you."

Anna believed him. Hands chained together, she awkwardly fumbled under the thigh-long tail of her Gore-Tex jacket. "I'm not going to try anything. Real slow. Here goes," she said pitifully. Reaching under the coat she unsnapped the leather keeper on the pouch where she kept her extra magazines. One snap sounds like another and she was satisfied. "Lifting it out," she said. His grip tightened on her coat, choking her with her own collar. The barrel of the revolver pressed hard into the bone of her skull.

"Dropping it," she said and let the magazine fall to the ground augmenting the sound it made when it hit by a surreptitious stomp. "Don't shoot," she whispered. "Please don't shoot."

Because of the jacket and the handcuffs, there was no way to retrieve her gun quickly. Anna had it in her mind to ease it out under cover of darkness while they walked, their joint movements she hoped would cover the groping for the Sig-Sauer.

"Show me your hands," Randy said and gave her a shake. The barrel of the pistol pressed so hard against the base of her skull that she could barely keep her head up.

She raised her hands.

"To your shoulder."

She did as she was told. In a movement as quick as it was brutal, he adjusted his grip till he held not only the back of her coat but the chain between her hands in one great beefy paw. Anna's shoulders ached, her wrists chafed. The inside of her left elbow, wrapped in a wet bulky Gore-Tex sleeve, was pulled hard across her face making it difficult to breathe. Claustrophobia reasserted itself despite the fact she was out of the car and under the sky. Darkness and constriction choked her mind with a cavelike sense of the walls closing in. Enough air could be drawn around the fabric to keep her alive, but still a sense of suffocation took hold of her mind. Her vision was probably impaired as well. As it was too dark to see, she set that aside and concentrated on not succumbing to panic.

"Now we walk. I'm going to handcuff you out in the woods. I got a plane to catch. Then I'll call and tell them where you are. You do what I say and I'm not going to hurt you. Just buying time is all."

The old joviality that had always set Anna's teeth on

edge was creeping back. A round of crying, a couple of
pistol shots, a chaser of physical abuse had restored his
confidence. Anna was relieved. In the car he'd been on the
brink of panic. Should he fall over that edge, shooting her
would be the obvious panacea. He shoved and she stag-
gered over to the rickety wooden gate that let the public
through the fence to the mound site.

Emerald Mound, though little visited, was one of the
true wonders of the Trace. It's magnificence put the modern structures—buildings from the eighteenth and nineteenth centuries that were so meticulously restored and
lovingly toured—to shame. For reasons of their own, and
eons before white settlers had come straggling up the Mississippi River, the Natchez Indians had created it out of
swampy forest lands. Dirt, the rock-hard clay and powdery
loess of the land, had been carried in, heaped up until a
mound over fifty feet high, longer than a football field and
at least half that wide, had been created. The top was flat
and level. On either end of this great elevated field more
dirt was piled, sculpted into two squared-off hillocks, the
westernmost higher than the eastern.

In summer this immense monument was green, emerald
green, covered completely in a thick carpet of grass and
tiny wild flowers. This night the mound was cloaked in
such darkness that Anna felt rather than saw it, a looming
presence in the night. As ever with ancient structures imperfectly understood, modern imagination had speculated
that the highest point was reserved for human sacrifice.
Stumbling toward the first steep incline, the winter grass
slippery underfoot, Anna wondered if she was destined to
reenact the role of the hapless virgin.

The path grew suddenly steep, the dirt trail augmented
by sections of four-by-four timbers set flush to provide
steps. Anna's booted foot hit the first of these. Sleet had
turned to ice on the wood. Slipping, she fell to one knee.
Arms and jacket were jerked hard, and she was on her feet
again.

Snippets from years of inadequate training and no practice flipped through Anna's brain, cue cards to be read and
discarded. If she tried to kick back, hit a knee—the best
way to cripple a big man—she would die. If she tried to
jerk an elbow free to strike she would die. Reasoning with
him would heighten his hatred of women in charge and she
would die. Many stories, and Anna did not like the end of
any of them.

Grunting, his breath coming hard from exertion and tension, Randy pushed her uphill. Several times he slipped,
and Anna was jerked roughly one way or another as he
used her as ballast to regain his balance.

A vision of herself laughing, excited, safe with Zach's
arms around her, whipping through Space Mountain in
Disneyland, a roller coaster in darkness, each turn a spine-
snapping surprise, surfaced from nowhere. Seeing Zach in
her mind's eye made Anna suddenly sad. Self-pity washed
up and threatened to unman her. Maybe the meek inherited
the earth but the pitiful inherited only a six-by-three-foot
plot.

Anna pushed the vision and the weakness aside. The effort of doing so caused her to cry out, a muffed squeak
very like a whimper. The grip on her chain and coat
seemed to loosen a little. Maybe.

Abruptly they reached the level tabletop of the man-
made mesa. Black plain, black rain, yet Anna could see after a fashion, enough to put one foot in front of the other,
enough to discern the earth from the sky. Even on such a
night as this, ambient light leaked through and the miracle
of the human eye gathered and used it.

Anna realized how acutely aware she was of life, past,
present and bleak future: how clean and cold the sleet
burning her face, the air sliding into her lungs, the faint
singing of the rain on her jacket, the pull of water-soaked
trousers over her thighs. She couldn't but wonder if this
overwhelming sensitivity and appreciation heralded coming death. She did not welcome it. Neither did she fear it

sufficiently. Perhaps the poet was wrong and one should go gently into that good night.

Not by this bozo's hand, an outraged voice reverberated through her brain.

Randy had set a course straight ahead to the foot of the wooden stairs set into the hillock that rose above the rest of the mound. The back of this rise was steep, falling seventy feet or more into the dense tangle of woods below. He would shoot her there and let her body tumble into the massed shrubs. By the time she was found, if she was found, the woodland critters, four-, six- and eight-legged, would have done their best to destroy any evidence of who had pulled the trigger. Not that there was any. Anna would die without defensive wounds, no DNA of the perpetrator beneath her fingernails.

Killed by Randy fucking Thigpen.

Anna whimpered again experimentally and said, "Please, please," in a broken voice. Thigpen's hold did loosen, if only a fraction. It hadn't been an isolated phenomenon. Female helplessness, degradation, soothed and comforted her erstwhile field ranger. Able by alchemy of familiarity and truncated eyesight, Anna saw the wooden steps a dozen yards ahead forming out of the sleet-driven darkness. For all the progress she'd made on any half-formed plan to better her situation, they might as well have been the steps to a scaffold.

Bidding final farewell to John Wayne, Anna burst into tears, pleas for her life riding brokenly on sobs. Thigpen talked over her snivelings. As she wept and begged, he shoved her forward, letting the invective of what he viewed as his months of servitude under her reign flow and voicing the bigotry he'd held in imperfect abeyance during that time.

Over the slosh of their boots through the wet grass, the hard rain on her jacket and the wet sounds of her own weeping, Anna heard him listing the rights women had robbed him—all men—of: promotions, training, dignity, pride, decency. Through it he used her as living proof of his theories, vilifying her for her tears, her begging, her cowardice, her small frame and inferior strength.

The more he talked the braver he became, brave and relaxed, full of his superiority and confident in his control over the sniveling hank of hair and bag of bones that Anna had become.

With a curse and a jerk, he started her up the steep wooden stairs leading to the highest point on the mound. Ice was forming on the wood. Anna shuffled in her abjection, guaranteeing she wouldn't lose her balance.

A little over halfway up she reached the step she'd been hoping for. Ice covered the surface. Anna shuffled carefully over it and stepped to the next. When she felt Randy put his full weight on its slippery surface, she cried out loud and wild and hurled herself backward with all her might and jammed the fists he held clamped at her shoulder with chain and collar back into his face.

Thigpen gave way in an avalanche of noise and flesh. Instinctively flinging his arms out to recover his balance, Randy moved the pistol from the back of Anna's head. The barrel, pressed so long and so hard into her skull, left a hot place behind when it was moved. As she fell with him she heard the shot as his trigger finger convulsed and he fired a round into the storm.

Falling seemed to take a long time. Anna felt her feet push off as she kicked away from the hillside, driving back into Randy's gut. She was aware of the small bones in her neck crackling when she slammed her head back, smashing the hard part of her cranium into his face. Then they seemed to float downward. Icy rain on her face, universal nothingness filling her eyes and mind.

Randy struck the ground. She smashed down, unbruised, onto his great soft belly. Time abandoned its petty pace. Anna had succeeded in knocking him down, but she wasn't free. He was still armed, still outweighed her by two hundred pounds.

Instinct took over and a sudden bone-deep desire not

only to survive but to win or, failing that, wreak as much havoc as possible took over. Screaming, spitting, hissing, Anna wrenched her chained wrists free and rolled off, kicking back to inflict what damage she could on shins and knees. Randy had lost control of her hands but still held on to the hood of the jacket. Cloth caught her around the throat. Instead of fighting against it, Anna rolled back toward Thigpen scratching, biting, butting, knees and elbows punching.

He let loose with a startled cry. She straightened her limbs and began rolling like a log, as she and Molly had done down summer-warm grassy hills. Shots rang out but darkness and speed were on Anna's side. Dizzy, but unhurt, she came to a stop several yards from the foot of the hill.

On elbows and knees, she crawled another ten or fifteen yards, then stopped and listened.

At first she heard only the pounding of her heart and the rush of the blood past her eardrums. Willing herself to breathe deeply, regularly, she listened past the raucous celebration of life in her veins. Rain. A huff. A splash. A booted foot on wood. Randy was up.

Mathematics was the first skill to vanish when guns were fired but Anna tried: two shots to cut her free of the shoulder strap in the Crown Vic, two—or maybe it was only one—when he'd fallen. Make it one. Safer. If he'd not lost the revolver in the fall, he had three shots left before he'd reload. Ideally a law-enforcement officer would take this down time to replace the spent shells with live ones. Gun battles were seldom ideal. Randy wouldn't risk reloading till he had to. Moving with care, she levered herself to her feet. Her keys were in her trouser pocket. The handcuff key was the smallest, the most difficult to maneuver with cold numb fingers and a mind shot full of adrenaline. Anna chose not to try it. Thigpen believed her to be unarmed. She had nine shots to his three and a second magazine. The first lay in the mud down by the car.

Anna unsnapped the keeper on her holster and, two-handed, lifted the semi-auto from the leather. It probably wasn't personal, merely leftover body heat trapped between her hip and the raincoat, but the butt of the weapon was warm, welcoming, more comforting than a father's hand.

Anna stood still a moment, letting dizziness pass, enjoying being free and alive. Clatter. Huffing. Randy running down steps. Wild-eyed Anna stared into the rain and darkness till she made out a piece of it that moved differently from the rest.

"Drop it, Randy. Give it up. The game's over," she yelled. The report of his pistol and a flash of muzzle fire were her answer. Anna threw herself to the ground and rolled, this time on level ground. Two more shots. Both wild. Randy was running, he'd fired at the sound of her voice.

Six shots, if she'd counted right. His gun was empty. Anna was on her feet running toward him yelling.

"Down. Down. Down. Get down, you son of a bitch."

Randy remained standing, a black hole in the night. Ten feet from him she stopped. "Give it up, Randy. I'm armed. Give it up."

"Bullshit." A glint gathered from the wan light of the house below the mound and across the road shone dully as he raised the pistol.

Firing wide to make her point, Anna squeezed off a shot.

"You lying bitch," Randy screamed.

Such was the shock in his voice that while being kidnapped prior to murder she would have the unmitigated gall to lie to him, Anna laughed.

"There's something wrong with you," Randy said again.

"Drop the gun, Randy. There's no bullets in it anyway. No sense getting yourself killed. Drop it now."

"Fucking lying bitch," he said, unable to get past her deceit. He dropped the gun.

Rangers weren't in the habit of carrying backup guns. It wasn't authorized, necessary, or more to the point, it wasn't the vogue. Still Anna was taking no chances. "Put your hands on your head. Interlace the fingers. You know the drill."

Randy didn't move. "Yeah," he said. "I know the drill. I'm unarmed. No threat to myself or anybody else. I'm not attacking you.

"Like you said, I've never killed anybody. Ol' Doyce fell by himself, Badger said. He and Martin left him hanging while they cleaned that doe. Thought it was funny. When they came back and found him dead they called me. I never killed anybody. I'm no danger. You can't use deadly force." With that he began backing away, his outline beginning to blur into the night.

Technically he was right. Probably he wouldn't get far. The highway patrol or the local police department would pick him up in a few days. Until then Anna could sleep with the doors locked and her gun on the nightstand.

He turned, began lumbering toward the trail that would take him down off Emerald Mound. Anna took her radio from her belt and called dispatch. "This is five-eight-zero," she said evenly. "I need backup and an ambulance at Emerald Mound." She dropped the radio into her pocket. Took careful aim and pulled the trigger.

For predators, compassion has never been an evolutionary advantage.

21

Randy was down, screaming. Anna felt no remorse. Chances were good he'd live. She'd aimed for a leg. Unless she'd gotten luckier than she'd intended and the bullet had severed the artery in the thigh, he'd survive. Given the breadth of the man's thighs, Anna thought a direct hit was unlikely.

Staying where she was, thirty feet from the shrieking lump of ranger meat and cloaked by the night, Anna put her gun in the pocket of her raincoat and, taking her time, retrieved her keys from her trousers and unlocked the cuffs with which Randy had fettered her.

That done, she took her little Mag-Lite from its place on her duty belt and, holding it away from her body, clicked it on. Randy was curled up on his side in the fetal position, clutching his right leg above the knee. In the black on black of the nearly lightless night, the beam of her flashlight sparked startlingly beautiful red from the blood oozing between his fingers and over the backs of his hands.

Anna closed the distance between them, stood over him

looking down. Anger, malice, even the cold precision of
the predator abandoned her. If she felt anything it was only
a sense of detachment, of being there without form or matter. "Boy, that must really hurt," she said.

Randy started screaming again; this time pain wasn't the
driving force but rage. When he'd run out of gender-
specific invectives he yelled, "I'll sue your ass. You won't
have a pot to piss in by the time my lawyers are done with
you."

Anna believed him. He might well win a lawsuit. Juries
were notoriously unpredictable. But she didn't think so.
"You ran the wrong way," she said. Had Randy run for the
woods, Anna might have let him go, knowing he'd not be
on the loose for long. He'd run toward the road, the patrol
car and the shotgun therein.

Till the first car arrived bearing Clintus Jones and André,
Anna did what she had to. Confident he wouldn't go far if
he moved at all, she left Randy lying in the muck, ran
down to the car and brought back a larger flashlight and the
first-aid kit from the trunk. Good sense and personal preference told her to let Randy bind his own wound. The pain
was acute, color was gone from his face and sweat
streamed amid the rain on his face, but he was sufficiently
conscious to remember the rudiments of his EMT training.
She hadn't tried to handcuff him, nor would she. From various bits of horseplay she'd overheard between him and
Barth she knew Randy was too big. The metal bracelets
would not circle his wrists. The leather bellyband more re-
calcitrant persons were chained to would not fit around his
middle.

Squatting on her heels in the rain, semi-auto in one
hand, the other holding the light on his wounded knee,
Anna watched him cut away the pant leg. Rain fell on the
exposed flesh and began to wash away the blood. Her bullet had struck about five inches above the kneecap and toward the inside of the leg. The entry wound was small and
neat. The exit wound had blown away a chunk of meat
nearly the size of a teacup.

It's only a flesh wound, she thought and smiled at the cliché. She considered sharing this with him but doubted he would see the humor.

There was enough blood for show but no arteries had been severed. Knee and ankle still functioned, and though he groaned enough to indicate otherwise, Randy was not incapacitated by pain. No bones broken. There was a lot of flesh to be got through on Randy Thigpen before a bullet could find much in the way of vital organs or bone.

To pass the time, Anna had tried to engage him in conversation, but after the final stream of abuse when she'd shot him, he'd said nothing except, "I want a lawyer." Anna was happy with that. She preferred the sound of the rain to that of the human voice. Curiosity didn't nag her. Most things she was fairly sure she'd figured out.

Randy had been charging locals admission into his own private hunting club on the Trace, probably for years. This season a client had died. He'd been asked to take care of it. Thigpen was too cagey ever to admit anything, at least not till the information could be used to gain him an edge in court, or prison, but Anna guessed he'd been the mastermind behind stripping Doyce and leaving him in the Mt. Locust Inn with the Bible text highlighted. At a guess, he'd used old Mack's wheelbarrow, the one he complained had been taken and not put away properly. Martin, Herm, even Badger had appeared genuinely baffled when the intimate circumstances of how the corpse had been discovered were relayed to them. Odds were good they had no idea till after the fact.

Thigpen, an opportunist, wouldn't have been able to resist. Fallen, quite literally, into his hands, was the corpse of the brother of his rival for the Adams County Sheriff's badge. Randy would have known anything smacking of a sex crime in the family would doom Raymond Barnette's campaign. When Anna and Clintus had chosen to keep the details under wraps, Randy had quickly leaked them to the newspapers.

At length Randy had managed a good enough pressure

bandage over the wound to lie back and rest from his labors. Supine he reminded her vividly of poor ol' Doyce, stranded for all time like a beached walrus.

Clintus Jones would be running unopposed. Anna could hire a new field ranger. Despite the mud and the blood and the unremitting rain, silver linings were popping up everywhere.

When Clintus and André arrived and Anna saw the car pull up at the bottom of the hill, she waved till their spotlight searched her out.

André, proud of his youth and strength, attempted to bound up the steep slope of the mound and ended up crawling over the edge in a bedraggled, grass-stained state. Clintus used the steps cut into the west end. Even in the rain he looked unruffled and tidy.

He started to apologize for letting Anna down, then thought better of it and paid her the compliment of treating her as an equal. "Good work," was all he said.

Lights and sirens broke up this wordless tête-à-tête.

For the better part of two hours, everyone was caught up in the circus that grew out of trying to get a three-hundred-pound crippled man down off a mountain of grass and ice.

In the end they loaded Thigpen onto a wheeled gurney, left in the collapsed state, and roped it up. Verbal once again, he was ordering ambulance personnel around and telling tales of Anna's wanton kidnap of and assault upon his person. The Indian mound had nothing that could be used as an anchor. It took six men and Anna to belay Thigpen to the bottom of the slope and four of them to lift the stretcher into the back of the ambulance.

Clintus and his deputy would ride with him to the hospital in Jackson, where he would remain under guard until the doctors released him to the legal system.

Sheriff Paul Davidson had arrived shortly after Clintus and his men. In the hoopla of packaging and transporting Randy Thigpen, Anna had been able to more or less ignore him. Because it was deemed she was shaken and because she had no energy left to resist, the men had kindly planned

out the next hour of her life. A deputy would drive her car
back to Port Gibson following the ambulance. Anna was to
ride with Paul.

"Are you all right?" he asked gently when the noise and
lights had faded and they were left alone together in the
privacy of his car. Both were drenched. The heater was
turned on high. Paul took her hand. "I was listening on the
park frequency. When you called in I couldn't not come."

Anna didn't know what to say. She was too tired even to
cry. For that she was grateful.

"Let's get out of here," she said.

He put the car in gear and trailed north in the wake of the
others.

Because she was afraid he would break the silence with
the news with which he had threatened her earlier, Anna
began to talk. She told him of the gun to her temple and her
backward tumble to freedom. She didn't tell him that her
gambit had called for begging and sniveling. That she
would never tell anyone. How much of it was acting and
how much cowardice she would never know herself.

"What set Randy off?" Paul asked when she'd run down.

Anna had thought about that. "He knew Clintus was
tracing the original owner of the truck that destroyed my
patrol car," she told him. "When Clintus radioed me and
told me to get to a landline, Randy must have figured it had
been traced. Clintus said the guy he'd talked to had sold it
to Badger Lundstrom. Lundstrom must have traded it to
Randy. He wouldn't say what for, so my guess is it was in
partial payment for his membership in Randy's private
hunt club. Clintus sent deputies out to pick up Lundstrom.
He'll stand charges for wanton disregard of human life,
reckless endangerment, poaching, conspiracy to cover up a
crime and, if we can prove he was with the men who
chased me, attempted murder, though that one probably
won't stick."

They were quiet for a time. Anna could feel Paul building up his courage to say something. It had been a trying

day. When he finally opened his mouth to speak, she
wasn't ready to hear him and cut him off.

"Barth and I made headway today on that cemetery
business," she said. "Looks like Mama Barnette's land
isn't hers. It was ceded to a black man, Lanford Restin,
shortly before the Civil War broke out. There's no record it
was ever bought back. Lanford died and the living Barnettes just absorbed it back into their own property lines.
The old newspaper said Restin chose to be buried 'back
with his people.' Barth thinks that meant in the slave cemetery behind Mr. Locust. There's several Restins buried
there. Barth got that from your deputy Lonnie. It fits with a
grave being dug up, Raymond building a fine tiny coffin
and reburying it on his mother's place. After all these years
there wouldn't have been enough left of Unk to require
much more than an infant's coffin. There's still living relatives. DNA from the remains could make a positive ID.
Lonnie and his new bride might be getting three hundred
acres of good farmland for a wedding present."

"Why would Raymond go to the trouble of making a
nice coffin, reburying the remains?" Paul asked.

"Whatever else he is, he's a good undertaker. He takes
his duties to the dead seriously."

Paul thought about that for a while. Covertly, Anna
watched him. The faint light from the dashboard tinted his
features. She'd known him less than a year, but already she
knew his face as well as she did her own and yet could not
read it.

"Before the end of the war, though Unk—Lanford—was
a freedman his Mt. Locust relatives would still have been
slaves. A slave couldn't inherit legally. Barnette will have
the law on his side in that at least," Paul said.

"Making reparations is big in politics at the moment.
Mama and Raymond will have a fight on their hands."

"You figure Raymond vandalized the graveyard signs to
make a point? Obliterate the name 'Restin'?" Paul asked,
trying to tie up loose ends.

Anna shook her head. Raymond was a lot of vile things, but she doubted he'd ever desecrate a cemetery. "My money's on Mama Barnette for that," she said, remembering Claudia's tale of the old woman mud-splattered and exhausted from some bizarre outing that sapped her strength. Mama fit with the profile of those who defecated on the goods of their enemies; there was a touch of psycho about both the woman and the house she lived in.

"Are you going to try and prove it? Prosecute?" Davidson asked.

Anna considered it for a moment then said, "Nope. She's old. I'm just going to hope she dies soon."

It was a distinctly un-Christian attitude, but Paul had chosen to lie down with heathens; it served him right if he got up with blasphemies.

They reached Port Gibson as the ambulance, followed by the sheriff's car, was pulling out of the gate. The sheriff's car stopped until they drew alongside to pass along the information that Anna's keys had been left atop her front tire on the driver's side.

Paul parked and switched off the ignition. Neither made a move to get out of the car. Heat and immobility wrapped Anna in lethargy. She didn't know what Paul's problem was. Didn't want to know. Not tonight at any rate.

"You look worn out," he said kindly.

For reasons pertaining to wives and "good talks," Anna resented the concern. "I am," she said curtly.

"Why don't I take you home, fix you something to eat and put you to bed?" he said and took her hand.

Anna snatched it away childishly.

"What is it?"

"You said you wanted to talk." Avoidance had become too tiring. Anna wanted to take the hit and get it over with.

"Why don't we get you something to eat—"

"No. Now is good," she said stubbornly.

Paul looked startled, hurt, but Anna was unmoved. Rage undiminished by the satisfaction of besting Thigpen—even of putting a bullet into his unwholesome carcass—welled up inside her, and she began counting backward from ten in Spanish to keep it from spewing out.

"Okay," Paul said, saving himself for the moment. "Though I'd pictured it differently, maybe candlelight and soft music." He smiled.

Anna didn't smile back.

"Okay," he said again. "Like I said I had a good talk with my wife."

Anna braced herself, kept counting.

"She's agreed to the divorce. It seems she's found a fella."

The words reached Anna's ears, but it was a moment before her brain could take it in. When it did, she exploded. "Why in the hell didn't you tell me that over the phone?"

Paul didn't rise to meet her anger. "I wanted to be with you," he said simply. "I was afraid once you knew I was free you'd run away from me."

"Fat fucking chance," she said irritably, her linguistic skills eroded by recent events. At least she retained the grace to laugh at herself. Paul laughed with her.

"A fella?"

"The one who's been pouring evil gossip into her ear about you, evidently."

The way to a man's heart might be through his stomach. The way to a woman scorned was through her bile.

"Steve," Anna said suddenly, his mysterious project all at once illuminated. "Steve Stilwell, the Ridgeland District Ranger is dating your wife. What a guy." Laughter, giddy from the relief at being alive and not alone, took Anna over for a minute, bubbling through at inopportune moments as she told Paul the story, piecing it together in her mind as she went.

When she'd finished he looked grave. "I'd hate to see her hurt," he said.

Anna wouldn't but she had sense enough not to say so. *Hoist on my own petard,* Stilwell had said. "I think Steve has fallen for her," Anna reassured him. "He's a good guy. She'll be all right."

Paul sat for a minute then turned the key in the ignition. "Home?"

"Home." For the first time since coming to Mississippi, the word didn't feel strange in her mouth or in her mind.

Turn the page for a sneak preview of
Nevada Barr's new Anna Pigeon mystery,

FLASHBACK

Available in hardcover from G. P. Putnam's Sons

Until she ran out of oxygen, Anna was willing to believe she was taking part in a PBS special. The water was so clear sunlight shone through as if the sea were but mountain air. Cloud shadows, stealthy and faintly magical at four fathoms, moved lazily across patches of sand that showed startlingly white against the dark, ragged coral. Fishes colored so brightly it seemed it must be a trick of the eye or the tail end of an altered state flitted, nibbled, explored and slept. Without moving, Anna could see a school of silver fish, tiny anchovies, synchronized, moving like polished chain mail in a glittering curtain. Four Blue Tangs, so blue her eyes ached with the joy of them, nosed along the edge of a screamingly purple sea fan bigger than a coffee table. A jewfish, six feet long and easily three hundred pounds, his blotchy hide mimicking the sun-dappled rock, pouting lower lip thick as Anna's wrist, lay without moving beneath an overhang of a coral-covered rock less than half his size, his wee fish brain assuring him he was hidden. Countless other fish, big and small, bright and dull, ever more delightful to Anna because she'd not named them and so robbed them of a modicum of their mystery, moved around her on their fishy business.

Air, and with it time, was running out. If she wished to live, she needed to breathe. Her lungs ached with that peculiar sensation of being full to bursting. Familiar desperation licked at the edges of her mind. One more kick, greetings to a spiny lobster (a creature whose body design was only possible in a weightless world), and, with a strong sense of being hounded from paradise, she swam for the surface, drove a foot or more into the air and breathed.

The sky was as blue as the eye-watering fishes and every bit as merciless as the sea. The ocean was calm. Even with her chin barely above the surface she could see for miles. There was remarkably little to soothe the eye between the unrelenting glare of sea and sky. To the north was Garden Key, a scrap of sand no more than thirteen acres in total and, at its highest point, a few meters above sea level. Covering the key, two of its sides spilling out into the water, was the most bizarre duty station at which she had served.

Fort Jefferson, a massive brick fortress, had been built on this last lick of America, the Dry Tortugas, seventy miles off Key West in the Gulf of Mexico. At the time construction started in 1846, it was the cutting edge of national defense. Made of brick and mortar with five bastions jutting out from the corners of a pentagon, it had been built as the first line of defense for the southern states, guarding an immense natural—and invisible—harbor; it was the only place for sixty miles where ships could sit out the hurricanes that menaced the Gulf and the southeastern seaboard or come under the protection of the fort's guns in time of war. Though real, the harbor was invisible because its breakwaters, a great broken ring of coral, were submerged.

Jefferson never fired a single shot in defense of its

country. Time and substrata conspired against it. Before
the third tier of the fort could be completed, the engineers
noticed the weight of the massive structure was causing it
to sink and stopped construction. Even unfinished it might
have seen honorable—if not glamorous—duty, but the ri-
fled cannon was invented, and the seven-to-fifteen-foot-
thick brick-and-mortar walls were designed only to
withstand old-style cannons. Under siege by these new
weapons of war, the fort would not stand. Though destined for glorious battle, Jefferson sat out the Civil War as
a union prison.

Till Anna had been assigned temporary duty at the Dry
Tortugas, she'd not even heard of it. Now it was home.

For a moment she merely treaded water, head thrown
back to let the sun seek out any epithelial cell it hadn't already destroyed over the last ten years. Just breathing—
when the practice had recently been denied—was heaven.
Somewhere she'd read that a meager seventeen percent of
air pulled in by the lungs was actually used. Idly, she wondered if she could train her body to salvage the other
eighty-three percent so she could remain underwater ten
minutes at a stretch rather than two. Scuba gave one the
time but, with the required gear, not the freedom. Anna
preferred free diving. Three times she breathed deep, on
the third she held it, upended and kicked again for bliss of
the bottom.

Flashing in the sun, she was as colorful as any fish. Her
mask and fins were iridescent lime green, her dive skin
startling blue. Though the water was a welcoming eighty-
eight degrees in late June, that was still eight point six degrees below where she functioned best. For prolonged
stays in this captivating netherworld she wore a skin, a
lightweight body-hugging suit with a close-fitting hood
and matching socks. Not only did it conserve body heat,
but it also protected her from the sometimes vicious bite
of the coral. Like all divers who weren't vandals, Anna assiduously avoided touching—and so harming—living

coral, but when they occasionally did collide, human skin was usually as damaged as the coral.

Again she stayed with and played with the fish until her lungs felt close to bursting. Though it would be hotly debated by a good percentage of Dry Tortugas National Park's visitors, as far as she was concerned the "paradise" part of this subtropical paradise was hidden beneath the waves.

Anna had never understood how people could go to the beach and lie in the sand to relax. The shore was a far harsher environment than the mountains. Air was hot and heavy and clung to the skin. Wind scoured. Sand itched. Salt sucked moisture from flesh. The sun, in the sky and again off the surface of the sea, seared and blinded. For a couple of hours each day it was heaven. After that it began to wear one down as the ocean wears away rock and bone.

Two dive sites, twenty dives—the deepest over forty feet—and Anna finally tired herself out. Legs reduced to jelly from pushing through an alien universe, she couldn't kick hard enough to rise above the surface and pull herself over the gunwale. Glad there were no witnesses, she wriggled and flopped over the transom beside the outboard motor to spill on deck, splattering like a bushel of sardines. Her "Sunday" was over. She'd managed to spend yet one more weekend in Davy Jones's locker. There wasn't really any place else to go.

The *Reef Ranger*, one of the park's patrol boats, a twenty-five-foot inboard/outboard Boston Whaler, the bridge consisting of a high bench and a Plexiglas windscreen, fired up at a touch. Anna upped anchor, then turned the bow toward the bastinadoed fortress that was to be her home for another eight to twelve weeks. Seen from the level of the surrounding ocean, Fort Jefferson presented a bleak and surreal picture: an overwhelming geometric tonnage floating, apparently unsupported, on the surface of the sea.

Enjoying the feel of a boat beneath her after so many

years in landlocked parks, Anna headed for the fort. The
mariners' rhyme used to help those new to the water remember which markers to follow when entering heavy
traffic areas rattled meaninglessly through her mind: *red
on right returning*. Shrunken by salt and sun, her skin felt
two sizes too small for her bones, and even with dark
glasses and the sun at her back, it was hard to keep her
eyes open against the glare.

The opportunity to serve as interim supervisory ranger
for the hundred square miles of park, scarcely one of
which was above water, came in May. Word trickled down
from the southeastern region that the Dry Tortugas' supervisory ranger had to take a leave of absence for personal
reasons and a replacement was needed until he returned
or, failing that, a permanent replacement was found.

Dry Tortugas National Park was managed jointly with
southern Florida's Everglades National Park. The brass all
worked out of Homestead, near Everglades. Marooned as
it was, seventy miles into the Gulf, day-to-day operations
of the Dry Tortugas were run by a supervisory ranger, who
managed one law enforcement ranger, two interpreters
and an office administrator. Additional law enforcement
had been budgeted and two rangers hired. They were new
to the service and, at present, being trained at the Federal
Law Enforcement Training Center in Georgia.

"Supervisory Ranger" was a title that bridged a gray
area in the NPS hierarchy. For reasons to which Anna was
not privy, the head office chose not to upgrade the position
to Chief Ranger but left it as a subsidiary position to the
Chief Ranger at Everglades. Still, it was a step above
Anna's current District Ranger level on the Natchez
Trace. To serve as "Acting Supervisory Ranger" was a
good career move.

That wasn't entirely why she'd chosen to abandon
home and hound for three months to accept the position.
Anna was in no hurry to rush out of the field and into a
desk job. There'd be time enough for that when her knees

gave out or her tolerance for the elements—both natural and criminal—wore thin.

She had taken the Dry Tortugas assignment for personal reasons. When she was in a good frame of mind, she told herself she'd needed to retreat to a less populated and mechanized post to find the solitude and unmarred horizons wherein to renew herself, to seek answers. When cranky or down, she felt it was the craven running away of a yellow-bellied deserter.

Paul Davidson, his divorce finalized, had asked her to marry him.

Two days later, a car, a boat and a plane ride behind her—not to mention two thousand miles of real estate, a goodly chunk of it submerged—she was settling into her quarters at Fort Jefferson.

"Coincidence?" her sister Molly had asked sarcastically. "You be the judge."

The fort had only one phone, which worked sporadically, and mail was delivered once a week. Two weeks had passed in sandy exile, and she was no more ready to think about marriage than she had been the day she left. But, given the paucity of entertainments—even a devotee could only commune with fish for so long—she was rapidly getting to the point where there was nothing else to think about.

Under these pressing circumstances, she'd done the only sensible thing: she stuck her nose in somebody else's business. Daniel Barrons, a maintenance man-of-all-trades and the closest thing Anna'd made to a friend at the fort, had a weakness for gossip that she shamelessly exploited.

He was a block of a man, with what her father would have referred to as a "peasant build," one designed for carrying sick calves into the barn. Perhaps in his late forties, Daniel covered his blunt face with a brown-black beard. On his left arm, seldom seen as the man wasn't given to tank tops, was a tattoo so classic Anna smiled whenever she glimpsed its bottom edge: a naked girl re-clining on elbows and fanny under a cartoon palm tree.

Given this rough and manly exterior, tradition would have had him strong and silent. Every time he snuggled down in his favorite position to dish the dirt, elbows on workbench, hindquarters stuck out and usually bristling with tools shoved in his pockets, furry chin in scarred hands, Anna was charmed and tickled.

With only a small nudge, Daniel had assumed the position and filled her in on why she'd been given the opportunity to explore this oddly harsh, boring, beautiful, magical bit of the earth. Her predecessor, Lanny Wilcox, hadn't taken an extended leave willingly. It had been forced upon him when he'd begun to come unglued.

"His girlfriend, a little Cuban number as cute as a basket full of kittens, ran out on him," Daniel had told her, his voice low and gentle as usual. He consistently spoke as if a baby slept in the next room and he was loath to wake it.

"Lanny was a terrific guy, but he was getting up there, fifty-one this last birthday. At his peak he couldn't a been much to look at. Hey, I like Lanny just fine, but, well, even he knew he was about as good-looking as the south end of a northbound spiny lobster. Five, six months ago he hooked up with Theresa. She's not yet thirty, smart, funny and a nice addition to a bathing suit. Next thing you know, she's living out here. When she cut out, Lanny just sort of lost it."

From what Anna had gathered, the old Supervisory Ranger's "losing it" consisted of increasingly bizarre be-havior that revolved around the seeing and hearing of things that no one else saw or heard. "Ghosts," murmured a couple of the more melodramatic inhabitants of the fort. "Hallucinations," said the practical ones, and Lanny was bundled up and shipped off to play with his imaginary friends out of sight of the tax-paying public.

On first arriving, struck by the beauty of the sky and sea, the fishes and the masonry, Anna couldn't understand what stresses could possibly chase even a heartbroken man around the bend. Piloting the *Reef Ranger* into the harbor, the glow of her swimming with the fishes burned and blown away, she realized that after a mere couple weeks of isolation, wet heat and scouring winds, she was tempted to dream up companions of her own. She needed a sense of connection to something, somebody to keep her on an even keel.

She laughed. The sound whipped away on the liquid wind over the bow. Soon she was going to have to relinquish her self-image as a hermit. Paul—or perhaps just the passage of years—had socialized her to some extent. Molly would be pleased. Anna made a mental note to tell her sister when next she phoned. It could be a while. Not only was the fort's only phone in much demand, but it also had a one-to-two-second delay, like a phone call from Mars, that made communication an exercise in frustration.

Red on right.

Anna slowed the *Ranger* to a sedate and wakeless speed as she entered the small jewel of a harbor on the east side of Garden Key. Eleven pleasure boats were anchored, two she recognized from the weekend before, *Moonshadow* and *Key to My Heart*, both expensive, both exquisitely kept. They were owned by two well-to-do couples out of Miami who seemed joined at the hip as their boats were joined at the gunwale, one rafting off the other. Anna waved as she passed.

At the end of the harbor away from the tourists, as if there were an invisible set of tracks running from Bush Key—Garden's near neighbor—to the harbor mouth and they had been condemned to live on the wrong side of them, two commercial shrimpers cuddled up to one another.

Commercial fishing and, much to the shriek and lament of the locals, sport fishing was banned in the park, but right outside the boundaries was good shrimping. The boats stalked the perimeters, the honest—or the cautious—keeping outside the imaginary line established by NPS buoys. Perhaps a few sought to poach, but there were plenty of shrimp outside. Most came for the same reasons ships had been coming for two hundred years, the reason the fort had been built in the middle of the ocean: the natural safe zone of flat water the coral reefs provided.

Shrimp boats, their side nets looking like tattered wings falling from a complex skeleton of wood and metal, were a complication Anna'd not foreseen. They sailed from many ports, most in the south and southeast, following the shrimp: four weeks in Texas, then through the Gulf to the Keys. Some boats were family owned, most were not. All were manned and kept in a way unique to an idiosyncratic and inbred culture. Daniel called them "bikers of the sea." Having spent an unspecified and largely undiscussed number of years in the land version of that violent fraternity before, as he put it, "breaking my back and seeing the light," he would know.

The shrimpers were a scabrous lot, not just the boats, which reeked of dead fish, cigarette smoke and old grease—part cooking, part engine—but the sailors themselves. The family boats were crewed by men and women, three or four to a boat. The others were all male, but for the occasional unfortunate who, like a biker chick out of favor, was passed from boat to boat, usually fueled for her duties with drugs and alcohol.

Anna had yet to see a shrimper with all his or her teeth. The violence of the culture coupled with months at sea away from modern dentistry marked their faces. A lot of them went to sea to kick drugs and found more onboard. A startling percentage had felony records.

This borderline lifestyle would not have affected Anna had not a symbiotic relationship sprung up between them and the tourists and park employees at the fort. Fresh gulf shrimp were delicious. The shrimpers were glad to trade a few for the culinary delight of those in the park. The problem was that the currency was alcohol—mostly cheap beer, but enough whiskey to make things interesting. Drunk, the shrimpers lived up to Daniel's name for them. They came ashore; they yelled, disrupted tours, urinated in public, knocked one another's few remaining teeth out, beat their women and occasionally knifed one another.

Her third day at Fort Jefferson Anna had been made painfully aware of a few administrational oddities of Dry Tortugas National Park: there was no place to hold prisoners and, though they were legally allowed to make arrests, it was highly discouraged by headquarters in Homestead. Two law-enforcement rangers keeping drunken violent shrimpers under guard in the open air for hours till the Coast Guard arrived wasn't a great idea. Transporting them three hours one way to Key West and so leaving the park without law enforcement or EMTs for a day didn't work either.

The best they could do was separate the combatants, bind the ugliest wounds and shoo the lot of them back onboard their boats.

The two shrimpers anchored in the harbor as Anna motored in were family owned. They'd never caused problems, and the lady on one of the boats had a terrific little dog she let Anna pet. Tonight should be quiet. Anna didn't know if she was grateful or not. With only one other ranger—Bob Shaw—in house, neither ever truly had a day off but slept with a radio ready to serve as backup for the person on duty. Quiet promised uninterrupted sleep. Anna supposed that was a good thing. Still, she would have welcomed something to do.

As she backed the *Reef Ranger* neatly into the employee dock, Bob Shaw walked down the weathered planking. Opposite where Anna tied up, on the far side of the park pier with its public bathrooms and commercial loading area that the ferries from Key West used, the NPS supply boat, the *Activa*, was moored. Like Christmas every Tuesday, but better, the *Activa* arrived with supplies, groceries, mail and Cliff and Linda. Cliff was the captain,

Linda the first mate. New blood was as exciting to the inhabitants of Fort Jefferson as fresh food. The crew of the *Activa* could be counted on to bring the latest news and gossip along with other treats and necessities.

"Teddy took your stuff up to your quarters for you and stuck the perishables in the refrigerator," Bob said as Anna cut the engine. She tossed him the stern line and he tied it neatly to the cleat on the starboard side. Wind was more or less a constant on DRTO, and the NPS boats were tied to both sides of their slips to keep them from banging into the sides of the dock. Fenders could only do so much when the winds flirted with hurricane force.

"I'll be sure and thank her. Is Teddy in the office?" Anna asked. Teddy, short for Theodora, was Bob's wife.

"Till five, like always." He stood stiffly to one side as Anna heaved towel, fins, snorkel and water bottle onto the dock.

Bob was a strange fit with the park. He'd been there for eleven years and clearly loved the place. He said, and Anna believed him, that he never wanted to work anywhere else and intended to serve out his remaining six years till retirement at the fort.

Anna suspected his desire to remain in this isolated post was due only partly to his love for the resource. A good chunk of it, she theorized, was because nowhere else could he live such a rich and rewarding fantasy life without coming head-to-head with the cynicism of his fellows.

Fortunately for her, Bob's particular brand of psychosis made him a great ranger.

Swearing he was five-six, though Anna, at five-four, could look him in the eye in flat shoes, he seemed bent on being the poster boy for a benign version of the Napoleon complex. Now, as he readied to go on his evening rounds—showing the flag, boarding boats he deemed suspicious, handing out brochures to newcomers and checking the boundaries because they were there—he wore full gear: sidearm, baton, pepper spray, cuffs and a Kevlar bulletproof vest. If the man hadn't been such a strong swimmer, Anna's greatest worry would have been that he'd fall overboard and his defensive equipment would sink him like a stone. The only concession he made to the cloying heat was to wear shorts.

Though Anna would never have dreamed of telling him so, they tended to spoil the effect. Not only was he no taller than Anna, but he couldn't have exceeded her one hundred twenty pounds by much either. Like a lot of men who take to the water, most of that was in his chest and shoulders. Chickens would have been insulted to hear his legs compared to theirs.

"Anything up for tonight?" she asked as they made lines fast. Mostly she asked for the fun of hearing Bob's answer. His fantasy, as luck would have it, was that he was the sole protector (she didn't count for reasons of gender, and Lanny hadn't counted for reasons Bob clearly had but was too honorable to speak of) of this jewel in the ocean. Like all other great and honorable lawmen of history, Bob was constantly in danger from the forces of evil. Each and every boat could be smuggling cocaine from Panama, heroin from the east, guns from pretty much anywhere. All shrimpers were ready, willing and able to knife him in the back.

Given that he apparently genuinely believed this despite eleven years in a sleepy port, Anna couldn't but admire his stalwart courage in facing each day, never late, never shirking. Having been exposed to this criminal-under-every-bush, Marshal Dillon under siege mentality the day she arrived, Anna was pleasantly surprised the first time she'd patrolled with him. Part of honor and duty—and natural inclination probably, though his tough-guy image would never let him admit it even to himself—required he be gracious, polite and, when he thought no one was looking, overtly kind. Seeing that, Anna had been quite taken with the man and made it a point to resist the temptation to tease him about the boogeymen that lived under his boat. She

didn't even resent his sexism. Respect for a superior over-
rode it, and it wasn't personal. There were no women patrolling the streets of Dodge City, flying fighters over Nazi
Germany or walking shoulder-to-shoulder with Clint East-
wood through the saloon's swinging doors.

Sans petticoat and fan, Anna simply didn't fit into
Bob's worldview.

"Did you see the boats on the south side, anchored out a
ways, not in the harbor?" Bob asked. He smoothed his
sandy-red and handsome mustache with one hand and
pointed with the other.

Vaguely Anna remembered passing them, but had paid
them little mind.

"I saw them."

"They've been here two and a half days. Never come
into the harbor. Never visit the fort. Something's up with
them."

Anna'd not noticed those things. And they were perti-
nent. Most folks, if they bothered to come to Garden Key,
made use of the harbor and at least paid a curiosity visit to
the fort.

"Good eye," Anna said and meant it. "I'll keep close to
the radio."

Bob jumped lightly into the second of DRTO's five patrol boats. Only four were working. The fifth was beached
behind the dock up on blocks. Bob took the *Bay Ranger*, a
twenty-foot aluminum-hulled Sylvan. He seemed to prefer it to the sturdier Boston Whalers. Maybe because it
was quieter, had a lower profile. All the better for sneaking
up on evildoers.

Anna shouldered the net bag she used to carry her dive
things.

"Oh," Bob said as she turned to go. "You got a big box
from New York waiting for you. Teddy said if there's
bagels in it, she'll trade you some of her homemade key
lime pie for some."

Anna waved Bob off, then stood a moment, habit de-

manding she do a visual check of an area after an absence
of hours. The campground, with space for only a handful
of tents and, other than flush toilets on the public dock, no
amenities, was quiet. Because there was so little dirt to be
had on Garden Key, overnighters were by reservation
only. Picnickers sat at tables nursing beers and sunburns,
talking among themselves, families for the most part with
lots of little kids scratching at mosquito bites, Kool-Aid
smiles adding to the clownish colors of beach towels and
bathing suits. Even Bob would have a hard time imagining
an evil nemesis in the bunch.

Savoring the fact that she wasn't in a hurry, that, once
again, her work for the National Park Service allowed her
to rest her eyes and mind on a wonder most people would
never take the time to see, she turned her attention to the
fort.

Bob's motor's drone a pleasant burr in her ears, as comforting as the hum of bees in summer blooms, she looked
across the moat at Fort Jefferson. More than the skyscrap-
ers of Manhattan, the Golden Gate Bridge or all of Bill
Gates's cyber magic, it impressed her with man's determination to fight the world to a standstill and then reform it
in his own design.

Seventy miles out in the sea, on the unprepossessing
Bush Key, the magnitude of the effort awed her. Jefferson
stood three stories high and was topped with earthworks
and ammunition bunkers. A coal-black tower, built as a
lighthouse but demoted to a harbor light when the taller
lighthouse on Loggerhead Key was finished, thrust above
the battlements. The black metal of its skin gave it an unearned sinister aspect. A wide moat, meeting the fortress
walls on one side and contained by brick and mortar on
the other, ran around the two bastions fronting the structure. Beyond was nothing but the Atlantic. At first the
moat had amused Anna. Only in the front and along the
eastern wall was it bordered by land. On the two other
sides its outer wall separated it only from the sea.

When she'd first seen it, it had struck her as a conceit, the architect slavishly following the classic castle moat theme though this fort was set in a natural saltwater moat thousands of miles on one side and seventy on the other. Duncan, the island's historian and chief interpreter, had disabused her of that notion. Moats were not merely to keep land troops at bay but ships with malicious intent at their distance.

Trailing a young couple so in love they didn't notice it was too hot to be hanging all over each other, Anna crossed the bridge. As she stepped into the imagined cool and welcome dark of the entryway she heard the shivery sound of children giggling and saw a small head vanish into a stone slot. Anna laughed because heat and boredom had yet to diminish the childlike glee the fort engendered in her: "secret" rooms where ammunition had once been stored, dark and twisted caves where arches met and clashed and crossed at the bastions, designed by an architect who must have foreseen the genius of Escher. The formidable structure was now dissolving back into the sea with infinite slowness. Lime dripped out of solution as rain worked its way through ancient mortar. Stalactites formed, growing like teeth in the long, long passages through the casemates. Standing at a corner and looking down arch after arch after arch, perspective skewed. It was easy to feel as if one were falling through time itself.